TO SWIM BENEATH THE EARTH

A Novel

Ginger Bensman

Horn Rimmed Editions

SALEM, OREGON

Horn Rimmed Editions
230 Hansen Ave. S
Salem, Oregon/USA 97302
www.website-url.com

Publisher's Note: This is a work of fiction. Names, characters, places, and incidents are a product of the author's imagination. Locales and public names are sometimes used for atmospheric purposes. Any resemblance to actual people, living or dead, or to businesses, companies, events, institutions, or locales is completely coincidental.

Book Layout ©2013 BookDesignTemplates.com

Ordering Information:
Quantity sales. Special discounts are available on quantity purchases by corporations, associations, and others. For details, contact the "Special Sales Department" at the address above.

To Swim Beneath the Earth/ Ginger Bensman. -- 1st ed.
ISBN 978-0-9962957-0-3

For Walt

Bone-biting cold descends in the Andes the moment the sun sets and—so the Incas believed—begins its nightlong swim beneath the earth.

—Loren McIntyre, *The Incredible Incas and Their Timeless Land* 1975

"Amor Fati, – "Love your fate", which is, in fact, your life."

—Friedrich Nietzche

THE EXTENT
OF THE
INCAN EMPIRE

1 TAKING FLIGHT

It's a long way from Denver to Bogota. I have an appointment at the antiquities department there at the National University. Jasper Corbin, the celebrated anthropologist, has informed me that one of the Elders will be there too. I understand it's a test. He wants to know if I'm for real—and so do I. It's the great riddle of my life.

Even as we leave my brother's apartment with the stars still sharp against the night sky and the headlights of his little Honda casting twin beacons through the silent streets, he reminds me that my tickets weren't that expensive; surely, I could get at least a partial refund.

"Charlie," I say, "don't," and then, "I'm sorry." I turn to stare out the passenger window, looking for something beyond my reflection and marking silence as we put miles between moments, moving along, until the repetitive hum of the tires rolling over the highway becomes a comfort, a sort of centering mantra.

I glance over at Charlie. His rusty curls still reveal the imprint of his pillow, despite his efforts with a brush; one more message that he's missing his coffee and shower. I'm compelled to tuck the tag of his rumpled shirt back in place, but I twine my fingers, press my palms together in my lap, and he takes no notice. He's watching the road, his hands intent on the steering wheel. His face is set in tight, stern angles.

"Thanks, Charlie." I say. "You're a good brother."

"You show up. What was I supposed to do?"

"You could have slammed the door in my face."

He grunts and shoots me a glance so sharp it feels like a slap.

"Mama and Claire would have," I say. It's a weak offering.

He sits there, straight, and implacably mute.

We're approaching daylight and the airport simultaneously. I've seen two road signs counting out the miles. In places, the recently empty grasslands are becoming peopled with construction crews. In the mellow half-light, hardhats with coffee cups are slamming truck doors and unloading materials.

My heart flutters. I check my watch, reach into my purse, and feel for my ticket.

An airport is a potent place, a point of reunions and departures. For the traveler, it's a crossroads at the moment of decision, a flash point that separates intention from retreat. I tilt my head one more time, trying to catch the last ghosts of the stars. I fix on a stark white light, probably a satellite. Sometimes it's hard to know what you're seeing.

Though the car has slowed to what seems a crawl, I draw in a breath and brace myself for each speed bump. I turn to Charlie. "You ought to see someone about these shocks."

I wait for an answer, but it's like he didn't hear me. He's maneuvered us into a loading zone, right in front of the terminal. I get out of the car, stoop to gather my bags, and turn to pull my long coat from the back seat. I expect Charlie to jump out and open the trunk, but he just sits there facing forward, the heels of his hands on the steering wheel.

"You're really going, aren't you? I can't believe . . ."

"Charlie, please. Don't." I grip the door handle.

"I know you think you're looking for something, but Megan, your timing sucks."

I bite the inside of my lip. There's nothing I can say, at least nothing he wants to hear.

He presses his shoulders against the back of his seat. His neck is flushed. "What about Mom? She's been through a lot. Who's going to be there for her? We've learned to put up with your little eccentricities, but for god's sake, you're twenty-nine. Grow up, Megan. I've never known you to be so selfish."

There, he said it: the *s* word. He turns his face toward the creeping traffic and draws in a sigh. I move to speak but he cuts me off. "Dammit, Megan," he mutters, pushing himself out the car door.

It's a stab through my heart. Not the words. The words I can handle, it's that Charlie said them. I waver on the hard edges of his opinion, fighting the urge to remind him that I'm not Mama's only child. Exactly who decided I was responsible for her life anyway?

He's pulled the bags out of the trunk and has turned them over to the skycap who stands waiting for me to produce my ticket. As the bags disappear into the terminal, Charlie and I both know a line has been crossed.

"There's no more time." I say.

Charlie cups my face in his hands and kisses me on the forehead. I think maybe he's going to tell me it's okay and that he loves me.

"Take care of yourself," he says. "Call me when you know where you'll be." Then he slides into his car and drives away, straight ahead, no wave, no smile. I'm left standing in his wake, the coat over my arm fluttering with the bursts of air that escape through the terminal doors.

I scan the overhead monitors checking arrival and departure times. I should have called to confirm my reservations, but it wouldn't have made any difference. I would have insisted on coming now anyway. It's like the suicidal man; sooner or later, he needs to come to terms with the precipice—sometimes you recognize a pivotal moment and you have to step into it.

They're boarding children and the infirm, and I follow close on their heels. I edge into my window seat and bend to push my carryon under the seat in front of me.

If Mama were here, she would insist on an aisle seat, close to the restrooms and the ministrations of the flight attendant. She's into comfort and security, and she likes to be noticed. But I've come for the long view, and I snap the metal tongue into my seat belt and lean back.

It spikes my mother's blood pressure that I won't listen to reason—her reason. She's become more militant now that Dad is gone. She takes my leaving as a personal affront, like I'm doing this to vex and humiliate her.

I picture her at home this morning, calling her friends, detailing her outrage beneath a veneer of motherly concern. I expect she's already phoned Dr. Vickers and asked him to refill my old prescription. I can almost hear the two of them conspiring. She's doing what she can to prepare for the return of a cowed and more repentant me. I'm leaving her with the two things she fears the most: embarrassment by association—what will her friends think—and losing her grip. Mama has always had trouble loving with an open hand.

I try to sympathize, muster a little tenderness. Since my father died, we've all been trying to relocate ourselves within the space of his absence. But Mama says I'm on a dangerous course. What am I doing?—She says I'm looking for my father in the pages of the National Geographic.

They've secured the doors and the engine is whirring, a hum so constant, that if it were to stop, silence would be a sound.

We're moving, taxiing down the runway. It's a thrill. I feel like a thief, as if I've stolen my own life. I'm sealed inside, protected, but I catch myself looking toward the airport windows and down onto the tarmac, half expecting to see Mama and Dr. Vickers running after the plane.

If I were home, I would refuse to think about Dr. Vickers and the way he runs the tips of his fingers over his lower lip when he does his hard, angry listening. I stopped our anguished little sessions years ago, but I still give him a wide berth.

Last week I was having lunch with a friend when the good doctor came into the restaurant. I got up and walked out, scraped right past him at the door.

It's no secret that my mother still calls him on occasion to bemoan my stubborn lack of family feeling. And I imagine Dr.

Vickers is glad of it, Mama's calls that is, even though her proper self has yet to see him without me as an excuse.

Dr. Vickers is a married man, and a psychiatrist with no humility. He told me that he's practically part of my family, and I know, every time he looks at my mother, he'd like to believe it's true. I'm not sure if he sees my father's death as a setback or an opportunity, but he's got his eye out, spinning webs wherever he finds an opening.

I'd be careful though, if I were him. Even with all his years of practice and those pompous credentials, my mother may not be the fragile lovely widow he supposes.

Thinking of the two of them, I smile to myself, a contemptuous little smile that sends a shiver of pleasure through my stomach. Someone should warn him, but it won't be me.

When I was a child, I believed Dr. Vickers would save me, that he would banish some deep misunderstanding and declare me sound. Instead, he did his best to confound me with his jargon, measuring just how far I miss the mark with his pack of inkblots and open-ended questions.

I confronted him once, asked him if he wanted me to lie. He was unsympathetic, shrugging and brushing me off like so much dandruff, with a quick flick of his bony wrist.

His main achievement in my case has been in the area of diagnosis. He even published me. He almost thanked me once, in front of my mother, preening at my expense.

"Intriguing case, yours." He had a rolled up magazine in his hand and he tipped one end at me. "I should probably thank you," he said, smirking and shifting his gaze to my mother. "My article, about Megan's case. It's been published in the American Journal of Psychiatry," as if the mere name of the periodical might take our breaths away.

He must have seen incomprehension, even in my mother's eyes, because he faltered.

"Perhaps you'd care to take a look." He pushed the issue toward my mother.

"I've used Erikson as a framework. I'd be pleased to sit down and take you through it. I realize the writing can be dense—very clinical."

A little unethical, I think. No names were mentioned, of course, but there I was in printer's ink, captured in an invented phrase that, according to Dr. Vickers, fits me to a tee: pseudo-savant with a florid Electra complex—an ugly mouthful. It's the "pseudo" part that has Dr. Vickers' chin in the air. He invented it. When I commented that "pseudo" made it sound as if the rest of the diagnosis wasn't real, he said he added it to separate my condition from the classical accepted notion of savant. But I have a theory that the pseudo is really a Freudian slip. Electra incited the murders of her mother and the man her mother was tantalizing; maybe that's where the pseudo really comes in, a little subconscious manipulation tossed in for his own protection.

My father never liked him. Dr. Vickers' presence in our lives was always a concession to my mother. Another psychiatrist might have implicated my mother, pondering her pleasure at my dysfunction, but she always manages to get off scot-free when it comes to men.

2 THE DOPPELGANGER

I've angled myself toward the window to secure more privacy. The man who's been assigned the seat next to me is settling in now, leaning back and oozing in my direction. He's sized me up and has embarked on the process of declaring male privilege by planting his arm on our common armrest and inching his personal space in ever-increasing increments in my direction.

I catch myself in the process of compacting to accommodate and the awareness chafes. But I stall, making excuses for him. He really is too large to fit in these meager coach seats. I try to let it go at that, but he hoists himself forward and pulls the inflight magazine from the seat pocket in front of him, then bumps back to a recline with a force that shoots an elbow into my rib. I jerk around. He smiles, embarrassed "Sorry," he says, and retracts slightly but maintains command, his arm in a relaxed arc over fully one quarter of my seat. Now I'm bold, a fuming crusader, though my words let me down. All I can utter is a puny "Excuse me." But then I push against his interloping appendage with my forearm, a militant little act that surprises us both. And I move in and plant my arm all over that armrest. It's going to be a long trip, and I know his kind. You have to take care of yourself. There are precious few who are capable of respecting the space of others, even those they say they love.

We're airborne now, cruising at a lofty altitude and the pilot announces that we can move about the cabin. The tray tables and seat backs no longer need to remain in their upright and locked position and neither do I. I push my seat back at an angle and close my eyes. And there, in the only place I can dependably find him these days, is my father's face, hovering right behind my eyelids.

Oh God, I miss him. It's both a prayer and a lamentation. He was a man open to possibility but impressed by the facts. For Mama, it's a combination that has always been a challenge. She complains that it's one way I take after my dad. Like Eve, Dad was too curious to be a good Catholic. Mama still frets about his mortal soul and beats her breast for us both at Sunday Mass. Of course I'm exaggerating; her prayers are nothing if not proper. It's just that I can't help but rankle at her presumption. I wish she'd just stick to praying for herself and leave my dad and me out of it. But then, I shouldn't speak for him either.

No child can comfortably contemplate the death of a parent, and I doubt that a little warning really makes it easier. If you know something's coming, you have a tendency to flinch. Flinching involves crouching and squinting, and that's no way to meet life.

Dad died in the jagged hours of a single summer afternoon, five days before my twenty-ninth birthday. He was hefting a box of waste paper into the trash bin behind his office when a hit-and-run driver struck him down. The instrument of death was bruise blue, the color of a metallic hyacinth. It rammed my dad up against the Dumpster and left a blunt-edged signature, a telltale lead to something on wheels that has yet to be found.

I keep thinking about him that afternoon, hurt and alone, without a soft touch or a cradling arm. That thinking makes me miserable. It feels like my fault, the curved weight of karma. If Dad were here, he would tell me that his life and death isn't about me, that I spend too much time dwelling on what can't be changed. He'd be right, of course.

I've made more than one pilgrimage to that alley, to sit with my back up against the Dumpster, flush with the point of impact. I know it's morbid, and that I can't draw away Dad's pain, but I suffer too. I want to enter that place at the moment the blow was dealt, to conjure an instant replay so I can locate blame and demand justice.

But my strange seeing doesn't work that way. Instead, I hear the whir and click of roller skates on concrete, the high-stepping crunch through gravel, and I see two young boys, alarmed and tender. I watch them agonize over how to help. One leans over my dad's face, thinking about mouth-to-mouth resuscitation, but he notices blood on the teeth and he's afraid. The other darts from stoop to stoop, pounding at back entrances, until a dark-skinned man in a smudged apron, head circled with a sweat-stained bandanna, throws open a door.

Help will come now. Still, the one boy sits close, tears in his eyes, whispering, "Don't die, mister. Please, don't die." The other hangs back, he wants a safe distance, as if the approach of death is contagious.

I'm left grateful and bereft at the same time, even a little jealous of the moments my dad's rescuers spent with him. I thank God they found him, but if only I'd been there, I'm convinced I could have done more. Even Mama and Dr. Vickers have stopped slandering me; it's not just intuition and herbs anymore. I'm a doctor now, the emergency room kind, with a legitimate degree and prescribing rights to patented potions. I wonder if I might have saved him. I might have saved Bella too, not because I'm a doctor, but because I saw it coming. When it comes to those I love, I'm denied the opportunity. It's my karma, the pattern of my lesson. It drags me down. I miss my dad and I want to hold Bella in my lap and smell her hair.

I catch myself sighing, loud enough so the guy next to me rolls his eyes away from his magazine. He's stealing a glimpse to see if that audible little exhale requires something from him. It doesn't. I don't want any inane questions about where I'm from, or whether I like airline food. And I certainly don't want to see the pictures in his wallet. I give us both a break, and turn my head toward the window.

It's a clear day, with puffs of drifting clouds hanging together above a grid of pasture and croplands, and now and then, a patch of blue where the water winks back the sky. We're above the weather up here, speeding through thin air, but pending too. Travel is always about transition, not to be confused with the real life that happens down there, next to gravity, beneath umbrellas and sunscreen.

There was no need for an umbrella the day my dad died. It was as hot as it can get in a Colorado mountain town, and I wore sunscreen that afternoon. In fact, I was standing in front of my bathroom mirror, dabbing the lotion over the pale freckles across the bridge of my nose when the phone rang. I listened to it ring with one ear, trying to decide if I could resist the urge to answer it. I expected Mama to be on the other end, ready to harp that I don't come home enough, or maybe she had an errand in mind, another one that only I could accomplish. Not today, I thought, she won't get me today. Anyway, I knew her real problem was with my dad, and I didn't want to hear it.

Dad and I had gone fishing every Wednesday that summer. Wednesdays were my day off. Dad would close his office at two-thirty or three, and we'd head off in my Jeep, toward the Piedra with our fly rods and hip boots, some tomatoes from his garden and a black iron skillet for frying up a trout or two along the banks of the river at sundown.

Mama usually tolerated our fishing excursions, but that particular Wednesday, Bill and Trina Martin were visiting from out of town and she and dad had been invited to a barbeque and a game of bridge in their honor. Mama had accepted the invitation and she didn't tell Dad about it until the night before, when she was certain it would be too awkward for him to refuse.

She had urged me to come over that Tuesday evening. "Megan, darling, please. The garden's overflowing. Your father and I won't make a dent. And bring your laundry. There's no reason for you to go to a Laundromat when you can wash your clothes right here." She wanted to make sure that I would be there to overhear when she informed my father that this particular Wednesday evening was committed. If he was reluctant to cancel our routine fishing expedition, she was certain I would insist he go with her in the interest of keeping the peace.

It was after dinner and I was in the laundry room, folding warm towels and stacking my cotton underwear in neat piles on top of the ironing board, when the conversation began. Mama was in the kitchen biding her time, clinking the dishes, organizing them inside the dishwasher. I heard the lawn sprinkler begin wheeling around with its repetitive pst pst pst, and the screech and slam of the screen door behind my dad.

Mama slipped the first words in like they were a reminder. "Will, don't forget; there's a barbeque. We're playing bridge at the Pierce's tomorrow. Bill and Trina will be there. Seven, I think."

"That's the first I've heard of it. Anyway, you know Megan and I can't get back by then. If it's tomorrow night you'll have to cancel."

"But Will, it's important to me. Trina and I have been friends for years. You know how hard it was for me when they moved."

"Look, Rose, if you'd asked me earlier, but not this week. Megan and I have something special going on and we just saw the Martins last Sunday. Go without me. Ask someone from your bridge club. Or ask Father Tim, he plays bridge."

"But they asked us as a couple. It may be our last chance to spend time with them before they leave on Saturday. Will, come on. You and Megan can change your plans this once." Her voice was rising now, becoming strained. I could feel her getting ready to reel me in. Still, I jumped when I heard my name.

"Megan, Megan darling, come out here."

I slammed the dryer door and stepped around the corner, but even before I had assumed the proper attentive demeanor, my father intercepted. He had his hand in the air, palm toward me like a traffic cop, his eyes hard, fixed on my mother.

"Stop it, Rose. Just leave it. If you want to go, then go. But tomorrow night, Megan and I are going fishing." He softened a bit, and glanced my way with a reassuring nod. But when he looked back at my mother, his stiff shoulders exposed the cords in his neck. "Damn it. Sometimes you surprise even me. If this is still about my plans for Megan's birthday, you're wasting your time. If you're really looking for me to rearrange a little fishing trip to accommodate a bridge game, then you have a short memory."

My mother stood there, looking wounded, tears glistening on the rims of those exquisite blue eyes, movie tears, enhanced by a sweet little lipstick pucker. She kept her chin up, courageously wronged, waiting for an apology. And my dad did stall, a glimmer of sadness there. I thought he would step forward and fold her in his arms, but instead, he turned on his heel and left. He closed the door to the garage behind him, not even a slam. My mother sighed and bit the corner of her lip. She tilted her head up to stare at a cobweb in the corner. Poor spider, I thought, he'd have to work faster, be craftier, to stay ahead of her. But for now, she was regrouping, gathering in her frustration.

I came forward to comfort her, but I wasn't the audience she wanted. She moved out of my reach, turned her back on me. She snugged in, next to the kitchen sink, looking away from me and out the window. I watched her lift her arms and pull her green rubber gloves over the polished tips of her fingers. She powdered the sink with a gritty chlorine cleanser, took up her sponge, and went to work, purging the porcelain.

I didn't go into the garden that evening. The kitchen window faces the backyard, and I was afraid my stomping around out there would annoy my mother. Anyway, I was in a hurry now. I wanted to go back to my own apartment, to be among my own things, in a place where I had a form and substance I could count on.

I put my laundry into a basket and wiped off the surface of the washer and dryer, the way my mother liked to have it done, and went outside. The day was spending the last of itself in a flame of pink that washed the horizon and tinted the sidewalk. My dad had the garage door open and was loading his fishing gear into the back of my Jeep. It seemed an odd thing for him to be doing just then, since our pattern had always been for me to come by the house and pick him up on our way out of town. I went around the passenger side and set my laundry basket inside on the seat. He came around beside me and put his arm across my shoulders, a smug smile on his face. "Take good care of my tackle box, Meg, it's got your birthday present in it. And no peeking. I thought you and I would celebrate a few days early, just the two of us."

As I backed down the driveway, I heard their phone ring and Mama hollered, "Will! Will, it's for you."

Dad stepped away up the driveway, but paused and turned with a wave. Then he straightened his stride and hustled toward the house.

I backed the Jeep out into the street and shifted into first gear, gave it a little extra gas. The Jeep jerked forward toward the stop sign at the top of the hill.

I grew up on a quiet street. The homes are old and well loved, just like most of the people who live there. It's a mix of older folks and young families, where kids still set up lemonade stands and their parents visit on porches or over the back fence. There are few interlopers and only the traffic of neighbors. But that evening, as soon as I left the driveway, I felt a car encroach and crowd me from behind. I glanced into my rearview mirror. Practically on top of me, lights on and out of sync with a summer evening, especially in this particular protected universe, was a steel grey hearse. I tapped the brake, warning him to back off. I had my hand on the Jeep's horn, was checking to size up the driver before disturbing the peace. I looked, and looked again, but it wasn't the driver that grabbed my attention. There, in the passenger seat, I saw myself.

I shook my head. My hands were trembling. I willed myself to turn and confront, but I couldn't summon the nerve.

The windows of the hearse were open. And though a brisk evening breeze was whipping loose strands of hair against my face where I sat perched in the driver's seat between the roll bars of my Jeep, the air in the hearse behind me seemed stagnant. Not a whisper rustled the scarf that kept the apparition's hair confined at her neck. And those soft wisps of dark blonde hair, the ones I smooth and straighten every morning, pulled loose at her forehead and cheekbones into damp curls. She sat there; looking listless, beyond tired and wilted, hanging a pale nervous fist outside the window grasping something. I couldn't tell what.

The Jeep pushed forward. My foot still pressed an uphill speed, but I couldn't take my eyes away. There was the sudden flash of a headlight. My doppelganger registered it too. She jerked her chin forward, head up. Our eyes engaged in the mirror. I startled and slammed on the brakes. The Jeep screeched into the intersection, across the path of an oncoming car. The driver rode his brakes and blasted the horn. He swerved to the side and up onto the curb shouting something I'm sure I deserved.

There was an instant when my foot pressed the floorboard that I waited for the screech and slam of the hearse to strike me from behind, but the hearse had vanished. Anyway, there was no need. I had already been stricken.

I was still trembling when I got home, rattled and a little disoriented. I pulled into the garage, grabbed my purse and the garage door opener and took off across the pavement, feeling pursued by the slap and click of my own sandals. My watch had stopped working again, but it must've been about 9:00 because the lights along the walkway outside my apartment were competing with what was left of the daylight. I had to hold one hand over the other to steady the key into the lock.

I slammed the door behind me, heaped my purse, keys, everything, on the corner of the couch and headed for the phone. I needed to talk to my dad, but the line was busy. I punched the button down, then dialed, over and over again. My mind was jumping all over the place. I wondered if he'd been on the phone since I left him, and I was stabbed by a thought—Charlie! What if something had happened?

At last there was ringing on the other end. "Oh please, please, don't let it be Mama," I muttered between my teeth.

"Halloo," it was Dad's easy offhand voice.

"Dad," I blurted, "I saw something on my way home. I saw me, the me I am now."

"Meggie, honey, slow down."

"I know, Dad. It doesn't make sense, but I know what it means. Something terrible is going to happen. To someone I love."

"Who, Meg? What kind of thing?"

"I'm afraid it's Charlie, or," I paused, then almost in a whisper, "You. You, Dad. Maybe it's you."

There was silence on the other end, and I reconsidered, but it was too late to take it back. Now Dad would worry, mostly about me.

When he spoke, his words were carefully chosen. "Megan, you need to get ahold of yourself. Settle down. We'll handle this. I just spoke to Charlie. He's in Chicago at a conference on the North American Wetlands. He's lecturing with his photographs tomorrow, staying right there in town with Claire and Jonathan. I know for a fact, that, at least for tonight, everyone's all right. And your mother and I are here, safe and feeling fine. We'll talk about this tomorrow, on our way out of town.

We'll pick it apart. Now tell me you'll relax, have a glass of wine or warm milk, whatever it takes. Please."

"Alright. But will you be careful?"

"I promise not to do anything crazy. And tomorrow I'll go straight to work. I'll take my fishing clothes to the office, change in the bathroom, so you can pick me up there. And if I feel sick or strange, I'll call you. Okay, Doc?"

"Thanks, Dad. I love you."

It was that next afternoon and I was getting ready to collect Dad at his office when the phone rang. Anticipating that it was Mama, I kept right on with what I was doing, slipped the sunscreen back into the pocket of my vest, then twisted my hair into a knot and tucked it up under my favorite fishing hat. I even took the time to look in the mirror again and admire my felt hat band, all spruced up with extra hooks and the flies I'd tied with Dad.

The phone kept ringing. That's just like Mama, I thought, she doesn't know when to quit. I was positively oppositional by the time I gave in and picked up the receiver.

"Yes."

"Hello. Hello, Megan?" the voice stumbled. "This is Joyce, you know, Mrs. Collins, from next door to your folks. I hate to trouble you."

Oh god, I thought, adrenalin numbing my fingertips, here it comes. "Yes, hello? Is everything okay?"

"No, dear, I'm calling for your mother. There's been an accident. Your mother's gone to the hospital."

"Is it serious? Is she alright?"

"No dear, I'm sorry, I mean it's not your mother. She's gone to be with your father. Apparently he was hurt and they've taken him to Mercy Hospital."

I could barely breathe. My mind flashed to the curtain behind the seat of the hearse. The details were already converging. My tongue felt too large for my mouth and I stood there, dumb.

"Your mother said to tell you she needs you, and to hurry. It may be bad. That's really all I know."

"Yes, well, thank you. I'm on my way. I'm leaving now."

I clicked the phone down, didn't wait for sympathy or farewells. That would come later.

On any other day, it's a nine minute drive from my apartment to the hospital, but that day it took less than seven minutes. I know because I didn't take the time to go around to Emergency. I used the front entrance, took the steps two at a time and burst right through the heavy double doors at the top and into the foyer, face-to-face with a recessed statue of a world-toting baby Jesus. The holy infant supported the earth in one arm and lifted his other hand in a benediction that pointed upward, a benevolent gesture toward the divine eternal. But more immediately, he directed my eye to the round etched face of a clock thoughtlessly superimposed on the decorative panel above him. I registered the time at 3:09.

Dad and I should have been on our way out of town, 'Gone Fishing,' like the sign I knew was hanging at the end of its chain on his office door said. Instead, I was stalled there in the hospital lobby, afraid of losing my grip, my own little world humming in my hands, gaining velocity and already spinning out of control.

They brought Dad in by ambulance. By the time I got there, he had already been moved to the intensive care unit. I rushed to his room, then hesitated in the doorway. They had him all wired up, and Barb Jennings, a nurse I knew, who sometimes worked with me in Emergency, was checking his vital signs and adjusting his IV. Mama was breathing in soft, managed sobs; one hand over her mouth, leaning up against the metal bar at the foot of Dad's bed. Even from the back, I saw her make the sign of the cross, opening a portal to God. She looked to Father Tim in his priestly collar and ceremonial stole. I knew what he was doing. Father Tim was at work, marking Dad with an oily thumb and the mumbled words of extreme unction.

I stepped to the side, behind the door jamb and out of sight. I couldn't bear to be part of this, not yet. I needed to gather myself into a solid center and come to this wretched thing on my own terms before Mama realized I was there.

It was in that half moment that Paul Neeley came into the hallway outside Dad's room. I'd had a hard time working with him lately, but it shouldn't have been that way. He'd been a long-time friend of my brother, Charlie. Our families attended the same church and we had a lot in common. He'd been hired as a doctor in Mercy Hospital's radiology department at about the same time I'd come on as a physician in the Emergency Room, both of us fresh out of residency. He was tan and blonde, with the kind of good looks that made him the lascivious object of gossip in the nurses' lounge. We had dated a couple times. He'd been pleasant and eager, for awhile, while I did my best to dodge him. But at the moment, what I really regretted was how unrelentingly rude I had become whenever he was around. Now I hated the awkwardness. I needed a friend.

He came to me, his expression serious, even tender. I thought he might take me in his arms, but at the last minute he hesitated and put his hands in the pockets of his white coat.

"Have you been in there?"

"No, I'm waiting for Father Tim and Mama to finish with their mumbo jumbo."

"Megan," I caught the beginnings of a rebuke but he changed direction. "Bailey's prepping for surgery, in case that's what you want. I don't recommend it. I don't think . . ."

Mama heard us. I registered her awareness, monitored her in the periphery as she emerged through the doorway. I saw her pull her spine straight, chin up. She pinched at the end of her nose with her handkerchief and stuffed the matted cloth into the folds of her skirt. She must have come from shopping or having lunch with friends. She swished into the hallway all nylon stockings and silk petticoats under a floral print, cinched to perfection with a wide white belt, and smelling of gardenias. But inside the flouncy outfit, this was a different mother that stumbled toward me. The usual sensuous blush she wore on her cheeks had turned garish, smudged over skin gone pale and translucent. For once she reached out to me, her chin quivering, pursing her lips into tiny trembles and puckers, "Meggie, honey, come see your father. He's been hurt and I can't get him to wake up. Please. He needs to tell us what to do."

I stood there while she clung to me, not the mutual embrace that soothes in times of trouble, but a desperate grip that clutched and smothered. Paul saw my discomfort and stepped close, murmuring words next to my mother's ear. He was talking, coaxing, trying to dislodge her. I don't know what he said, by then I had stopped listening.

I had tuned in to a faint drumming and whooshing, coming closer, sounding like the flutter and whistle of a wind that whips and eddies at the mouth of a tunnel. For a second, I expected it to ruffle the curtains and freshen the air, but then I caught a flash, the approach of a radiant swirling breach, an invitation into that veiled and insubstantial place that is no place.

I twisted away from my mother, pushed her toward Paul, and shot into my father's room. Father Tim was finishing, making the sign of the cross. "Move," I said, and thrust myself between Father Tim and my dad.

Father Tim arched backward then righted himself, stepped off, and recoiled toward the door.

Dad was lying there, white and smaller than I'd ever seen him. I took his hand. "It's okay, Dad," I said. But I knew it wasn't.

3 REQUIEM

We buried Dad on my birthday. The Mass was packed. I think everyone in town was there. Even Reverend Howard, the Baptist minister who spent one summer years ago coaching little league with my father, took an inconspicuous corner in a back pew.

Father Tim threw the church doors open and had extra fans brought in to churn air across the congregation. Still, the day hung on us like a mantle. And while Mama insisted on a funeral program of heavyweight paper embossed on the front with a Constantine cross, her tasteful statement was lost on friends and family who seemed more appreciative that a sturdy card like that could be put to use as an efficient personal fan.

The organ ceased its mumble of familiar Sunday hymns and the mourners stood upright in the pews. A black-robed Father Tim swept down the aisle and gave the signal, then waited at the mouth of the church between the heavy double doors while the pallbearers slid the coffin from the back of the hearse and hefted it up the steps, feet first. When the casket crossed the threshold, the pallbearers halted in place and Father Tim opened his arms, marshaling the forces of light. "Come to his assistance, you saints of God. Come forth to meet him, you angels of the Lord. Receive this soul and offer it in the sight of the Most High."

We, the bereaved family, gathered at my father's head. Only Mama had the benefit of her prayer book. She gripped it next to her stomach together with her rosary, and listened as Father Tim and the congregation chanted back and forth, inducting Dad into the hereafter.

Father Tim finished and led the pallbearers and their burden up the aisle. One of the ushers waited for us to cluster and steady, then he escorted us to a pew at the front, close by the polished wooden casket, already flanked with banks of flowers and marked off with drooping loops of black crepe.

Mama marched at the usher's back, her slender neck emerging from a prim and collarless dress into a swirl of black netting that enveloped her face beneath a brimmed hat. Her public persona seemed to glide along on Charlie's arm but I could feel her exerting a gravitational pull. And right then, Charlie was her object. Charlie was white with fatigue, but he was tender with her, caressing her grip with his opposite hand and mincing his lanky steps to reconcile with hers.

Behind Mama and Charlie came my older sister, Claire, grown up angular and sophisticated, successful in all the ways big sisters are supposed to be. Claire paced forward on the sleeve of her husband, Jonathan, a suave city stockbroker whose other arm supported a rosy-cheeked toddler. Baby Toby was glassy-eyed and tenuous, missing his nap.

I dragged along behind, a loose end in a stiff black dress that Mama had Claire pick up for me at Graden's Department Store.

Claire presented the dress to me in one of those plastic hanging bags and I took it, too numb to care. But when I put it on, the shoulders were too snug and the armholes chafed. The unyielding feel of it in the heat made me irritable. Perspiration gathered around the neckline and under my arms. In the places where I oozed or trickled, the fabric clung to my skin like a poultice.

In front of me, Baby Toby sucked his thumb and drooped against Jonathan's neck. Toby, I thought, would miss his grandpa, or more likely, I'd miss his grandpa for him. Dad would have insisted on taking his grandson home, saying a funeral is no place for a child. I pictured him in the garage, searching out our old wading pool and filling it with the hose. While Toby slept, Dad and the water would wait and warm in the sun.

Our little procession rustled into the reserved pew and the organ began to play. Choir voices chimed. "Holy, Holy, Holy, Lord God, Almighty," and a cloud moved, or the sun slid a notch, and a shaft of blue light streamed in through a stained glass window tilted above the altar. The light dazzled the polished coffin and refracted against the metal bands and handles. The beam spun off fragments that shimmered around the room. One angled over Toby's curls and across my face. Toby squinted and buried his head in the curve of Jonathan's neck, and Jonathan slid out of the brightness closer to Claire.

But I stayed where I was, soaking it up, feeling a quiver at the back of my heart like the leftover vibration of a percussion instrument. I could sense Dad in the light—God and Dad all mixed together.

It was to be a High Mass, a typical celebration of its type, but with personalized ornamentation. Claire swallowed an extra Valium from Mama's stash so she would be able to sing the Ave

Maria before Father Tim delivered his sermon. Charlie's job was to stay beside Mama. And from me, Mama wanted something from Mozart before the consecration of the bread and wine. I acquiesced under pressure, with the single stipulation that she not expect me to learn something new.

It seemed right anyway, that I would play for Dad on a day that was supposed to be about him, though Mama's selection wouldn't have been a special request of his. He liked folk music and country western best. When the two of us put our guitars together Mama would pick up her stationery box and leave for the library or go shopping. Now my guitar sat alone and lonely on the wide carpeted steps in front of the choir box, propped there beside a little wooden music stand. How was I going to survive without my dad?

The good priest and his solemn little entourage took their places around the altar with their backs to us and the standing congregation kneeled. As Father Tim chanted Latin prayers, the sheets of my music, stacked loose against the lip of the stand, began to rustle and dish off, one after another, lofted by currents of air from the freewheeling fans at the front of the church.

Some skipped over the carpet, then wavered on the other side of the communion rail until they were caught by a current and blown against the carved base of the altar. They hung there like litter against a roadside fence until Father Tim, at a place where the ritual would forgive him, lifted a finger. An alert altar boy bustled to a genuflect, made the sign of the cross, and removed the offenders, jamming them under the weighted base of the music stand.

Later, when Father Tim nodded for Claire to come for her solo, he pulled his eye along our family pew, punctuating the sweep of his vision with a pause and a sharp look for me, as if I had set the fans spinning or placed those pages where they would be peeled off by the breeze.

Mama's perfect child, my stunning sister, Claire, stood and squeezed past Jonathan and me, careful not to disturb the sleeping Toby. She didn't stand where I thought she was going to, but placed herself on the step in front of my guitar with her shiny black heels tight together. She arched her back and lifted her chin, drawing air in a vast inhale, inspiring, then exhaling her clear bell-like prayer above our heads and into the rafters so the melody resonated there before it settled on us like a soothing mist.

Her last note struck silence and there was a pause. The congregation began to shuffle in their seats. Father Tim left his stiff-backed chair and swept into the pulpit.

Claire took advantage of that shifting moment to attempt a discrete gathering of the rest of my scattered music. She scooped a page from the floor in front of our pew, then stooped to retrieve another from among the banks of flowers surrounding our father's casket. She dislodged the page, and along with it, her grasp having been a tad imprecise, she liberated a single daisy from a spray that bunched daisies with pink snapdragons and sprigs of heather. She grasped the flower with the music in one hand. I think she intended to return to her seat, but she used one of the brass bars that supported the coffin to balance herself back onto the tilted arches of her sharp-heeled shoes, and hung there, staring at the bow of the wooden lid. A deep concerted silence rippled over the congregation. Jonathan stiffened beside me and I heard someone in the back ask, "Is she all right?" Everyone was primed, but nobody moved.

She put her cheek against the coffin, and then her ear. Mama leaned around Charlie to Jonathan and me, "For heaven's sake, one of you, have the good sense to help her."

I pushed out of the pew, genuflected, and moved toward Claire. I was making a show of rescue, but mostly, I was trying to buy her some time. I expected she wanted to listen, maybe she was hoping for a knock from the other side.

I laid my hand against her back. She registered my touch and twisted, faced me, stark, her eyes gathering tears. "I meant to call him last week. He needs to know I love him."

I wrapped her in my arms and held her head against my neck, fighting the choke of sympathy. "He knows, Claire." And I knew he did.

She straightened and wiped her cheeks with the back of her hand and offered me my hard won music and that single drooping daisy. When we eased back into our pew she squeezed my arm and whispered, "I'm sorry."

I was sorry too; sorry that she was embarrassed, sorry that Dad was dead, sorry that we would have to go on living in a world without him. But it seemed to me that being sorry was the only real thing about loving Dad that had happened all day. The rest was performance, sterile and unrelated to us, like somebody else's medication.

Father Tim leaned forward in the pulpit and cleared his throat. He started his eulogy with the comfortable words, "Come unto me all you that travail and are heavy laden, and I will refresh you." Then he talked about my dad as a husband and father, a member of the Knights of Columbus and a champion of children. But his words were general, devoid of loving detail. It was Mama that Father Tim knew by heart. Father Tim might have been the priest in Dad's parish, but he was not his friend, or even his confessor.

Still, Father Tim tried, comforting us with the story of Lazarus, and how Lazarus's good friend, Jesus, took pity on the bereaved family and dried their tears by bringing Lazarus back from the dead. The story came with a disclaimer at the end, that it was a miracle, the impossible made possible. "We Christians," he said, "must look for our serenity in the promise of peace and faith in the life after this one."

His sermon left me chafed, an irritation that stayed with me as I marched the shallow steps to my guitar, wagging my rumpled pages with the daisy crushed against them.

I stood behind the little music stand and looked out over heads and hats, then paused to run my eyes along our pew. Mama's expression was masked under her veil of netting, but she sat upright, expectant. Charlie dipped his chin, as much of a smile as the occasion could muster. Father Tim cleared his throat. I glanced at him and nodded.

I pushed the music stand forward and shoved the pages in my hand underneath with the others, dropped the daisy on the wooden lip and picked up my guitar. I plucked a few tuning notes and hummed alongside them until the blend was right, then stepped next to the casket, making a shallow genuflect to God on the way. It wasn't my intent to be disrespectful.

I strummed a little intro. Mama pushed up higher in her seat. It didn't take long for her to figure out it wasn't Mozart I had on my mind. I tried to give her a gentling look as I hummed to tell her to relax and trust me, but she shook her head and shrugged, then dropped back against the pew.

I blanched and the sweat under my arms turned cold and clammy, but my sense of her disapproval only galvanized my intent. This was my remembrance to Dad and I went right ahead, ignored Mama, and broke into a song my dad and I used to sing, our mutual version of "Morning Has Broken," a hymn full of soaring praise for God and the natural world that my dad loved so much.

Early on, I saw Charlie, his face stark with emotion, put his arm around Mama. I took it as a sign of his approval, and I sent my voice out, strong and encouraged.

Later, when I looked again, Mama was shaking, emitting low keening moans. She crumbled into Charlie's arms. Charlie wept too, bent and ruined.

I held a note, then let it trail off into a long and awkward hush that, every now and then, churned up a whisper or a muffled sob. My heart puddled into my shoes. I had gone too far, stolen Mama's dignity, and inflicted my need to be purged on others who might have been better served by a slow cure.

Mama told me once that I was her child, more like her than either Claire or Charlie. I had been incensed, but I was getting a new perspective. Intolerant and sometimes too stubborn, maybe I needed a dose of humility myself.

I left the unplayed pages of Mozart where they were and picked up that poor, sad daisy, a lone straggler just like me. I beat a path down the carpeted aisle toward the heavy double doors at the mouth of the church, through a gauntlet of perplexed stares and unintelligible murmurs. I could feel sobs working in my chest, and blood throbbed in my head. I took long, quick strides, gaining speed, until I burst out into the gathering swelter.

I clomped down the church steps hating the heels on my shoes and panicked by the sting of embarrassment. First I worried that someone would come after me, then I worried that they wouldn't. I got to the bottom step and pushed into a shaded corner where the building met the concrete banister, leaning into whatever coolness might be left in the shaded stone. I stood there listening and scolding myself. How could I be so smart and so stupid at the same time?

Seconds passed; I counted them like heartbeats. I heard the firm thump of a man's shoes against the stone steps and held my breath. The footsteps halted and then scuffled, moving the width of the stairs and back. My name pierced the air, elongated, "May-gun. Hey, kid, come back. Megan, please. Where the devil are you?"

It was Charlie. Oh God, he sounded so exasperated. But he had come for me; Charlie, always the hurt-soother, Charlie the peacemaker. Wasn't I too old to expect him to come to my rescue? I started to move away from the wall so he could see me, but it was too late. All I caught was a glimpse of him throwing his hands in the air on his way back into the church.

I stood there dangling my guitar. I was thinking that I should just go home. It meant not seeing Dad through to the end, but I wasn't sure how I fit here anymore. Then, from up the street, I heard a car door slam. Someone I recognized, Jeff Burgess, came stepping around the back of the hearse, out of the truncated shadow of the church. Jeff had managed to come by the only real pocket of shade on either side of the street. He was wearing a chauffeur's hat and carried a dark jacket draped across a bent arm. The neck of his shirt was open and he'd pulled the knot of his tie slack.

"Megan, I thought that was you. Are you alright?"

"I'm okay. Just don't ask what I'm doing out here. I can't go back in there, but I can't seem to leave either."

"This heat's a killer. At least come sit in the shade until you decide." He angled his head toward the hearse. "Wish I could offer air conditioning, but today when I could use it, it's not working."

I trailed close behind him. He opened the door on the passenger side. It took a minute before I could bring myself to get in, but Jeff held the door and waited, as if he expected a little skittishness. "Yeah, a lot of people are reluctant to get into a hearse."

It wasn't quite on the mark, but it was more understanding than I got from a lot of people. I nodded and handed him my guitar. He put it in the recess behind the seat, and I ducked in. He let himself in on the other side, slipped under the steering wheel and left his door open on its hinges. "I was having a soda. Want one? They're not cold but they're wet." He reached around behind the little curtain in back of the seat and pulled a Coke out of a paper bag. He held the bottle over the gutter outside and removed the cap. It whooshed and fizzed, then settled. He handed it to me.

He could have talked about old friends, or asked me what it was like being back from medical school and Pennsylvania, or told me about his new wife, but he didn't. We just sat there, leaning against the seat, both of us watching for signs of life from the church, and now and then pulling swigs from the rolled glass lip of our Coke bottles.

The church bells began to peal and Jeff sat upright in his seat, buttoned his shirt to the neck, slipped the knot of his tie in place and jostled into his jacket. "It's show time." He tugged his lapels straight, started the engine, and jerked the hearse door shut. "You're welcome to ride with me—with your dad. It's doubtful anyone will notice you, unless you want them to."

Jeff backed the hearse up, close to the steps. From the front seat, I couldn't see the pallbearers, but I felt the heaviness of the casket as it was hefted and settled. The door slammed shut, and Jeff came back around and hopped into the driver's seat. He turned on the headlights and stuck his arm out with a signaling movement.

The hearse rolled forward at a dirge-like pace through town toward the cemetery. The engine jogged and shifted into a lower gear, pulling uphill, then halted at the last stop sign, just before the gates with the marble angels on either side. I felt a pang of guilt, wondered about Charlie and Claire—and Mama. I put my hand out the window to feel the breeze on my arm, and let my eyes drift to the rear-view mirror, expecting a glimpse of the limousine behind, but the angle of the mirror caught my own reflection and flashed it back at me—my face, pale, and damp with perspiration. The mangled daisy drooped from my fist; its petals fluttered in the breeze. The breath caught in my throat, I made a sharp little sound and yanked my fist back inside—not a surprise exactly, just that the details were so precise.

Jeff turned, "You okay?"

"I just saw someone," I said. "But I knew she would be here."

I stayed to the lonesome end, stood among the aspens and cedars up the hill and watched like Daddy's guardian angel, until the hydraulic frame that supported the casket over the gouged earth lowered its burden and was rolled away and folded in on itself. By then I was the only mourner left, unless you counted Jeff, who waited in the hearse. I wandered back down through the gravestones, reading the names of Daddy' s new neighbors, then made myself step to the edge of the gaping hole. It smelled like digging potatoes in Daddy's garden. I dropped the daisy on top of the fistfuls of earth thrown in by Mama, and Claire, and Charlie. I was having desperate thoughts.

I heard the lumbering drone before I saw it, a heavy duty engine chugging along the hard-packed incline, drowning out the chirps of insects and the faint hum of traffic drifting up from the highway. Close-in, the vibration was thick enough to jar loose soil from the walls of the grave onto Daddy's coffin. The sound was huge in the silence, but at close range, the backhoe was small, a miniature road machine operated by a lone workman. The sun-burnt man bumped along as if he were in a saddle, managing the machine's gears with gloved hands. When he saw me between him and his work, he jerked the machine to a standstill beneath the shade of a nearby tree. He perched there, looking at me from under his baseball cap. I suppose he was trying to show a little respect, but he kept the engine running. Nobody needed to tell me that I had overstayed my welcome.

I blew my dad a kiss and whispered, "See you later, alligator," the same way I'd been telling him goodbye since I was four. I felt around in my pocket for a tissue and walked back to the hearse, slid in next to Jeff. And as if we were already gone, the workman crossed our path with his little yellow burying machine and hopped down. He hoisted, then flipped the tarp, to get at the mound of dirt underneath, remounted, revved the engine, and slid the controls to swing his bucket.

Jeff took me home the roundabout way. We had to stop by the mortuary to leave the hearse and get his car, but he insisted on delivering me to my door. He waited at the end of my walkway for me to wave him off, idling against the red upholstery in his little white Corvair. I had my key ready, slipped it in the lock with a measured push, then turned and lifted my hand. He gave a sloppy salute, really more of a high sign, and drove off. I stood against the door, holding the knob, and watched him take the corner, disappear, then reappear, far removed and merged with the traffic heading across the bridge.

It must have been about 3:30. A breeze was kicking up, massing and rolling out a cloud-cover that dimmed the light and deepened shadows. The atmosphere sagged with a glow that seeped into bricks and grass, even the concrete, everything washed in the somber sheen of a minor key. Heat lightning flared in the distance and rumbled, once and then again. I counted the seconds between peals. Relief was coming.

4 THE TACKLEBOX

I leaned back against the door, felt it click shut behind me. It was a relief to fill my lungs with air that had the familiar smell of my own things. I set my guitar in its stand and lobbed my purse onto the couch, flexed one foot then the other, flicking my clunky-heeled shoes with a snap that sent them across the carpet. I padded to the refrigerator for iced tea, held the pitcher next to my face and absorbed the wet coolness, tilted it up like a giant mug and chugged big gulps that sloshed over my chin. The phone started to ring but I didn't hurry. By the time I got across the kitchen and was picking up the receiver, I had peeled that insufferable dress down to my waist and was shaking my hair free, letting it fall in a mass around my shoulders.

I used my free hand around the back of my head to pull my hair away and pressed the receiver to my ear.

"Hello?"

"Finally. You left the church in such a state. Where have you been?"

"I'm not in a state, Mama, but I'm sorry if you worried.

"Everyone's been asking about you. You should be here with your family. I was afraid you'd gone off again. I'll send Charlie."

"Mama, don't. I need some time alone. Please. Don't send Charlie."

Those last words went nowhere. She'd already hung up the phone.

I laid the receiver back in its cradle and shimmied into my jeans and an old madras work shirt, grabbed some thick socks and my hiking boots. Outside, heavy drops, lonely and methodical, began to thud and splash off the metal awning over my kitchen window.

I stuffed my rain gear and an extra tarp into the top of my backpack along with a few dehydrated dinners, a bag of gorp, and several oranges. My bedroll stayed hitched to the bottom of the pack frame, part of my standard equipment, but I covered it with some plastic. The only thing left was my fishing pole, and it was still in the Jeep, along with Dad's pole and his tackle box.

I drew the blinds and locked the door, was crossing the parking lot to the garage with my gear when Charlie drove by in his little red Honda. Paul was with him.

I ducked into the half-shed that housed the trash cans and crouched down behind the cedar boards, scraping the metal frame of my pack against the can lid on my way down. I froze into position and watched the two of them pull the collars of their suit coats up as they ran through the raindrops to my front door. There were minutes of quiet when I knew they were ringing the doorbell. Charlie pounded and called my name. I hunched lower, shame beginning to seep into my confidence. Why was I making everyone who wanted to love me work so hard? How would it look, me rising up among the trashcans? And then what?

The two of them dashed past me, heading back to Charlie's car. I heard the doors slam and the tires spin up water. I hunched there for long minutes, drawn in on myself and feeling lonely.

I drove out of town in a torrent. The windshield wipers worked double-time and a change in the temperature had scared up a breeze that swept through the piñon pine and spruce, bowed the aspens and made a wet whistle that blew beads of moisture through the little gap between the rubber and glass on the driver's side. I watched the eerie droplets coalesce and snake across the top of the windshield, then burst apart, too ripe for their own good.

I thought about my dad and his first night underground. I had touched him yesterday, held his lifeless hand and emptied myself into his deaf ears. I felt myself trembling and steered off the highway onto the first dirt road that left the highway. I lodged the Jeep in between some scrub and a barbed wire fence, then let go and bellowed, rolled down the window and wailed into the wind and rain, wallowed in unsociable, ugly tears until my insides were dry and limp.

My private purge exhaled into a deep dampness, and I blew my nose and wiped my eyes. The rain had stopped and late day sunshine dazzled drips still clinging to the scrub. The smell of sage and pine needles spiked the air. I straightened in my seat to listen. A magpie jeered at me from a fence post and mosquitoes, bobbing and humming through the open window, searched me for patches of bare skin. I slapped one against my neck and wiped my hand on my jeans, cranked the window closed. I mopped the fog off the inside of the windshield with an old tee shirt, started the engine, and turned on the defroster. Afternoon was turning into evening, the sun already pinking up the snow-capped peaks. I was frittering away daylight and I had it in my head to make it to a certain lean-to. I jerked the Jeep into re-verse and whipped backward in a stroke, hit the highway and pressed ahead with a resolute lurch.

The wide, barren patch next to the trailhead was already oc-cupied by a truck hitched to a double horse trailer, and I had to park farther away from the trail and closer to the road than I'd wanted. I locked the doors and went around to the back, pulled out my pack, and decided to take my dad's fly rod and his creel instead of my own. I popped open his tackle box to get at his reel, and there, with a "Happy Birthday, Megan" scrawled across it in Dad's flat condensed handwriting, was a manila en-velope.

It had crossed my mind once, earlier in the day, that it was my birthday, but the thought had so little weight to sustain it that I'd let it drift. Now, here it was again. The envelope had the heft and thickness of multiple pages and a bulk at the bot-tom that felt like a folded letter or packet. I held it close to my nose but the only smell was the one it shared with the tackle box, a faint scent of old metal mingled with salmon eggs.

Inside, I expected to find a gift certificate for new gear, or maybe Dad had finally committed us to a winter vacation in Yellowstone, our reward after the expense and effort of medical school. I was tempted to open it right then but I decided I'd wait and open it by firelight. I tucked the envelope and the short rigid tube that held the pieces of Dad's fishing pole into the side-pocket of my pack. I grabbed his sheath knife and hooked it onto my belt, finished closing up the Jeep, and hoist-ed the pack onto my back.

I began hustling along the edge of the road, a hundred yards or more, and started to climb at a place where a snow-fed spring, swollen with rainwater, gurgled down into a culvert beneath the asphalt.

The last smudges of daylight would be fleeting and I decided that getting to the lean-to was out of the question. The best I could do was trudge upstream and find a grassy place to bed down.

The clouds were clearing and there would be a moon; I was counting on it, a waxing gibbous moon, bright and lopped on one edge. Dad would be proud of me for knowing my moons.

How long would it be before I stopped anticipating his presence? Even the heavens seemed less hopeful without him.

I took off at a clip, hiking along the edge of the trees. I didn't have far to go before I found a stretch of smooth earth shielded from the intermittent breeze murmuring across the tops of the aspens and pines.

The sheltered cove was almost a nest, thick with old pine needles and matted in places where a deer might have slept.

I spread my tarp and unrolled my sleeping bag, pulled out extra clothing, my toothbrush and the insect repellent. I put the pouch of gorp, an orange, and two packets of hot cocoa mix in my pocket then I flung a rope over a sturdy tree limb and anchored my pack out of reach.

I began breaking the dead, scaly limbs off evergreen trunks until I had a stack of sticks and kindling. The branches snapped and cracked in the quiet, oozing pitch that made my hands tacky. A better prepared camper would have used her gloves, but I didn't mind. The resin smell gave me a heady connection to Dad. I licked a finger to get closer to the bitter pine.

Tree trunks stood like sentinels in the firelight and somewhere an owl hooted. I breathed in the chocolate scented vapor coming off my cocoa then set my tin cup on a flat place close to the fire and went to stand under my hanging pack. The pack dropped on its rope and I lifted the flap, took the curious manila envelope in my hands.

I held my dad's gift up in the smudged light. "Happy Birthday, Megan." I fingered the letters, pictured him writing, the pen pressed into service between his thumb and the arc of his slender fingers.

I took my flashlight and went to sit by the fire. The moon was bright now, lustrous and silver. I added wood to the fire. It smoked and flared. I put the flashlight in my jacket pocket and removed the pack of papers from the envelope, laid them on my lap. The thickness stuck at the bottom of the envelope and I left it there, wanting to unpack this last message slowly.

A first pass was puzzling. It looked like business correspondence, some on letterhead stationary from the University of North Carolina's Anthropology Department. I read it more than once.

January 14, 1973

Dear Mr. Kimsey:

Thank you for your last letter and the accompanying documentation that I requested. I was most intrigued by the photographs of quipu and your daughter's interpretation of the knots. I have taken the liberty of keeping these for further study and have forwarded copies to several of my colleagues, including Professor Eduardo Sircusa, who currently serves as the Minister of Cultural Antiquities to Peru and holds a visiting faculty position in the Antiquities Department at the National University of Colombia in Bogota.

Frankly, I don't know what to make of your daughter's claims.

There are a number of puzzles here. Given the background you describe, it is difficult to understand where she may have acquired such specific and esoteric information concerning the more obscure peoples of the Amazon and the Inca Empire.

Some information you provided, i.e. plant names with appended drawings and detailed descriptions are well documented folk medicines. However, others are not known to exist. Some are extinct, and some of the herbs, barks, and mixtures detailed in the notes as having medicinal and practical uses have no referent at all, much less any recorded history. I have questions that only your daughter can answer. However, I understand your desire to shield her from inquiry until some of her claims can be substantiated. That is what I am now attempting to do. Rest assured, I will be contacting you as soon as I receive responses to inquiries I have made among my colleagues.

Regards,
Jasper Corbin, Ph.D.

Along with the letter were six 8 x 10 photographs. Each photograph was broken into four separate images. Some were pictures of my drawings, mostly plants and birds. Others were patterns and designs with notes taken from some of my old sketchbooks.

There were shots of the knotted counting cords I kept as a child. Dad had arranged each group radiating from its center, then photographed them on our old pink tablecloth for contrast.

It made me smile. Dad had always been curious and respectful about my projects. The significance of each knot and color was still immediate to me. One represented an evolving description and tabulation of the tropical fish in my fish tank; another counted and gave a succinct characterization of the children in my third-grade class, including a large black and white knot with an intentional fray at the top representing Sister Mary Agnes. All these years, Dad had kept them.

I was touched and curious, but I couldn't figure out what this odd assortment of childhood artifacts had to do with me now.

Dad had included a National Geographic, more than a year old, with the photos and letters, its cover folded back, the table of contents on top. Circled in red ink, was an article about a Peruvian dig with text written by Jasper Corbin.

I flipped the pages for a look at the article in question, and there, staring me in the face, was a glossy picture of a flat golden circle with an emblem that could have been the twin to one of my sketches. The opposite page featured some knotted strands, quipu, scavenged from a burial site. In method and character, these were strikingly like my own.

I reached inside the manila envelope and removed the remaining fold of papers, a conference program, Pan American Primitive Societies, and airline tickets, TWA; there were two. I opened the ticket on top as if it were a pamphlet. It had my name and a departure date of August 27, 1973. The destination: Bogota, Colombia. The return fare was paid but the date had been left open. I knew without looking that the other ticket was Dad's.

.

5 THE DREAM

That night in the La Platas, I lay with my sleeping bag zipped up to my chin and my eyes open to the heavens, prospecting the universe for answers. I'd send up a question and wait, hoping for some celestial event, a quirk in the clouds drifting across the moon or a meteor streaking through the sky. But there were no messages, just trails of vapor and stationary stars, fixed points in the darkness.

At the stroke of dawn, a cherwill pierced the silence, then chirrups and chirps, squawks and caws. I covered my head, scrunched down inside my bedroll, blowing into my hands to warm the tip of my nose. My toes were blissfully warm, but I had been lying on the ground too long, sleeping in one position over pebbles and mounds that had become boulders and hillocks. I couldn't stay submerged. I wiggled to the surface and pulled myself halfway out of the bag, up onto my elbows.

The rising sun was putting on a show, edging sketchy clouds with touches of pink and shades of glowing orange. I could see the new light working its brightness across the mountain, beaming down and melting over the landscape.

I'd rolled up my jacket and used it as a pillow. Now I shook it out and put it on, sat and pulled on my boots. I thought about making a pot of coffee, but changed my mind; decided I'd wait for brunch, or lunch, when I had a few miles under my belt and a fish to fry. I packed my gear, doused last night's cinders, and bit off the end of the orange that was still in my pocket. The juice dribbled into my mouth, and I began working the night out of my bones, making my way back to the trail.

I scrambled along rocks and boulders at the edge of the water, sometimes picking my way through the brushy willows and walking among the slender, white-barked aspen that pushed up in clumps along the bank. There would be a fishing hole ahead, a sheltering lie that I knew by heart. This was a place where my father liked to work the river, where large speckled trout cruised beneath the burbling surface. If you were still and focused, you could catch their glide and shimmy above the stones of the riverbed.

The lie pooled to the side of a blistering current where the streambed curved around and took on the downhill spill of a seeping mountain spring. I eased along the incline where water and moss slicked up the rock, steadying myself with a few sprigs of scrub and the mossy hump of a toppled tree, making my way toward a granite ledge. I wanted relief from my pack, to lean back and rest in my shirtsleeves, to dangle my legs.

I hoisted myself up, dropped my pack, and propped it beside me. The sun was baking the boulders at my back and I rubbed my shoulders and leaned into the heat, took off my hat and shook my hair loose. My tongue felt thick and dry, and I lifted the canteen, filled my cheeks and swished water, spit and licked my lips. I leaned back with my eyes closed, a breeze brushing against my skin and water murmuring all around, listening to the earth breathe.

I had passed hunger an hour ago and was feeling a little shaky. I ate what was left of the gorp in my jacket pocket. I would still have fish, but it would be for dinner.

I checked out the tied flies on my hatband and dug into my pack to liberate my gear, then eased myself over the side of the outcropping and began to clamber down. There were water skippers and minnows darting and flashing in the shallows along the water's edge. I crouched to look, then stepped into the stream.

The chill and pressure of the current moving around my boots and ankles was a tame thing but it gave me a thrill. I picked up a rock and turned it over to examine the bottom, to see what kind of insect the fish would be searching out for lunch. Then I stood downstream from the lie to wait and watch, expecting to see a trout rise and leave a bubble behind. Sure enough, they were feeding on dry flies, my signal to begin casting upstream, just like my dad had taught me.

I could hear him coaching, "Upstream, Megan. Be systematic. Take your time and cover the ripple." He was a stickler when it came to body mechanics, "Don't jerk and snap like that. There's grace in your arm, girl. You're part of nature out here. Act like it."

I pulled my forearm back, waiting to arc, thumb up, hand easy, just enough flick forward to loft the line. The cast streaked out and skipped like a live fly. I watched, cast once, twice, three times; made myself still inside and listened with my wrist and the tips of my fingers. I held onto the cork grip of Dad's rod, launching and holding where his hands should have been, missing him with a whole new batch of tears.

That afternoon, I netted a dozen trout, maybe more, big browns and a few rainbow, using a barbless hook and reeling them in by degree. I was in a groove, matching the play of the pole and staying right with the fish, countering each tug that flashed and slapped against the water's surface. I dispatched two of the smaller fish, striking their heads on a rock and put them into a vest pocket for my supper; the rest I eased off the hook and supported in calm water until they were settled enough to swim out of my hand.

By three that afternoon I was trekking again in earnest, anxious to gather wood and begin setting camp for the night. My path took me next to tangled masses of watercress with their tiny white flowers creeping along the stream bank, and into drier rocky places where new dandelions pushed up, looking miniature compared to the ones Dad spent his summers digging out of our lawn. I collected handfuls of edible leaves wherever I found them, layering them in the saggy net pocket of my fishing vest. There were wild currant and bilberry bushes to pick through too, but most of the fruit had already been carried off by the birds and chipmunks, or foraged along with some of the leaves by browsing deer.

The sun was dipping behind the crests of the mountains when I took up the last climb over a little rise that I knew would open into the glade that my father had always called Megan's Meadow. It was an untamed territory with a broad outlook, a clearing where the breeze perpetually rustled in ribbons across the grass. I stood at the edge of the trees and watched the quivering carpet roll out in front of me, a sea of feathery green all speckled with alpine sunflowers, little stars of blue gentian and, here and there, the bold red-orange heads of Indian Paintbrush.

I assembled a makeshift shelter not far from the trees by throwing my tarp over a log whose east end I propped on an old stump. There were plenty of rocks around to secure the canvas where it draped the ground, and buckets of fine dry pine needles to spread over the floor to cushion my bedroll.

I gathered wood and loitered, found a place to hang my pack and did the few small things that were left to prepare for the night. And then I took a break, slouched against the stump at the mouth of my shelter, and chewed on the sweet nib of a blade of grass. My eyes were aimless, and I opened my ears to the husky whispers moving across the meadow.

Later, well into dusk, when I took my pail to the creek for water, I stumbled onto the rounded tracks of a large cat. The tracks were old, at least several days, but I toned down my movements and craned my neck for a look around, understanding in a fresh way that I was blundering around in someone else's territory. The knowledge kept me vigilant.

That night, nestled among the pine needles, my mind sent up images of a tropical place, clear and luminous, so vivid I was conscious of the soft muggy feel of humid moisture next to my skin. In my dream, I knelt at the edge of a wide pool, wearing the single heavy braid of my childhood and my grandma's flimsy cotton chemise, the one she liked to wear for summer sleeping. I felt a moment of concern, a need to touch and look, to make sure that those were my own familiar curves and reedy legs underneath Grandma's nightgown.

Small silver fish streaked through the shallows just beyond my toes. And further out, where the water turned a hazy opaque green, there were rippling eddies and blind depths. I stepped into the pool, waded out several paces, gripping with my toes in the slick and squish and feeling for the ledge along the mossy rock. I paused, inhaled, and arced forward, pulled my body into a straight line and sliced through the water, heading down into deeper green, bottle green, fronds and tendrils. On the rebound, and rolling to my back, I watched my barrette plumb past. I spread myself flat, let the water lift me, felt my hair billow into a blooming mass as fine as seaweed.

I drifted, arms and legs sporadic, frog-like, coasting the languid current. I floated past a heron strutting in among the Banyan trunks and a family of capybaras surveyed me from the bank.

The rhythm of my dream shifted at a place where the flow of water swerved around a rocky spur, piled up on itself and spewed froth and mist as it funneled into a canyon. I found myself swept, jarred along and bouncing feet first at a clip that required full concentration to dodge stumps and piles of jutting rocks.

I was measuring each nuance of the river's surface, panning the banks for a place to pull out onto dry land when I spotted the feline apparition of my childhood, her looming presence licking a paw, keeping tabs on me from a scooped out cleft in a rocky outcropping that channeled the river. Our eyes locked and my heart lurched into a wild flutter. She pulled her massive body up from a recline and growled a throaty truncated warning that was half snort.

The scene shifted to a grassy steppe-land battered by harsh winds. Now I tramped behind the puma up a vertical slope paved with loose cobbles that slipped beneath my feet. We climbed upward through a sea of living grass the color of straw to a bare and rocky terrain. Everywhere around, wind howled, gray peaks and ice pierced the sky.

I trudged after her through clouds of gauzy mist until we came to a ledge where two stone towers supported the braided cables of a hanging bridge. We stood between the anchoring piers, staring out across the ravine. A thick stillness numbed the world and I was afraid.

The lioness went ahead without me, padding her way between the woven grass ropes toward a mist-shrouded presence waiting at the center-most point of the crossing. The cat turned and glimpsed back at me.

I felt alone, about to be marooned, and lunged after her. No more than twenty feet into my decision, the wind whipped and bounced the bridge. It warped and yanked against its own underpinnings. I grasped the ropes on either side and pulled my way forward.

The fog started to gust off in scattered patches and the chop and jerk eased up. I began to get my bearings. I had charged along farther than I supposed and found myself at the most pendulous point, swaying over a vast ravine, the river below less than a slim gray squiggle at the base of a broad canyon. The view down made me dizzy and I looked up with a start—into the waiting gaze of an ominous presence on the bridge.

From somewhere, I remembered his name, but when I parted my lips to utter it, he put his hand across my mouth and wrenched me close, bound me next to him inside his billowing cloak. He smoothed my wild hair and pressed me hard against his broad chest. And he began to breathe in gusts with his mouth wide and his nostrils flared. He gripped me tighter and tighter, puffing faster and faster, until the sounds of moving air and the clamorous thumping of his heart fanned against my ears like great beating wings.

I started to cry out, but felt myself losing substance, becoming translucent, nothing more than a hissing plume of swirling vapor.

There was vibration and the heaving sigh of a vast inhale, and that enigmatic other sucked me up whole. I was that plume and yet distant, watching the last of me roaring down his gullet and expecting to feel dead, but I didn't. Instead, my steamy remains seeped behind his eyes and bulged at the walls of his lungs.

His seeing and breathing rippled through my moving molecules in a chain reaction that turned epiphany. I was in his eye, seeing clear, and with a new edge. And I hurt with a fierce desire, a yearning so hot and urgent that I jerked out of my sleep, bolted upright with a screech.

The wind had whipped up, yanking at my tarp. One corner pulled loose; it snapped and twisted. The chill air wailed. I hitched the sleeping bag tight around me and snaked toward the breach, grabbed the flapping corner and rolled over it so that my bagged body anchored the canvas hem against the ground.

Inside, the darkness pressed around me, dense and soft and too big for my little tent. I tried to calm myself, to clear my head and force my thoughts into a neutral place. Now and then I drifted close to sleep, approached the border like a silent shadow, but it was no use.

Each time my mind began to float and scatter, it came lurching back, tethered to the dream. I surged into periods of alert panic and ruminated, dredged around in a parade of surreal images that tumbled up from the depths of some barely tested reservoir.

I glimpsed landscapes and people's faces, summoned up the fragrance of heavy scented night-blooming flowers, and aimed the pangs of my empty stomach toward edible concoctions and tastes that, just yesterday, would have made the American sensibilities in me gag. The images flashed past then gathered together, coming up and up to burst into my brain like dislocated memory.

In a single moment of crystalline awareness I paused in mid-thought and realized that I was no longer thinking in English. Instead, the whole curious experience was coming to me in a language more fluid, more playful. I paused to grasp and understand—spoke the name of the speaking, "Runasimi," out loud and into the night so that I could bolt it down and own it with my own tongue, with my flesh and blood ears. "Runasimi. It's Quechua," I said. "It's the man's mouth, the voice of the people."

If my facility with the language struck me as odd, my pronouncement regarding its nature seemed even more outlandish, and I had to stop and wonder what had come over me. I tried to take a mental step back and approach myself as if I was my own patient. There was a possibility that I had snagged some kind of hallucinogenic weed with the handfuls of watercress that had been part of my salad for supper, but that was unlikely. The leaves had been washed and picked through and there was no off taste; there had been no nausea, no headache, no dizziness or characteristic color flashes.

Next, I tiptoed around the loathsome prospect that I might be having some kind of psychotic break. I felt clear-headed enough, at least for the middle of the night, was oriented times three; I knew who I was, where I was, the date and approximately what time it was. I didn't really think I was someone else; it was more complicated than that.

And then there were potential issues around delusions and language acquisition. In medical school I had done a rotation in psychiatry. I knew that among the deranged, it wasn't unheard of, or even particularly uncommon, for an individual to take on the persona of Socrates, or Napoleon, or especially Jesus of Nazareth. But in no case had I ever heard of the unwitting imposter suddenly becoming fluent in Greek, or French, or Hebrew. Certainly, fluency was something I could verify.

Then I diverged, took my thinking deep rather than wide, testing the language, translating. First simple phrases like, Hello. When do we eat? And I fish with flies. That last made me smile, because, although I could transfer the words and the meaning, I could comprehend how meaningless it was in Quechua. In the Quechua world, flies might be fish food, but a man caught fish with a net, or a quick and silent hand. And it occurred to me that I could almost feel the strike and grasp of my fingers around the fish, that I intuitively knew that sort of detail about some other time and place.

That knowing, and understanding that I knew, tossed my mind again, and I was plagued with the weight and tension of a thousand potential memories. Were there droves of them, waiting, even pacing in the wings, each one wanting just the right kind of coaxing to send it forward? My mind began to probe around among bits and pieces of whatever I could summon from childish visions and dream-life, looking for triggers, specific associations. Every time I located one, it would usher in a brazen surge of euphoria along with a rapid-fire blitz of images. I was frantic with the effort; and the faster it came, the more I wanted.

I felt for my flashlight, beamed it at my backpack and rummaged, searching for the birthday envelope from my father, then grasped and slipped a photograph of one of my sketches from between the airplane tickets and Dr. Corbin's letter. I was on my elbows, positioning the light so I could get a clear look. The drawing featured tiny tongues of flame lapping at the edges of two distinct plants. "Yes," I shouted into the night, "Megan, you idiot. Of course, this is a recipe."

The tent could barely contain me; I wanted to scream and shout and dance around. The penciled leaf patterns seemed so obvious, ayahuasca vine and yaje. And the small encircling flames around the pictured sprigs signified a special kind of slow fire. I sensed that if I were to find myself in the jungle, I would know where to search out these herbs, and how to prepare them. What's more, these came with mental images, images of things that weren't pictured; the one safe way, the kind and size of clay cooking vessel; and that, if prepared properly, the resulting brewed extract could summon potent visions.

I was out of control, and I knew it, could hardly breathe and my heart was lurching in my chest. There was a sense of guzzling, of not being able to get enough. Now I wanted my sketches, all of them, my quipu, and my father's notes about our conversations.

I thought of Mama, already consulting with Claire and Charlie. I pictured them with their heads together making plans, plans that were sure to include me. My siblings were sticklers, well aware of the burdens of responsibility; they would want to have the details of Mama's everyday life settled before they traveled back to their own. I had the feeling I was about to regret being a hometown girl in ways that even I couldn't anticipate.

Most disconcerting of all, now that my father was gone, there wasn't a single person anywhere that I felt I could trust. I thought about Charlie, but his priority would be Mama right now. And to be fair, any rational person might wonder if I wasn't too self-absorbed to see what was really happening. I promised myself that I'd work this out alone, make plans with my mouth shut. And I would do my best to be scientific, keep my wits about me and review each piece of evidence as it presented itself, in painstaking detail and from as many points as possible.

I was up at sunrise, pulling my gear together to go back into town. Funny how my demons had shifted overnight; all I could think about was my sketches. Mama might already be sorting and dispatching the books and papers in Dad's study. One thing was certain; if she came across Dad's notes and my things among them, she would throw the whole bunch out with yesterday's trash. And she'd do it with a clear conscience, glad that I wasn't there to interfere.

I headed out to find a crossing in the creek, intent on making an efficient descent. On my way up the mountain, the absence of my father had emptied time, created a pensive and lingering surplus; but my sense of the moment was ticking again, funneled and urgent in a way that shoved me from behind.

It hadn't been part of my plan to follow the mountain lion, but I crossed the creek at a place where I had seen the cat's tracks the night before. I balanced my way above the current, treading the back of a sheared off tree trunk and hopping some jutting rocks.

Later, probably no more than a mile or so downstream, I ran across more of the distinctive paw prints, this time obscured in a mishmash of chaotic patterns. There were horse tracks there, and the imprint of boots.

I was making my way into the thicket when I took in a whiff of something foul. A scavenger crow came swooping at me through the brush, screeching and beating his wings so that I reeled backward. I batted my arms above my head and shooed. And he retreated, squawking, then settling in the upper reaches of a nearby pine. But the bird stayed and I could feel him watching me, sizing me up sideways and pulsing the air at intervals with piqued screeches and eerie screams.

Several steps more and I came on the cat's carcass, robbed of head and hide, and flung at the base of a knee-high boulder. What was left of the puma had been ditched there to rot like so much refuse, a feast for the cloud of flies that swarmed the stench like a second skin. The smell and the droning buzz assaulted my senses and I wheeled away, cupping my nose and mouth with my hand.

A trapper had done this. The peg he used to secure the trap was gone, but the vertical tunnel where it had penetrated the earth was still there, a fulcrum that dictated the distance the cat could move in any direction. I stooped to examine the patch of earth where she'd dug the base of the steel snare back and forth across the mud. Her going and coming left a pattern that rayed out in a contained arc. The shape and depth of the gouged impression made me think of a wing, the wing of a snow angel, the kind children make lying flat on their backs, flapping bundled arms up and down through fresh powder. But there was no joy in this wing, and no flying away, unless you count the release of death.

I pictured the cat, the bone and flesh above one paw dragging the blunt steel jaw, tugging and lurching back and forth until her captor came. And at the end, she probably snarled and challenged while the trapper took aim and finished her off with his rifle.

I picked up the spent casings and sniffed the sour burnt smell, then kicked around behind the rocks and in the bushes. While I was looking, I stumbled on the stiff and battered remains of what must have been the puma's cub. The skull was smashed in on one side and the eye sockets were vacant, probably picked out by birds. The putrid little carcass struck a chord with me, left me pensive and wondering if the kitten's mother tried to comfort him from the snare. Did she fluff his fur, lick and groom as if it were any other day? Encourage him to snuggle close and take milk when she was spent of railing against her chain?

I knew it would be unusual for a mountain lion to produce less than two kittens in a litter, and I began a directed search on the off chance that an orphan might have been left behind. The den was there, about fifty yards away, cozy and concealed, but not concealed enough; a crushed cigarette butt was tossed in the bushes not far from its entrance. And while on the surface, this was a place of still blue sky where a clean breeze brushed across the tops of the aspen, and winged grasshoppers went on clicking about their business, the savage ghost of exhilaration drawn from pain still blew through the grass and settled there in an uneasy pall.

I was sure that the tattered little rag of hair and bones left behind had a counterpart somewhere, a twin that had been nabbed and taken out of the LaPlatas alive and in the back of a truck, with traps and guns, and the hide of its mother. Some fates are worse than death, but I already knew that.

Before I left, I took a piece of shattered bone from the puma's leg and cut some snips of fur from the cub's neck. The bone, I wrapped in my handkerchief and pocketed, but the fur I spread in my palm. I puffed over the fluff with my living breath until every last follicle was joined with the prevailing breeze. I had an urge to wish the trapper harm, but I stopped myself. There had been damage enough, and that kind of venom has an ugly way of splashing backwards.

6 BELLA

Sometimes carrying around little snatches of other times and places feels akin to having my own crystal ball, but I'm no gypsy, and I'd never wish my little windows of clairvoyance or visionary hindsight on anyone. Most glimpses catch me by surprise, and each sighting comes with its own raft of unexpected, and often unpleasant, consequences. It's a little like stepping onto the sidewalk in front of Woolworth's and finding out that your best friend's been using your pockets for shoplifting. Besides, looking into the future mostly doesn't make sense until after it's happened; and I've learned that even small specks of understanding are burdened with a shadow-side. Some shadows are so dark and sad when they wash over, that they're liable to swamp your soul. That's what happened to me when I lost Bella.

Mama still treats my nervous breakdown like it's a family secret, and certainly, she did everything in her power to keep the details that came with it under wraps, but in a way, the whole town went right over the edge with me. I was the one, though, that ended up with my name in the newspapers, and not just the Durango Herald; my story went national to the really big presses, like the Denver Post and the Chicago Sun Times. The whole life-shattering event got pared down to a poignant little human interest story all summed up in less than two dozen lines and squeezed into a single column. The day the story appeared was the day I disappeared, and I was gone for several months. Despite Mama's overt concerns about my personal privacy, it didn't take a genius to figure out that I hadn't gone away to finishing school.

Bella froze to death on New Year's Day in 1960. She died early that morning, probably hours before the sun came up. I was only sixteen then, and to this day, if anyone has the nerve to bring up the way I crumbled, Mama makes it clear that the breakdown was an aberration specific to me. "Mental illness doesn't run in our family," she'll say, "never has."

In a strange way, Mama took possession of the tragedy. She wrapped her efficient sort of comfort around David and Dodie Cannon, managing their necessary and immediate affairs until members of Mrs. Cannon's family could navigate airline schedules and winter travel delays. Mama says it took them a day and a half to get from Wilkes Barre, Pennsylvania, to Durango. And it was Mama, standing in for me, with the Chief of Police who was interviewed on the Six O'clock Albuquerque Evening News.

I remember the first time I saw the baby Isabella, all swaddled in a thin flannel blanket through the nursery window. Mr. Cannon took our eighth grade honors biology class, all six of us, to the hospital to meet his "Bella" the day after she was born. We marched through the hospital lobby that afternoon behind our teacher, single file like a line of fledgling ducks.

And when we got to the elevator door and the group clumped together, I made sure I stepped in next to Mr. Cannon. I had been watching him from the second row of seats in our classroom all year, and I was more than keen to catalogue his details close up. I latched onto every little thing: the black toes of his polished wingtips, the way the cuff of his shirt sleeve pushed beyond the arm of his tweedy sport coat, and those broad, intelligent hands. I watched him extend his finger to press the elevator button, noticed the creamy moon of his fingernail going whiter with just that measured instant of pressure.

In tight quarters, and with the door shut, I angled closer and brushed my shoulder up against him. I told myself it was okay because I didn't really have a choice; it was so crowded in there. And when he felt my touch, he looked at me and smiled, then stepped back a pace, crowding Bobby Peck and Max Robbins, so that everyone gave me a little more room. But his smell lingered, Lux Soap and a late-day whiff of some musky shaving lotion that I wished would rub off on me. And on that point, I wondered, even hoped, it was customary to shake hands when you congratulated a new parent.

Mr. Cannon's wife was waiting for us in front of the nursery. She wasn't exactly the sultry beauty I'd expected. In fact, she wasn't sultry at all, but dark blonde and not quite slender, just an ordinary sweet-faced woman wrapped in a mottled silk bathrobe that drooped down over fuzzy pink slippers. We all tried to act nonchalant while he greeted her. I knew I should look away, but I just stood there bold-faced, watching him bend close with his fingers spread in her hair. He leaned in and delivered the softest brush of a kiss across her mouth and she smiled back, straight into his eyes. She stood there, fondling his shirt button between two fingers, and I heard her whisper, "Hey you," a sweet nothing that shot a charge of bitter longing straight through my heart and right to the pit of my stomach. I looked down at the speckled tiles on the floor, then sidled over by Penny Shultz, thinking I'd ask her if she'd ever been in a hospital before.

Mr. Cannon introduced us to his wife. Her name was Dodie, Dodie Cannon—Mrs. Cannon to us. Afterward, the eight of us ebbed, in what must have looked like a single motion, to the other side of the hallway. We bunched up in front of the nursery window around Dodie Cannon, all of us peering through the glass, and her guiding our attention with a gesture, helping us hone in on the sweet new apple of her eye.

Altogether, there were seven newborns in the nursery that day lined up in hygienic bassinets, each little bed affixed at the end with a file-sized card chock full of vital statistics and color coded, pink if the occupant was a girl and blue for little boys. And for visitors who might be colorblind, the message was repeated in big letters stamped across the top, BABY GIRL or BABY BOY, followed by a place for the nurse to write in the family name. I scanned the pinks for BABY GIRL Cannon, and sure enough, Mrs. Cannon had directed us to her own in a heartbeat.

We arrived just in time to see Bella begin to rouse from her newborn stupor. She stretched and mouthed her little fist, grimaced and grew red-faced, working herself up until her baby arms were flailing air. Though the sounds of her caterwauling were vague on our side of the nursery window, we watched her screeching distress ignite one infant after another until the whole nursery was in an uproar. Mrs. Cannon was agitated too, wanting her arms around that baby girl, and indignant that she should have to remain on the outside, separated from her infant by an arbitrary glass wall and hospital protocol. Mr. Cannon looked from her to the baby and stepped off to get a nurse.

We watched him lurch toward the nurses' station and halt there, a forward arching angle that loomed across the counter. He wasn't yelling; if he had been we would have heard. But he jabbed the air with his finger, stopping just short of the nurse. And in no time at all, that stiff-capped nurse was hustling toward us down the hallway with Mr. Cannon in pursuit, doing her best to keep the heels of her industrial strength shoes at least two steps ahead of his shiny black wingtips.

There was a common sigh of relief as the nurse stepped in with the babies and closed the door behind her. And Mr. Cannon, having achieved his desired end, pushed back in among us to take his place beside Dodie. I watched him slip his arm around her shoulder, and she slumped in close and tilted her head so it dovetailed just under his chin, an exact fit. I looked away, down the hall, into the nursery, anywhere. There was a hot blush blooming over my face, and it took everything I had to squelch the way my unruly thoughts wanted to elaborate on that fitting together part.

The nurse wedged her white clad presence between us and the object of our attention. "She's checking her diaper," Dodie explained, briefly panning us for understanding. We nodded, some of us marking time on the balls of our feet, and the boys, every now and then, erupting in an exchange of surreptitious jabs. But the baby Bella continued to complain. Unwrapped and re-wrapped, patted and jostled, that professional baby-handler went through her entire repertoire of tricks short of breaching the established feeding schedule; until finally she relented, at least enough to offer the agitated infant a stubby bottle of sugar water. Bella hit that amber nipple in a single strike and settled right into the nurse's arms, her greedy little cheeks puffing and contracting in a rhythm of vigorous pulls.

With the baby occupied and quiet in the crook of her arm, the nurse approached the window. She thrust the sucking Bella right up to the glass in front of Mr. Cannon. With that, he gave the nurse a nod of approval and turned to his students, throwing his arms in the air, scooping us in, "Hey gang, here she is. This is your chance. Gather around and have a look."

We jammed in, shoulder to shoulder. I was so close to Mrs. Cannon that I could feel her clean-scented warmth emanating through the silky folds of her bathrobe. She dislodged her arm from between us and reached up with her hand, extended a finger, close-clipped and unvarnished. She tapped the glass and cooed. I followed her gaze, watched her probe Bella for a response.

I tried to imagine my own mother tapping the glass, wondered if she haunted the nursery window after Claire was born, but I couldn't picture it. Dad might have lingered in front of the bassinets on his way to and from my mother's room, but after what she had been through to make him a father; Mama would expect him to spend his time with her.

Once, when she had me serving cucumber sandwiches to her Wednesday bridge club, I heard her advise an obviously pregnant card player that being catered to in the hospital was a new mother's reward. And Mama recommended bottle-feeding, "So hygienic," she'd said, "and it lets the nurses manage nearly everything so you can catch up on your beauty rest. Heaven knows there's not a time in your life when you'll want it more."

But it wasn't beauty rest Dodie Cannon had on her mind. And Bella, she didn't even know how lucky she was, being dropped there smack in the middle of all that love.

The baby swigged the last of the water and released the nipple. She stretched and shot startled arms into the air, opened serious gray eyes, and pulled her little mouth into a perfect o. I caught the motion, and for the first time I was engaged by the baby herself and stunned by my own attraction. I marveled out loud at those tiny fingers; and when I did, Dodie Cannon tilted her head to look at me. I looked back. I could feel her approval. It surged clear down to the tips of my toes. In unison, the two of us turned our attention back to Bella. Dodie reached over with her glass-tapping hand and set it to rest on my shoulder.

Three weeks later, between bells, I was rushing to pull assignments and papers together with my notebook and searching around for a missing pencil when Mr. Cannon called to me from up by the blackboard. He had his back to me, working his way across the day's lesson, guiding a felt eraser in long methodical sweeps. "Megan, could you please stay after for a minute?"

I jerked to a quizzical kind of attention with my chin up as my classmates hustled around me toward the door. Mr. Cannon took his time, finished his erasing and paused to check the calendar on his blotter before he stepped toward me. He stooped in front of my desk to pick up my pencil. He held it upright, "Yours?"

I bobbed my head and reached out to take it. With a sleight of hand, he evaded my grasp and slipped that smooth yellow writing tool into my hair and behind my ear. My pulse thumped and fluxed in my chest and my knees felt mushy, but it was the rush of blood to my cheeks that did me in.

I looked down at the desktop and fiddled with my papers, neatening things into a stack while he worked to squelch the way his face wanted to smile at my expense. "How would you like to baby-sit? I mean—you wouldn't be alone. Dodie, Mrs. Cannon, would be there if you needed her. She just wants someone to come in late afternoons to help out. She's quite a seamstress, you know. Wants to get back at it."

The two of us agreed that I would show up to help out with Bella on Tuesdays and Thursdays after school, at least until school let out for the summer. When the time came, if I wanted to quit or we needed to consider a different arrangement, we'd talk about it then.

Mr. Cannon offered me directions to his house and I feigned a need to know, even took pains to write down the address and the cross street. But I think we both knew that I had already figured out where he lived.

The next day was a Thursday and I rushed home to change my clothes and get my bike. I pushed out of our garage, heedless of Mama clucking behind me. "The roads are slick. You'd better walk."

I launched my bike from the side and swung onto the seat rolling forward, acknowledged her warning with a stingy quarter-turn of my head. "I'm late, Mama."

The gutters were clotted with sanded ice, but where the streets and sidewalks had been plowed and shoveled, the concrete was dry and bare. Still, I kept an eye out for black ice, zoomed my bike along the sweep of Third Avenue and across the incline of a sloped driveway at a speed that allowed me to coast the rest of the way along the sidewalk and right up to the base of the Cannon's front porch. At the end, I let the bike glide forward at a measured speed until I felt the tire bump against the bottom step.

I took my time going up the steps. The bristly mat at the door announced "Welcome" from a two-tone curlicued box at its center, and I wiped the bottoms of my shoes in several directions across it. There was a handwritten sign taped over the doorbell, "Baby inside, please knock softly." None of this seemed real. I worried that Mrs. Cannon would answer the door and give me a blank look. What did I know about babies anyway? I'd never even held a baby; in fact, at my house, I was the baby.

I unhinged my wrist and hammered out a soft series of staccato raps, then waited. I heard a scuffle inside.

The door swung open and there was Dodie Cannon, no longer the sweet-faced dowdy hospital patient, but transformed. I stood there like a dummy, staring into those sparkling hazel eyes. Her taffy colored hair curled every which way, and the oversized flannel shirt she wore probably came from Mr. Cannon's side of the closet. Mama would have used words like "unmanaged," or "sloppy." But I thought she looked perfect.

"Megan, right? I remember you from the hospital. Come in. You can call me Dodie."

She scooped me in with one arm, almost a wide hug, and pushed the door shut behind me. She spread my coat and muffler across the radiator.

She chatted, talking for both of us, as I followed her across the camel-colored carpet and into the living room. "Bella's not really on a regular schedule yet. She's sleeping but she'll be telling us that she's wet and hungry anytime now."

Dodie led me to a ruffled bassinet sitting on one end of the sofa. She put one finger to her lips and with her other hand she beckoned me to look. Bella was nestled inside, sleeping on her stomach, framed in white wicker and surrounded by creamy colored flannel dotted all over with tiny pink rosebuds. I bent next to Dodie and became still, straining to discern the rise and fall of the baby's breathing and touched by the soft fuzzy down of her blonde head and the relaxed curl of her little fists.

I barely got to do my job that afternoon. Instead, Mrs. Cannon—Dodie, and I worked on feeling comfortable with each other. I followed her around and found myself talking while she punched down a yeasty smelling bowl of risen bread dough and re-stoked the fire. When Bella finally screeched for attention, Dodie showed me how to hold and diaper a baby in a slow and methodical way that let me know she was happy to teach.

And then I sat across from her on the couch, mesmerized, as she hoisted up that oversized flannel shirt and led Bella to the nipple of one of her hard, beautiful breasts. While the baby mouthed and sucked the one that was offered, its vacant counterpart trickled milk too. Dodie was overflowing. I reached out with a clean diaper and she tucked it up under her pocket to catch the stain and smiled at me, then at Bella—a smile that spread over the two of us like sunshine.

I stayed for supper, even though Mama cautioned me not to overstay my welcome. I held Bella, rocked her in my arms and patted her at my shoulder with a nose to her sweet smelling head. I kept company with Dodie while she rolled out tiny homemade noodles and minced fresh basil that she snipped from a flowerpot on the windowsill above the kitchen sink.

When Mr. Cannon came home, he greeted me with a hand to my shoulder, stooped to coochie-coo Bella and went straight for Dodie, grabbed her from behind, nuzzled her neck and tickled. She shrieked and twisted around, and grasped his hands with a sharp agreeable, "David, behave yourself."

"Just say hi," he said, tilting his head to plant a kiss, and Dodie leaned to meet his mouth. I was thinking I should leave the room, but as I turned for the door, she gave him a good-natured push backward. "Why don't you take your daughter so Megan and I can finish making your supper?"

He made a pleasant show of snatching Bella from my arms. Later, I could hear his voice coming in playful fits and starts from the living room, "Mares eat oats and does eat oats and little lambs eat ivy. My Bella eats ivy too, wouldn't you?" I knew the song, but it was the only time I ever heard the words parsed out like that.

Their house was like a delicious foreign country and I stayed longer than I should have, past sunset, to the very edge of twilight. David offered to drive me home but I had my bike; there were streetlights and it wasn't far. We stood by the door saying our good-byes, chatting while I bundled against the cold. The radiator had done its work, and the cozy residue of heat that bathed the lining of my coat and muffler felt fragile the moment I stepped out into the icy evening.

David flipped on the porch light behind me and when I flicked my head in acknowledgement I caught a glimpse from the side that took my breath. I thought I saw someone slouching in the corner of the porch, slumped down where the porch rails come together with the board siding. I looked again, but it was just a bag of rock salt propped against the sweeping half of a broken broom. I turned back for reassurance. David had his arm around Dodie and she lifted Bella's tiny hand to wave at me from behind the glass of the storm door.

My name was among Bella's first bona fide utterances, though really only recognizable to Dodie and me. To be honest, it came out sounding more like Maymay than Megan. And when she wasn't learning new sounds, Bella was impressing us with feats of physical agility; dropping clothespins into the rolled glass opening of an empty milk bottle or pulling herself up to a stand and teetering around the blunt wooden edges of the Cannon's mahogany coffee table. That baby held the three of us, David, Dodie and me, spellbound just learning to be herself.

So, neither Dodie nor I were surprised when David extended Bella's celebrity to school as well. He arranged for Dodie to bring Bella to class at regular intervals. We students were to chart her accomplishments scientifically, demonstrating in measurable terms that every child's progress is, as David put it, "A little window into the evolution of the whole human race." And to her father's absolute delight, Bella proved to be a glorious prop, charming the class and keeping pace ahead of her promise. She was so fetching, so coy and cute, that during "demonstrations," students wandering the halls and teachers from adjacent classrooms, even the janitor and school secretary, would poke their heads in to get a glimpse. And nothing pleased me more than, at the end of each performance, with all the pairs of arms thrusting and coaxing, all the, here Bellas, and the Come see mes, Bella would smile demurely and reach out for me.

By the time spring came, I was already working every afternoon except Wednesdays, helping Dodie around the house and watching Bella while Dodie worked on sewing jobs and alterations for Graden's department store and a few regular customers.

As far as Wednesdays were concerned, Mama made it clear that they belonged to God. And in my case, God and I had a standing appointment to rendezvous in the church hall at Newman Club where a well-meaning Mr. Jeffers and Father Tim droned on and on, talking about church etiquette and leading us through a study guide and its companion workbook. Mostly I stared out the window or drew vines in the margins of whatever page I was compelled to focus on, thinking about Dodie and Bella, and wondering how they were managing without me.

When school let out that summer, I spent most of every morning pushing Bella ahead of me in her stroller or pulling her from behind in her little red wagon. She leaned into the future, a pint-sized explorer, craning her neck and gripping the rolled edges of her conveyance, every now and then locating some point of interest with an eager finger and a babble.

We'd stroll down Main Street and stop at City Market where Eunice Spencer, who managed the in-store bakery, waited for us behind the counter with a huge complimentary sugar cookie that she'd break in half for the two of us. What was left of those mornings, before lunch and Bella's nap time, I spent dogging her across the blacktop of Mason School's deserted playground, Bella mincing her steps up the slide's steel ladder, or my arms supporting her so she could sense her weight dangling from the monkey bars. I circled myself around her.

By the next summer, Bella had taken command of the playground, directing me with a sassy little finger. Mostly I laughed and she smiled back. She refused her hat and frequently dispensed with her clothes altogether. And while I was chasing her around, trying to keep suntan lotion on her busy little body, my own skin mellowed in the sun, took on a golden sheen that made me look again each time I passed myself in the hall mirror. There were other changes as well. In spite of a year and a half of Dodie's wheat berry-bread and raspberry kuchen, Bella and I lost our baby fat. Bella got leggy under her warm weather rompers and I shot up cool and tall as a glass of iced tea, but with a hint of some budding curves, the beginnings of my very own breasts.

If they had announced themselves during wintertime, I would have added a T-shirt and gone on about my business, at least for a while. But my summertime apparel let me down. It was just the sort of thing Mama was apt to notice, though we never really spoke about it. One night while I was down the hall getting ready for bed and brushing my teeth, she simply deposited a J. C. Penney shopping bag on my pillow. It was one of those rare times that Mama and I were home alone. When I discovered the sack, I stuck my head into the hallway and hollered out to ask her about it. There was no answer, just the click of the bathroom door and the rasp and thump of the tub faucet turning on.

The contents of the bag were self explanatory—sort of: a box of sanitary napkins and an elastic belt to hold them in place, a thin booklet with daisies printed all over the front and a title that promised to tell What You Need to Know: Becoming a Woman, and last, but of most interest to me, two new training bras. I examined the flat-chested model on the package. She wore a copy of the brassiere inside; her picture looked back at me with a smile that seemed almost boastful.

I closed the door and picked up the booklet, expecting something – diagrams, maybe hygienic talk about the physical changes of growing up, or even more titillating, some straight talk about men and women making babies. But the whole thing was about sanitary napkins: how to wear them, when to wear them, what to do with them after you wore them.

Next I undid one of the cardboard flaps and slipped the bra out of its box. It was just a flat strip of fabric with stretch panels sewn in and three hook and eye fasteners that were supposed to come together at the back. I doubted that my new breasts were trainable, and any lesson these contraptions might have to teach didn't look that comfortable.

I held my misgivings over until morning. In the spirit of giving it a try, and because Mama would expect it, I started the next day wearing my new bra. But no matter how much I let out the straps or how many times I sneaked a finger up under

my shirt to give the fabric a stretch, it felt like Japanese tor-
ture, the old fashioned breast-binding kind.

In early afternoon, after Bella was down for her nap, Dodie
caught me coming out of the bathroom with the offender wadded in my hand. She was stepping down the hallway with a
stack of folded towels on her way to the linen closet.

"What's that? A problem?"

I was always blushing.

Dodie stashed her armload on the shelf above the sheets in
two neat piles. She closed the door softly and nudged it with
the flat of one palm until the latch clicked, then turned with
her hands out. "Here, let me look. Maybe I can help."

I handed her the bra. She unfurled it right there in the hallway, examined the tag and glimpsed my chest. "Come on. Let's
check this out in my sewing room." She paused, "If you want."

I nodded and said I guessed I did.

Her sewing room was a cluttered cubbyhole, really a convert-
ed walk-in closet off one side of the bedroom she shared with
David. I stood in the doorway between the two rooms taking in
the filtered light, the way the pattern in the lace curtains
moved across the bedspread, dappled and skittered with the fan
and the puffs of warm air pushing through the window.

Dodie rummaged around in her sewing basket looking for her
tape measure. "Let's see how big a bra that fits you would need
to be." She stretched out the tape. For some dumb reason, it
took me a second to register that she was waiting for me to take
my shirt off.

"Oh, okay." I said.

My fingers fumbled over the buttons but I was unsure. Even
my doctor listened to my chest in patches, lifting my clothes in
the back or pulling them to the side in the front, searching out
skin for his stethoscope. I tried to focus on my finger work,

avoiding Dodie's eyes. I peeled off my shirt and handed it to her. She tossed it on the corner of the dresser and I was left exposed, standing in someone else's bedroom.

Dodie unfurled the measuring tape. "You'll have to lift your arms away from your chest or I can't get your dimensions." My arms shot out like posts, but low and together in the front, still shading my breasts. Dodie took a step back, "Megan, sweetie, try to relax just a little. You know, we don't have to do this. Maybe we'll just figure with your clothes on and subtract some."

She handed me my shirt. I felt instantly wretched. "I'm sorry. I want to. I do. Please, I'll stop."

She tilted her head and looked at me, standing there with my shirt clutched to my chest. "All right, we'll try again, but first, I thought I heard Bella. Let me go see if she's still sleeping. I'll be right back."

I backed up and plunked myself on the corner of the bed. The barrette that clasped my hair had gone cockeyed and I dropped my shirt in my lap to fix it. I could feel the bed wobble under Dodie as she sat down behind me. She peeked over my shoulder and gentled a smile into the reflection that beamed back at us from the beveled mirror above her dresser.

She lifted my hair away from my neck. It fell loose over my shoulders and she tilted my chin so that I saw myself reflected, dark blonde hair splayed and tumbling into wisps that brushed over my new nipples. Dodie met my eyes in the mirror. "Look at you, Megan, at who you are when you're just being yourself. You're so beautiful you break my heart."

It was the first time I saw myself that way. I was my mother in lighter hues, younger and softened. But the eyes were wholly mine, not those vivid blue signature eyes, but tender opalescent green, the shade of deep forest pools. I smiled at Dodie and absorbed her appreciation, swelled up like a thirsty plant plumps with the rain.

The next moment, Dodie whisked around me with her tape measure and helped guide me back into my shirt. "See, that wasn't so awful. And in case you were wondering, you're an absolutely perfect thirty-four "A", and I'll bet that's just the beginning."

The next morning she was waiting for me with two new bras, soft cotton with snug little lace-edged cups. "These are for you, a present. Because we're friends."

I stepped into the bathroom to try one on and kept on wearing it. I never showed my new bras to Mama, although she might have seen them in the laundry. If she noticed, she kept it to herself.

The weather forecast that Halloween called for snow mixed with rain; another reason, Mama said, for me to stay home. Even now, I can't think about that night without wishing I'd listened. Mama never did like Halloween; the underlying concept of unsettled dead, wherever she encountered them, disturbed her well-ordered Catholic sensibilities, and she considered the hoopla of children going door-to-door no better than begging.

That particular Halloween, Mama reluctantly agreed to let me spend the evening at Penny Schultz's house. Penny's parents were going out, and Penny wanted me to keep her company and hand out treats. In the meantime, the two of us planned to pop some popcorn and watch an old Boris Karloff movie on television. Mama said I could go, but she spent most of the week harping on her reservations. She was still repeating herself as I headed up to my room to get ready. "You bundle up. The weather's going to turn cold and messy. Make sure Mr. Schultz brings you home. Who knows who'll be out wandering the streets? Understand?"

I was looking for my sweatshirt when the doorbell rang. I heard a scuffle downstairs, chortles and the muffled vibration of conversation humming under the floorboards. Laughter and more laughter. Dad hollered to me from the bottom of the stairs. "Megan, come down here. There's someone to see you."

I stepped into the hallway and peered over the banister. There was Bella, her small face tilted, her eyes wide, stock still with anticipation that came undone the moment she saw me. "Maymay, see my tail. See my tail." Bella went into a dither, twisting in a tight circle until she had secured proof with a firm grasp of the puff attached at her padded bottom.

I laughed out loud. We all laughed, and our laughing sent Bella into spasms of performance, engaging little jigs and giggles that split our sides with pleasure.

To an outsider, Bella must have looked like the Easter Bunny on Halloween, but I recognized the costume as Dodie's version of Babbit, Bella's toy lop. Dodie had dressed Bella head to toe in creamy plush, her baby body zipped into a footed jumpsuit and those blonde curls snugged into a close fitting cap that sprouted huge pink satin-lined ears that flopped to the sides.

Some children suck a thumb; others fix on a favorite blanket. When Bella was tired or out of sorts, it was Babbit she relied on, the stroke of his silky ears against her face and fingers. She fondled that poor toy to tatters. Her dependence left Dodie following close behind, hovering, waiting for sleep or an occupied moment, to sneak her baby's stuffed companion into the wash or patch a frayed seam. But even a mother's love can't turn back the clock, and Babbit was fast becoming a mere and matted impression of his former self.

That Halloween, I remember Bella as Babbit, Babbit with a plastic pumpkin instead of an Easter basket, Babbit brand new. And, I noted the real Babbit, worn and drooping, clutched under David's arm.

I charged down the stairs and swooped Bella off the floor for a hug, but she was much too busy to spend time in my arms. She was greedy and anxious to knock at every door on the block.

The Cannons hung around for a few minutes chatting before they struck out again. I left for Penny's right behind them, in time to see David and Dodie standing on the walkway next door, holding themselves back while Bella managed her plastic pumpkin and took the steps up the neighbor's stoop one at a time.

Penny was waiting for me at her house, anxious to pull the drapes and switch off the living room lights as soon as I arrived. The two of us settled into the evening on her couch. We huddled under blankets and let the eerie glow of her television flicker over us, mesmerized by black and white images of the mummy, profaned and run amok. The specter of the embalmed and his unnatural and angry resurrection charged us to our nerve endings, so that we all but jumped out of our skins every time the doorbell rang.

About nine o'clock the sleet Mama had predicted started to fleck and scatter against the windows. I was primed to ask Penny's dad for a ride home, but about half an hour later, when Penny's parents pulled into the carport, they kept the engine idling and we could hear them arguing, at least her father was yelling. The car door slammed and her mother burst through the kitchen. She headed right past us without a word and stormed straight to the back of the house. Outside, the car revved, then screeched and accelerated, humming off down the street. In the instant of stillness that followed, Penny went to the window and pulled back the curtain. She whispered to me over her shoulder, "Maybe you'd better go now."

The sleet was mixed with snow by then, heavy and falling fast. It streaked through the glow of street lamps and left a fine mush on lawns. But on the roadways and sidewalks, the soggy crystals melted where they touched, then pooled, or seeped away to gurgle along the gutters. I was late and practicing a speech for Mama; the same way I was sure she was practicing one for me. If things got too desperate, I had leverage to fall back on, a tidy little morsel of gossip about the Schultzes.

I dove forward, heading into the weather with a gloved hand clasped at my collar. By then my loafers were taking on moisture; soaking up slush that seeped in where the leather was stitched to the sole. Longer, more decisive strides seemed prudent, and I began to count the suck and squish of each step as a marker. Half way home and crossing the street at the block where the Cannons lived, the wind changed and I tilted my face skyward, expecting movement in the clouds and searching for a speck of starlight. But as far as I could see, there was no heavenly light, not even a ghost of the moon.

The odd thing was, that when I leveled my chin to look ahead, the walkway in front of the Cannon's house appeared washed in angled moonlight, moonlight made twice as bright by drifts of undisturbed snow. I could feel myself seeing with more than my eyes, and I stalled, trembling inside my coat sleeves.

There, emerging from the tapering shadows cast by the bare and boney limbs of a huge old elm, I spied Bella. She wore a ruffled nightgown, plaid, and made of some supple material that bunched in folds on the surface of the snow, giving an intermittent impression that she was buoyant, her small form drifting in effortful waves toward the house.

I stood, bolted where my feet met the concrete, unable to believe our baby could be outside at night without her coat on and not a light on in the house. And where were David and Dodie? My mouth opened to call out; I had words in my throat for Bella, stacked up and waiting, but no sound came. Instead, my voice turned inward, it fluttered across my heart and settled there uneasy, to perish without a whisper.

Just then, the Cannon's Chevy motored up the street and turned up the driveway. The harsh beams of the headlights exposed me where I stood, and I lifted my forearm to shield my eyes. David eased on the brakes and pulled to a stop in front of me, close enough that I heard him sigh when he rolled down the window. "Megan, what in Sam Hell are you doing out there? Go on, up on the porch where it's dry."

I waited for them by the door, amazed to see Dodie maneuver out of the car with a drowsy Bella in her arms. David followed close behind, lugging the diaper bag in one hand, and Bella's bunny hat and plastic pumpkin in the other. While David fiddled with the key, Bella roused against her mother's shoulder; she bobbed her head and looked up to see where she was, then drooped again, still clutching Babbit to her chest and mouthing a thumb, her baby cheeks ablaze, tinged with sleep and the bald warmth left over from the car's heater.

David brought me home that night. I kicked my shoes off on the mat by the door hoping they would dry unnoticed. Mama was waiting for me by the kitchen table, scraping the tip of a spoon around in the dregs at the bottom of her teacup, but we didn't say much. I let her go on thinking Mr. Schultz had driven me home.

I often wish I had told my father or even Penny about seeing Bella out in the snow that night, but I kept what I had seen to myself. The vision stalked me in a way that was too potent for words and I was afraid.

Over and over, I summoned up that moonlit image of Bella pushing through the snow. I recorded it in my journal and dated the entry, then parsed it out, isolated every detail; the depth of the snow, the fact that Bella wore a nightgown instead of her usual footed sleeper, the leafless limbs of the tree, the still and lifeless windows of the house. But what troubled me most was the part that defied description, the utter aloneness that came with the image.

The next day was a school day, an interminable day to live through, since my whole focus was to get past the last bell to four o'clock, and to Bella and Dodie. All afternoon, I perseverated on the vision, scolded myself; summoned up my mother's practical voice, then tried to dead-end my thinking by taking the role of Dr. Vickers, anticipating how he might try to puncture my phantoms with his sure-footed probing. Any clear thinking person could see that I was being fanciful, silly; the whole thing must be a product of too much candy, that creepy Boris Karloff movie, the effect of Halloween on an impressionable brain. Maybe it was just a bad dream, but I needed something more concrete than mere logic to convince me that I was an idiot.

Minutes before four o'clock, I was poised with a fist at the Cannon's front door. I could hear Dodie's sewing machine humming overhead, so I waited, paced my knock to coincide with the silence at the end of a seam, then rapped and listened to quick footsteps squeak across the floorboards above the porch.

Dodie stopped me at the door and warned me not to remind Bella about her plastic pumpkin or last night's stash of candy. There had already been a series of demanding little tantrums over Dodie's management of the Halloween goodies; the last outburst coming to an abrupt halt with the candy filled jack-o-lantern deposited on top of the refrigerator and Bella banished to her bed. Bella was still in her crib when I arrived; but her bedroom door had been left ajar, and I could hear her stirring from her nap, chattering to herself.

Dodie wore the day on her shoulders, but she brightened when she heard Bella call out, "Mommy." Minutes later, Dodie came bouncing back down the stairs with Bella perched on one hip. I watched the two of them on the landing, Dodie hoisting the baby close to her face for warm little Eskimo kisses. Tip-to-tip, their noses touched, both of them laughing.

Dodie kissed Bella on the forehead and set her on her feet in front of me,

"Go on now; play with Maymay. Mommy has too many dresses to make."

And she did. The bundles of fabric, the patterns and notions, were piling up in Dodie's sewing room. She'd spent the last month stitching Halloween costumes, now she was taking orders for holiday dresses and still trying to keep up with alterations that Graden's department store sent her way.

"Almost enough for a down-payment on a house," she'd say.

Lately, she'd boasted her hopes out loud whenever we walked to the bank or saw a "For Sale" sign on someone's front lawn, proud that her sewing money was adding up. And she made me feel like I was helping too, not just as her babysitter, but as her friend, almost a part of her family.

I hung around close to the bottom of the stairs playing pat-a-cake with Bella, listening for the scrape of Dodie's chair and waiting for the sounds of the sewing machine to fall into a rhythm. Then I snatched up my playmate and made a beeline for the nursery. I pulled one toy and another out of the toy box, tempting Bella, until she finally settled on her building blocks. While she was stacking and demolishing on the floor beside me, I rummaged through her dresser drawers and closet, hunting for the nightgown that had billowed around her in my vision. If I came across its real-world counterpart I'd know it. The scene, like a sliver, had lodged itself in my mind's eye so that the slightest mental movement triggered a kind of sore awareness. I looked everywhere, but there was nothing to find, no nightgown of any sort, just well-worn footed sleepers and cotton pajamas.

A week or two later, I was relieved once again when Dodie announced that she and David had tendered an offer on a house just down the street. Old Mrs. Manka was moving to Phoenix to live with her son and daughter-in-law. The place was huge and decrepit, but the price was right. Dodie and David had always loved the neighborhood. The actual move was a month or two away, maybe at the end of Christmas vacation. School would be out then, and David and I would have whole days to help with packing and lugging. Dodie smiled, "What could be better?" I had to agree; one by one, my phantoms were slipping away, and I began to believe I'd just had some kind of waking dream. I started to ease up, even laugh at myself.

The nightgown arrived a few days before Christmas; delivered by the postman. For almost a week it lay camouflaged, one of a dozen presents gussied up with curls of ribbon in red and green and stashed at the base of a fir tree that winked, cheerful with colored lights and tinsel.

I was there with my parents on Christmas Eve, wishing the Cannons a happy holiday with a gift of Mama's special cinnamon rolls. We were all sitting around sipping from cups overfilled with hot cider when David invited a pajama'd Bella, fresh and still damp from her bath, to pick out the present from Grammy Cannon. The baby had been training for this moment all week, and with one or two reminders, Bella brought the gift to her father with commendable restraint. She placed it in his outreached hands, her own small hands practically vibrating with anticipation. David crouched off the edge of his chair on a level with Bella, and read the tag out loud,

"To my sweet Bella. With love, Grammy Cannon. To be opened on Christmas Eve."

He handed the gift back to Bella, "Now. Go ahead Bella, you can open it."

Bella looked first to Dodie for a nod, then ripped through the paper, but she struggled with the ribbon until David stooped down to help. The exposed box lid was secured with two or three smallish squares of tape, and when Bella yanked, the package burst apart.

The moment still comes back to me in my dreams, always in slow motion; the soft plaid flannel tumbles into a heap on the floor and I suck in a breath of air so sharp it sets me choking. The cup of cider in my hands breaks loose, bounces off my thigh and onto the floor with a thud and a splash.

Dodie went for towels and my dad escorted me into the kitchen to help me mop the cider off my clothes. By the time I made it back into the living room, Bella was wearing her new nightgown, all plaid flounces and rosy smiles, and David was snapping her picture next to the Christmas tree. I was so noticeably white and nervous that my parents hurried me home.

I didn't see Bella again until the day after Christmas when I went back to help Dodie with the packing. By then I had lulled myself with the idea that I had been given the vision for a reason, and I prayed about it, desperate to believe some kind of cosmic logic was at work, a merciful logic that had singled me out as a remedy.

Weather-wise, the week between Christmas and New Years blew in cold and dreary, but I spent it snug with Bella, keeping her out of harm's way. Mostly we rattled around in the confines of the nursery, serving orange juice for tea from Bella's tiny tea set, or playing "babies," the two of us mothering Babbit and Bella's new Tiny Tears doll. Downstairs, Dodie and David stuffed boxes and stacked them against walls and in the vestibule. All the while, the woodstove crackled and scented the air with smoky comfort.

Bella's things were packed last to be unpacked first, but there was disagreement about her bed. It was the only time I ever heard the Cannons argue.

The issue was a big girl bed that already waited, dismantled and in crates at the Sears warehouse downtown.

A week or two earlier, I was there when Dodie ripped a picture of bedroom furniture from the catalog. She helped Bella tape the page low on the refrigerator door, and together they made a circle in bright blue ink around the photo of Bella's new bed and its matching dresser. From then on, each time Bella passed through the kitchen or clambered out of her chair, Dodie called attention to the pretty white spindles on the headboard, or the exceptional bouncy-ness possible on that grown-up mattress.

I was standing at the front door in my coat and boots, zipping Bella into her snow suit and adjusting the cuffs around her mittens, when a crash and the sound of shattering glass jarred loose from the kitchen. Bella gaped into my face, her little mouth open and a quiver in her chin. She was off toward the commotion in a flash with me a step behind. But she screeched to a halt in the kitchen doorway when Dodie yelled, "Bella, no. There's broken glass. Stay out."

"Megan, could you come get her."

I swooped Bella up in my arms and turned to take her out-side but not before I noticed David and Dodie struggling with the chaos—crates and cartons everywhere, dishes and glassware set in stacks and lined up in rows on the kitchen table and along the counter, and Dodie crouched with the whisk broom, sweeping what was left of a crystal wine glass into the dust pan. David stood above her wearing his frustrated teacher face, all puffed up and adamant, though his hands worked at taping the box in front of him. His words were clipped and low, and I had to rein in my movement and strain to hear.

"Craig and Violet need the crib now. Why would we move it just to have them come in a week or two and take it away?"

Dodie's voice arced back, "It may be practical, David. God knows you're always practical, but it's not the transition we planned. You're so smart—you stay up with her all night. It's not good if everything is new and strange."

It didn't sound as if Dodie was backing down, but early in the morning on the day of New Year's Eve, before David left to go get Huey Martin's pickup truck, Craig came tramping up the shoveled walkway, leading a pregnant Violet along with his gloved hand. I knew they had come for Bella's crib.

I hugged a bundled Bella close and squeezed between Violet and the boxes in the foyer, saying hello and goodbye at the same time. But Violet wanted more, and she pressed her face next to Bella's and uttered a string of condescending coochie-coos with sour breath. Bella jerked away and struggled in my arms. Her cherub face puckered and she wailed for her mom.

Dodie managed a tolerant smile and made excuses to Violet. She pushed past her and ushered me onto the porch. She pulled the door shut behind us and leaned in to smooth Bella's tears away with her fingertips and plant a kiss in the curls on her forehead. "Shh, now you be a good girl. Go with Maymay.

You'll have fun at her house and Mommy will see you tonight. We'll make you sketti for supper."

But when Bella and I arrived at the new house that evening, Dodie was lurching around in her nylon stockings. Her hair was pulled up in a festive knot and she wore a sleek black dress, sequined in layers that dazzled when she moved. She stopped for a brief hello and to pinch Bella's cheeks, then continued to rummage, peeking beneath box lids and mumbling to herself. She charged up the stairs grousing about the whereabouts of her patent leather pumps.

And David, handsome and smelling fine enough to make a person swoon, perched on one end of the couch in his blazer and slacks, fingering the coins in his pocket. He smiled at us. When Bella ran up to him, he lifted her onto his lap and leaned over her with a kiss, but it was an absent kind of kiss, and in a minute she jumped down to trail Dodie up the stairs. I asked David how the day had gone, but he glanced at his watch, not really listening.

I was the one that made macaroni and cheese. I couldn't find the box with the cans of Spaghetti or the cartons that packed the dishes, so Bella and I ate off paper plates. We were sitting at the kitchen table when Dodie swooped in wearing her fancy fur jacket. She posted the name of the supper club where they were expected for dinner and the telephone number for Percy's Lounge. They'd be back, she said, probably about one or two in the morning. Bella held out her paper cup for more milk and Dodie made a move to take it, but David grabbed her by the arm, "Let Megan get it. We've got to get going. Come on, the roads are probably a mess." Dodie lifted her eyebrows in an unspoken apology and sang out a cheerful "Happy New Year," on her way out the door.

I held Bella up to the window and we pressed our faces next to the cold glass, watching the car back into the street. The wind whistled and thumped against the house and the tires spun over the ice at the edge of the driveway. David and Dodie sped off into the smoky evening, windblown snowflakes streaking toward them through the headlights. Bella and I stood there taking turns breathing fog on the windowpanes and drawing pictures with our fingertips.

We rambled through the house peeking into every room, then played hide and seek until bedtime. Dodie had Bella's new bed made up with cheerful flowered sheets, smudges of white baby's breath speckled with bright blue forget-me-nots all smooth and crisp on pale blue muslin. But the drawers of her new dresser were still empty.

Bella was at my heels when I pulled a pair of thick training pants and a footed yellow sleeper from the laundry basket we found at the bottom of her closet. She was out of sorts by then, tired, with blazing cheeks and sucking her thumb, and she countered by dragging out her Christmas nightgown. I put it back in the basket and closed the closet door, but Bella puckered to cry; she made me feel cruel and foolish and I let her open the door and get back into the basket and put on the nightgown.

I expected a rough night; we couldn't find Babbit and Bella wasn't too sure about her new bed. The thing was fine for jumping on and she enjoyed dangling her feet over the edge while we read a bedtime story, but she refused to sleep and she cried for her mom. I cuddled and kissed her, and promised that Dodie would be home when she woke up in the morning. I coaxed her, and the two of us lay down together. I fell asleep with Bella nestled in my arms, her hot little breath dampening the crook of my neck.

It must have been past two when I roused to the smells of old cigarette smoke and the swish and perfume of Dodie's skirt. She touched my shoulder and blew my name across my ear until I fluttered an eyelid and focused. The moon beamed in right through the naked window, nearly as bright as the slice of light that followed Dodie from the hallway. Her shadow stretched across me and she smiled. She pressed a finger to her lips while I worked my arm from under Bella.

The car's engine purred and my mitten stuck to the frost on the door handle. Fresh snow covered rutted ice and the car jogged and shimmied along vacant streets. David pumped the brakes to a stop in front of my house and idled in place while I tromped up the steps and let myself in. I didn't wash my face or brush my teeth. I hurried into my pajamas and left my socks on, then curled up between my sheets and shivered. I felt like I'd never get warm.

I was sleeping hard, dreaming an effortful dream about scrambling along a ridge at the top of the world, struggling to breathe, and afraid, trying to hurry. In my dream, I twisted to look behind me, still lurching forward, and when I turned back I stumbled and slid. A ringing sound bounced across the canyon walls, and small pebbles, then chunks of stone, began to sheer off the rock face. I grappled for something to hang onto. My own scream echoed inside my head and I felt myself caught by the shoulder. I sat, bolt upright in bed, almost bumped heads with my mother.

Mama stood there in her bathrobe, somehow managing to look severe and concerned at the same time. "Megan, settle down, you were dreaming. Come on, get up. There's a call for you."

I muddled into the kitchen still stunned with sleep. Daddy was up in his pajamas, thrusting the telephone receiver in my direction. "Megan, it's David Cannon; the baby is missing. They've been looking and can't find her. Can you think where she might be?"

My hand trembled, and I took the phone, pressed it to my ear. But there was a vacancy there, a scuffle and distant voices, breathing, the sound of someone half-listening.

"David? Hello, are you there?"

"I'm sorry, Megan. I'll have to call you back. The police think they've found something outside. Oh God. I've got to go."

I was left with the hum of the dial tone and my heart thumping in my ears. My parents stood there, riveted, silent questions on their faces.

I tried not to cry, but my voice had gone all croaky. "David had to go. The police were talking to him." Then I pleaded, "Daddy, please, will you drive me? I think I know where she might be."

He nodded, "Come on, let's go."

Mama's voice wedged in, "Well, I'm coming too." But she headed for the stairs.

I looked at Daddy, desperate, and he hollered after her.

"Hurry, Rose, or we'll leave without you."

Still we waited for Mama with the engine running, us in our pajamas with our parkas and insulated galoshes hanging on us like afterthoughts, so she could scribble a note for Charlie. When she finally pushed through the door, she stepped out smartly in her winter dress boots, the ones that matched the black leather purse she clutched close to the nubby surface of her coat. She slid into the back seat behind us and slammed the car door, removed her gloves and snapped her compact open. I watched her in the rear view mirror, using the new light of that awful January morning to guide her lipstick and fluff her hair. The day was coming on clear, bright ice blue, with wind that whistled and churned loose snow across the ground in little squalls and eddies. I kept checking the clock on the dash-board; its glass dome marred with spidery cracks that sprawled in every direction from a tiny pit near the center. Underneath, black hands inched from seven-thirty-seven to seven-fifty-two, and still we crept along the scraped swath of pavement. I listened for the hum of a snowplow, but the only sounds came from the spin and crunch of tires on ice.

The morning felt oddly vacant, and I remember wondering if I was still dreaming; there were signs of life, but no one living. And as if to answer myself, as if I invented him, a bundled paperboy appeared from around the corner ahead of us. He kicked snow and hustled along, working his way and puffing into the cold. I don't know who he was, we drove past him without a greeting, but the back of him in his tan overcoat, the bulge of his bag to one side, is the last thing I remember before things, the way I knew them then, began to unravel.

7 THE FROZEN CHILD

I think I know what it must have been like for Bella; it's no trick to understand her logic. Our poor baby was just looking to find her way home, struggling to get back to what she knew. And though her aim was perfect, she was a day too late. Time had already barred the door.

The image of her passing still comes to me at unexpected times, and I've stopped resisting. I stumble right into that old hurt and heave myself over the top—barely a heartbeat beyond, that's where I find her.

The wind must have whispered around Bella that morning, or maybe it followed behind her in gusts. There was no clue; not a footprint going up the porch steps or an interruption in the line of crusted snow that ran along the length of the railing.

I gripped the car's door-handle, white-knuckled the whole way, waiting to catapult myself in the direction of my premonition. But by the time my dad had maneuvered the car into the ice ruts in front of the Cannons' old house, I was losing my nerve. The car idled and my parents leaned in, wordless, waiting for me to make a move. Little prickles of panic crept under the skin of my arms and shot down my spine. There was a moment when I couldn't seem to get my breath and I looked at my father and started to cry, "I'm scared, Daddy. I don't know if I can go up there." He tucked a stray hair behind my ear, "Megan, it's okay. I'll go. Up on the porch? Is that where you want me to look?"

I shook my head; "I have to go, Daddy. I think it has to be me. But please—will you come?"

I expected my mother to insist on coming too, but she listened without comment and stayed where she was.

The house stood over us, its stark windows inert as blind eyes. A dusting of snow covered the steps and powdered the painted floorboards. And I thought to myself that Dodie must have forgotten to tell the newspaper they were moving, because the morning edition lay rolled in its rubber band by the front door. Somewhere in the distance, the ponderous creak and snap of an ice-burdened tree limb pealed through the silence. I twisted toward the sound; my eyes swept to the end of the porch. She was curled into a corner where the board siding met the porch's railing, her little knees drawn up under her Christmas nightgown and her head at rest on folded hands.

I stood stunned. My father's voice rasped behind me, "Oh my god." And he hollered toward the street. "Rose. Dammit Rose, roll the window down. Get the blanket out of the trunk. Bring it. Hurry."

I hovered over Bella. "Bella, baby, wake up. Bella, it's Maymay." But there was no response. I stooped to warm her inside my coat. Her small frame was stiff and awkward in my arms. I managed her bony edges and scooped her close, curled myself around her and nuzzled her cool blonde curls. Daddy made a move to take her, but I refused to loosen my grip. He stooped and checked her wrist for a pulse, then lifted an eyelid. He must have seen that she was dead because he let me be. I turned to the wall, hunched in tighter, so that when Mama came with the blanket, Daddy took it and draped it over me. He sent Mama for help, and without a word, he squatted next to me and put his arm across my shoulders.

I remember starting to sway, rocking and rocking. Maybe I was rocking Bella, or rocking to comfort myself, and all the while groping with a brain gone slow and fuzzy. I prayed that the thing I feared was some mistake, that time would turn back or turn away, that God would reconsider, take something or someone else, just not Bella.

I was rocking and praying, rocking and praying, taking quick little breaths, warming puffs of raw air between sobs and blowing them into Bella's nose and mouth. And though I could feel the chill of her passing into my bones, no pink burnished her lips, no eyelash fluttered.

What I achieved instead, was a dizzy sort of weightlessness that came with its own strange perception. It seemed I was crouched holding Bella at the center of a floating sphere, a sphere as light and fragile as a bubble. I drew her tight against me and we drifted, hovering inside the silence of a long hush. There was an instant in that sense of stillness when the thump of my own heart surged in my ears and the corners of my hearing picked up a vague rattling, the clack and clatter grew, expanded until it could barely be contained inside my head. I must have groaned or complained, because I felt the warmth of Daddy's hand move to the back of my neck and I lifted my chin.

There, outside the sphere, came a golden child. He entered my line of vision, his figure refracted in multiple images that flashed and shimmered over the membrane's crystal curvature. The bright stripes of his woven tunic streaked behind him as he danced, hopping on one foot and then the other, pivoting and dipping in graceful circles, each circle winding him closer and closer.

In the beginning my head hurt, overfull with the hollow musical clatter of his bangles, adornments of pounded silver and seashells threaded on the thin bleached leather thongs he wore around his ankles and wrists. But as he spun near, glancing at me with each twist of his head, his thin reedy voice advanced in a chant, a language that registered as lyrical and strange but I understood. The drone of his singing grew in intensity, high pitched and insistent, a child's song that arched across my consciousness in a memory without context:

"Little beetle, little beetle

Back so shiny black.

Has your mother left you here?"

He planted his feet and looked past the milky separation between us. His face questioned Bella, cradled and inert in my arms. He stared into my eyes and repeated his song. He stopped again at the very same word, drew the tone out so it hung in the air, tense and expectant. I knew what he wanted, and I rasped in answer, no more than a hoarse croak.

"Is she coming back?"

That bit of song was barely past my lips when the beautiful black eyes of that bronze child grew cold and accusing. His lower lip puckered in an unsteady tremor beneath his stare, "Tayta, when are you coming?"

The child's name spilled off my tongue, Kantu. And with the speaking, the weight of a grievous offense descended on me.

Though the substance of the fault still loomed outside my grasp, I could feel it begin to tunnel, to snake and gnaw at my insides.

My misery was acute; clinging to one dead child and accused by another. I gripped Bella tight with one arm and reached out to that sad little boy. As my fingers thrust toward him, the separation that was between us dispersed. The baby body I embraced sagged in my arms. When I glimpsed down to bring Bella closer, to pull my coat tight around her, it wasn't Bella at all, but the frozen body of the golden child. Even his hair, a mass of slender braids crowned with a cluster of red and yellow feathers; the black tips of his eyelashes were dusted with fine beads of ice.

Out on the street, a car door slammed and a raw gust of wind charged the porch. Dry leaves and tiny twigs came dislodged from a gutter that ran along the porch's roofline. They tumbled through the air and skittered along the frost on the painted floorboards, gathered against the front door and in the corners next to the house. Off in the distance, I thought I heard a mourning wail and howling beneath the wind.

The slam of more car-doors and the shuffle and noisy silence of withheld conversation pressed up the sidewalk. The first boot hit the wooden planks of the steps and my heart lurched in my chest. Daddy nudged me. I felt David's presence and I twisted. He stood there stalled, staring without focus. Our eyes touched, and as he came close I slid Bella sideways in my lap, angled her so my coat blossomed out around her head. David fell to his knees and reached out with a gloved hand, stroked her cheek and tilted his head, looked into her small face. A snowbound stillness pressed in on the edges of the wind and I held my breath. My ears were tuned; in the quiet they picked up a soft little noise that erupted from the back of David's throat. He choked, "Bella, Bella baby." But Bella had nothing to give back, nothing but the unrelenting peace that had settled at the corners of her mouth.

A policeman in a business blue parka had stomped onto the porch alongside David. The officer hung back and let David go ahead of him.

At the last, David's head dropped and he whispered, "Oh, my poor baby." His chin took on a quiver and he wretched a moan so low and wracked with hurt that his sobs choked in my own throat. I craned my neck, blinded by tears and sniffing, desperate that David should have help, but the policeman had moved. I saw the back of him from the side, blocking Dodie's way as she came up the steps. There were tears in my father's eyes, and he sank down next to David and pulled him tight against his shoulder.

Dodie came then, stumbling past the policemen. Her hand brushed David's back as she dropped in front of me. She'd brought a blanket, and Bella's toy rabbit dangled in the crook of her arm. She looked down at Bella and uttered a no . . . spoken so softly that it could barely be discerned. She reeled and made a wan, stunned little grimace and fell onto her knees. I cried out to her, "Oh, Dodie," and lifted my arm to circle her neck, but she shunned my embrace. "Please," she said, and "Thank you," as if she barely knew me. "I'll take her now." She gave a half turn of her head. "David, please. Take us home."

The shrill whine of the ambulance throbbed into earshot. The policeman was at Dodie's elbow before she was back on her feet.

My father and I stood next to the railing of the porch and watched through the tree branches as the driver threw the doors at the back of the ambulance open. David, and Dodie with Bella in her arms, were flanked and hustled to the inside.

Metal on metal, the latch on the door clicked into place, and the idle of the engine took on a moving tempo. No siren sound or flashing lights marked their departure, just the boxy edges of the ambulance lumbering away from us on the snow-packed street.

Daddy sighed and put his arm across my shoulders, handed me his handkerchief. "Let's get you home, Pumpkin, and get warmed up. We could all use a cup of cocoa."

Daddy had it in his mind to leave right then, but there were people congregating at the front of the house. I recognized the neighbor from across the street and her new daughter-in-law, edging closer and closer, stomping off the cold and peering out from under puffy hoods puckered tight around their faces.

Next door, the curtains rustled and parted; cold winter sun glinted off the glass, and I looked in. But the spectacle was on the outside; I was part of it. Bold as day, the Sniders and their son, Randy, a sometime friend of my brother Charlie, massed at the window to mouth their coffee mugs and gape.

The arrival of the Channel 8 News van on the heels of the ambulance drew everyone who had heard or seen.

Mama was on the sidewalk; poised like she was waiting her turn, while Maureen Dunn, our town's celebrity from the Channel 8 News Team, pointed her microphone at the policeman.

"From what I've seen, Miss Dunn, it looks like the Cannon child got out of bed and walked out the front door while everyone was sleeping. They'd just moved from this house yesterday." His eyes moved to the porch and to me. "The babysitter found her." He pegged me long enough that Maureen Dunn turned her head to look.

The camera man panned the porch; he caught Daddy and me, unkempt and unprepared. I winced backward and pushed my cheek against my dad's coat. My father's hand squeezed my shoulder, a grip that asked me to endure. Even that little bit of kindness, and my grief was on me again.

They all seemed to surge toward me then. Maureen Dunn lurched ahead with her microphone; "It's Megan Kimsey, isn't it? You're the Cannon's babysitter. Is that right?"

Daddy pushed in front of me "Go. Get in the car." And I meant to do it.

But as I hurried down the steps, a gauntlet of onlookers closed in from every side. More than one person called my name. Still I moved. I was almost there—the car door, barely an arm's length away, when a man with a camera stepped in front of me. His shutter snapped and so did I.

My mouth parched and my breathing quickened. The muscles in my legs twitched. My insides thought they were running before the balls of my feet began to hammer the snow-packed pavement. I skirted our car and made a beeline across a neighbor's yard, heading toward an unplowed alleyway. I pressed for speed and wept, bawled until I sucked in enough icy air to make me wheeze, then I yanked my scarf up, tightened it over my mouth and ran. I became a piston, energy and impact whipped to double time and slogging through the snow.

It wasn't until the church bells began to peal that I had a direction in mind. It was a holy day, the Circumcision of our Lord. And it occurred to me that my whole family was missing Mass; even more remarkable, Mama was missing Mass. I pictured Father Tim in his robes striding behind the altar boy, making a stately parade toward the front of the church. I could almost hear him invoking the Holy Trinity, chanting the words while I was loping through the snow. I knew the response by heart and I heard myself say the words out loud; "I will go to the altar of God." I changed my course then, began to run parallel to Main Street, heading for the church, not for the altar, but for the soft deserted darkness of the confessional.

The streets were ghostly empty that morning, still, I did my best to stick to places where the snow had been plowed or packed. Closer to downtown, I traveled next to buildings and slipped along alleys, sometimes I paused in doorways, and for a while, I crouched behind a parked truck to rest and listen. I hunkered, my sense of absence complete—no sound, no color, no Bella, just silence and snow.

The hum and scraping metal of a truck pushing a snowplow rumbled into the quiet. I poked my head around in time to see the snow coming off the street in a curl that slumped and set-tled in a waist-high mound across the mouth of the alley. Minutes later there were boys, four or five of them, carrying sleds and pulling a toboggan. They goaded each other, shrieked and lobbed globs of snow. When they'd gone past, I stepped around the corner and leaned against the wall, watched them until they became mere specks of bobbing color.

My path took me in the opposite direction, toward the cen-ter of town. I stopped in front of the Wagon Wheel Donut Shop and looked out across the river. The snowplow had cleared a path down Main Street and scraped a slender swath over the bridge. There were cars by then, some treading the ice in chains, and one or two spinning and slipping; all of them puff-ing white plumes of exhaust into the chill air. At the bridge, one-by-one, cars crept across between the banks of snow, snow that heaped over the cut stone railing of the bridge's pedestrian footpath. The little cause-way was obliterated.

I stood there and stared, numb behind the eyes. Inside my gloves, the tips of my fingers ached with cold. I wiggled them and rubbed my hands together, then thrust them inside the pockets of my coat and shivered. My fingers fumbled over a half-eaten roll of LifeSavers. Yesterday, Bella had taken great pains to peel the wrapping back. She'd liked the red ones best. "No, Bella," I'd said, "It's not polite to be so picky. You must take the one that's offered." And she'd pried the green one from the top and crunched it between her teeth, looking from me to the cherry o that came next. "Later," I'd promised.

I shoved the roll of candy with the cherry one on top back in my pocket and took off down the hill. I went the back way across Main Street, toward the old power plant, aiming to cross over at the swinging bridge.

Closer to the banks of the river, the pathways lay hidden, mantled in the softness of snow. Only a jackrabbit had left traces that darted in a zigzag across the surface of white.

In the summertime, the leafy boughs of cottonwoods and willows crowded along the banks of the river, arched over, shimmered and dappled the wooden planks of the bridge. On those warmer days, I was more apt to be under the bridge, meandering along the banks or fishing with my father, than passing overhead. I seldom crossed there. The give and sway of the bridge unnerved me in a way I couldn't explain.

The day Bella died I stood at the mouth of the bridge staring down the length of it, one board and then another, each heaped with its own half-moon of snow. I measured my reluctance. It seemed inconsequential; more habit than fear, since the worst thing I could imagine had already happened. When I'd walked almost halfway across, a gust of wind rushed the river. The cables rasped and the bridge shuddered. I halted, steadied myself with a broad gait and a hand to the railing. Snow shoved up my sleeve and I shook the arm of my coat. The motion was abrupt and sent a mound of powder pitching toward the river. I watched the mass drop and disperse in a mist of crystals that sparked and dissolved on the surface of the current.

I looked down past my feet at the water that coursed below. The river's relentless hum drowned out everything but a kind of bottomless sadness.

I couldn't imagine what tomorrow would be like, waking up to a life without Bella. I pulled out the pack of LifeSavers but I put it back in my pocket. The slivers of wrapper would remain exactly as her fingers had left them.

David and Dodie and I, we were the lost souls in this world, left adrift without our anchor. My sweet Bella had already taken her place among the found. I hoped she was sleeping in certainty. Maybe she was dreaming about us.

Daddy said it was a miracle he caught sight of me perched, squatting on the exposed ledge beyond the bridge's railing. I remember his voice, firm and directive, "Megan, don't move; stay right where you are. I'm coming to get you."

I must have climbed, even struggled, to post myself in such a precarious place, but like a sleepwalker jarred awake, I was as stunned as anyone to discover my own predicament. Even if no one believed me, and no one did, my memory was absent regarding whatever impetus or effort had moved me to roost there overlooking the river.

My father's words jarred my ears at the same time a beam of new sun flashed off the surface of the river. My eyes blinked and I came aware, rudely apprised that I mustn't move. The whole weight of my body crouched, teetering and balanced on nothing more than the balls of my feet. An involuntary gasp of raw winter air exploded inside my lungs and I glanced down. I held my breath and coiled toward my center, afraid even to tremble.

Daddy came for me. He stepped out onto the bridge alone and I felt the bridge grate and wobble beneath me. He was careful to ease his weight forward, one foot at a time. He kept talking, saying how I was doing fine, just another minute, and one more, until I heard him speaking at my back.

"Megan, I'm right here behind you. I want you to turn, slow and careful, then reach out and take my hand. No jerky moves. Can you do that?"

I was crying by then, my heart thundering in my chest, but I began to inch my way around. He reached out and took my arm to steady me. He bent across the iced-over railing, grasped under my arms. I felt the lift and jerk of his embrace and slumped forward against his shoulder.

Charlie was waiting by for us by the car. He didn't ask to drive. He just slid into the backseat and thumped the door closed. I sat in front next to Daddy with the steady sigh of the heater blowing the chill off my woolen overcoat. I looked at my hands then watched out the window. Charlie reached up and squeezed my shoulder. No one said a word.

We rounded the corner coming home, and big as day—there was Dr. Vickers' Lincoln Continental, huge and black and parked right in the middle of our driveway. I felt my father stiffen in his seat. He approached the driveway and nosed in, half of our station wagon still out in the street. Dr. Vickers' car had been left at a careless angle that managed to block access to both garage doors. Daddy jerked us backward and we swerved in parallel to the heaped up snow at the curb. My father muttered something, got out, and slammed the car door. But he was pleasant with me and Charlie, a hand to each of our backs as we took the steps and walked onto our front porch.

From the window, we could see Mama's slender arm and part of her shoulder, a flick of her hairdo, nested inside the arms of the wing chair. Dr. Vickers leaned toward her from our couch, elbows on his knees, chin forward. I didn't need to see him up close to know his face was full of her.

Daddy huffed in stomping the snow onto the mat by the door. "Go on now." He was talking to me. "Go upstairs and get in the shower, change your clothes. I'll make you some eggs and toast. How about it, Charlie, you want some?"

Mama's teacup clinked on its saucer; she set it on the coffee table and stood up. "Will, Henry Vickers is here." And then to me, "Megan, wait. I called Dr. Vickers. He's come to see you," as if that was somehow supposed to please me.

Charlie raced past me on the stairs, taking two steps at a time. The latch on his bedroom door clicked. I stopped where I was, sagging, wishing I were some inanimate object, the newel post or maybe a paperweight.

Mama turned back to my father and repeated herself. There was a blush growing in her cheeks. "Henry is here. I've been in such a state, worried about Megan. And that poor Cannon child."

Daddy sighed. "Yes, Rose, of course you have."

By then Dr. Vickers was in front of my father with his hand extended. "How are you doing, Will? This must be upsetting. I came as soon as Rose called."

Daddy met Dr. Vickers' waiting handshake with a disinterested grasp, but Dr. Vickers was a two-hand shaker, he was determined to show his concern. My father pulled away before Dr. Vickers was ready to let go. He arched his back in a stretch; his tone was tired. "Yes, well . . ." He made a move to head toward the kitchen.

"Will, please," Mama was pleading. "We've been waiting, worried and anxious to hear where you finally found her. Henry was the first person I thought of when Megan went tearing off like that."

Daddy twisted toward me, reminded then that I was stalled on the stairs. It was the first time that morning that I'd really been still and focused enough to see him. His eyes looked dull, and there was an angle of resignation in the tilt of his head. I wanted to hug him, to tell him I was sorry, not to worry. He smiled at me, as if he heard my thoughts. "You can go now, honey. Go take your shower."

I locked myself in the bathroom, stood in the steam and let the spray beat against the back of my neck until I was worried that someone would start to knock and complain that I was using all the hot water.

When I was back in my room, Daddy brought me the eggs and toast that he'd made. I ate, not because I was hungry, but because he'd looked so hopeful when he set the tray on my dresser. Then I stayed in my bed and slept, or sat on the window seat and stared out the window. I left my door open a crack, listening for the phone to ring and thinking of Dodie, always Dodie.

I asked Daddy about the Cannons, if Mama had seen either of them, if she would be taking a casserole or calling their house. I knew Daddy had something difficult to say, because he sat down in my rocking chair, and in spite of my being grownup and gangly, he opened his arms and beckoned me to sit. I plunked myself there on his lap and dropped my cheek against his shoulder, taking comfort in the vague spicy smell of his shaving lotion, and we settled into the steady pitch and glide of the chair working back and forth over the floorboards.

"Mama's already been to the Cannons' house. She spent part of the morning there, helping out, mostly calling relatives and making travel arrangements. Right now, Dodie's mother is on her way from Pennsylvania. This is going to be hard for you to hear, but tomorrow or the next day, as soon as the weather clears so her mother can get here, the three of them, Dodie, David, and Dodie's mother, are getting on a plane. The Cannons are leaving Durango."

"But Daddy," I choked on my words, "Why would Dodie's mother come if they are just going to turn around and leave? And what about Bella?"

"Dodie's having a hard time, Megan. Even worse than you might expect. She won't talk to David. She won't let him anywhere near her, and she won't go home. She's refusing to leave the mortuary. David's devastated; he doesn't know what to do. He's hoping that Dodie's mother will be able to help."

More than anything, I wanted to go to Dodie. But I remembered how she'd looked past me when she took Bella from my arms, and my heart hurt for David. Their argument flashed across my mind, the shattered wineglass and the angry words. I knew what Dodie was thinking. What if the big girl bed had stayed in its crate a few days longer, if David had waited just a week or two to give Bella's crib away, if David had remembered to put the chain on the door after he took me home? Dodie was using hindsight to locate blame. If blame was the issue, I knew I didn't deserve to be her friend.

I cried again, cried and cried and cried. My dad held me and we rocked without words. I was ready to tell him about my premonition, but all I managed was a weak, "If only . . ."

He shushed me. "Stop it, Megan. We all need to grieve sometimes, to come to terms with our losses. If only is dangerous, it has a way of stealing from the present; it turns the past into poison."

He spoke with such authority that it made me wonder what he had to regret. He kissed me on the forehead and told me to rest. He left my room. I waited for him to take the stairs, stood there motionless until I heard his voice engage with Mama's. Then I closed my door. Still, I couldn't keep myself from listening for the telephone.

Later in the afternoon, when a smoky dullness was all that was left of the day, Dr. Vickers steered his black monstrosity back into our driveway. He came to see me. We sat across from each other, alone in Daddy's study. He cleared his throat and pursed his lips, folded his hands in his lap. "I think we should talk."

I bit my lip and looked down at my feet, let my eyes wander from his shoelaces to a chip in the paint where the molding met the floorboards.

He warned, "If you don't tell me otherwise, I'll have to make assumptions based on your behavior. Is that what you want?"

I lifted my head and stared past him to the shelves of Daddy's bookcases, not really seeing, fighting the sting and pressure, not wanting to cry again. I closed my eyes, squeezed them shut, still, tears oozed out the corners.

"And Megan, I need to know, are you a danger to yourself? Are you experiencing hallucinations again?"

Even as an adult, I come back to that moment and want to mount a defense. Moses saw the burning bush and heard the voice of God. The Angel Gabriel visited Mary. I want to tell Henry Vickers that not every aberration is a disease, and normal is nothing extraordinary. But I also know that nothing I said would have made a difference. For him, it was always about Mama.

8   BREAKING FREE

I unloaded the Jeep and dumped my gear by the front door, made meticulous work of my grooming, even put on my white slacks and twisted my hair up in a knot. I rattled around in the bathroom drawers looking for mascara and a dab of lipstick. It wouldn't do for Mama to get sidelined on a technicality, not when I had something I wanted her to hear.

I called to tell her I was home; I was coming. But it was Charlie who answered the phone. I faltered a beat, steeling my nerve. "Charlie, it's me. Is everyone furious?"

"Try worried out of our minds. What the hell happened?"

"Under duress I guess, thoughtless, stupid. Do you think Mama will talk to me?"

"Hard to say. She's not here. She and Claire went to the grocery store. It's just Jonathan and me. Toby's down for his nap. Look, things have turned to crap here."

"Like what?"

"Dad's dead and Mama's drinking gin out of a teacup. Sounds like I'm making a joke, but it's not funny. Claire was looking in Mama's makeup drawer for fingernail clippers and found three different prescriptions, two for Percocet and one for Valium. That doesn't count the Valium Mama keeps in her purse, or the way she's been guzzling gin and tonics. Claire confronted her. You can imagine how that went over."

"Does Mama seem all right to you?"

"God, I don't know; she just lost her husband. You're the doctor. Please come home."

"Okay. I'm coming." I could sense his relief. Already, there seemed to be less room for me to breathe.

The Jeep was dusty from sitting by the side of the road, but it couldn't be helped. I got in, careful not to get my white pants dirty and thinking I might try to hose the worst of it off in Mama's driveway before she could get home to disapprove.

Mama's driveway, the phrase stuck in my brain. Already, she was filling the spaces where my father used to be and he'd only been dead a week. I struggled with the thought but now was not the time. I had my airplane ticket to think about and an odd feeling that I knew where I was going and why; I just couldn't remember, not yet. My senses were charged, so keen they were almost painful. There'd been a change in my perception; it was as if I'd discovered a new color and I caught myself looking for signs of it everywhere. And the language, the Quechua, was coming without effort. I wanted to speak to a *runa*, a native speaker. Until there was conversation, I couldn't be sure.

Toby was watching for me at the window, part of a curtain bunched on his shoulders. By the time I'd pulled the Jeep up close to the curb, he'd burst out the screen door and was running toward me across the lawn, breathless, his cheeks still blazing from sleep.

I scooped him into my arms and swung him in a circle, then tickled him until he giggled and begged me to quit.

The screen door swung on its hinges and Jonathan stepped onto the threshold. He stood there, a shoulder against the door-jamb holding the door with the heel of his hand. "Whoa, Megan. Pretty bold. Popular wisdom says you ditched us for the mountains and your fishing pole."

I shrugged, "Yeah, well you know my family. It gets hard to maintain a sense of mystery." I left it at that, and he pushed the door wide and stood back for me to duck through with Toby riding on my shoulders.

Jonathan's lips flattened in a grim smile. "It's been pretty tense around here."

"Charlie told me."

"I'm glad you're back."

That little bit of friendliness felt like a gift. I'd always liked Jonathan; Dad and I both liked him. The three of us had been fishing together more than once. Dad gave him a hard time for catching his fish with angleworms and salmon eggs, called him a *worm-dunker*. And when Jonathan and Claire had come to visit earlier in the summer, my father and I had made a big deal about taking him to the Piedra for his first fly fishing lesson. My brother-in-law was good-natured, he let us coach while he cast and recast his line. Still, the only thing he took away that day was a story to tell on the golf course. He'd had fun, but there'd been no conversion.

Jonathan's attention shifted above me, to Toby. An open smile spread across his features. I took in that flicker of tenderness and it lingered around me, like the comforting brown and savory smells of the pot roast Mama had simmering in the oven. I let my eyes drift to the worn upholstery of Dad's easy chair and remembered myself at Toby's age, sitting in that chair on my father's lap, me on one leg and Charlie on the other. We, all of us, were outside the circle of his arms now.

Toby wiggled on my shoulders and I could feel his small fingers working the bobby pins that held my hair in a knot. I swooped him down in front of me and onto his feet. "All right you rascal, hand over those pins." I held out my hand but he was off squealing and running, ducking behind a chair.

"Ah, well," I sighed. I smiled at Jonathan and shook my hair, tried to tame it with my hands. "Where's Charlie?"

I had barely uttered his name when Charlie stepped in from the kitchen, his hands over the two halves of a Popsicle still inside its wrapper. He glanced at me and snapped the frozen pop at its center, then stooped to withdraw one of the blunt red spears and held it out to Toby. "Want a Popsicle, buddy?" Toby peeked around the side of the chair, eager, bobbing his head. He dropped the pins he'd been playing with and came around to claim his treat.

Charlie straightened to face me and his expression turned irritable. He lifted the remaining spear on its stick and bit the top off.

"Jeez, Charlie," I said. "Don't be mad."

"How am I supposed to feel? You ditched me. You could have waited—at least long enough to say you were all right. I wouldn't have stopped you."

I was mouthing some words, forming an explanation, when the garage door creaked open, wobbled and began to slide up on its tracks. Charlie thrust his Popsicle at me and pushed the wadded wrapper into my empty palm. "Duty calls," he said. He stepped in the direction of the garage, passing Mama and Claire on their way inside with their purses and parcels.

Mama hollered after him, "Charlie, make sure you get the frozen food first. It's in one bag at the front."

Mama looked from me to Toby and back again. Her eyes fixed on the Popsicle in my hand. "You're back," she said. "I don't appreciate your serving snacks to a three-year-old in my living room."

"Sorry Mama," I said, and without thinking, the good and ardent child in me bit the rest of the Popsicle off of the stick, a huge bite. The cold shocked my teeth, went right from the roof of my mouth and up my sinuses to the gray matter behind my eyes.

Claire called to Toby, "Take that out to the kitchen. Now." As he passed her, she plunked her purse on the end table and steered him toward the kitchen with her hand on the back of his head. I followed Mama, shuffled along in the wake of her scent and the tidy clip of her heels. Toby sat at the table sucking his Popsicle and dangling his feet, thumping them, first one and then the other, against the horizontal rungs between the chair's legs. He was watchful, searching faces, Mama's and mine. I smiled at him as I stepped off the rug and onto the tiled floor. He looked down and I hesitated. We both honed in on the descent of my sandal, watched its touchdown corrected and safely executed. *Step on a crack, you'll break your mother's back*, a game we'd played before, zigzagging and hopping over the fissures and molded lines in the sidewalk outside.

I put a hand to my mouth and exhaled a "Yikes," a dramatic little gesture that made Toby's eyes shine and crinkle up at the corners. I thought Mama was going to say something, but she only gave me half an ear. She was already putting on her apron, working her hands over the bow at her back, her shoulder blades so distinct that they might have been the beginnings of angel wings hiding underneath the fabric of her blouse.

She seemed older that afternoon, her skin sallow, her makeup less artfully applied. Even so, she was arresting. No friend or suitor of Claire's, or mine, or Charlie's, had ever come to our door without gaping at her. She looked more like a model on the cover of a magazine than a mother; she'd never cultivated the kind of warmth that children crave. I remember the dumbstruck look of those other children, and I knew they were thinking how lucky we were, the way folks looked at us when Mama was holding one of our hands, or how tall we must feel at church, sitting in the pew beside her. They didn't know how long and cold her shadow was; how each of us had to struggle one way or another just to keep the chill of her from seeping into our bones.

In every way that mattered, we had been our father's children. That we were left with Mama was small consolation. Everyone's world had shifted and I felt myself teetering on the edge of a fault line, more than a crack, a chasm.

"Megan, move. Now you're blocking the door." Mama's hands went to her hips. Charlie nudged me from behind with softer tones and a forearm wrapped around a bag of groceries. "Excuse me little sister, but you're in my way."

I took a sideways step and Charlie slipped past me. He hefted the groceries onto the counter by Claire who was already pulling cabinets open, rearranging cans and boxes of cereal. I went to stand next to her, lifted a box of Cheerios out of the bag. "Shall I unload these on the counter or hand you things?"

Mama stepped between us and the bags. "I'll put things away." There was a sharp edge to her tone. She took the box out of my hand and I stepped backward.

Behind us, Jonathan cleared his throat. Claire gave him a turn of her head. He was holding a six pack of beer in one hand and Mama's car keys in the other. He tossed the keys on the table next to Mama's purse; they landed in a clatter. "Come on, Toby, let's go outside. You can help me water the garden. Let's ask Uncle Charlie if he wants a beer."

The screen door slammed and I looked over at Mama. Her back was stiff and her head erect. She was facing the counter but I knew she was punishing me with silence, making me wait.

Claire faced me, her arms crossed under her breasts. "Are we supposed to ask where you've been?"

"I'm sorry if you worried," I said.

I glanced out the window that faced the backyard. My heart was pounding in my ears. I couldn't think what else to say. Toby was in the garden, standing small next to the stalks of corn, barefoot, his toes splayed in the mud. He was holding the hose in one hand and blocking the nozzle with the other, amusing himself with the jets and limp dribbles that eddied out at the edges. Jonathan and Charlie were hovering on the patio, close by the open door. I could feel them listening.

"Dad left me a birthday present, an airplane ticket," I blurted. "I'm going to South America."

"What?" Claire almost laughed.

Mama wheeled around. "I spent most of yesterday looking through your dad's things, trying to find those tickets, still hoping I could head this off at the pass. You and your delusions, your odd irresponsible behavior." She shook her head. "I can't do this anymore. This hair-brained trip is the biggest fiasco of all. You have an important responsible position at the hospital, a chance for a great life, but you can't seem to get beyond this one gaping blind spot. Now here you go, determined to walk right into it."

"I've got it covered, Mama. I'm taking a leave of absence. Give me some credit."

Claire shot me an incredulous look. "What's this about?"

"Dad made arrangements for me to meet some people at a conference in Colombia," I said. "He was going to go with me."

"Megan," Claire lowered her voice a notch, "we need to talk. You don't know what's been going on around here."

"Charlie told me about the Valium and Percocet."

The corners of Mama's mouth took a hard little downturn. "My prescriptions are none of your business."

But then she pursed her lips and faced me. "Okay," she said, "Here's the deal. You give me the plane tickets, promise to level with a psychiatrist and follow any course of treatment he pre-scribes. It doesn't even have to be Henry. If you do that, I'll go cold turkey—the Valium, the gin, everything your snooping sis-ter's been harping about. Everything."

Claire gave me a hopeful look, as if I had achieved some-thing.

"Mama, I can't do what you are asking. I'd be dead inside. You know I can't."

Mama scanned past me with a snap of her head. "Then I give up." She thrust out her arms and grabbed the bag with the ice cream, turned away from us, and yanked the handle on the freezer door. It flew open on its hinges, trailing a burst of cold air. Mama burrowed in, unloading and rearranging boxes of fro-zen vegetables.

"Mama," I said, working on my tone, trying to keep it even. "Can we at least talk?"

I stood there with my arms hanging down while she made a place for the ice cream on the freezer door and thumped it shut. "Mama." My voice was strained. I could feel a quiver coming in the back of my throat.

Charlie looked in through the screen door and made a move to come inside but Mama pushed the door open and stepped past him.

I watched her through the mesh, watched her sit down in one of the lawn chairs. She slipped off her shoes and crossed her legs at the ankles, leaned back and closed her eyes. That was the last I saw of my mother, reclining in the late afternoon, the sun glinting off her earring.

I made tracks for the front door with Charlie at my heels. "Megan, stop. We can work this out."

I shook my head and reached for the doorknob. "I don't think so."

Claire came out of the house as I was stepping off the front porch. "South America can wait. You can go another time. Mama needs you now."

"Mama will be fine," I said. "She has friends." I thought of Henry Vickers. "She's not alone."

9 THE TOTEM

We're making our final descent into San Francisco. It's not so bad; rubber thumping the runway, contact, a brief careen pulled into a lurching recoil, and we ease up, roll forward—a bus with wings.

My seatmate pushes into the aisle, up and panting the instant the captain has turned off the fasten seatbelt sign. He pops open the over-head bin, stretches an arm to rummage, and the belt of my coat flops down. I hop into the seat beneath him.

"Please, could you hand me my coat?"

He grunts, gathers, and drops it into my lap, then delivers a black leather attaché case that thumps on top of it. I start to protest, but the case is scooped up by the aisle-dweller behind him, a little old man mumbling in an accent I can't understand, and the line jostles forward.

The crowd thins. I stand and start to fold my coat over my arm. Dammit, there's a greasy looking smudge—that old man's case. I touch the black streak. It smears on the tan gabardine

and leaves a residue on my fingertips that reeks of petroleum—
probably shoe polish.

I loop my daypack on my shoulder, fold my coat over my
arm, and hold it against my chest with the stain exposed so it
will be easy for the stewardess to see. I explain and she offers
me the little cove with the sink, gives me a towel and some club
soda, but it's no use.

The corridor from the jet-way spills into a bright-windowed gal-
lery. I press past the gauntlet of greeters. None of these craning
smiles is waiting for me. I scan faces, not sure whether to feel
free or empty. It's an unhinged feeling deep enough to wallow
in, but I counter by reminding myself that this trip is a gift
from my dad. He would tell me to buck up, to pick a next step,
to stay focused.

I hang back, make a detour, and stop in one of those tiny
cafes that scallop the edges of every airport promenade. This
one's a coffee shop with a French moniker. The sign wears a
tilted black beret. I pass an empty table and toss my coat on
top.

I pay the cashier for a croissant and coffee. The coffee quivers against the roll at the cup's brim and I step lightly, balancing, and let my purchases guide me back to my table.

My dictionary of Spanish phrases is in the zippered pocket of
my pack. I open the book and lay it out in front of me but my
mind is too unsettled to study. Instead, I blow across my coffee
and sip in a kind of rhythm, watching the rush of people going
by.

Shrill beeping pulses the concourse and I prepare with an
image, expecting to see a cart hum past supporting a wizened
old woman too small for her clothes, or a mother with an arm-

load of toddlers and a mountain of luggage. Instead, the cart glides into view tugging a train of tagged wooden crates and conveying a tall bulk of a man in his late-forties, most striking for his broad shoulders and erect posture. He wears a leather vest over a regulation white business shirt and rests an arm on the seatback behind an attractive young woman dressed in tan slacks and a silk blouse. She must be half his age. The cart halts in front of the coffee shop. The man speaks close to her ear, almost a nuzzle, and she attends with such a rapt expression that I know she's definitely not his daughter. She slips her fingers beneath the man's vest into the pocket of his shirt and pulls out some folded bills in a money clip, then hops off the cart and hurries past me to the counter.

The man turns his head to follow her and pegs me watching. I look down, pretend to focus on my book, but I sense his eyes and look again. As if he's been waiting for that second look, he sums me up with an ogling gaze and a slow smile—and winks. I jerk back to the Spanish phrases on the page in front of me and scold myself for feeling stung and flustered, but I can't keep my mind from hurling a string of silent insults: pompous, self-important, womanizer. I glance up in time to see the young woman hand him his drink and slip back into the cove of his arm. The conveyance jerks, starts to roll forward.

I exhale, mutter, "Good riddance." The words have barely left my mouth when the cart halts and the young woman jumps off and comes running back—to me.

"Excuse me," she says, "I've been asked to tell you that you have a huge smudge across the front of your blouse."

I flinch and look down. My skinny knit shirt, usually one shade of shell pink, is sporting an obnoxious black streak across my breasts. I snap my head up, a searing blush exploding in my cheeks. And she makes a smart turn, hustles off and hoists herself back onto the cart. The man is watching from his seat. He flashes a smile and dips his chin. I lift my hand in a reluctant wave.

As soon as I'm sure they're gone, I snatch my coat and put it on, clutch it closed at the front.

I ditch my half-eaten pastry in the trashcan and take one last sip of coffee. I think about what's in my suitcase. I didn't expect to need a replacement for the shirt I'm wearing.

The magazine shop across the way has racks of shirts, sweat-shirts, and T-shirts. I choose a cream colored T-shirt with a ti-ny insignia at the top, a miniature Golden Gate Bridge in a little red circle, give the clerk my money, and head for the re-stroom and one of those white enameled stalls. On the way out, my pink shell goes in with the garbage. Painful, I liked that blouse, and I'm unsettled; I can't shake a superstitious worry that the black mark is somehow a strike against me.

I'm quick-stepping and in a state of alert when I turn the corner into the open cul-de-sac that functions as customs for interna-tional arrivals and several departure gates. My eyes make a sweep looking for where I belong, but come to an abrupt halt.

Standing under the overhead customs sign with a uniformed official by his side, is the man in the cart. He's wrapped himself in some kind of serape and is having his picture taken by a TV news camera. A smart looking female reporter angles a micro-phone close to his mouth.

He's flanked by eavesdropping onlookers but I mind my own business. I find my gate and take a seat, focus outside, beyond the windows where luggage carts and mechanics bustle in loops around airplanes priming on the tarmac.

I'm settling in, getting up to take my water bottle to a fountain for a refill, when static garbles through the loud speakers. The projected nasal tones of a woman's voice reels off a string of names and insists, "Please come to a white paging telephone."

The call dissipates, but comes again. This time a singular name rivets my attention and I hone my ears, willing a repeat. "Jasper Corbin. Dr. Jasper Corbin. Please come to a white paging telephone. Jasper Corbin."

I'm electric, eyes sweeping the concourse. I scan faces trying to anticipate the noted anthropologist among us. I can recite every word in the letters Dr. Corbin wrote to my father and I've read almost everything he's published. I expect him to be weathered, strong and dignified, with a sensitive face—as smart and wise and kind as a favorite professor—or my father.

I touch my pack over the zippered pocket where his letters are stowed looking for a psychic connection, but there's no energy there, and the one white paging telephone close-by remains un-peopled.

Then I see the female protégée of the man in the cart step up to the telephone and pick up the receiver. She hangs up and waves her arms. Her voice threads the distance, aiming for her arrogant cart-riding associate. "Dr. Corbin, you need to call the Colombian Consulate about your speaking engagement."

I feel like a balloon with the air spewing out, and definitely not entitled to the disappointment I feel. This is not the Dr. Corbin I wanted.

We are boarding single file, moving two steps at a time then waiting. I've been greeted by the stewardess and am stalled. The First Class passengers around me are already enjoying a snack served up on real china plates. I scan the wide seats and glimpse the manicured woman at my hip. She glares back and I refocus, stare ahead and take another step. I sense someone's eyes and turn to look. It's Corbin, reclining by the window. He pours amber liquor from a tiny bottle into a whisky glass, lifts and tilts his drink in my direction. "Nice shirt," he says.

I nod and smile, get prodded from behind and move on down the aisle to the cheap seats in the tail section, already scolding myself for not commandeering the moment and standing there long enough to introduce myself.

I find my seat and snag one of those little airplane pillows and a blanket from the overhead, then situate my pack, flop in, and fasten my seatbelt. But the plane is slow to take off and I'm restless—feeling unfocused, and a little desperate. I unsnap my seatbelt, bend, and reach to unzip my pack and rummage to get at a pack of gum that's worked its way to the bottom. The movement is a bit of a ruckus in such a tight space and it draws attention from the old mestizo woman who has quietly settled into the seat next to me. While I've been fidgeting and fretting, she's been sitting with her worn brown hands folded against the uncompromising colors of her woven skirt, bright-eyed and silent, watching people, or just watching.

The stewardess moves down the aisle offering magazines in transparent vinyl covers. I choose an *UTNE Reader* and settle in for a long and tedious flight.

It takes my Indigena companion's delight that the stewardess has been kind enough to bring her a foil bag of peanuts and a can of Coca-Cola, to give me fresh eyes. She savors her peanuts one at a time, smelling and chewing and licking the salt off her lips. Her gusto is good manners, part of her gratitude, and with a pointed glance she chastises me for the unopened packet on the tray in front of me. So we eat our peanuts together, and with more pleasure than I might have expected.

We aren't talking, though we both suspect we might. She smiles and I smile. It's a conversation waiting for a place to begin, and she points to the zippered compartment in my back-pack.

"*¿Puedo ver?*" she asks.

I bend and unzip, pull the gap open so everything's visible. She points beyond my Spanish book to the bottom of the bag.

"This?" I ask.

She bobs her head in a series of pleased and vigorous nods. I grasp my prize and guide it out, flex back into my chair holding it gently with a closed hand, the way one would hold a small bird. She smiles at me, coaxing, and I lay my palm open, present the bone fragment and feather, each hooked with its own special knot, attached to dangle like a charm from a slender decorative braid made from my own hair.

She's instantly engaged and reaches to slide the tip of one finger along the polished surface of the looped and knotted strand. She takes stock of the hair on my head and shifts back to touch the bone. And with loving care, so it stays nestled in the center of my hand, she fingers the fragment, her skin warm and close to my palm.

"Chuqui Chinchay?" she asks—Quechua words. And in my mind's eye, I understand she's talking about a cat-shaped constellation of stars in the night sky, the cat that bridges heaven and earth.

I answer, the victim of unbidden tears and mixing the languages because it comes awkward. "Si, abuela, Chuqui Chinchay."

I lift the relic, offer it to her, and she accepts, holds it with a kind of considered reverence, cherishing the knotted strands that fall away from it with the tips of her fingers. And for an instant, I flash on my own grandmother's pale hands working the beads of her amethyst rosary, so unlike these wise brown hands and yet the same.

She's fixed on the knots; they're unorthodox, quipu and not quipu. These strands carry markers, the gatherings of a past. *What's past is prologue,* Shakespeare's words; and I've mulled them over with a thousand thoughts of my own.

"This gringo girl," that's what has her stumped, wondering what the fetish in her hand has to do with me. She lifts her chin, gathers the lines of her weathered face into pursed lips and a squint over probing eyes. And I engage, willing myself wide open.

She's testing, and in Quechua she asks, "*Maytataq rinki?*" She wants to know where I'm going; small talk is full of stupid questions. We're on the same plane: of course I'm going to Bogotá. But on another level, without even thinking, I surprise myself and respond with Quechua words that match hers. I tell her I'm going to Bogotá. And then I tell her that I have a long way to go.

She sizes me up with a shake of her head and a, "well, aren't you the damnedest thing" kind of look. And she comes back, a one-up of sorts, this time in English, her consonants tenderized around the edges, softened with the sounds of Spanish, "Your Quechua, it's an odd dialect."

So now I know she's more than local color, and I'm not so eager to share. "Yes, well . . . I suppose I'm a little rusty."

I turn away to look out the window and let the silence crackle between us. She reaches to touch my shoulder and offers me the puma bone, but when I move to take it, she pulls back a little, "I think I know who you are."

I raise my eyebrows, waiting.

"You're the girl from Colorado who thinks she's an Inca."

Where did that come from? I feel like I should check my wallet; or maybe there's some mark on me. I'm cautious now, and not just a little irritated. My words come out clipped, "And you are?"

"My name is Koyam. I hope I didn't insult you. I work with Dr. Corbin."

And that explains just about everything except this particular seat assignment, at least a remarkable coincidence.

I reach to receive the puma bone, lay it in my lap, and offer my hand. "Well, Koyam, you've taken me by surprise. In case you don't already know, I'm Megan Kimsey."

Her touch is hot and dry, her grip overlong, so that when I pull back she continues to clutch my fingers. She cranes her neck, thrusts her face close so we are practically nose-to-nose, stares into my eyes, and then beyond. It's as if she's fixed on a bird traveling the horizon or the stones in the depths of a pool.

"You see something," I say. "Tell me."

"On your journey, you will come to my house. I will consult the coca leaves. And perhaps, you shall read the stars."

And I know this is true. In my mind's eye I see the shadow flickering across the orange glow of her cool stucco walls. I can almost feel the heat from her little brazier.

She grunts, releases me, and sighs, leans back into her seat and her eyelids droop. Then she startles me. She lets go a sharp chuckle. "You're going to scare the hell out of Dr. Corbin."

10 Touch Down

It's a rude rousing; touch down, three bumps, and a lurching skid before we settle into a waddling roll on the runway. And I wonder if the pilot's been sleeping too. Koyam is a flurry of motion beside me. She's already burst out of her seatbelt and has pulled her large woven satchel from under the seat in front of her; she's practically straddling it, ready to spring to a stand.

The flight attendant's voice anticipates impatience in the cabin, asking us to sit, to wait—but she knows it's hopeless, that she won't get Koyam or any of the other passengers who are popping up all over the plane to get back into their seats.

Koyam perches, listening with her whole body for the plane's engine to stop. I'm still blinking off sleep when she pushes into the crush. She makes a half turn, twists and speaks to me over her shoulder. "*Tupananchikkama*," she says. "Until we meet again."

I raise my hand in a salute. "Goodbye," I say, but she's already gone, and inexplicably, her absence feels like a loss. I think of Roy Rogers and Dale Evans on television, singing, "Happy trails to you, until we meet again. Happy trails to you, keep smiling until then." And I can't get the song out of my head.

I dawdle in my seat. Now that I've arrived, I'm reluctant. Colombia's a famously dangerous place. This would have been a different trip if my dad were with me. I scan the line of people pressing toward the front of the plane and finish fiddling with the zippers and tiny combination locks I brought with me to secure my backpack. The crowd thins. When I finally swing into the aisle, it's behind an older couple in matching flowered shirts and tan shorts. "Tourist, *Americano, Gringo*" – just like me.

The hollow thump of my feet on the metal walkway that connects the plane to the airport is all momentum, one foot and then the other, like the steady beat of a heart. But when I arrive at the open end of the Jetway, I stall. It's that last step, stepping into a new life that has no form, a sort of utter freedom that feels more like a deep lonesome than wings. For a second I wonder if I made the right choice, me, a woman with a passing grasp of Spanish, alone in the heart of drug cartels and guerilla warfare. I coach myself, looking for a little comfort, but stop short. I don't even bother asking, "What's the worst that can happen?"

I look for an overhead monitor and a map or a sign that points me toward the baggage claim and customs. I've checked two bags, a small suitcase and my medic bag. For a conference and a week or two of sightseeing, the medic bag seems superfluous, but I might decide to stay.

Mama almost had a heart attack when I told her once that third world medicine might agree with me. Just thinking about trench work, sanitation, and pot-bellied babies makes her want to wash her hands.

At the other side of the baggage claim, I fall in line. I wait my turn at customs, still wearing my backpack, lugging my suitcase in one hand and gripping the folded leather pouch that carries my letters of introduction and passport in the other. The customs officers are smiling, making small talk. The room is alive with the steady whir of machines, the muted intermittent hum of passengers chattering among themselves. Then, precipitously, chatter ebbs, the noise drops.

Though my chin's pointed in the right direction, I can't see what's going on, just the aftermath. A man in a tailored suit, a fellow passenger, is hustled toward a door behind the customs station. The man yanks his arm away from the customs official striding close by his side, as another, following along with a briefcase and bag, presses in from behind. The passenger angles his head. He shouts, "I want to see my consul." The ragged edge in his voice sounds an alarm.

The answer is muffled, emphatic, "*Cállese. Cálmese, señor.*" And more coaxing, "*Por favor, señor*, quiet. Please. We have a telephone inside." The door is thrown open and shut, shadows move away from the milky glass of the door's window. An uncomfortable rustle and whispers pass from one person to the next. A report from the front of the line says the agent had used a knife, or maybe it was a razor, on the inside of the man's suitcase. Perhaps money? Drugs?

The slow and steady shuffle begins again. Now I'm worried that the few medical instruments I've brought with me will be a problem, make me look suspect, or like I have something worth taking.

The officer signals for my papers. I hand them over and watch the expression on his face as he unfolds, examines. He's dark skinned, with lumbering shoulders that overhang seeping patches of perspiration under the arms of his uniform. The edges of his mustache bush out, peppered with coarse gray quills. He hands my visa and letters back in a careless stack for me to refold and organize. But before I can get a grasp, he points to my suitcase and slaps the Formica in front of him. "*Arriba y abierto.*"

I want to ask him to wait a minute. I open my mouth, but change my mind. I shove the pouch and the handful of papers under the waistband of my pants, heave my suitcase up and onto the counter.

He gestures at my backpack. "*Esa también.*"

I wiggle out of it, drop it beside my bag and unlock my suitcase, splay it open with the fabric ribbons that keep things neat and folded dangling over the zippered edges. I pull my hands away and he begins to finger through my shirts and underwear, to pile them in short stacks away from the medic bag nestled at the heart of things. He pulls the medic bag's hinged aperture apart, removes my sphygmomanometer and stethoscope and sets them aside. He's interested in the small supply of antibiotics I've brought along. He gathers two or three of the vials in his palm, lifts one and looks at the label.

"You saw my letters." I say. "I'm a doctor. *Soy medica. Americana.*"

He slips the pills into the pockets of his uniform; the cylinder shaped containers bulge under the fabric. "*Pero señorita,*" he says, his face transformed with a swaggering smile, "This is America."

He's tongue-tied me with semantics and that little pocket trick of his. I'm still groping for a response when a hand from behind clutches my shoulder. My mind flashes to the passenger compelled to the door and I jerk my head to look.

The hand belongs to a man—Latin, bronze, with quick eyes, and not much taller than me. He's wearing a suit, no uniform— and that's a relief—a summer weight pin stripe, tailored and obviously expensive, garnished with a bold red tie. "Excuse me *señorita*. Dr. Kimsey is it? I believe we've been waiting for you." He extends his free arm, exposes the crisp white cuff of his shirt and one of those high-tech watches with dials, the kind that divers wear. He points. And there, beyond customs, non-chalant and leaning against a cement pillar, is Dr. Corbin with Koyam next to him. She's occupied, looping the handles of her satchel over the metal bar of a luggage cart, prodding and se-curing the stack of custom leather bags underneath. She glances up and dips her chin, a sign for me to trust what's happening.

The man is all business and I'm clearly a problem to be managed. He steps forward to engage the customs officer. The two shake hands and the officer introduces himself with an agreeableness that borders on servility. The current of Spanish that passes between them mixes with head nodding and smiles. After a quick palm to palm pass of folded currency, the officer smiles and motions for me to pack up my things and go. He's already scrutinizing the next passenger's papers.

I start to stuff things back into my open suitcase, but I re-member those vials of antibiotics that are still in the officer's pocket. I lean across the counter, ready to open my mouth, but the stranger nudges my arm with his elbow. He reaches across me and tosses the rest of my things into my suitcase. His voice, accented and firm, buzzes against my ear, "Please, mind your manners." He folds my suitcase together on its hinges, runs the zipper around the edges, yanks it up, and steps off toward Corbin. Things will be a mess when I unpack. I hoist my back-pack onto my shoulder and follow along.

Corbin pulls away from his post, stands straight, holding his briefcase in front of his knees, waiting for us. I look for Koyam, but she's gone. There's just Corbin wearing an overlarge smile, like a kid who's just given his teacher the right answer, and for some reason, his expression annoys me. But when we're face to face, I take the hand he offers and smile.

"So you're Miss Kimsey; it's really Dr. Kimsey, a medical doctor. Right?"

I nod. "And you are Jasper Corbin, the illustrious anthropologist, and also a doctor." I'm trying to be playful, but it comes out sounding unnatural and a little too cute.

"And so," he says to the man who's taken charge of my suitcase, "Our mysterious repository of ancient Incan wisdom turns out to be a fetching young woman. Imagine that."

"Yes, well . . ." the man turns. He's still lugging my bag; his other hand is in the pocket of his pants, jiggling his keys. He glances past Corbin, preparing to offer me a perfunctory hello.

"Dr. Kimsey," he says, and this time he really sees me, does a sort of double-take. He lifts his chin, his jaw softens, and the nervous hand in his pocket is suddenly still. For an instant, long enough to make us both feel awkward, the dark centers of his eyes fix on me with a doe-eyed stare. I look down at my feet and blush, and he blinks and clears his throat. "*Mucho gusto, señorita.* I'm Eduardo Sircusa."

"Dr. Sircusa," Corbin corrects.

Sircusa gives a perfunctory smile and shrugs off the title. "It'll be rush hour soon. Do you mind if we walk and talk? Come. I'll drop you at your hotel. The ride will be tight. I hope you don't mind. It's better than a bus or taxi." And he takes off at a clip with Corbin and me hustling to keep up.

His car is parked in an adjacent garage but we've taken our lives in our hands to get to it. The thoroughfare that runs along the street side of the airport is choked with traffic—busses and decrepit cars, motorcycles, all in intermittent motion; doors slamming, horns honking, the hydraulic hiss of bus machinery, and everywhere, the smell and dingy pall of exhaust.

"Over here." Sircusa points to a buffed and polished, cream-colored Austin Healey, yet one row away. I hang back. Corbin hesitates with me. There are three boys, cocky adolescents, loitering around Sircusa's car but he doesn't slow a step. He strides up to the one who's leaning against the front fender. "*¿Está todo bien?*" he asks. The four of them converge. There's a brisk exchange, muted and none of it intelligible. But I understand the clip of folded currency the doctor pulls from his jacket pocket, the murmur of settled accounts.

The boys leave and Sircusa unlocks the car doors and tosses my bag in the trunk, motions for my backpack too. "I apologize," he says, "I hope you won't be too uncomfortable."

Corbin opens the passenger door. "You'll have to squeeze into the back; your legs are much shorter than mine." I don't object; I have no problem with the laws of physics.

We are making our way out of the garage. It's stop and go, a busy place. Even so, up a tier of cars and not far from the exit, I notice the same young men Sircusa paid to watch his car, two of them crouched and prying the hubcaps away from the whitewalls of someone's convertible.

"Dr. Sircusa," I say, "do you see what they're doing?"

"This is a complicated country, Dr. Kimsey. Let's concentrate on getting you to your hotel. Where are you staying?" His eyes flash on mine in the rearview mirror.

I dig for the piece of paper that's in my pocket and read the name. "*Hosteria de la Basilio* on *Calle Nueve*."

"It's in the old part of the city," Corbin says. "It's a small hotel. I recommended it to your father. I think you'll like it."

"Are you staying there?"

"Not this time. My graduate assistant found me an apartment, but I don't expect to be around much. I'm starting my sabbatical."

"Will you be teaching at the National University here?"

"Oh no." He turns his head enough so I can see the smile lines around his eyes. He looks at Sircusa. "Eduardo and I have secured funds for an expedition."

"That's fantastic. Where are you going?"

"Part of the money comes from a German drug company with a requirement to look for plants and organisms of potential medicinal value. That means varied terrain, some rainforest, and we've had to hook up with a pharmacologist. Still, there's a lot of latitude. Eduardo and I are headed to Ecuador and ultimately, southern Peru. The high point will be taking on the Andes, looking for sacrificial burial sites."

"*Capa cocha.*" The words come out of my mouth in a whisper, vague and steamy, like smoke off dry ice. For me they hang in the air, somewhere between utterance and thought.

"You know about *capa cocha*? Well then, you can imagine what kind of find that would be, a child sacrifice—a classic time capsule."

But I *don't* know; it's more like a vague ache.

It's late in the day, past rush hour and into evening. The traffic's thinned and there aren't so many buses to challenge us on every side.

"How much farther?" I ask.

Sircusa speaks over his shoulder. "Ten minutes or so, not far."

I rearrange my knees; try to move the kinks around so I won't get stiff.

This part of town is local color, a swatch of collective memory, stuccoed churches and colonial houses situated at the edge of narrow, tiled streets. But present need lurks here too. Street musicians and even a contortionist vie for an audience. And there are beggars, palsied and poverty-stricken, some of them children, who plead from doorways and on the stairs and stoops of steepled churches. They tug at my conscience—one girl in particular, maybe thirteen or fourteen, who sits at the corner of a building, practically in the street, a dangerous place. We pass so near that I can see the nervous whites of her eyes. The sign that's hung around her neck says, "*Tengo hambre, soy ciega,*" announces the obvious; she's hungry and blind. And I notice about her, above those thin, brown legs and under her loose, plaid dress, a soft roundness. She's pregnant, I'm sure of it. I start to ask Sircusa to stop, but I worry that he'll accuse me of being gullible. Anyway, if I give her money, someone will take it. She didn't find that street corner by herself. I tell myself, maybe tomorrow, in broad daylight, I'll search her out, bring her something to eat.

Sircusa pulls his car close to the curb in front of a whitewashed building, turns off the motor, and steps around to get my bags out of the trunk. Corbin lets himself out the passenger door. He stands holding it for me. "Well, what do you think?"

I boost myself out and onto both feet, stretch to a stand, and take my eye the length of the building. Door, balcony, window frames, all painted the same rich green. Grates of ornate wrought iron latticework cover the door and the tall windows on either side are clotted with vines and abutted by huge urns overflowing with pink-blooming plants. The sun is glowing low on the horizon, almost gone; but what's left plays up and down the street in a rosy wash.

"It's perfect." I say to Corbin. But I'm thinking of my father, picturing the slouch of his shoulders in his old suede sport coat, his camera dangling from a leather strap around his neck, lugging our suitcases up the steps to the hotel as if they weigh nothing. He's there at the door, pausing, turning slightly, a look back to catch my eye. And then he disappears—gone on ahead of me.

Sircusa gathers my things and comes to stand beside me, and inexplicably, his presence feels like ballast. He pauses, giving me time, proud of his country and pleased that I'm agog. And I do my best to reward him. "It's charming," I say. "Thank you."

He nods and smiles. "Come, I'll give your bags to the bellman. Do you need help checking in?"

"No. Thanks. I can take my things now. It will be good for me to struggle with my Spanish."

But he strides beside me to the reservation desk anyway. The clerk is turned away from us talking on the telephone. Sircusa clears his throat, demands attention, but the clerk rounds his back and steps close to the wall where the hotel's room keys hang on small brass hooks. The doctor sighs and drops my luggage at his feet, thumps the brass call bell with the flat of his hand. It chimes a clear and solitary note.

The clerk flicks his head to his shoulder and emits a sound, terse and husky, "Un momento," then hunches back into his conversation.

"I'm in no hurry, really," I say to Sircusa. "I can handle it from here."

But the good doctor looms across the desk, his voice louder than necessary. "*Señor Clemente, dónde èsta?*"

The name he's uttered has the desired effect. The phone hits its cradle and the young man pivots, practically stands at attention. Words fly between the two men. The registry is pushed across the counter. I make a move to sign, but Sircusa's arm prevents me. Instead, I watch him sign my name. "Excuse me," I say.

"It's no problem," he says.

The clerk sounds the bell, and a bellman, mestizo, short and older, in a crisp white cutaway jacket, reports front and center. He dips his head to Sircusa and then to me. The doctor offers him a coin and the money disappears into his jacket pocket. The clerk hands the bellman my room key, instructs, "*Vientiuno.*" The bellman hoists my backpack, grabs my suitcase, and my bags are gone.

The whole transaction feels like it happened without me, and I'm doing my best to manage a rising prickle of resentment. I tell myself that it's no big deal. I'm just tired and getting desperate for some time to myself. I make a move to disengage, "Thank you again. Before you leave, I owe you some money." I pull the money clip out of the front pocket of my pants. "How much? For customs; for getting me out of what could have been a jam. And for taking care of the bellman just now."

He shakes his head. "You can thank Koyam. She was quite insistent. And the tip, it was nothing." His smile is pleasant, intentionally official, and he offers his hand. The palm is dry and warm. "I'll look forward to seeing you at the conference tomorrow. *Buenas noches*, Doctor Kimsey."

"Yes, *hasta mañana*." I'm practically heaving a sigh of relief, imagining the expansive stillness of being alone in a hotel room, the feel of having my shoes off, the hot bath I'm going to take.

Sircusa and I are just turning to part ways when Corbin comes toward us. He puts a hand on Sircusa's shoulder. "I've had the most remarkable idea, Eduardo. Why don't we invite Megan to your little soiree tonight?"

Corbin looks incredibly pleased with himself and Sircusa and I are stopped in our tracks. Sircusa puts his hands in his pockets; he nods. "Yes, of course." He smiles at me. "Please. I hope you'll forgive me for not thinking of it myself. I've invited a few colleagues to a party at my sister's house tonight, a sort of *bienvenida*, an informal get together before the conference begins tomorrow. You're welcome to join us."

"Oh, I don't think so, Doctor. I've been traveling since early this morning."

Corbin interrupts. "But you must come. You see, we have a game we play when we get together. Each of us brings an obscure artifact. We challenge each other, a sort of stump the archeologist. I think you'd find it interesting."

"Thanks for thinking of me, but I'm not sure I'd fit in. I'm an emergency room physician, not an archeologist, and I'm fresh out of artifacts." The words come out too flip, almost arrogant, but they've left my mouth before I can catch them.

"Then why did you come here? You claim to know things. Think of this as an opportunity to convince us."

"I don't know what you discussed with my father. I know you mean well, but I need to be clear. I don't claim anything. I have an interest and some questions. That's all."

Sircusa throws a hand up in front of Corbin, a signal for him to be quiet. "Doctor Kimsey, please. I assure you, the reception—it's purely social. Jasper has put you off. Now you must come. How else can he redeem himself?"

I'm left in a sort of social cul-de-sac, reduced to making excuses. "I don't mean to be rude. It's just that I'm tired. And I'm not prepared to be someone's parlor trick."

"No preparation is necessary." Sircusa smiles.

I shrug.

"Then it's settled," he says. "I'll send a driver for you around eight."

11 THE ARISTOCRATS

The night breeze rushes along the narrow street; it flutters inside my open coat and blows the scent of rain against my face. The driver holds the limousine door open and I gather myself inside, pull my coat around me and smooth my hair. We are underway, motoring who knows where. My whole life's become an act of faith.

The rain comes in earnest now, spattering in hard, wide drops against the metal rooftop, wet-shining the pavement and spinning off the tires. Oncoming headlights swipe past, Dopplers of light, and none of this seems real. I lay my head back and take a deep breath, but I can't relax. How long, I wonder. How far? My wristwatch is in the pocket of my suitcase, left there in favor of a fake gold bangle. Black nylons and slender strappy heels—my basic conference banquet finery already called into service. Maybe this is a masquerade; I feel as if I'm dressed as someone other than myself.

We've turned off the highway, traveling up a narrow avenue toward a lighted gate framed by trees. Their wet leaves shimmer silver, backlit in the dark. And just beyond, stands a huge house, luminous inside and out, an island of honeyed light in the rain and gloom. The gate is drawn apart and we roll forward. The driver guides the car along the paved semi-circle, pulls in close to the curb, and stops where the steps lead up to a broad doorway. I'm stunned, gawking. The driver's already out, opening my door. He flicks an umbrella; it bursts into a canopy and I slide out, put my feet on the pavement and stand. The air is sweet, heavy with the scent of bruised magnolias. And somewhere, dogs are barking. I stall, twist to look behind me, but my guide is firm; he has me by the elbow, piloting me toward the door. He rings the bell. A chime resonates inside and the driver is gone. I'm left, feeling orphaned on some stranger's doorstep.

The heavy double doors swing apart. Framed there in the center, holding onto the brass handles on either side, is a woman, striking and cosmopolitan, sleek in a gown of ivory satin. The dress is bold, revealing, and so like lingerie that it can only be designer. Her hair is a managed cap of short, dark curls. She takes me in at an angle, looks me up and down with a practiced kind of impertinence, and fingers the diamonds at her throat. The slow smile she aims my way feels more like a cataloguing of my deficiencies than a welcome.

"I'm Megan Kimsey," I say.

She takes a step backward and ushers me in with a sweep of her hand. "I know who you are," she says, and raises her voice above her shoulder. "Asunta." A maid, a dark-skinned girl in a crisp black dress and white apron, steps away from the wall.

The girl slips my coat off my shoulders and carries it away.

"I'm Martina, Martina Sircusa Marquez. Eduardo is my brother." My hostess offers her name but she's less generous with her hand; instead she twines her fingers, suspends them close to her body just below her waist. "You've been the talk. How do you say? Your ears, they are on fire."

I smile at her syntax, and because I don't know what else to say.

"Come," she says, "you shall see." She turns and I fall into step behind her, marching along in the shadow of her dazzle, her bronze back and the sensuous sway of her slender hips. We are moving toward music; a harp and flute provide background to the rustle of Martina's satin skirt, the rhythmic swish of her silk stockings as her thighs pass against one another. I tell myself that she will be my savior, that in her company, I am rendered invisible.

I'm all eyes and ears; I know this music. It's Brazilian, Villa-Lobos, done simply. I envy the musicians; I miss my guitar.

We step through an arch and into a room with a soaring, coved ceiling and elegant, expansive rugs. The floor, where it's visible, is pieced together from huge slabs of some dark and ancient wood. And across the room, by the glow of oil lamps and candles, servants are laying a table of small foods on china plates—platters of thin sliced meats rolled into tiny funnels, bowls of dates and sectioned oranges sprinkled with ivory flecks—maybe almonds, maybe pine nuts. The atmosphere is dense with warm smells: bees' wax and cumin, a tang of cinnamon; the whole mélange reminds me that I've barely eaten all day.

The musicians are stationed near the door. Their music is heaven and they're something to watch. The harpist is tall and loose-limbed. He straddles his instrument and labors in a kind of musical stupor with his eyes closed, swoops in on his strings and retreats, straightens his back and flares his nostrils, pluck-ing notes in rapid succession, registering each ping and tremor as it escapes from beneath his fingers.

His flautist partner provides a subdued counterpoint, a sweet lament among the strings. There's no strut or preen. He simply cups his upper lip and plies breath across the mouthpiece. The sound is pristine, and I stop to watch and listen. But Martina is impatient. She puts an arm across my shoulders, speaks close to my ear. "Come along, chica. I have orders to deposit you with my brother, but trust me; his friends," she raises her eyebrows, "they are boring. You'll want a drink in your hand."

We've been spotted. Corbin breaks away from a chatting threesome and comes striding toward us, spreading his arms. "Welcome, Dr. Kimsey. And Martina, what a picture, the two of you, the sun and the moon. Spectacular." His speech is loose and there is a bloom in his cheeks. He's had a few drinks al-ready.

"Pero, Jasper," she says to Corbin, "am I now to think I'm not the only star in your sky?" Martina gives him a feigned pout. "Watch out for this one, amiga. This professor, how you say? He likes to teach the ladies."

"Yes, watch out." Corbin winks at me. "Observe however, that although she complains, our hostess remains immune to my charm." He shrugs and smiles. "It's not fair, a bruise to my ego. But tonight we have business. Come, Dr. Kimsey, let me introduce you. We should get started."

Martina sighs, shakes her head. "The food's just been set out, and Dr. Kimsey must have a drink. At least invite every-one to fill a plate before you start impressing each other."

She turns to me, "You're a medico, not an archeologist, true?" I nod. She looks straight at Corbin. "You'll see what I put up with. They spend too much time digging in the dirt, disturbing the dead. These tontos, my brother as well, no manners at all."

"She maligns us, but we keep coming back." Corbin raises his hands, playing at keeping Martina at bay. "I promise, a drink for Dr. Kimsey, and I'll prod everyone toward the food before we shut ourselves in the library to study our treasures."

Corbin leads me toward a server who's circulating with a tray. I take a glass of white wine but the bourbon he wants is not on offer, and he excuses himself with a promise to come right back.

It's a relief to have a drink in my hand. Just a sip, a whiff under my nose, is enough to blunt the edges.

I count eleven of us in all, including Martina and myself, a small number considering the elaborate table, the music. No wonder Martina complains.

I survey the crowd and gravitate toward the one woman in the room who seems to have professional standing among these men. It's her laughter that draws me, tumbling through the junctures of the conversation she's having with Dr. Sircusa and a young man who wears the rumpled sport coat and open ardent face of a student. It's eavesdropping I have on my mind, but Sircusa sees me and beckons. "Dr. Kimsey. Come join us. Let me introduce you to my colleagues, Dr. Henriette Polmo and Mr. Justin Foley." He dips his head to the two of them. "May I present Megan Kimsey? She's an emergency room physician from the United States, and the author of that puzzling little sketchbook that's been making the rounds tonight."

"My sketchbook?" I can feel the tension setting like cement along my spine. "You've been passing around my notes and drawings?"

"Don't worry. Your work is safe. It's probably in the library by now. Jasper's taken a personal interest this year. I'm sure everything is under control. "

Dr. Polmo extends her hand. "Yes, leave it to Jasper. He's been bustling around gathering in everyone's treasures, nesting with our shiny objects." Her grip is firm and somehow reassuring. She smiles.

On someone else, all that cheer might play as a nervous habit, but Dr. Polmo has an affect that is far too grounded, too meticulous, to be so skittish. Everything about her is managed, solid, from her glossed-back hair and smooth forehead, to the sheer ballast of her presence, wide shoulders, broad hips, all tempered by pinstripes and tailored silk, even the buff on those plain, flat shoes. As far as I can tell, the only concession she's made to look festive is the single magenta carnation that's pinned to the lapel of her suit. She registers that my eyes are on it.

"Oh this." She brushes the flower with a fingertip. "Martina's touch. Our hostess worries that my work is making me dull."

"Impossible." It's Corbin, already back at my shoulder. I twist my head and catch his eyes along with a blast of the bourbon that's on his breath. He grins at me then scans the group and dives into our conversation.

"Henriette's a pathologist turned archeologist, anything but dull. But you'll see for yourself. And Justin here is a graduate student angling to get in on his first South American dig. In real life, he's a regular farm boy from Montana."

"It's a ranch, and it's in Wyoming." Justin raises his eyebrows but stops short of rolling his eyes. He takes a drink instead.

"Wyoming, Montana, Colorado, all cattle country." Corbin looks to me for confirmation. "The Wild West, right?" But he's already on to something else, craning his neck, surveying the room. "I'm afraid you two will have to catch up on cowboy country later." He claps his hands together and broadcasts around the room. "Everyone, take advantage of Martina's beautiful table. Fill a plate and make your way into the library."

The line at the buffet is instantaneous, the feasters as eager as insects. My appetite's sharp, almost painful, and that glass of wine has gone straight to my head. But I wait my turn; listen to the buzz of conversation, the clink of silver on china.

Finally, plate and napkin in hand, the banquet is at my disposal. The first significant morsel I come across goes right into my mouth; shredded beef and chilies all tucked inside a tiny tortilla. I stand right there and eat another, take two more and a mound of seasoned rice, pile the edges of my dish with fresh strawberries, sections of oranges, some fingers of cheese. I take my time and let the others move on ahead, until even the musicians are gone, and it's just me, my shadow looming out ahead of me in that cathedral of a room where the silence has settled like ashes.

A gust of wind rattles the shutters and spits rain down the chimney. There's sizzle and smoke, a whiff – reminders of childhood campfires and old fireplace picnics. I move in close to the hearth where I can watch the flames, feeling unsure and homesick, wanting to be left alone, to be dazed by the heat and wine. Behind me, a waiter passes at the table removing platters. He comes to ask if I need help—then insists. Reluctantly, I follow—a few steps down the hall, a turn to the right, and he ushers me to the threshold of the library door.

I take a deep breath and do my best to slip inside with an unobtrusive step. The entire entourage is settled along the outer edge of three polished mahogany tables custom-made to fit together in the shape of a wide horseshoe. There is a projector positioned at the center facing a huge expanse of white wall.

Already, Henriette is beckoning from where she sits. She shifts a briefcase from the seat next to her and angles the empty chair, an unmistakable invitation.

"You look a bit uncertain. Did you get lost?" she asks.

"Just slow. Mostly tired," I say. "And, to be honest, a little out of my element."

"Don't worry. There may be posturing, but no one bites. I always enjoy this room, actually the whole house, a shrine to Martina, don't you think? Breathtaking really." Henriette smiles at me, being generous.

She lifts her chin. Her eyes beam to the far end of the room and an immense portrait of a girlish Martina set inside a gilded frame. The artist has rendered our hostess soft and ethereal, dressed in innocent eyelet and bathed in the dew-fresh light of early morning, her arms brimming with pink and white peonies.

Henriette is silent, waiting on my assessment.

"It's arresting—the light." I say. "Martina looks like an angel."

"The painting was commissioned as a wedding present, a gift to her from her husband. The Sircusa family, the whole lot of them, comes from old money, hacendados, part of the oligarchy left over from the conquistadors. And Eduardo," she continues, "it's ironic, but what he wouldn't give now to bring back just a few of those precious pieces his ancestors melted down for trade. I'm afraid he's chosen a line of work that makes his heritage hard to live with."

I scan the room, looking for Eduardo. That little teaser of information has me thinking he might be more complicated, more interesting, than I expected. I locate him shutting the door to the library just as Corbin announces we are ready to begin.

Henriette moves to a seat behind the projector and clicks in her carousel of slides. "Eduardo, please, if you'd like to begin, I'll manage the photographs."

Chairs scrape and adjust. Eduardo makes his way around the table dangling a pointer in one hand and gripping a folder of documents in the other. He glances around the room then nods. "As most of you know, Henriette and I have spent much of this year excavating in the Lambayeque Valley."

He moves close to the screen.

There's an instant of darkness. The projector begins its hum and emits a beam of watery light. Henriette fiddles with the focus. The image draws together, solidifies, and I pull up in my seat, lean forward across the table, as if recognition depended on inches, trying to hone in on what about this photograph seems so familiar.

On the screen, a multitude of huge mounds dominates an unrippled landscape of fertile flatlands. Cultivated patches and strands of fruit trees, but signs of life stop abruptly where the monuments begin. In the distance, the blue shadow of the Andes unfurls across the horizon.

"A view of the site," says Eduardo. "Tucume, virtually a metropolis of pyramids. At this point, we have linked the occupation of Tucume to three distinct periods with radiocarbon dates that span from around 1000AD to the Spanish occupation some years after the Inca were overcome in 1532. The verification of successive cultural periods is the subject of the paper Henriette and I will present tomorrow at the symposium. But that's old news to most of you. Tonight," he says, his eyes seeking our faces in the dark. "Our intent is to incite discussion. Next please."

Henriette flashes a series of photographs, each a grouping of clay vessels, the largest no more than four inches tall and etched around the rim. But most are smaller, less than an inch in height and unadorned.

Eduardo continues. "These little receptacles are called crisoles, quite common. To date, in this dig alone, we've recovered literally hundreds. Lights, please."

We all shift in our chairs, blinking off the sudden brightness, and Eduardo begins unpacking a small box of the featured vessels onto the tables in front of us. He sets three crisoles along the center of the table in front of me. I reach toward one and look up at him. "May I?" I ask, and he gives an approving nod.

Nestled in my palm, this one's smooth, coated in a warm brown glaze. And with the heft of it, a jumble of images crowds my mind. Crisoles, mundane, comfortable little things, bona fide creature comforts, hardly different from looking at some excavated English discards—perhaps tea cozies or toothbrushes.

A cascade of memories—tucking baubles like these into the interior pockets of a shoulder bag, nesting them in hot coals to absorb heat, warming medicine and morning brew, heating a gourd of milk for a child, all moments un-troubled and common—but out of sync with my time and person. It's a discontinuity that's difficult to bridge. I set the vessel back on the table next to its fellows and lean into my chair, look up and realize that Eduardo's been watching me.

"You know these?" he asks.

I hesitate, but I can't commit. "I'm fascinated." I say. "I'm waiting to hear what you have to say about them."

Eduardo dismisses me with a smile and opens up to the group. "There are varied opinions regarding crisoles, what their use might have been, certainly no consensus. But we have some new evidence, and from an unexpected source. Before I go on, please, would someone be kind enough to give our guest, Dr. Kimsey, some history?"

Corbin steps away from the wall, squares his shoulders, and tugs the lapels of his jacket. "I'll do it." We all shift in our chairs, watch him amble into the cove where the tables come together. He picks up one of the little vessels and turns it in his hand. "Crisoles show up in almost every dig. They are numerous as ritual offerings, entombed with the dead and in shrines. But we are just as apt to find them when we excavate individual living quarters or tambos, way stations along Inca highways. Manufacture and use of crisoles predates the Incas and appears to have been widely disseminated even before the earlier Moche and Chimu civilizations came on the scene."

He stops and pours himself a glass of water from a pitcher on one of the tables. He pauses and grins at me. "My students usually take notes." There's a swagger in his comment. I give him the required smile, and he continues. "Some archeologists have proposed that crisoles were used as vessels for ritual liquids, though the interiors of most are conspicuously absent of residue. As sacred offerings, crisoles frequently appear to have been ritually broken or interred with the dead in an unfinished state, sometimes before the clay has had time to harden and dry. To date, there's been no satisfactory explanation. Frankly, we don't know what they were used for. That's it in a nutshell. Unless there are questions, I say it's time to put Eduardo on the spot, hear this new evidence he thinks is so compelling."

Eduardo and Corbin exchange places. I watch, willing Eduardo to have figured it out, and if he has, to tell us what got him there. There's an excited burnish under his olive skin. He clears his throat. "I'm a great fan of Occam's Razor, a rule that says the simplest answer is usually the best. But I've gotten ahead of myself. Let me back up a bit.

"The natives who live in the Lambayeque Valley are very superstitious, convinced that the pyramids are inhabited by guardian spirits. They believe anyone venturing near the monuments is in mortal danger, that anyone who sees one of these spirits is doomed to die. Fear among the locals is so pervasive we were forced to recruit labor from as far away as Chiclayo. Please understand, the poverty in the area surrounding the site is extreme and these are an industrious people. Under other conditions, they would be clamoring to have lucrative work.

"As you can imagine, the stories of these guardians captured my interest and set me wondering if they might, in some way, resonate with what would be unearthed by the dig. I began to ask questions and engaged an interpreter, a native boy of Chimu descent who seemed to be related to everyone. Whenever I could get away from the site, Paulo and I made the rounds in the village, chatting with anyone who would stop and talk. But it was his father's ancient uncle, a frail old man, who became my source.

"The old man lived with an elderly daughter in a shack somewhat removed from the town. He spoke Quechua, probably other local dialects as well, but no Spanish. Being in his presence—I can't tell you what that was like."

Eduardo's voice wavers; he clears his throat. Henriette pours him a glass of water. He takes a sip and hands it back. "Give us the next slide, please."

Projected in front of us is a hut, mud bricks and a thatched roof. Over the doorway, posts pounded into the ground support a ramshackle awning. The figure of an old man sits underneath.

The next photograph is a close-up of the old man, gnarled and propped upright in his swathe of shade. He sits with his back against the sunbaked bricks looking beyond the camera, his face a network of furrows and crevices; his eyes, the piercing watery eyes of age. Flies probe the old man's tunic and one has settled on his cheekbone, still his hands remain at ease, one resting on each of his knees.

"We called him Machu K'ak'a, meaning old uncle. I spent many afternoons and evenings with Paulo and Machu K'ak'a in this smoke-saturated hut.

"There will be more to say later about the local myths and our source's commentary, what we found at the site, but back to the crisoles. I had been visiting with this old man for several weeks, was leaving the site to go see him one afternoon, and it occurred to me to see what he had to say about crisoles, so I stuck a couple of them in my pocket.

Machu K'ak'a smiled when I set them before him. He touched them and called them good, good for making medicine. He said they were used when he was a child."

Eduardo holds one up. "Go ahead and handle one. Note how small they are, and hollow. Occam's razor, my simple answer. Crisoles were used to heat liquids, placed among the hot coals to take on heat, then lifted out of the fire and set to float, to dissipate their warmth in a cup or bowl of some liquid, most often chicha, Inca corn beer. And the little finger holes," Sircusa dangles one on his own finger, "these make them easy to drop in and remove, with a stick or tool of some sort, possibly by hand once they are cool and have done their job."

There's clapping all around and Corbin pronounces, "Well done."

I'm pleased for Eduardo. He's beaming, so is Henriette.

"Your response is gratifying, but the credit really goes to Machu K'ak'a, and to Paulo for translating. I am merely their recorder. When you see what Henriette has to offer, you will understand our frustration that we didn't happen upon Old Uncle sooner."

Henriette moves off to a corner of the library and comes back with Corbin, each of them supporting one end of a flat, lacquered box. They set it down on a table not far from the screen. "Eduardo, please," Henriette asks, "if you would talk about the guardian, the feathered shaman. I believe it would set the stage for what comes next."

"Of course, let me get my notes." He strolls around the table, picks up a folder, and along with it, he grabs my sketchbook. He comes toward me and stops across from where I'm sitting, lays it open and bends down, stoops and whispers, "I think you'll find this interesting."

The page he's selected has a simple geometric design on a background that's textured for softness. It's in pencil, just a doodle; quickly executed, and done so long ago I can barely remember. I lift my head, give him a shrug, but I'm not feeling as casual as I pretend.

He steps backward and begins. "In talking with the villagers and Machu K'ak'a, I recorded composites of three distinct entities that were said to inhabit the pyramids; guardians if you will. But for our purposes tonight, Henriette and I will focus on one, the spirit of the feathered shaman. He is said to be an ancient, older than the pyramids, born of both man and bird, and with the rattle of a venomous snake. Oral legend has it that the shaman's plumage is so striking, that anyone who comes upon him is powerless to look away; a lethal twist, since any unfortunate who sees him is also doomed to die.

"Fear among the natives is so pervasive that all the dwellings in the village are oriented away from the monuments. No one wants to chance coming out of his door some morning and getting a glimpse of this birdman in the sky."

Eduardo nods to Henriette. She's radiant with what she's about to tell us. She produces a pencil from behind her ear and uses the sharpened tip as a pointer. "What you see on the screen are three mummy bundles as we found them inside this unusual stone chamber. Unusual because it's the only room in this entire complex constructed in characteristic Inca stonework."

Something in the photograph sets me groping. The room on the screen, it's too spare, not right, a needling dissonance, and my head feels fuzzy. Too much, I think, crisoles, and that projected vista of pyramids against the horizon, Machu K'ak'a, this scribble of mine. And the despair of a feathered shaman – what is a haunting, I ask myself, but despair?

The images begin to vibrate against each other inside my brain, like single notes sounding one after another before a melody comes together. There's sadness, and a squeezing sense of panic that has my heart colliding with my ribs. I think about leaving, but I can't seem to pull myself together. I'm not even sure I can remember the name of my hotel.

Henriette is lobbing her words, or maybe it's just me, catching them through some kind of fog. I pinch the back of my hand, wanting the pain, to feel something immediate, something real.

"These three bundles were discovered in an interior stone chamber, a departure from the sun-dried mud bricks and plaster that constitute the rest of the site. Because of the location, and the fact that the mummy bundles were found with some artifacts of distinctly Incan origin, we speculated that all three lived during or at the end of the Incan period.

"The problem, or rather, a more interesting discovery, came to light when we began to examine these individuals in the laboratory. X-rays of one of the mummies turned out as we expected, but the other two appear to be ceremonial re-interments of two individuals who were originally buried in a prone position. By the condition of the remains and some of the offerings found with them, we can extrapolate that these two, a man and a woman, lived much earlier, during the Lambayeque period."

The next slide clicks onto the screen, a picture of leathery remains and bone unraveled from its cocoon. Henriette explains. "This high ranking individual was wrapped in eighteen layers of textiles, sixteen decorated and of finely spun vicuna wool of a type usually reserved for the Lord Inca himself, and one, an elaborate cloak of feathers. Note a great curiosity, the carved wooden rattle to the left. It was found inside a scarred pocket incised in the flesh of this man's thigh."

I try to pay attention, but I can't seem to stop trembling. I cross my arms and rub them, pull in and remind myself to breathe.

Henriette moves to stand behind the lacquered box, removes the lid, and takes out a piece of soft fabric. She spreads it on the table, and then reaches back inside for a necklace of abalone shells and a large conch trumpet. She takes her time arranging them on the cloth. I keep waiting for her to comment. Instead, she goes back into the box. "I've saved the best for last. Eduardo, please. Of course, this is a copy of the mummy's cloak, a labor of love, recreated for a North American museum tour next summer." Eduardo moves to help her. He holds one side for display and Henriette continues. "You can see the beautiful work."

There's an audible intake of breath; the guests all pull upright, lean forward in their chairs. Eduardo and Henriette flank a fabulous cloak of white and pale green feathers, the center done in an overlapping pattern of diamond shapes, the design itself in shades of scarlet and emerald green. I glance down at my drawing; it has to be the same, the motif, and in context, the soft repetitive pencil strokes take on the texture and definition of feathers. I feel Eduardo's eyes on the top of my head.

"Come, Dr. Kimsey," he says. "Your artwork, you tease us with tidbits, little open-ended hints that you know more than you're telling." He and Henriette still hold the cape. "Please, I'm anxious to hear if you make a connection between this design and your drawing. Would you pass it around so the others can see?"

I surrender my sketchbook. It's Justin Foley, the American graduate student, who's first to look. His face gapes puzzlement, "I don't understand. I thought Dr. Kimsey was a medical doctor, not an archeologist."

"You're right, Mr. Foley, absolutely right," says Corbin. "But Dr. Kimsey has other qualifications, which I don't presume to understand. Maybe she'll be good enough to clarify." His eyes shift to me.

My first instinct is to equivocate. "It's hard to explain." I say. "I can only tell you that images like this come to me, some of them I recorded in my sketchbooks. Snippets of things, faces, sometimes whole scenes. It's like living in and out of a dream. The drawing of the cloak, I can barely recall. I must have been twelve or fourteen, in junior high, when I drew it."

Corbin's standing next to the table where Henriette's displaying the large shell and neckpiece. He reaches around, picks up the conch and offers it to me.

It's polished and perfect. The sense of calm that comes with touching it feels like a blessing. My mind drifts for a second, imagining the conch nested in silt amid pulpy tendrils and fine grassy blades, suspended in muffled silence.

"Go ahead; show us how it's done. Blow it." Corbin's words jar me; they're rude, abrupt. I don't respond and he urges, "Go on. When I talked to your father last spring, he said he'd seen you make one of these sing." Corbin's posturing, being flip.

"You don't know what you're asking."

"Then why don't you tell us."

I hate him for putting me on the spot. I open my mouth, uncertain, but when my words come, they push back. "To sound a conch like this one is a sacrament, such an act without preparation, without intent . . . Think me superstitious if you want, like the people who build their houses facing away from the pyramids."

Corbin tightens his chin. He fixes his eyes on me. His expression is calm and penetrating. He's so sure of himself. And for an instant, Corbin and Dr. Vickers seem the same.

12 Stone Eye

Eduardo's watching the road, driving. He's unsettled, silent, but then, what do you say to someone who speaks in tongues?

I would have been just as glad to take a taxi, or have Martina's driver deposit me back at my hotel, but Eduardo insisted. We left the guests speechless, all but Corbin, who walked with us as far as the door, making it his business to come along. But it was the Austin Healey that Eduardo asked the servant to bring around, and this time, he sent Corbin back inside, to help Martina with the guests.

I ask Eduardo if he minds, could I roll the window down, and he nods.

The air is fresh and damp. What's left of the rain is all mist that hovers over the highway. It rolls out in a billow that hangs just beyond the headlights, as if the clouds have come to earth. Above us, the night is clear and speckled with stars.

My consciousness is spreading roots, organic now, drawing from two worlds. There's wonder to it, even grace, I think. If only I can give up resisting.

I keep rewinding the evening, over and over, combing my psyche for details, repeating so I don't forget before I can get back to my room and put it all down on paper. Even so, some things will be difficult to record.

My catechism came back to me tonight, potent with natural symbols—Inti, the sun god, and Killa, the moon, Mamaqocha, Mother Sea, and Ukhu Pacha, the depths at the door of the dead. It came on the heels of Corbin's demanding, and I knew the conch, felt myself absorbing its cool power. Saw ribbons of pink flash behind my eyes, coalesce and spread in a rosy glow above a steel blue ocean seething with whitecaps. That restless sea roiled with a soft roar that smothered sound. And then, in a chink of illumination, I witnessed myself baptized in light at the moment of death. And in that instant, like Lot's wife, I knew I had turned to look back.

I could hear Dr. Corbin, but nothing he said seemed relevant—nothing. There could have been an earthquake, and still, I would have remained in that chair, mute, absorbing from the inside.

When I did engage and look around the table, it was as if I was seeing with new eyes. All those gaping faces, Martina's guests wondering if I was having a seizure, or maybe they thought I'd gone crazy. I didn't care. It was their appearance that grabbed me, how tall they seemed, and pale, and the hair on Dr. Corbin's face, his beard. Time had turned me around and jarred my bearings; had me looking through an altered lens. People like these—I remembered them, lurking in the omens, part of the pestilence prophesied to Atahualpa—become flesh and bone, and I among them.

I set the conch on the table in front of me and examined my hands, the color of my skin, my class ring—Villanova; there had been no lapse in memory, only some twist in perception. I pushed back in the chair and looked down, through the smoky colored nylon, at the smallness of my toes, the stretch of black fabric across my thighs. I thought to touch my breasts, but I didn't. What I wanted was a mirror. I grappled for the word but couldn't think of it. I couldn't grasp the equivalent in Quechua, and I was thinking in Quechua.

Eduardo spoke close to my ear, "Megan, your skin is flushed. Would you like to step out, get some air?" He reached across the table for the pitcher. "Maybe a glass of water?"

'Would you like,' his words. What? And then it came—first in darkness as thick and soft as sleep. Ache and seeping chill— toes, my toes, wretched numbness—and muffled, the brush and slap of feet trodding pavement, inexorable trodding, and still I had no eyes.

My distress must have been evident because Eduardo intensified his efforts to give aid, and somewhere in back of me, I heard Martina ask, "What's wrong with her?"

I responded for myself, my voice hoarse with insisting, "Ch'in. Saqey."

What I got in response was Eduardo scrambling. "Escuchen. I think it's a dialect of Quechua; telling us to stop, to let her be. Can someone understand what she's saying?" He yelled across the room. "Ortega, you're the linguist. Get over here and see if you can tell us what she's saying."

I heard a chair scrape and Dr. Ortega came and sat beside me. In Quechua, he asked me to tell him what I saw, what was happening. As if I'd been sleepwalking, his request became part of my dream.

I remembered in slow motion, the way one picks apart a tragedy, and Dr. Ortega began to decipher my account from the Quechua.

The speaking was electric and I trembled each time I paused to let Dr. Ortega catch up. What I said, or how well the translation rendered what I saw in my mind's eye, I don't know, but in that vision, I became the man I was then.

At first fog, and bobbing in every direction, luminous halos, torches on the move. Fingers hurting, stiff with gripping. We thrust our flames high and forward, advanced in unison, weary men marching, lungs aching, powered on drafts of rheumy air and the sharp repetitive "haugh, haugh," of the sinchi, Ruminaui, a dangerous general, who, in every quarter, was known as Stone Eye.

We were aimed toward a tampu. I'd been there before, a lonely outpost along the road in the midst of a sea of yellow grass and thin air. No markers that night, only mist and numbed feet groping, until a gong shuddered, limp and distant in the fog. The sentries had seen us. Our ears were tuned and we surged on the sound of each hollow toll.

At the gate, we relinquished our torches and shivered, pounded our shoulders and stamped for warmth, while Ruminaui grunted to the guards. The moment dangled; regimented positions waited and prepared to shift.

Ruminaui beckoned and I took my turn with the others, ducked through a narrow portal in the stones and crossed the courtyard to congregate in a broad reception chamber. By then, little mattered to me. Though I put one foot in front of the other, I was already dead.

I passed the night inside the walls of the tampu sequestered in a chamber specially furnished with a warm fire. Two hammocks hung in that room, one for Ruminaui and one for me.

We retired in our marching clothes, and the captain ordered his men to lodge with us, sleeping end to end and side by side so that every space beneath my bed was occupied. I lay suspended, the object of the general's dozing eye. If I slept, I dreamt of being awake, my thoughts circling the fire, gathering sparks.

I stopped speaking, slipped deeper inside the vision, and the whole of my awareness funneled to a single point—behind familiar eyes and privy to thoughts I could almost remember. As if I willed him to do it, I, he, the one who was me and not me, slipped a furtive hand beneath his cloak and fingered for the slight bulk of a leather pouch secured to his belt. He cupped its weight in his hand and closed his eyes in a blur of thought that stilled on the figure of a woman. He mouthed her name and its sound slipped through my lips. "Citllali," I said.

"Shining," Dr. Ortega's translation dropped into silence, and I could feel Corbin, Eduardo, all of them, listening.

Citllali spread across my awareness, slowly absorbed yet already present. That she had a name, and the physical sense of her, paralyzed me with want. 'Profane. Not right,' warning words lodged somewhere in my head urged me to harden my psyche around her, to leave her untouched, but I couldn't look away.

Her countenance, radiant endurance, the icon of my rosary beads. Hail Mary. Didn't every child put a face on the mother of God? I felt myself small again, Megan at four, five, six, lace trimmed anklets and patent leather shoes, propped deep in a stone-hard pew, Mama's harsh whisper at my ear, her grip on my thigh, "Stop it. Stop fidgeting." And when I closed my eyes, chanting, yearning one bead at a time for grace and some unspecified forgiveness, it was Citllali that came to me, an otherworldly image crowned with dozens of coiled black braids.

God's princess, holding vigil in my prayers, a study in benign distance, the blessing distance of transcendent beings.

And how, I struggled, was the angel Citllali to be reconciled with the bold and physical longing that stoked this other mind?

The memory of her presence shimmered, a mirage in desert heat, my lover, my wife, holding back the drapery to my apartments. Another man's woman might run to meet him, but not Citllali. She would wait and lean, shoulder and hip to one side of the doorway, a reminder that always, it is I who comes to her. And when we were but a breath apart, she watched me still, unmoving and wide-eyed. Her skin glistened in the swelter. I bent to kiss her on the mouth, but she tilted her head and offered her neck, a small evasion that hardened in my jaw. I caught the slender cord she wore like a necklace with a soft jerk that brought her face to mine. She hung there, suspended and without struggle, until, with a twist, I grasped the soft leather pouch that hung next to her heart in my fist.

"Where is he?"

"Your son—he's with the amautas, getting his lessons."

I let loose a shout, and Inquil, Citllali's old servant woman, appeared from inside. I pointed to a stool outside the chamber's entrance. "Sit," I said, "and don't let us be disturbed."

I remembered Citllali's hand, the cupped warmth of her palm against mine as I led her to my cot. The taste of her was cool and salt, and she smelled of crushed carnations.

A rustle of fabric, perhaps Martina's satin skirt slipping into a seat close by and Eduardo's voice funneled into Dr. Ortega's ear, fractured my attention.

"Ask her. Who are these people? See if you can get her to give a location. Everyone knows Ruminaui, he's no trick; his name is in the chronicles, but find out who's telling this. How does she witness these things? Who does she claim she is?"

Ortega prodded in Quechua, demanded a name, a place, while I groped to hold on to the thought of Citllali. But in the dissonance, a sharp ache stabbed at the back of my eyes and I winced.

The whip and flutter of blown fabric, clacking, and a scraping tap—tap, tap, tap, the sound of bone testing metal, vague at first. An acrid wind blew across my consciousness, hot and dry and tainted with old smoke and decay. I covered my mouth and nose, tilted my mind's eye.

Eduardo moved closer. "Megan, please. Tell us. What do you see?"

That he spoke my given name registered somewhere, and I uttered words in English that sounded foreign to me.

"Stone pavers. I'm standing on a road of huge stones, a highway. The temple's been destroyed. My teacher, the old oracle. Now I see. Oh god, they've severed his head." My voice caught in my throat and I stared, gaped at his body, draped on a silver plated pier at the gates with a tangle of hair lodged in his withered fist. Every wind that blew filled and flapped his vestments. He dangled his own head like a benediction. And the shells, tiny scallops and pieces of abalone, sewn in bands and circles about his robe, scraped and tapped, scraped and tapped.

Martina brought me back with a cool hand to my forehead and a pungent jolt of ammonia salts. A huddle closed around us.

I must have scowled, blinking off Martina's Spanish and my confusion because, when she spoke, her tone was defensive. "No hay de que," she said, a sharp, "don't mention it." She came close to my ear. "You should thank me, chica. That last, you didn't drool, but it wasn't pretty."

I pulled my shoulders up against the back of the chair, picturing myself a spastic mess. My mouth was dry and all those eyes . . .

Corbin stood a space apart from the rest. He moved off to reappear with a glass of water, pushed past Dr. Ortega and offered it to me with no words, but there was a smug fullness around his mouth that warned me. I took the tumbler, brought it to my lips, but didn't drink. I waited for what he had to say.

Sometime during the evening he'd loosened his tie and dispensed with his suit coat. He crossed his arms, clamped them down over patches of perspiration. "Are you well? Is there something you need?"

I shook my head, "I'll be fine."

"Then I'll ask," he said. "What do you propose we make of all this?"

I stared at him without comprehension and he waved his hand, pretending to draw out his next words, "Your display."

"I don't understand."

"Or seizure, or attack, or visitation, whatever you call it."

My reaction must have pleased him because he made an effort to keep from smiling. "No one would argue that what just transpired here was precisely archeological, perhaps psychological. Or if you must—parapsychological."

A sort of wounded muteness lodged in my throat and Martina settled a hand on my shoulder. I shot a glance at Eduardo. I expected him to speak but Dr. Ortega startled everyone with a strident huff.

"I couldn't disagree more. Linguistically, at least, Dr. Kimsey is precisely archeological—her Quechua, pure, archaic, totally innocent of Spanish. Impossible, maybe, but I recognize it when I hear it."

Silence settled. Eyes flitted from face to face.

"More concrete details would help," Henriette said. "Ruminaui could be the marker. We have dates for him, affiliations."

Eduardo pulled his chair next to mine, "Ruminaui, you mentioned him. Megan, think. What can you tell us?"

My inner demons stalked me. I didn't chase them. Best gone and soon forgotten, except they never really went away, and now I'd involved other people. I regretted it.

Again, "Please, can you describe him?"

I wanted my hotel room, walls around me and a door to shut. Even more, I wanted my dad to be here with me, to tell me I didn't have to do this, that we could go home now. But it was just me, and I couldn't get past being a guest, crippled by my own good manners. I closed my eyes and trained my focus on the man Ruminaui. Like the blind depending on touch or smell, I only sensed that I'd known him in many places. But I remembered my vision, the general in firelight, the way I'd seen him that night on the puna, and I forced the thought of him forward until the flint hardness of his eyes stared back at me.

"He's thick-chested, the trunk and legs of a soldier, and his skin, it's pitted, pock marked, scars left from the sickness."

"Sickness?" Henriette asked, but the memory was shallow and I didn't respond. Impatience, I felt the room shrug around me.

"How would we know he's the general," Eduardo asked, "not just one of the soldiers?"

"Earplugs and the braided headband, the llauto, and the canipu. His forehead medallion, silver, etched with a desert serpent."

The specter of Ruminaui, his ugly strutting arrogance, triggered a bitter taste in my mouth. I knew that I straddled some invisible line. Quechua thoughts assailed my English and my gums hardened around a sneer. "His earplugs are trifles, painted wood. He's hahua, a long-hair pretender with high-placed friends and a talent for cruelty."

"And you, what were you to him?" Corbin asked.

I brushed my earlobe with my fingertips; a boast poised and ready puffed into my mouth but dissipated on my lips. The apparition at the gates blew across my mind again, the sway of the headless ancient; something necessary lingered there, restless, yet patient as death. I tried to shake it off, shake them all off.

"I want to go back to my hotel now," I said to Eduardo,

He nodded. "I'll drive you myself."

13 FUGUE

Eduardo's at my elbow, the protective pressure of his hand is warm against the sleeve of my coat. He walks me through the hotel lobby. It's dim, deserted except for the clerk who looks up from his book.

Up the stairs and part way down the hall, I crowd the door to my room and Eduardo waits while I finger inside the edges of my handbag. I produce the key and hold it up for him to see. "I'm safely delivered. Thanks. I can take it from here."

"I'd feel better if you'd get your things and let me bring you back to Martina's."

"I'll be fine," I say, but I'm so weary I'm dazed. What I want is some clean sheets and to be rid of these damn high heels. It's an impulse; I flick them off, splay and firm the bones of my feet against the cool flat floor.

Eduardo speaks but I don't understand. I'm sorry," I say. "What?" I turn and tilt my chin to meet his eyes. For a dizzy instant, we are face-to-face, so close I can smell the starch in his shirt, the brandy on his breath. His eyes, I think, are deep enough to drown in, and neither of us can look away. I don't move, don't breathe. He puts his hands on my waist and brings his mouth to mine in a soft brush of a kiss that sends a sweet thrill, like the giddy lift of a Ferris wheel, to the center of my stomach.

"Everything about you is a surprise," he says. "God, you're beautiful," His gaze has the soft dazzled look I've seen on the faces of men when they look at my mother.

"This has been a strange day," He says.

"Strange, yes," I say, "and long."

He shrugs and smiles, then stoops to retrieve my shoes and holds them out to me. "I should get back. You're tired, and Martina will be wondering where I am. I'll have my driver come for you in the morning. You can join Jasper and me for breakfast before the conference begins."

"Thanks, but I don't think so. I'm having second thoughts about the conference."

"You're not coming?"

"I need to think, figure out what happened tonight and make a plan for myself. The conference—this whole trip, was my dad's idea. Now? Well, I'll have to decide."

"Megan, please. Tomorrow, after the conference, at least let me take you to dinner. You have to eat."

I don't protest, and he assumes.

I shut myself inside and step across the darkness to the balcony windows, watch Eduardo cross the street. He pauses to look up before he slips into his car and drives away. I sit on the edge of the bed with my face in my hands, trying to quell an unnerving sense that my life is skidding off the rails.

The priest intones in Latin, tedious immutable words that slip like ghosts along the rafters. And I sit, inert in the shadows of a dim alcove banked with cupped candles whose lights flicker with each wet gust at the vestibule doors. I ran here through the marketplace. Rain was blowing, slant and cold, and every wet surface reflected steel gray beneath a pall of low-hanging clouds. I reached the church steps still unsure and found my silk scarf wadded in my coat pocket.

Last night I slept the sleep of the dead, if the dead sleep, courtesy of pills because I couldn't trust my dreams. Midmorning, the maid pressured me from my room and I took to the streets and walked the marketplace with a dull appetite and muscles nervous with unspent adrenaline. I should have been reveling in the cobbled streets, the Spanish spoken in doorways; instead, scenes dredged up the night before thronged my mind. There was even one sharp instant when I turned and looked behind me; sure I felt Ruminaui's rank breath at the back of my neck.

The decapitated ancient, his infernal tapping, woke me early and followed me through the morning. I'd shake him off, be onto something else, but he would find me again, the shells that embellished the hem of his robe, clicking, scraping, tapping. The hem, the bloated purple feet, and always the shells. I'd left my room, indecisive, wandering. I sidestepped a puddle of murky water iridescent with oil and stopped to stare—the same silver blues and purple pinks that mingle over an abalone shell, and the image of the ancient came again. This time he walked the shoreline in sandaled feet, a whole and younger man, searching the sand for small flat shells and bits of abalone. He lifted his head and looked down the beach, a benevolent smoothness spread across his forehead and he smiled. I was the small boy who ran toward him, barefoot on sunbaked sand with a handful of prizes to add to his sack.

The moment shot through me and evaporated. But for an instant I knew what it was like to be that running boy, uncomplicated and warm and loved. I stood there with the breeze tugging at the back of my coat, watching the ripples of turbulence at the puddle's surface morph and swirl the streaks of oil. I felt misplaced in the universe, enraged and wretched. I wanted my dad. I clamped my mouth shut against a bellow rising in my chest. The muscles of my larynx convulsed and grew rigid, and I swallowed a tremor of short, jerky sobs. A businessman in a poncho and an old vendor stood away from me and stared. They were smart to keep their distance.

Maybe Mama was right; this time I'd gone too far, crossed hemispheres, and some invisible line even more difficult to navigate. I might have called Charlie, just to hear his voice, but I couldn't lie to him, and he was already short on sympathy. One inkling of remorse and he would make it his mission to come after me, a long-suffering rescue with coils of string attached. I started walking, no sense of direction, just walking.

A fresh gust spiked with ozone and a smattering of raindrops caught me standing at one end of a large plaza. I thought to head back to my hotel room, but the street signs were foreign and I hadn't been paying attention. I felt light-headed.

A bright ochre charge flared and backlit low hanging clouds. I listened, long seconds, for the muffled groan of thunder. An uneasy chill filled the air, and a sudden onslaught of hail tapped and ricocheted off walkways and walls. I stood in the open, receptive. Maybe God was slapping me to my senses. And then, somewhere close by, I heard bells, peals of bells.

Some things endure—mumbled prayers, the smells of damp wool and melting wax, the ceaseless vigilance of a carved wooden cross. Today is August 28, the feast of St. Hermes, an obscure Roman noble beheaded for freeing Christian slaves. Tomorrow it's John the Baptist, a whole season of headless saints. God, I have questions. What am I supposed to do?

I watch for Eduardo from my balcony windows, my coat over my arm. He's late and I'm ambivalent, but I move to greet him, lock the door from the inside and pull it shut behind me as he steps into the hallway. He's weary, fatigue pressed into shadows beneath his eyes. He's dispensed with his tie and his collar is open, an extra button undone. "I'm late," he says, "Sorry." He reaches for my coat and holds it for me.

"You look great," he says. "*Muy guapa.*"

"Thanks," I say. "But you look tired. Are you sure you're up for this?"

"Dinner with you, I'm sure." He smiles.

We walk, Eduardo following close behind me, down the hall, down the stairs.

"You'll be interested to hear, there was a lot of excitement about the birdman. His cape was a big hit with the press. *National Geographic* is doing a feature."

"Congratulations." I say. "You must be pleased."

"Yes. And Henriette is beside herself. This kind of thing attracts attention and access to grants, more opportunity."

"So what comes next? Will the focus be more excavation of the Tucume site?"

"It may be that you help us decide."

"I don't understand."

"It's complicated; we'll talk over dinner." He clips the sentence shut, a small liberty that prickles.

I find my niche in the passenger seat of his little car. We blurt small talk at first then lapse into silence. And I'm content, couched in the smooth swell of leather, my face to the evening as it slips past the window.

We pull off the street and cruise to the center of a broad cement semi-circle, slow to a stop and idle in front of vast glass doors and a waiting valet. I anticipated local color, not this regulation American-style Hilton. True, as we move inside, there are native touches—green leafy plants crowded into faux adobe planters, Colombian art in the lobby and along the walls.

The place is a hive of activity, groups in threes and fours, and loitering singles on couches or at the banks of telephones. Eduardo attracts an instant orbit of eyes. His affect, appreciative but cool, keeps the lookers at bay. Still, they lurk. Name badges, everyone's got one. And then it clicks, this hotel, of course, it's the site of the conference.

Eduardo's hand guides at the center of my back and he feels me stiffen.

"Don't worry," he says. "We're headed for the restaurant. Good food, great entertainment. You'll like it."

The host flourishes menus and leads us to our table. The room is dim, all white tablecloths and burnished colors; every surface warms to candlelight. Eduardo and I settle across from each other in the tight arc of a booth. He gives a grim smile. "I should have warned you that we were coming here, but I thought you might back out." His eyes flick above my head in search of a waiter. "I need a drink. Shall I order wine or would you prefer a cocktail?"

"Wine would be nice."

He orders with authority, an imported Merlot, and we slip into the business of menus.

"I might as well be at home," I say. "Everything's dubbed in English."

"We can speak Spanish if you like, or you could challenge me with Quechua, though it would prove frustrating. My grasp of the language is limited."

I smile.

"You left us breathless last night," he says.

"Ah, what Dr. Corbin called, 'my display.'"

"I'm afraid Jasper may take more convincing."

"And it's important for him to be convinced because . . .?"

"I think you may have potential to illuminate artifacts, to help us find lost connections. I'm hoping we can help you too, but Jasper's buy-in is crucial. We can't be working at cross-purposes. Last night, you already knew about the crisoles, their use, didn't you?"

I feel the blood flash in my cheeks.

"Would you have corrected me if I was wrong?"

"I don't know."

I'm grateful when the wine steward and waiter converge at our table, but their business is quick and Eduardo is back on task, pulling a business card from the inside pocket of his suit jacket and handing it across the table. "For you from George Ortega."

I take the card, "Remind me. Who is he?"

"The linguist who translated your words last night. He's hoping you'll meet with him. He wants to record and analyze your Quechua."

I slip the card into my purse then take a sip of wine. My fingers trace the stem of my wineglass.

"About Jasper, you're an educated woman. Your situation, it's a lot to take on faith."

"So where is this conversation going?"

"Jasper suggests we offer you a hypnotist. Certainly, you must have considered the techniques of parapsychology, the work of Edgar Cayce, a guided opportunity to probe, substantiate."

"Past life regression with you, Henriette, and Dr. Corbin asking the questions?"

"In a nutshell, yes."

"Why would I do that? Open myself up in ways I can't control, to a group of people I barely know who have their own agendas?"

"That stings a bit. I thought I was seeing signs that we're becoming more than strangers. And in defense of my colleagues, are you the only one who's allowed to have an agenda? You come here expecting something from us; I'm not sure what. Now you seem offended when we want more information. "

Our waiter arrives with small dishes of minced shrimp in salsa heaped on tiny toasted corn cakes but Eduardo's practically cantilevered over the table, intent on drawing a response.

"Pardon," the waiter says and Eduardo sits upright and silent while the waiter places the plates and pours more wine into our glasses.

"There is a difference," I say. "For me, this is personal. Full disclosure—I had a nervous breakdown once. What you're asking feels like a risk. I'm here alone and my dad's not around to help me pick up the pieces if I fall apart." I turn away, swallowing hard against the anguished little flutter expanding in my chest, and already wishing I could take back every word I just said. I direct my attention to three musicians assembling in an arched alcove across the room, but I can feel Eduardo's eyes watching me.

For a strained moment, neither of us speaks, and then he says, "I want you to know, I defended you today."

He reaches across the table and takes my hand but I have trouble looking him in the eye.

"It speaks volumes that I need defending," I say.

I expect a rebuttal, instead, he says, "These performers, I'll be interested to hear what you think."

Three men, slight and bronze, in simple white shirts and dark trousers, launch into a native melody. I'm mesmerized, not by the antique synthesis of sounds, but by the instruments themselves.

"What do you know about these?" I ask, "The flute and the horn, the ceramic whistles."

"Pre-Columbian, everything but the tiple." I understand that he's referring to the odd guitar, obviously Spanish. "Use of the reed flutes, panpipes or *flautas*, very wide spread. The conch-shell horns, *futotos*, from the coastal areas. Ceramic whistles, *capadores*, probably coastal as well—and the *guacharacas*, notched gourds, like the reed flute, very common."

I'm out of my seat, floating on a sense that my own move-ments are beyond my control. I approach the musicians, so close I can sense their discomfort. Still they play and I listen, socializ-ing my compulsion, but the ache is there. I want the conch in my hands; the reed flute has something to tell me.

An instant before the last strain dissipates, before they can tell me to move away, I call back to Eduardo, "Ask them. Will they let me examine the horn and flute?"

He's up and approaching them, speaking quickly. He reaches into his pocket and liberates a fold of bills from his money clip. Other diners stare, even the waiters, perturbed—this spoiled gringo girl, being indulged. Even I'm surprised at my own sense of entitlement, how little I care what anyone thinks.

I wipe the mouth of the conch, blow a clear tone once and again, and then give it back. The instrument is plebian, nothing compared to the conch Corbin taunted me with the night before, more distant than distant cousins. The musician dips his head and smiles, congratulating my modest display, and the flute is handed to me. When I bring it to my mouth, a rote sense takes over. No hesitation. I close my eyes and begin to push breath across the flute's openings in a syncopated restless rhythm. The hollow melancholy that emerges sweeps through the corridors of who I am with a homesickness I can hardly bear.

When the song is done and my eyes are open, I'm left displaced, relinquishing the instrument and uttering my thanks. The musician, his expression stark and pale, extends his flute once more, this time a request with an open hand, but I decline. There's an instant of stunned silence, and then stray clapping. I feel the penetration of all those eyes and I pull myself erect, step among the tables with studied nonchalance, the way one moves in the presence of a dangerous animal. I'm out of the restaurant, rushing through the lobby but Eduardo catches up with me.

"Wait. Don't go." He grasps my arm. "Come back inside, please. Don't run away."

I feel dull, confused, as if I'm emerging from a migraine. He puts his arm around my shoulders and I let him guide me back to our table. For awhile we sit across from each other, drinking our wine, using our knives and forks on the edges of our food, saying nothing. And then he gazes into my face from across the table, with such an earnest expression.

"So you speak flawless Quechua and play beautiful pre-Columbian music—what else, Megan? Talk to me. What just happened?"

"Forgive me," I say, "I don't mean to be rude—or dramatic. It's just—the reed flute, even before I touched it, its music was singing inside my head. Sometimes it's like I'm someone else."

"That's why you're here, isn't it? This kind of thing's been happening all your life."

"I think my father wanted me to face my demons. Do you think I'm crazy?"

"Crazy people don't just happen to speak an obscure dialect of Quechua or stumble across an indigenous reed flute and play like you just did. As an archeologist, I'd be more apt to wonder if you weren't trying to pull some kind of stunt, looking for media attention, but I know that's not true. Look, you must want to know, need to know. I'm urging you to consider. Tonight, a short elevator ride, Jasper and the rest are waiting for us with a psychiatrist who's experienced in past life regression. I was going to let it go, not even bring it up, but after what just happened, I think you might want to consider the possibility."

"Tonight? You made arrangements without asking me. I should refuse on principle. It feels like a trap."

"You're right. We jumped the gun. But where else will you find a group of people who have a mutual interest? Whose intentions are so transparent? What if this is the way you get to some answers that help you understand what's happening to you? In your words, to 'face your demons.' I promise, any limits you set, everything you ask . . . Give me a chance to prove myself. No one can replace your father, but at least—let me be your friend."

14 THE HIEROPHANT OF TUMBES

Martina swings the door wide, "¡*Por fin, chica*! We were getting impatient." She slips an arm across my shoulders and scoops me inside. Eduardo lags behind. I glance back, see him close the door, and drop my coat across the back of a chair. I scan the room looking for familiar faces. I count seven of us in all, and I'm surprised how relieved I am to see Henriette standing at the bar with the man who must be George Ortega, the Quechua linguist.

Corbin and the man he's conversing with rise to greet me, as if a lady has entered the room. I feel a pang of plainness next to Martina as she propels me toward them. Corbin grips his lapels and makes an effort to contain the width of his smile. His associate has the cerebral look of psychiatry; he's older than Corbin, all tweed, tall and thin with a shock of white hair cut blunt and parted a little too far to one side.

"Finally she comes," says Corbin, "Dr. Felix Lester, may I present the object of tonight's inquiry, Megan Kimsey." Martina releases me, but stays.

Dr. Lester offers his hand. "I'm fascinated and anxious to know more. May I call you Megan?"

"Why not?" I give the smile that's expected and shrug. "You're the hypnotist?"

"Yes," he says. "Have you been regressed before?" He stares straight into my eyes—as if there might be signs.

"No. I'm not even sure I believe it's possible."

Corbin wags a finger. "Now that could be a problem, if even the patient has doubts."

"On the contrary," says Dr. Lester, "other than a bit of resistance, it merely means we are starting from the beginning."

Martina nudges, "*¿Quieres algo beber?*" She motions toward the bar.

"No, nothing to drink," I say. "But thanks. I didn't expect to be here, and it's late."

Eduardo comes to stand beside me, puts his hand on the center of my back, and I turn to Dr. Lester. "Can we just do this?"

"Of course." He points to a black leather chair, a huge winged thing angled close to the sofa where he and Corbin have been sitting. "Megan, if you would take a seat."

Corbin claps his hands to get the room's attention. Everyone converges and I take my place in the lap of the chair.

I'm dwarfed; my feet don't even reach the floor. Dr. Lester moves to accommodate with a hassock, and Martina brings a glass of water to the table at my elbow. There's a tape recorder there. She clips a small microphone to the neckline of my dress and stands ready to press the *on* switch. When Dr. Lester comes back he's carrying a small wooden chair. He sits and inclines forward. "Are you comfortable?"

"Please," I touch the microphone; enunciate my words. "Eduardo promised, any recordings would be mine. And, Dr. Lester, I want to remember everything that comes to me tonight. Can you make that happen?"

"A post hypnotic suggestion. I'll do the best I can."

I nod and lean back, bracing myself. "What do I need to do?"

"Just sit comfortably, but as upright as you can."

I push into the chair and pull my spine straight.

"That's good," he says. "Let's begin by having you focus here." He touches a spot just under his right eye.

I do, and he fixes his gaze, an unblinking stare, straight into my pupils. His irises are flecked shades of green emanating from golden coronas, each with its own black and mesmerizing center.

"Now, begin taking slow deep breaths."

I inhale, exhale.

"That's right," he says. "Notice a pleasant stillness in your body, a sense of inner calm. Every breath is slow and effortless. You feel safe. There's nothing to worry about. Your hands and arms, the muscles in your neck, you feel them becoming loose, at ease. Steady breathing, in—and out. Feel the calm, incoming, like an ocean tide.

Dr. Lester's drone is buoyant, feather light. "Inhale. Exhale—gently, evenly. Your toes, your feet and legs are warm and relaxed. You are sleepy, unbearably sleepy. Your eyes are drooping, closing—so heavy."

His words circle, slow, monotone, almost murmuring. "You're sleeping now, but when I say the words, *wake up, Megan,* you will open your eyes and remember everything you saw, how you felt, and what seemed important while you were asleep."

I'm drifting, gaining mass, dreaming. No, not a dream. Pushing through blackness, and then thrust up, as if on the shoulders of water and beneath a blinding sun.

A voice coaxes. "Tell us. Where are you? What do you see?"

I do—I see. And it's like looking through a child's View Master 3D, the depth is deeper, the colors brighter.

Mother Sea. I've come home to my mother's country. My eyes are his eyes and both of us have been homesick. Quotidian blue, water and sky, cloudless, flecked with birds and an armada of bobbing reed boats. Calm—but not right.

"What's not right?" asks Dr. Lester.

I scan, try to organize an answer but what's in my mind is too diffuse.

I see women in thatched hats fishing, working the nets. A few pilgrims chat and recline, sheltered from the sun inside ornate porticos and beneath awnings. But everywhere, I sense a glint of some anxious face peering back.

Dr. Lester's voice comes again, demanding, "Tell us. What's not right?"

I feel my heart quicken. I shake my head—war, earthquakes, premonitions. . . Pachatikray, the world is overturned.

Dr. Lester asks, "Pachatikray?"

"Andean folklore," explains Corbin, "the promised dissolution of the world at the end of an era, a divine cataclysm."

Questions, they keep asking, but I'm caught in my own bleak transference, becoming feverish with that other life.

Vague, Corbin asks, "Can't you be more direct? Who does she thinks she is? I want lineage and tribe. She says she's in Tumbes; we all know that's an ancient coastal city, part of the Moche culture before it was confiscated by the Incas. No trick, it's in the history books. Pizarro came ashore there. See if she can come up with something obscure. Give me some details I can verify."

The hypnotist turns the question softly. "Tell us. Who are you? What's your name, your lineage?" His voice sounds far away.

"Illapa. I am Illapa." I repeat for myself and the cadence gives convergence, like the single vision of two eyes. "The son of the Inca, Huayna Capac, and his consort, the Capullana, Rhian, high priestess and governess of Tumbes."

"Tumbes." The breath of it makes a soft familiar buzz against the roof of my mouth.

A ripple of whispers. Corbin, incredulous, buzzing doubts that skitter across my consciousness.

"The lords Atahualpa and Huascar are your brothers?"

I feel a surge of irritation—and caution. "There are many brothers."

"You are in Tumbes. What do you see?"

Ocean washed in copper light. Time has slipped a notch. It's twilight. The gulls have gone to roost, but there are stragglers, white sparks in the twilight. From up the beach, Kantu, my child, comes running toward me on his sturdy little legs. His mother has given him a tallowed catkin. It smokes and glows against the evening and he carries it like a wand. He stalls to check for her behind him. Citllali shoos him forward, and I wonder, is their coming a peace offering or does she mean to twist the knife. He rushes to greet me, but when I kneel with my arms outstretched he refuses to be lifted. Instead, he charges the shore and scrambles onto an igneous shelf exposed by the tide.

Citllali comes to stand beside me, each of us self-conscious, beaten down by argument and trouble, too bruised to touch.

But side-by-side, we watch Kantu ascend the granite pinnacle. He slashes his small torch at the dusk and the breeze swirls the friable ash around him like a thousand glistening fireflies.

Citllali covers her mouth with a hand to stifle a sob, and then she turns on me. "You're supposed to be a man of prophesy and power." She spits the words. "Do something. Make there be another way. Why can't we run away with him tonight and be gone? Just disappear."

"And what would we leave behind?" I reach out to touch her but she recoils, stiffens and tilts her chin to examine my face. Her eyes, the color of clear dark honey, shine with desperation and something infinitely more bitter. I brace myself, expecting, even wanting, her to strike me. Instead, she wraps her arms around my chest and clings, her ear pressed against my breast-bone. I hold her, brush her forehead with a kiss. I wonder how we will manage to get through the night, and if the days left to us will be worth living. "I'll find a way," I say.

The hypnotist's voice insinuates, "Something's wrong? Tell us."

I resist. But Dr. Lester urges.

"Atahualpa requires it," I say.

"Requires what?"

"Proof of loyalty—capa cocha, a child sacrifice. Not a child from the compounds. He insists; it must be Kantu, my son. I'm to lead the ritual journey, to make the offering myself."

Whispers prompt the hypnotist but I've slipped into my own turmoil, losing track of my inquisitors. *Tumbes* . . .

I'm sleeping in my apartments in Tumbes, a wretched spastic sleep, and then a grip, a jostle. I flex upward, eyes wide. Citllali leans over me, the heavy ropes of her hair touch down like coils of silk against my chest. She whispers my name, "Illapa." Her face is bleak.

I'm disoriented. I only meant to doze. I drop back on my cot and tug Citllali down beside me.

"Be still," I say. "Lie with me." She's uneasy but she settles and I wrap my arms around her, wanting her warmth, to meditate on the smooth slide of her skin. Every moment's become singular and rare, freighted with the passing of time.

She nestles her head against my shoulder. "Is it true?" she says. "When Atahualpa was imprisoned at Tumibamba, did the gods help him escape? Did Inti really reach down from the sky and turn him into a snake?"

"Be careful what you ask," I say. "Truth can be treason."

"Tell me," she says. "I'll keep the secret."

"It wasn't Inti or any other god, just a common girl, tending his cell. She brought him a metal pick and he spent the night gouging his way out. I bandaged his blistered palms myself."

"And the girl?"

"Strangled. Before daylight, Atahualpa had his roaches scurrying the streets searching for her. Two days later, at sun up, Atahualpa entered the city as a god, flanked by his armies with his hands in the folds of his tunic."

The hypnotist's questions come like phantoms, demanding, "Tumibamba, tell us."

"Tumibamba is obliterated—only bodies and toppled stone."

"What happened? Be there."

Marching—through the city gates behind Atahualpa's palanquin. I'm sick at heart, but only one among his counselors. He's fueled on revenge and past advice. We come to witness.

Citizens flank the streets, every Cañar, man, woman and child, many of my friends among them, ordered out of their homes. Heads bow as we pass; only the babes stare, fixed and alert in their mothers' arms. There's dew. It's early.

Wooden pipes suspended in clusters clack together—make a hollow sound. A light breeze rustles the treetops.

Atahualpa's attendants carry his ceremonial stool to the center of the stone dais. From here, the city slopes into the fields and beyond. Atahualpa takes his time. He squats and sits, leans forward and props his forearms on bent knees. His generals stand on either side, both of them smirking above the crowd.

The city's dignitaries approach, prostrate with apology, and then an embassy of children, their arms outstretched with wreathes of feathers and baskets heaped with pouches of fine-milled coca. Next, a confluence of light-skinned girls from the *acllahuasi,* each one a prize decked out in scarlet and hyacinth blues, waving their arms in fluid arcs, dancing in columns and swaying. And at the end of their dance, dropping prostrate onto the cold stones.

Atahualpa's bloodshot eyes roam the supplicants. Once or twice he nods approval. He calls one of the dancers forward. He orders the medallion removed from around his neck and presents it to her. She beams and blushes, genuflects. For the people of Tumibamba, this appears to be a flicker of hope, and the mood trembles. But those of us with a view from the dais can't dismiss the steady march of troops that continue to approach the gates and amass at the outer walls of the city.

Only Atahualpa's judgment remains. He bows his head, makes us wait. For a moment, a benediction seems possible. But when he looks up, his jaw is set. *"Maruy."* He spits the word.

The generals, Challcochima and Ruminaui, incite the charge, shouting, "*Chaya! Chaya!*" A tumult of scrambling soldiers assails the population. "*Haylli! Haylli!*" Battle cries collide with tortured screams and a wave of moaning that goes on and on.

I've stopped speaking, gone numb, but Dr. Lester picks up the thread. "What else do you remember about that day?"

"Late in the afternoon, from our camp in the hills, the ruins of Tumibamba were visible in the distance, glowing like cinders against a darkening sky. Atahualpa sat down next to me and we watched for awhile. A wind blew out of the west, gritty with ashes and smoke. I don't know what he was thinking, only that he sat erect, fingering his medallion."

Dr. Lester urges, and time slips a notch.

"Something's changed," he says. "Tell us. Where are you now? What are you doing?"

"Hiding—in the shadows of a maze-like corridor. Waiting. It's the middle of the night. Citllali should be here by now."

"What city? Why are you hiding?"

"I've come home to Tumbes. Atahualpa's soldiers have taken control of the city. They've imposed curfews."

Citllali steps around the corner, her face is white and exposed in the moonlight. I take in a sudden breath and exhale. I'm almost weak with relief. My stomach feels like it's in my throat. I reach for her hands. The night is warm and humid but her fingers are cold. Her words tumble out in a rush of anxious whispers, promising that she's been careful, that no one has seen her, that Kantu is safe with Inquil. When she left, she says, he and the old woman were sleeping.

I put my hands on her shoulders. "Now we need to get from here to the beach and find the others," I say. There's fear in her eyes, the flit of nervousness, but she draws her spine upright, swallows and nods. I kiss her on the forehead. "We should go," I say.

We start moving, staying close to the walls, aimed for the abandoned sector of the city, forbidden now and decrepit with long disuse.

As promised, the massive gate has been left ajar. We slip through the slender opening one at a time, into a cathedral of crumbled altars and spires spread out beneath the sky, their shadows meant to intersect in rotating patterns with the nocturnal tilt of heavenly bodies. One corner of the terrace is collapsed, broken and tumbled into a recess below. Nothing but depth and the lapping sounds of ocean ricochet through the hollow darkness.

We grope for footholds in the rubble. When we reach the bottom we stop, stunned by dappled phosphorescence, and the glimmering waver of moonlight on surf sloshing into the cove. Waterlogged sand churns grit across my feet. I tug Citllali by the hand. We run.

Four old women, the last remnant of a governing council that, in living memory, has always numbered nine, are convened in an inlet cloistered by cliffs. Their silhouettes warp sharp and frenetic against the shuddering glow of a driftwood fire. Citllali and I drop to our knees on the sand to watch and wait. Tonight, the music is strained and discordant, and I have a sense that everything is off-kilter; the whole world wobbles when it used to spin.

The men are gone, dead of the festering sickness or conscripted to Atahualpa's war, but the ritual goes on. These four, old aunts and ancient cousins, have been among my teachers. I have known them all my life.

Maita breathes the quivering undertones of a melody across the apertures of her flute, and Tuya beats the drum. Laban, a stark albino, devoid of color and gaunt as death, throws her white hair back and works her lungs like a bellows, forcing spaced tones through the conch. And Auqui, the guardian, crouches on her withered legs, coddling a mound of flickering coals as if they are chicks that might escape.

The focus of all this unsettling harmony is my mother, Rhian, waist deep in the surf. The white folds of her tunic billow around her. Her arms stretch out of their sleeves, luminous and stark as shorn branches in cold light. She dips her head in turns toward sea and sky. The mesh cap of her silver headdress, its tiny hanging tears of abalone, glint sparks. She wails a chant and removes a small ceremonial pouch from around her neck, empties fine coca dust onto her flattened palm and blows. The breeze takes some, the rest settles upon the water. And then she trudges out of the surf, her waterlogged garments dragging at her legs.

Maita and Tuya rush to replace her drenched tunic. Citllali and I tramp across the sand to join them. We embrace and sit. Auqui ladles small cups of warmed chicha from a clay vessel. For awhile, we sip in silence, staring into the fire.

Laban begins the speaking; her red rabbit eyes flit from face to face. "The augury—the white llama that was singled from the herds this morning—my knife overreached and pierced the heart before it was removed. The organ was still beating when I pulled it from the animal, but while I held it in my hand, small gray worms began to issue from the cut."

This is stunning, desperate news that freezes in our veins. Rhian spreads her arms to calm us. "Harden yourselves. We will hear no good news tonight."

Maita shakes her head. "Omens multiply in every part of the empire. Birds fall from the sky, dead before they hit the ground—earthquakes and the festering illness annihilate entire villages. And the doomed war between brothers goes on."

Tuya lolls her head from side to side, seeming to loosen the muscles in her neck, then pulls her head erect. "The white Viracochas return to Tumbes. Even now, storms pound their lumbering vessel. They fight among themselves, but they come. *Pachatikray.* The sacrifice of a high born child will not change this."

Citllali jerks out of the circle, runs, first toward a pier of rocks then veers and stumbles toward the surf, stopping short of the tide. Her shoulders droop and she covers her face with her hands.

"Bring her back." Rhian says.

I'm already on my feet, coming to stand beside her. I put my arm across her shoulders. "If you can't trust me, then trust the prophesy," I say, "How many times have you heard it repeated? That Kantu shall lead his people out of a time of great upheaval and want. To do that, he must live to be a man. I promise you, I will scorch earth and storm heaven to see that he does. You worry that Atahualpa has sent me to bring our son for sacrifice, but I'll take great care to protect him. Atahualpa has earned my hate. He is not my god or my sovereign. You must believe me."

"Kantu is so small."

"I know," I say.

She looks down at her feet. "What do you want me to do?"

I lift her chin and wipe her tears with my fingers. "Come back to the fire and listen," I say. "Speak your piece."

We take our places back in the circle.

Rhian brings out the pipe, lights it with the flaming tip of a dry reed. She mumbles ancient words, puffs and blows, inhales a lungful. Each of us takes a draw. The smoke singes at first, hot and acrid, but very soon it's soft and cunning, filling every inward space, smudging boundaries—until we are diffuse, unbodied, mingled.

In the firelight, Rhian's face is all angles and tired hollows. "A legion of forebodings bears down on us. Now Illapa comes to us with more evil news. Atahualpa plots against us. We must choose, either we submit Kantu, the last heir of our natural nation, to Atahualpa for sacrifice, or incur Atahualpa's wrath and join Tumibamba. Surely he will raze Tumbes and kill us all."

Laban is incredulous. "Aren't our decimated numbers proof that we aren't traitors? That he should demand Kantu makes no sense. The compounds are filled with suitable children. He loves the child."

"Laban," I say, "consider Atahualpa's motives. It's the prophecy he covets. The war has reached a final pitch and he must have every cosmic power aligned to himself. If Kantu is sacrificed to insure Atahualpa's victory, he achieves two ends; Kantu's mana becomes part of Atahualpa's triumph, and Atahualpa rids himself of a future threat. The child is dispatched— and any possibly disruptive promise with him."

Auqui fingers through a heap of driftwood. She selects slender sticks and bunches them together with a handful of dried moss and flings them onto the glowing coals. The heat whispers and licks through the tinder. There are curls of smoke, a whoosh and sudden flare. Her eyes are mirrors. "Better we destroy Tumbes ourselves, topple every last stone and leave Atahualpa and the white Viracochas with no one to greet them."

Suffocating darkness, thunder cracks and rumbles into distant peals. The air's gone stagnant, and from some remote somewhere, colliding voices advance in waves. I struggle to stay fixed, but the current is strong – the murmurs insistent. Someone slaps the back of my hand.

"Listen to me. Megan. Wake up. Megan, I'm going to count backwards from three again. You must wake up. Three, two, one. Now. Open your eyes."

Darkness billows to powdery gray. Light sears. I wince and jerk my hands up to cover my eyes.

"Get that damn flashlight off her face."—Eduardo's voice.

It's Corbin, brandishing a pocket flashlight. He shifts the beam downward to Dr. Lester kneeling at the chair's arm. Dr. Lester's face glows up at me, conspicuous with relief.

I glance around, trying to penetrate the darkness.

"There's been a blackout," Corbin says, watching me as if he expects something. "The storm's shut the power down."

"Oh," I say, coming to grips – a surge of wretchedness swelling to a knot in my throat.

Dr. Lester slips his hands into the pockets of his suit coat. He stares at me, seeming to puzzle over the contours of my face. "Most subjects see their past lives from a distance, like they're watching a newsreel or a movie."

Corbin runs his tongue under his lip. "What's your point?"

"I might have been too quick to agree . . ." Dr. Lester's voice fades to a mumble. "I should have taken a history, done a preliminary work-up."

"What work-up? What are you talking about? Is something wrong?" Eduardo scans between us.

Dr. Lester bends close. His shadow wags across the ceiling like a dark finger. His breath is humid on my face.

"Megan, do you recognize me? Do know where you are?"

"Send me back," I say.

"That's impossible right now. We're in the dark here—in more ways than I can count. Just sit quietly for a moment; get your bearings." He pulls a business card from an inside pocket and presses it into the palm of my hand. "Tomorrow, I want to see you in my office. You must come. And bring that tape recording. Don't listen to it alone."

Corbin stoops next to the table. He focuses his flashlight on the recorder, presses the button, and ejects the tape. Eduardo takes it out of his hand and gives it to me.

"Of course. Well, I'd like a copy," he says. "Maybe after you've listened to it."

The smells of matches and butane hang sluggish in the air. The air conditioner has stopped, and a hush, unnatural and too complete, inhabits the room.

I clutch the tape together with Dr. Lester's card, and sit, dislocated and gaping – stunned by a paralyzing sense of loss and distance. The imprint my body makes against the chair is overly-warm. The back of my dress is damp. I lean forward but I don't get up. Where would I go? I touch my palm and bring it to my nose, half expecting Citllali's scent to linger there.

The others are bunched in twos and threes, coping with the darkness. Eduardo and Henriette stand by the hotel-room door conferring over the fragile blue flame of Henriette's cigarette lighter. Eduardo grasps the knob and opens to gaping blackness. But there are sounds – other doors opening and closing, muttered voices that fall away. The door is shut again, and locked.

On the other side of the room, someone sweeps the drapes along their track. Martina stands, looking out, her silhouette backlit by the pale glow coming through the window.

Eduardo lays a hand on my shoulder. "We can go to Martina's. I'll take you. There are generators. It will be more comfortable. Please, I insist. You mustn't be alone tonight."

There's scuffling in the hallway, rapid pounding on the door. Corbin shines the flashlight through the peep hole. He opens to a bellman carrying a cardboard box stacked with flashlights and some candles in hurricane lamps that look like they've been rescued from table centerpieces.

And while the bellman lights lamps and tells the others that he has no news, that the elevator isn't working, I fix on the gaping door, get up and step across the carpet and out into the hallway. A couple pushes out of a room across the way, and the door that should click shut, or slam, doesn't. They lug their suitcases behind the beam of a flashlight toward the stairwell. I count my steps in threes—three, six, nine. I'm across the hallway and inside, pushing the door closed with barely a sound, feeling for the bolt, sliding the chain. When I'm still and alone in the dark, I make up my mind; I have to get to Tumbes.

15 Heading South

"You understand the risks?" The official at the American Consulate signs and puts his seal on the letter I asked for, but he secures it on his desk beneath his hand. "Miss Kimsey, respectable women in this part of the world don't travel alone." He puckers up around his words and surveys me with a chill expression that insinuates; just my being here is an insolent act.

"Then what do you recommend?"

"Take some extra days, recruit a male friend, hire a reputable guide—or tour a few museums and go home."

"But I'm only going to Tumbes—on the train."

He folds my letter and thrusts it at me.

"You may want to check with the station master. U. S. tourists often have unrealistic expectations of local transportation."

I stand there for a moment, thinking he might explain, but he licks the tip of his index finger and uses it to leaf through a packet of papers on his desk. When he looks up, he seems surprised that I'm still there. "Is that everything? You got what you came for?"

"I suppose so. Yes, thanks." And I walk out holding my letter, feeling off balance and irreparably naïve.

Back at my hotel, there have been inquiries. The hotel clerk said one of the men waited for over an hour. The messages, from Dr. Lester and Sircusa, might have been composed together. "I hope you are all right. Please call. I must speak with you."

Mama and Dr. Vickers would have a field day with my behavior last night—a textbook reprise of my most desperate moments. Megan Kimsey, under social and psychological pressure, splits, exhibits paranoid behavior, flees from a controlled situation into—what? I'm not proud of my record as a social coward, slipping off and hiding, listening while the others called my name up and down the hallway, and then this morning, watching as they scuffled past my peephole on their way to the stairwell.

But I don't owe these people anything—they're strangers. And now I have my own starting place—some pieces looking for a place to fit, and a name that can be found on a map. And this morning, something hopeful crept into my consciousness. I don't know what it means, but it helps.

When I checked out, I placed both notes, neatly folded, into an envelope with the tape recording of me under hypnosis and addressed it to Sircusa. Whatever he makes of it will be all right.

It's late in the day and the cab driver zigzags us through a maze of concrete. He uses one hand to steer while the other manages a smoldering cigarette and periodically darts out the window to test and adjust a rearview mirror that's been grafted in place with black electrical tape. His view is a concern for both of us, and there's a wobble in my legs when he finally opens the door and deposits me on the curb.

I climb a bank of tiled steps to the train station. Inside, the rectangular waiting room is lined with heavy wooden benches that could double as church pews, and the smell of urine is so old and pervasive that it must be cured into the cement floor. I wait in line at the ticket counter, ready with a finger in my Spanish-English dictionary. No need, the uniformed official only has to look at me.

"*¿Habla inglés?* You want a ticket, miss?"

"*Sí,* I mean yes. Tumbes, one way."

"It's not possible."

"I don't understand?"

"I can sell you a ticket to Cuenca, but from there you will have to find another way. Maybe a local bus or mototaxi. Check with the desk in Cuenca."

For a moment I feel uncertain. I picture myself stepping off the train into a dusty nowhere—and without an inkling of what comes next. But I give him my money.

I sit upright on one of the benches with my backpack between my knees, feeling conspicuously gringo, a white woman in pants. And then the dark-eyed children begin their assault, in groups of twos and threes; they hound me for money. "*No dinero,*" I say, and empty my pockets of butterscotch candies and gum. It's not enough and I turn my pockets inside out. "*No mas,*" I say. But the children stand their ground. Then, inexplicably, they suspend their efforts and drift away. I'm caught by the gaze of a policeman patrolling the edges of the room. He tilts his chin and inflates his chest—gives me a complicit grin. I answer with a brief nod and make a mental promise; first thing in Cuenca, I'll buy myself a wedding ring.

The call comes for boarding and I take my time. The stories about gringo women in crowds who've been pushed and robbed—or groped, have me on edge. My fingers are cold and bloodless when I work the zipper to put my book back into my backpack. When the train lurches away from the station I'm still navigating my way down the center aisle, hunting for a seat. I'm into my third car when a mestizo man with bad teeth takes pity and offers to move his caged rooster.

The bird objects—squawks and flutters, beats his wings and tosses up a flurry of seed hulls, wisps of down and dust. The man smiles up at me and pats the vacated upholstery. I nod and sit, resisting urges to sneeze and scratch while he settles the animal, speaking softly, almost crooning.

He covers the cage with his coat. When he leans back, his expression is pleasant, undemanding. Then he folds his hands over his lap and closes his eyes. I gaze past him, out the window. The evening has turned a murky yellow and already, the click and wobble of the train begins to soothe. It's been an endless day, all mixed up with yesterday and the day before.

The landscape flickers past. I settle, slack, and skimming sleep. With a jerk, I'm upright, shock still and aware, my face practically nuzzling some mounded belly and repelled by a cloying whiff of bourbon and the smell of cotton, starched and hot with perspiration. The consulate's warnings flash along my nerves.

"What are you doing?" I blurt.

But it's only the conductor, leaning across me, taking the rooster man's ticket. He steps back a pace, presses his chin in stern folds against his collar and extends his hand.

"*Billete?* Your ticket, miss. May I have it?"

I'm all nods—relief and humiliation. As I flex and draw my papers from my pocket, a young man with slicked black hair, barely more than a teenager, gives me an assured smile and speaks from across the aisle. His accent is thick but I comprehend. "Relax," he says, "I'm looking out for you."

"Thanks, but don't bother," I say, "It's okay—really. I'm fine." Then I make a point of ignoring him, and hide behind my book. It's dark outside, and when I glance at the window, his reflection looks back at me. My seatmate, the rooster man, is dozing again, his raspy snore stops and starts with a rattle.

Soon, I slip into a deep and oblivious sleep that ends with a dream. I dream that I'm alone on the train, not in my aisle seat, but slumped against a window. The glass is cold against my cheek and I'm wrapped in my old chenille bedspread. I pull it snug around my shoulders and gaze outside at the snow hurling past. The power lines strung along the train route sag. Trees and endless grasslands—everything is suspended and brittle, caught in crusts of ice and crystallizing in the chill fog. My dreaming eyes blink, stunned by whiteness, and my sleeping self sits up straight—something out there is moving.

The dream shifts. I'm upstairs in my parents' house, panicked and searching from my bedroom window. I fumble with the window latch, push and rattle, push and rattle, until inertia gives and the sash vaults open. A bead of snow that's been accumulating on the sill knocks loose and explodes into air so frigid it hurts to breathe—and then I bellow into the snow-muffled silence, "Bella, wait. Bella. Where are you?"

I jerk awake. The train's stopped moving. The rooster-man and his caged bird are gone and a short line of passengers presses through the forward door that empties onto the platform. It's still evening. How long have I been asleep? The young man in the aisle across from me pulls out of his seat. He's chewing gum. A smirk of arrogance twitches at the corners of his mouth and I have the creepy sense he's been watching me.

"Where are we?" I ask.

"Cuenca, this is where we get off. Give me your things. I'll carry them."

"I can manage," I say, still muddled with sleep and haunted by snow and loss, my chest hardened around a sharp longing for Bella.

He waits—and shrugs. "Suit yourself," he says, and snaps his gum with a sharp bite. He saunters toward the front of the train. I scoot to the window seat and watch him cross the platform and pass through the station doors. And then I fill my lungs with moist stale air—and sigh. The coach is deserted, its vinyl seats bruised and indented, the floor flecked with litter—chicken feathers and hair stuck to a squashed gumdrop, a discarded paper cup . . .

Hollowness permeates the pending quiet with a deep-down loneliness, and for a fleeting second, I consider going home.

The station door is a gaping wooden arch, ancient Spanish and painted an aqua-tinged blue. I pass through and stall, let others dodge around me while I search for someone capable of advice. I scan and catch that same young man glancing at me from a bank of telephones. I peg his gaze and he looks back, unabashed.

The clerk is standing on a stout ladder, his back to the counter. He's posting adjusted arrivals and departures. The blunt tips of his fingers slide numbered tiles along tracks carved into a huge black panel. I wait, an endless wait, with my backpack at my feet and my hands stuffed into the pockets of my pants. When he finally climbs down and pivots, I think I'll try my questions in Quechua, but instead I ask, "Excuse me. Do you speak English?"

He steps to the counter, wordless but willing.

"Please," I say. "Could you recommend a hotel? And how can I get to Tumbes?"

"How much? *¿Mas dinero o pequeño?*" he asks.

I shrug. For one night, it doesn't matter.

"Americans usually prefer the Hotel Flores. You can ask a taxi." He points to a series of doors at the street entrance. "A taxi can take you also to the bus terminal."

I hoist my backpack and turn. Less than three steps away, the young man is standing in the line behind me. I avoid his eyes and keep moving.

I step through the station door and gasp, unprepared for this view of Cuenca—not the quaint Spanish buildings, the eruption of church spires and whitewashed walls, but the way the city is snugged into a landscape of peaks and plains, the late-day burnish of light.

A bloom of feeling vibrates above my heart and swells to a knot in my throat. I feel dizzy and press my eyes shut. When I open them again, the rush of familiarity is gone.

All through the night, in fits and starts, I scan the neon face of my travel clock. Until finally, six minutes before five, I sit upright, toss back the covers, and grope for the lamp switch.

The carpet in the hotel lobby is pale green, dense and covered with patterns of vines that terminate in tendrils and lush drooping flowers. My footfalls make no sound.

The night clerk has slipped away from his post behind the mahogany counter, or maybe he's gone home and someone else is on the cusp of arrival. I move through the deserted lobby. A waitress with a burgundy apron over her arm steps into a wedge of the rotating door just as I step out. I imagine her inundated with the warm hotel smell of French-milled soap just as I'm breathing in the dew-chill of a fresh day. For an instant, everything seems locked into place, well oiled and synchronized.

I put on my hat and check inside my shoulder bag—water, compass, and my binoculars. And then I waver on the balls of my feet. How do I pick a direction? A whiff of something baking scents the breeze and I accept my hunger as a sign.

Less than a city block away, street vendors are shaking out their blankets and setting up their wares. A few shops are throwing shutters open and propping doors. I follow my nose toward breakfast and maybe some hardboiled eggs and fruit to stuff into my bag. I step to a broad, open window where a husky mestizo woman is plucking dough from a crockery bowl. She beckons, urges, "*¿Le gustaría tener una tortilla?*" and rolls a lump between her palms and drops it onto an iron, presses it flat until sweet-smelling puffs of steam rise from the edges and evaporate.

She gifts me with one of her potato pancakes, delicate and crusted in lacy patterns. We agree on a price and she layers several to take and wraps them in waxed paper. But there are no boiled eggs. Instead, I settle for apricots and a pocketful of shelled almonds.

Back on the street, the sun is glinting off rooftops, spilling stripes and patches of pewter-colored light. Around me, the scuff and drone of humans converging—wheels turning, motors humming – begin to swarm the tiled avenues. I wander, more osmotic than conscious, wearing my senses on the surface of my skin—and then, in the distance, a train exhales a thin plaintive hoot and I stop to listen.

High above the narrow street, white clouds advance across tepid blue sky in a pattern of arched ridges stacked one after another like smudged fish bones. There, skimming the belly of the fish, a flock of small dark birds, sure as winged arrows, glides in formation. On some imperceptible signal they disperse, swooping and chattering, to roost in the crannies of a huge domed steeple.

I crane my neck, watching, until dome and sky become an impulse, and like a sleepwalker, I'm moving, nimble but oblivious—passing storefronts, crossing streets, dodging pedestrians. At the base of stone steps that lead to the heavy wooden doors of the cathedral, I hesitate, and then I take the stairs two at a time.

I grip the carved handle and pull. Inside, the vestibule is cavernous and dim. The door behind me falls shut, a solid click. A scrape of footsteps—a priest in dour trappings comes to peer down the center aisle of the church. He pivots. His scan looks through me and beyond, as if the place where I'm standing is vacant.

I wait, unsure and immobile in my boots, listening as the priest's movements rustle and recede. And then I begin to search. Less than eight feet away, tucked around the corner of an adobe wall, I find the passage I want.

The stairwell to the bell tower is steep; it channels a draft of raw air. I climb from cramped landing to cramped landing with my pulse fluttering in my throat. The final flight is crowned with a corona of light beaming in around the edges of a rough wooden door. I yank. The door creaks on its hinges, lists open to stunning blue sky and a gust of wind that beats in my ears and whips my jacket. Birds startle and erupt in frenzied flapping and I step into their wake, pass the huge mute bell, to stand at the iron railing.

The far horizon—muted green hills rimmed in an aura of diaphanous blue. A surge of connection floods my chest and my throat erupts in an anguished little cry; another lifetime, before Cuenca, Tumibamba was here.

I pull out my binoculars and scan the wide grasslands from Cuenca to the foothills. There are still llamas, a few, strutting amid flocks of squat wooly sheep, and the wide Inca highway to the coast has been replaced by a streak of pot-holed asphalt. But I find remnants there too—a length of wall and some unwieldy Inca pavers, upended and presiding like tombstones.

My fingers are cold. I let the binoculars fall on their strap around my neck and rub my hands together, cup them and blow warm air into my palms. Then, from the bottom of my eyes, my hands look wrong. I spread my fingers, turn them front to back, examine the pale sheen of the fingernails, the slightness of the curled knuckles when I make a fist—a woman's hands. Are these the hands I wanted? I stare at them with a stunned looking that warps to foreboding and shut my eyes.

When I look again, Cuenca is gone; her tiled roofs and Spanish cobbles are nowhere. Instead, the valley before me is bleak, a vast grassland littered with stunted lonely pillars and huge heaps of toppled stone. Not a breeze frets the grass. For a moment I'm claustrophobic, starved for air. And then, across the rim of distant mountains, a thread of lightning flickers. I wait, attuned and counting—one, two, three. A smoldering rumble undulates through the stillness and on its heels comes a brilliant flash that illuminates the sepia-toned valley in a greenish charge. The hair on my arms stands on end. My soul lurches into my throat and quivers. Wild air begins to stir, full of the smell of rain. I see them, souls emerging by the thousands, wisps drifting close to the ground like fluid tails of smoke, all moving in one direction, toward the source of the storm.

I stand mute and trembling, a desperate want swelling inside the circumference of my ribs, as if my chest is full of stars—hot points of light spinning faster and faster. I wince and shut my eyes, brace to burst apart and shower this netherworld in a deluge of sparks. Velocity, pitch and static build until the air ignites and explodes in a discharge of searing light. The stone pillar beneath me fractures in an earsplitting crack, reverberates and sways.

I fall forward and clutch the iron railing, expecting oblivion, but instead—I hear birdsong. The ambient purr of traffic drifts up from the street, and a metal clip, knocked by a soft wind, clangs against a flagpole.

But it's no relief, and not Cuenca that confronts me. I look over the city and beyond; the nagging déjà vu that dogs me begins to harden and hurt. Within these hills, this singular valley still coursed by four ancient rivers, Tumibamba is what I crave, lush and vibrant—and disappeared. An anthropologist would scrape Cuenca's mud foundations and dig beneath her streets for pottery shards, the odd fragment of stone, heaps of bones, surely bones. I think of Eduardo, I could ask him. There must have been excavations, but it doesn't matter. I know, Tumibamba was here, as palpable as a foot, or leg—or my hand.

When I open the fist I've gripped close to my heart, there's a fiery slice that's oozing blood streaked across the palm, and I see that the railing in front of me is twined with razor wire.

I wrap my hand in a handkerchief and shove it into my pocket then glance down at the street. My eyes go straight to the figure of a man tucked into the shade of a shallow doorway. His head tilts up in my direction. His features are smudged by distance, but I recognize the cocksure attitude of his slouch, the sheen of his black hair. He's following me and he's been waiting awhile. It's time he answered some questions.

I descend the steps in double time, shaking some sense into my legs. As I round the final landing, the priest is at the bottom. He's poised to speak, but the only utterance is mine – a stalled and breathless, *"Gracias, Padre."* I hurry past him—burst through the huge double doors.

Bright sunshine stuns my eyes. I squint, aiming my attention across the street and come gaze-to-gaze with my stalker. He lifts his chin and straightens his slouch, raises an arm in greeting.

A ping of doubt ricochets through my resolve. Already, he's surprised me. Beyond confrontation, I have no plan. But I step quickly, sure of one thing, I can't afford to look weak. I plant myself in front of him and cross my arms. "You're following me. What do you want?"

"Buenos días." He smiles.

I press my elbows tight over my hands. "No small talk. Speak English and answer the question."

"But, senorita," he says, "I am your guardian angel."

"I'll go to the police. I mean it."

He shrugs. The black centers of his eyes make a bead straight into mine. "And what will they do, but agree with me? A woman alone in this country is asking for trouble."

"So what—you just saw me on the train and made me your project?"

"*El professor*, Dr. Sircusa, I'm working for him. It's no secret; I tried to talk to you on the train. "

"Well, talk to me now."

"Call me a guide. My name is Guillermo Santos. Ecuador is my country. I can help you."

"And what about Dr. Sircusa? What does he get?"

"*No sé.* Perhaps your safety. He thinks you are going to Tumbes. If he can, he'll meet us there."

An urge to send him packing hardens along my spine and I conjure a message for Eduardo, short, and rude—something about being presumptuous.

"I don't have time for this," I say. "I need to find a pharmacy. I've hurt my hand."

"*A ver,*" he says, "let me see."

"Are you a doctor?"

"No."

"I didn't think so."

I take off, walking at a fast clip, and he follows close behind.

"This isn't settled," I say.

I ask vendors on the street about a place to get medicine, bandages; and they direct me to *La Clinica*, a weathered building on the edge of town with its shutters thrown open and no glass in the windows. A bunch of locals, mostly Indians and poor mestizos, congregate around an open door.

Guillermo sees me hesitate. "Come," he says and grabs my wrist. He tugs me into the crowd.

"*Pardon. Pardon,*" he says. He wedges us between bodies and delivers me to the center of a small waiting room. He points to a makeshift privacy curtain. The words "Peace Corps" are printed across it in thick black letters.

Patients line the walls, waiting on benches and old kitchen chairs. The room is a stew of rancid smells—sweat and sebum, urine, old cigarette smoke. The bitter tang of rubbing alcohol coats the back of my tongue. I take shallow breaths and shove my hands inside my pockets to keep from covering my nose and mouth. Across the room on a window sill, a limp breeze rustles the leaves of a potted fern and I wait for a trace of freshness that doesn't come.

I turn to tell Guillermo I'm leaving, that I only wanted disinfectant and a ribbon of clean gauze. But I'm distracted and not quick enough. He's already stepped away.

My hand smarts, the pain working the nerves like the probe of a clutched wasp. I'm overwhelmed with heat and fatigue. The sense of open-mouthed wonder I felt gazing out from the bell tower seems less convincing now that I'm here in the midst of all this misery with my feet on the ground. I look at my hand. There's swelling and heat; infection's a possibility. I keep thinking of myself at home in my little apartment, turning on the kitchen tap and filling the chipped porcelain sink with cold water and clots of cubed ice—I'm fixed on a merciful plunge, my hand submerged, cool and clean and numb. Coming here was a mistake. I should have gone back to my hotel.

Maybe Guillermo will scare up a doctor—unlikely. As far as I can tell, the medical staff consists of one woman with an efficient bristle of short grey hair and a lab coat. She moves from patient to patient with her clipboard—asks questions, stoops to inspect a swollen knee or a bug bite, pulls the lid back on an inflamed eye. And with each observation, she writes. But no one is invited behind the white curtain.

Guillermo presses in on her. When she finally turns, her shoulders droop and she tilts her head. "*Siéntate*," she says, and motions for him to sit down, to wait like everyone else, but he won't go.

"Guillermo!" I shout his name across the room, "Don't bother. I'm leaving."

He glares at me, as if I've interrupted something that's none of my business. He can do what he wants. I turn to go back the way we came, threading my way through the crowd. An instant later, I smell the waxy citrus of Guillermo's pomade close behind me.

We are nearing the door when the jolt and slam of a crash outside stuns the waiting room and an agitated woman lurches past us holding her face in her hands. Everyone bolts outside to see what's happening.

Guillermo whispers and crosses himself. The car wreck is so close it's a lesson in providence. That it's a near miss is on everyone's mind. The driver might have veered a little to the left and plowed right into the clinic, through the spot where we stand.

Guillermo and I jockey to see from the clinic's stubby veranda, but the view is blocked and we push into the throng of patients and passersby that are gathering around a decrepit Plymouth. The front third of the car is crumpled against a stone retaining wall. Two men dodge jets of steam spewing from under the hood. They work together to dislodge the driver's door, yanking and prying at it with a tire iron.

Hushed chatter ripples through the crowd.

"It's the American doctor," Guillermo tells me. "They say he was called away last night, a chemical spill at a refinery."

The men force the car door open and the injured driver bobs against the steering wheel. Frantic, he rears back, gasping, clutching his chest. His skin is sallow and tinged blue.

The woman in the lab coat comes running. The crowd parts to let her pass and I barge through close behind with Guillermo on my heels.

"Malcolm," she says, and halts in her tracks, one arm hugging her stomach, the other clasping a cupped hand to her mouth.

I plunge past her hollering to Guillermo. "He's suffocating. Tell them I'm a doctor. You'll have to help me. Get these men to lift him out, away from the car. Lay him on the ground. Hurry."

I take the lab-coated woman by the shoulders. She's stalled, shivering.

"I think his lung's collapsed. We'll need a standard intravenous needle and alcohol or iodine, something to disinfect. If you can't come up with those in less than two minutes, I'm going to take the guts out of the ballpoint pen in my pocket and use that."

She turns away, dazed but nodding, and goes to search through the car's windows while I squat to examine the doctor. The men have cleared debris and gravel by sweeping with the edges of their boots and laid him on the ground. He's wheezing, hard desperate gasps, and the veins in his neck are bulging. I clutch the fabric of his shirt below the collar and yank. The buttons snap back at me. The chest is misshapen—distended on the left side.

The lab-coated woman returns with an old leather medical bag. She opens it and fishes out the items I asked for—an envelope of gauze pads, a small glass bottle of iodine, a needle still in sterile packaging. She glances at the doctor's bare chest then takes hold of his hand while I wipe a yellow-orange smudge high on the bulging side of his chest, a holy unction of sorts—be safe, Malcolm, deliver thee from harm.

I probe with my fingers to locate the space above the third rib, then chart an intersection directly beneath the collarbone and insert the needle. A hiss issues from the puncture and immediately his pallor turns flush. His breath evens and he opens his eyes. "Elizabeth?" He looks from the lab-coated woman to me.

"Who are you?"

"An emergency room doctor from the States. Let's get you inside and see what supplies you've got to fine-tune the job. I expect your chest hurts. I think you've broken a rib."

"Did I hurt anyone?"

"Except for you? I don't think so."

"Guillermo," I say, "find a gurney or a stretcher, let's get him inside."

The lab-coated woman rises to her feet. "I'll show him where the stretchers are. Thank you."

Malcolm protests, not my methods, but that he's flat on his back. He squints and frowns, the skin around his eyes and mouth bunches like crinkled parchment from decades of too much sun. He makes an effort to push up on an elbow but drops back on a rolled jacket that's been supplied as a makeshift pillow.

"You'll be fine," I say. "Give yourself a day or two."

"Where's Elizabeth? Who's going to take care of my patients?"

"I don't know," I say.

A rusted pickup truck that's come to take Malcolm home backs close to the clinic's entrance and pumps a chugging plume of oily exhaust through the door. Elizabeth hollers in Spanish, but the driver insists the engine is unreliable, if he turns it off, it might not start again. The truck's driver and another man carry Malcolm on his stretcher into the exhaust. I fret about Malcolm's lungs but hold my tongue and they load him onto the weathered flatbed. He's not my patient, not really.

Elizabeth dithers and deposits her clipboard with a plump-cheeked native woman wearing a white muslin apron that's probably been stitched from an old bed sheet, then comes to give me a stiff hug. She uses the truck's trailer hitch as a step up and hoists herself in next to Malcolm. Her voice strains above the engine noise. "I won't be back today." She points to the woman with the clipboard. "Anna can get you what you need. She'll lock up." The truck belches another gust of noxious smoke and pulls away.

"Thank you," Elizabeth hollers. "Tomorrow. Come back tomorrow."

Malcolm's departure leaves a void and his patients begin to mill and scuff. We all sputter and cough. Everything smells of exhaust. Anna gets a towel and starts fanning fumes toward the open doorway, and the crowd, along with the smudged air, begins to disperse. But not everyone is content to go. A few stragglers who saw me revive Malcolm come to plead.

Guillermo translates and I tell them that this is Malcolm's clinic, that I've never practiced field medicine, that I can't even speak passable Spanish. But there are a few who persist.

A small, copper-colored man with a recent bruise on his face and a swollen lip, wags a rough-slung forearm at me, implores with a string of words. "He says that a mule did this," Guillermo tells me. "One kick and he's still dizzy. He's worried about his arm."

A young girl, maybe nine, jostles a wailing infant and points to a woman slumped in a chair. "*Allichu*," she begs. She tells me that her mother is bleeding a lot and that the baby was born yesterday. Now the girl's afraid that her mother will die.

I nod a weary "yes," and sigh. "Okay, okay. Move. Give me space." I approach the girl's mother and look in her eyes, check her fingernails. She's pallid and weak, consistent with a loss of blood. I ask Guillermo to help me get her behind the white curtain. Then I take stock; ask Anna for analgesic, splints, tools to set a bone, something to instigate uterine contractions. "Like Pitocin," I say. It's then, when I impose a modern medical term—that it dawns on me that I'm hearing, speaking, even thinking in Quechua. I've known, of course, but without practice to verify. Someday, I tell myself, with enough exposure, I'll take this strange gift for granted.

The clinic's treatment options are limited, but lined up on one shelf are dozens of bottles and some small gray fiber bags coated in wax. Each is labeled in Quechua with an English explanation. Indigenous herbs and tinctures of herbs, the names seem familiar and strange at the same time. One says, "Ibenkiki: for migraines, causes uterine contractions."

"Anna," I say, "Where do these medicines come from? How does Malcolm get these?"

She hesitates so long, that I don't think she's going to answer. And then she gives a gruff whisper, "Koyam." One utterance, as if the name alone is more than I need to know.

.

16 THE MAPMAKER

Anna throws the bolt on the clinic door and secures it with a padlock, the last of a ritual of closures and locks that probably won't deter anyone. It's early afternoon, barely two o'clock, and somewhere a bird trills. But human sounds are remarkably absent. I gaze out toward the empty road and the hills beyond. I wonder about Malcolm.

Guillermo nudges my shoulder and I turn to see what he wants. Anna stands facing me with her hands pressed flat against the skirt of her apron. "She's waiting for you to tell her to go home," he says.

Her wide brown eyes tilt up, full of dazzle; she's endowed me with powers I hardly merit. In Quechua, I urge her, "Go home, Anna. Rest. I know you must be hungry. Elizabeth will need you tomorrow."

She's descending the porch's shallow steps when I call her back. "Anna, wait. Can you tell me? The woman who supplies the medicine—Koyam, where can I find her?"

Anna studies my face, as if my request is somehow beyond common sense. "The *cura*," she tells me, "she comes when she comes." She cocks her head and waits to see if I'm satisfied. I nod, because I don't know what else to say.

"You need something?" It's Guillermo.

"I was asking about Koyam, the person who supplies the native medicines. I met an Indigena on the plane coming into Bogotá, an acquaintance of Eduardo's. Her name was Koyam." I shake my head. "It would be an incredible coincidence."

"Dr. Sircusa—he expects me to be in touch. I can ask."

"Let's go to my hotel. You make the call, but I want to talk to him."

The reception attendant at the hotel sends us to a heavy wooden phone booth at the far end of a broad alcove outside the restrooms. Guillermo feels in his pocket for change, steps inside and presses a coin into the slot. He speaks to the operator in Spanish and begins to tap an impatient finger against the scarred shelf where a phonebook should be.

"He may not be there," he tells me.

I shrug; it's a wonder any of us are anywhere.

He asks for Sircusa, and then, with a blunt authority that drives me a step backward, he thumps the booth's folding panel shut. I fume. Who is he to insist on privacy when it's me they're discussing? I consider walking away, going upstairs to my hotel room and shutting the door behind me; one exclusionary thump deserves another. But I don't.

I'm remembering Koyam on the plane, the hot fierce grip of her hand on my wrist, the way she looked out for me at the airport.

Behind the booth's glass panels, Guillermo fidgets and straightens, pushes a limp shock of hair off his forehead. He gives me a furtive glance then hunches around the receiver. I back off, move against the wall opposite the phone booth, to lean and wait.

Beneath the crisscross of Anna's gauze bandage, the center of my palm emits a searing ache and the soles of my feet are hot. I search around for the shelled almonds I bought this morning and eat six or seven of them, picking them one at a time from where they've settled amid lint and sand in the seams and corners of my jacket pockets.

Then all at once, Guillermo beckons. "*Tome*," he says, and thrusts the receiver at me.

My vital signs surge in a blushing rush and I stand upright, dust my hand against my pant-leg, lick my teeth, and swallow—grip the phone and edge past Guillermo into the booth. I shut the folding panel and press the receiver to my ear.

Nothing but feathered silence and strands of white noise—then clicking. "Eduardo?" my utterance so tentative it comes out like a plea.

"Megan? *Hable mas alto.* Louder please, I can't hear you."

"I didn't say anything."

"That's better," Eduardo says. "A bad connection."

Eduardo clears his throat. "So you're going to Baños."

"Am I?"

"That's the most likely place to find Koyam. Her house is too remote for a telephone. If you'll hold off a day or two, I'll come to Cuenca and take you myself."

"It's not necessary. Just Koyam's address, even the general vicinity should be sufficient. If she's not there, I'll hang around and see the sights. Or do something else. Besides, I have an escort. I want to talk about Guillermo."

"I've made a mistake. You're not pleased."

"You should have asked."

"And how was I supposed to do that? You left me a note. Listen Megan, I'm trying not to crowd you, but you can't just disappear. Felix Lester is very concerned that he should have taken more precautions with the hypnosis session; he's worried about you. And Jasper's been parsing the tape, researching the details; he's obsessed, vowing to track you down."

I stall, tongue-tied and claustrophobic. The booth is stagnant, humid with Guillermo's exhalations and the residue of old pipe tobacco. I lift a hand to ease the door a breath, but Guillermo encroaches. He peers at me through the watery warp of the booth's window. Suspended there between us, my eyes settle on a tiny bubble entombed in the glass.

"Megan? Hello. Are you there?"

"What do you want from me?" My voice sounds more strident than I intend. "I don't mean to be rude, but I didn't travel all this way to become someone's science project."

"God, Megan, I'm trying to protect you? And Jasper—would it be such a bad thing, if the end result gets you what you want? We are asking the same questions. Is there observable evidence? Could your connection to the past lead to new knowledge, new archeological discoveries?"

His intensity almost generates heat.

"I'll think about it," I say, wanting a cold drink and desperate for fresh air. "I'll call you from Baños. I have to go."

"What about Guillermo?"

"I'll think about him too. Goodbye, Eduardo." I set the receiver back in its cradle.

For a dislocated instant I stare at the phone—unsure and alone, craving my dad's flannel-clad arm across my shoulders, almost able to smell the bristly whiff of Old Spice on his cheek.

I could dial; his phone number still inhabits my fingertips. If only we could talk, even for a minute. But talking to the dead is like shouting into a well, the only voice coming back is your own.

Outside the booth, Guillermo cocks his head and lifts his eyebrows. "What gives?" he asks—a phrase so unlikely I wonder if he learned his English watching American television.

"News flash," I say. "If you want to keep your job stalking me all over Timbuktu, then you work for me, only me. Understand? Whatever Sircusa's paying you, I'll match. If that works for you, then tomorrow, we leave for Baños."

"*No sé*. I'll talk to Dr. Sircusa."

"No, it's up to you. If you can't commit right now, then I'll find myself another guide and tell Eduardo to call you off, that I don't want you spying on me."

His eyes give back a brazen glint. "Why not?" he says. "The job's the same."

"Alright then," I say, making it up as I go along. "We'll talk terms tomorrow. You've got Koyam's address?"

"I know the way."

"We'll need transport to Baños. See what you can arrange, nothing fancy. Meet me back here in the morning, around nine. I'll be packed and waiting on one of the couches in the lobby."

I watch the back of him as he moves toward the door, his gait so restrained, so deliberately casual, I don't need to be a mind reader to know he's on his way to make another, more private, phone call to Eduardo.

The hotel elevator heaves a mechanical groan and lurches to a halt. I scan the lobby. It's after nine and Guillermo is nowhere. I settle my suitcase, prop my backpack, and perch on the forward edge of an oversized armchair, fingering the room key in my pocket and checking the time—fifteen minutes—thirty minutes—three quarters of an hour.

I surrender my key and ask the hotel clerk the best way to get to Baños. At first he thinks I mean the baths in Cuenca, but when he understands, he offers the bus station. But maybe, he cautions, I shouldn't be so quick to give up my room. The bus can have mechanical problems. And the schedule, he shakes his head—it's not so good.

He directs me to the street, Calle Larga, where I can buy a ticket, then stows my suitcase with my medic bag inside it and my backpack in a cavity under the reception desk for safekeeping.

I push past the hotel door into bright sunshine, take a deep breath, and exhale. A silken cool frets the morning's warmth, and I think about Guillermo and wonder if I asked too much.

It doesn't matter. I can find Koyam by myself.

Koyam entered my sleep last night, a rustle beneath dreaming. She called my name and I woke with the hoarse whisper of her voice still alive in my ear. The night was soft and dark and I got out of bed to stand beside the open window and watch a patient drift of clouds obscure the last sliver of a waning moon. A feeling of dread seeped into my bones and I shivered. For the first time, I sensed that I was at the center of something past changing, as fixed and solid as if it had already happened.

I stall in front of the hotel and tell myself that Guillermo's defection is a sign that my options are open; what I need is a plan.

I set off for the market to buy breakfast, food to take and some semblance of a wedding ring, not the gold band embedded with seven tiny garnets like Mama's, or the platinum partner to my sister Claire's diamond solitaire. Mine will be the anti-wedding ring, more like a necklace of garlic.

Not far, there's a bakery. I choose a spiral of cinnamon bread and the clerk hands it across the counter in a paper sleeve. The crust is crisp, but the inside is fresh and elastic. I tug with my teeth and dislodge a rain of tacky sugar, then brush and flick, lick my lips, lick my fingers, step back outside, alert and inexplicably leery. I scan left and right, make a full turn. No Guillermo. I hustle along, keep walking.

I stop to look into a jewelry store window populated with mannequin body parts, forearms that wear Swiss and German watches, sloping alabaster torsos festooned with pendants and etched lockets. And there are rings, most in sets of two, each pair tilted upright in its own plush little box. I wipe my hands on the front of my pants as if I'm preparing to handle the goods, and notice, reflected in the glass, a man approaching behind me.

He's native, a patient from the clinic. I recognize the blunt nose, the strange smile, so wide it could double as a grimace— and his eye.

In Quechua, I ask if it hurts, is he using the salve I gave him.

He tells me it's improving, but I doubt it. The eye bulges, wet and glossy, the lid swollen, rimmed a wild pink, an infection that will take a while to resolve.

He pegs me with his lopsided vision and wipes his mouth with the back of his hand.

"We came to find you," he says, and points with a bob of his head to a man who smiles at me from across the street. "Hernan's cousin, the man who hires us, is hurt. Could you come?"

"A hospital or local doctor might be better."

"*Por favor*," he says. "A short way. Not far. We can't move him."

I'm reluctant, but he wears his concern with such gravity. "My medic kit is at the hotel," I say.

He gives a grim nod and we step off in unison, my one-eyed patient walking close beside me, his friend a pace behind.

My Indigena tagalongs stop short of the hotel and insist on stationing themselves in the shade of an awning several doors away. "It's a gringo hotel," they explain and shoo me off.

"*Hanqa. Hanqa*," they say. Hurry. Hurry.

I make a beeline through the lobby to the reception desk. Before the clerk can crouch to lift my suitcase from behind the counter, Guillermo appears beside me, ridiculously stern, a hard glint of accusation in his eyes.

"Where were you?"

I'm distracted, searching the corners of my pockets for the suitcase key. "I waited for you this morning, for nearly an hour. I got hungry."

The key is tiny, clumsy in my fingers. I angle it left, then right.

"I'll do it. Give it here," Guillermo demands with his hand out.

"I'll get it." I wave him off, doing my best to manage a mild rush of irritation.

I insert the key, one click, then press the latches with my thumbs. The lid pops open.

"I got bus tickets to Baños," Guillermo says. "We leave this afternoon."

"We'll see," I say. "I came back for my medic kit. I'm making a house call."

Inside, my medic bag occupies nearly one half of the suitcase. The soft leather slouches, its position painstakingly secured by underwear, my long coat, my black dress. I lift the bag out and hand it to Guillermo, shut and lock the suitcase. As I tilt the suitcase upright and push it back toward the clerk, I can feel the contents shifting.

My one-eyed patient squats, his hat tipped to avoid the light. His compadre, Hernan, acts as lookout, leaning against the stucco wall, his attention patiently aimed in the direction of the hotel. He sees us coming and nudges his friend's thigh with the toe of his boot. The two stand together with a single focus, eyeing Guillermo with a penetrating squint.

Up close, I introduce, explain. "Guillermo is my assistant."

But Hernan shakes his head. "We can assist." He motions between himself and his companion. "He can't come. It's not possible," he says, "only the doctor."

"Then I won't come," I say, feeling a warm rush of solidarity with Guillermo. "Guillermo, let's go back to the hotel and get my bags. We have a bus to catch."

But Hernan has a change of heart. He tells me that, of course, a gringo woman, even a doctor, must not travel by herself. He smiles and emits a soft laugh, places his hand on his friend's shoulder and gives a firm squeeze.

"*Vámonos,*" he says, adopting a tone that scolds us for wasting time.

We follow them for several blocks, to a side street and a decrepit car pocked with rust, its paint sun-cured to the dull red of tomato soup. Only the doors on the driver's side work. Hernan hustles everyone inside. I scoot across ridges of brittle springs and frayed upholstery while Hernan slips behind the steering wheel and cranks the starter. Guillermo purses his lips and shoots me a bitter look just as the engine roars to life.

We skirt the edges of Cuenca then turn onto the highway going south, away from the city for ten, maybe twelve, miles. I look over Hernan's shoulder to the dials on the dashboard but the odometer is stuck in a series of endless zeros.

"How much farther?" I ask.

Hernan throws a hand up, a message to sit back. Moments later, he pulls the car to the side of the road and tosses Guillermo a sack made of dark fabric and an old blue bandana. He orders him to tie the bandana around my eyes, then put the bag on his own head. Guillermo stiffens, ready to refuse, but Hernan's one-eyed friend foists a gun and levels the barrel on the seatback.

Hernan's eyes gaze back from the rearview mirror.

"*Cálmense,*" he says. The blindfolds, he insists, are necessary. He urges us not to make a problem.

I stiffen, lean forward stunned and a little disoriented, ready to tell them this is a huge mistake, but Guillermo grips my arm. "*Por favor,*" he says, willing me to cooperate, to stay calm. "Let's just get where we're going."

I comply, turn and sit upright while he smoothes my hair and ties a knot. We reoccupy our seats on either side of the hump in the floorboard and settle back, worried and riding blind. Beneath us, the car jerks back onto the highway. Soon pavement turns to rutted earth. The chassis bucks and shudders. Each time the axle meets stone, I wince. We're off the map; even Eduardo won't be able to find us now.

We lumber to a stop, bones rattled, and Hernan tells us that our blindfolds can come off. I squint. It's past midday. Stark high altitude sunshine glints off the windshield. We've come to the roof of the world. Thatched grassland pebbled with boulders and light-colored stones falls away in every direction. Hernan motions toward a ramshackle enclave of hovels constructed of mud bricks and corrugated metal. But before we can get out of the car, a pair of frenzied dogs bolts up the hillside issuing a torrent of ruptured barks. They peer in at us and snarl, drool on the glass.

Hernan rolls the window a crack. "Alma," he shouts, and a young girl, maybe eight or nine, an indigena, with a wide brimmed felt hat and a single thick braid that trails halfway down her back, emerges from the cluster of buildings. She brandishes a stick and calls to the dogs, swings but doesn't strike. The dogs withdraw, slink around her legs and sniff the doorway. They paw at a filthy rug and lie down.

Hernan orders us out of the car. We troop past Alma into one of the buildings and through a makeshift vestibule stacked with boxes, bulging baskets, some old chemical drums.

Hernan hands me a small paper bag. Inside there are glass ampules and some syringes. "*Morfina*," he says, "*para Manuel. Está alli.*" He points to a worn curtain that serves as a door and makes a brusque exit.

I pull the curtain back and get a stale draft from inside, a nose-full of old smoke and hard liquor.

I step across the threshold with my medic bag into a patch of daylight, truncated slats of sunshine that edge through a small shuttered window close to the ceiling. The room is dun colored, a mud brick den with a hard-packed dirt floor and a fire pit gouged into the back wall. Nothing much, some rough wooden shelves littered with bottles and rags, a narrow pallet where a man dozes and frets beneath a coarse woolen blanket.

My patient is native, middle age, with a thick neck and a head of dense black hair. For a wavering instant, I wonder if we've met before. I step close to his bed, unsure what's expected. He mutters, twitches, sleeps but doesn't rest. The bronze hollows of his face are taut with managed pain. A fly probes his forehead near the hairline and I stoop to blow, a light puff, and flick it away with the back of my hand. My patient opens his eyes.

"*Allillanchu*?" I say. "How are you?" and lay a hand across his forehead.

He gazes up, struggles to telescope his focus to the universe of my face. He draws me in, sees and is seen, and in that instant, the shadow of sorrow, like a dark wing, passes between us.

He licks chapped lips, speaks in Quechua, "I'm not dreaming, am I?"

"I don't think so," I say, but how would I know if I was in his dream or he was in mine?

"Hernan brought me," I tell him. "I'm a doctor."

His energy wanes—he closes his eyes and curls toward the wall. His voice is dull. "Call Alma; tell her to get my lock box. I'll give you what you came for."

I turn, expecting to ask Guillermo to go find the girl, but she's already there, watching us from the doorway.

"You're from Tayta's dream," she says, her face a mask of defiance. "You want the eye. I don't care, take everything. We're sick of dead things. Leave us alone."

"Alma, please. This is no dream. You saw me get out of the car with Hernan. I came to help. Your father has a fever; look at the color of his skin. He's shivering."

Alma's face puckers. She puts the tip of her little finger between her teeth and bites down hard. She's saved herself from crying, but her misery is contagious. I feel it, anxious and fluttering against the walls of my stomach.

Guillermo is losing patience; he makes a move to get Hernan to deal with the child.

"Don't." I talk in Quechua, meaning for Alma to overhear. "This is Alma's father. She decides."

Alma turns on Guillermo, regards him with a slow and bitter stare.

"The police shot Tayta's leg," she says, "I helped Hernan; we cleaned the wound with trago."

"Alma," I say, "I brought medicine." I squat, lay my medic kit open on the floor, display the assortment of vials tucked into the pouches that line its walls. "Maybe there's something here that could help your tayta—but we won't know until I can look at his leg."

She considers in silence, then goes to touch her father's shoulder. "Tayta," she says, "the gringa has medicine. Let her look at your leg."

His skin is moist with sudden perspiration. He spasms, an involuntary jerk, then moans. Alma pulls back a step, paces herself, newly familiar with this grim rhythm. When he's eased, she holds his head and administers a swig of trago. He grasps the child's hand and kisses the palm then sinks back on his pillow.

Alma makes herself tall and official. She steps to the end of the cot and carefully folds the blanket up from the bottom, exposes her father's legs, and with them, the reek of rancid flesh. Alma removes her hat, beats the air—embarrassed but determined. She sets her hat on the shelf and comes back to the cot, primed for duty.

The left tibia is roughly splinted and wrapped with an ooze-stained cloth that's been secured with strips of knotted rag. I hand Guillermo my medic kit and ask him to shine the flashlight. Alma steadies the foot. I begin to unwrap until a moan catches in the back of Manuel's throat. He flinches, mumbles profanity, holds himself steady again.

The wound is ripe, gangrenous and spreading, too late for antibiotics or amputation.

Manuel studies my face for a sign. "Not good?"

"I'm sorry," I say. "I have morphine."

I ask Guillermo for new gauze and begin to rewrap the leg.

Alma's face blanches. "You're useless. You're not going to fix his leg, are you?" She makes fists of her small hands. I think maybe she'll hit me, but Manuel tells her to stop, insists she bring him his lock box.

"Morphine," he says to me, "but not much at first. I want to talk."

I fill a syringe and tie off Manuel's arm with a strip of elastic cloth, expose the vein just below the elbow. A thumb's pressure, and his muscles ease; he slumps, exhales.

"Enough to take the edge off," I say, withdrawing the needle, touching his shoulder. "You'll want more."

His eyelids droop but he resists sleep, smiles for Alma when she returns carrying a rectangular metal box secured with a small padlock.

"Did Hernan see you?" he asks.

Alma shakes her head and comes to deposit the box on the cot beside him, but he tells her to take it across the room, to put it on a bottom shelf. "For now," he says, "push it back. Scatter rags on top."

Alma is scrupulous in her efforts to please. She comes back to him with a tiny key that she pulls from inside her skirt pockets. He closes his hand around it, slips it beneath his pillow, then seems to relax—the morphine damping his nerves the way white noise covers sound.

Slack silence—a rustle, the hinge on the outer door scrapes and sighs, admits a chill draft that skitters loose stalks of straw across the floor. Hernan steps into the room. He's transformed himself; now he wears a camouflage jacket and billed cap. I notice his boots, well used and overlarge, military issue, with laces made from strips of twisted rawhide. He takes stock of the room.

"Alma." Hernan's tone is edged with irritation.

Alma stiffens, then scurries, crouches in front of the fire pit, methodical—arranging handfuls of brittle grass, kindling, chips of dried manure. She pokes around with a stick, exposes smoldering coals and blows until they glow and sputter a small blue flame. She adds bundled fuel, situates for a slow burn, but before she's finished, Hernan reminds her to hurry; she has another fire to stoke and food to prepare.

Alma slips behind Hernan and disappears through the curtained door, unobtrusive as a mouse.

Hernan motions toward Manuel. "What can you do for him?"

"Nothing, "I say, "Try to keep him comfortable."

"How long?" he asks.

"Tonight, maybe tomorrow."

Hernan turns to Manuel. "Are you going to die tonight, Manuel? Should we watch, then, for the mapmaker?"

Manuel's eyes come to rest on my face with the glazed look of a patron. "The mapmaker is here."

The misty glow of twilight gives everything a fuzzy edge, or maybe it's the smoke from Alma's fire.

"Manuel," I ask, "what does it mean to be the mapmaker?"

Hernan sneers. "It's the medicine, Manuel. You're grateful—or hallucinating. She's a foreign doctor, a white woman. Jorge found her at the missionary clinic. I brought her here, blindfolded in the car. She didn't come looking for you."

Manuel struggles to rise up on his arm, his face pinched with conviction.

Hernan becomes solemn. He motions for Manuel to lie down. He mumbles, curses, and shakes his head, then turns on his heel, takes two strides, and bats the curtain aside—on his way to get the map.

Manuel listens for the hinge on the outer door to creak, then asks Guillermo to bring him the lock box. He pulls the key from beneath his pillow, unlocks and tilts the box. A worn envelope stuffed with currency falls onto the blanket. Manuel beckons, insists I take it. He cups my hands inside his with a pressure that's firm and gentle, as if we are holding something fragile.

"For Alma." His tone is hushed and urgent. "Take her to Cuenca, to the nuns at Todos los Santos. Say you'll do it."

I hesitate, my thoughts flashing to the gun aimed from the seatback, the blindfolds, the sense of disturbing intention I felt when Hernan was in the room. What if Alma refuses? All by itself, Manuel's secret wad of cash could be enough to get us killed.

Manuel firms his grip on my hands. "Promise," he says. "Let me hear you say it."

"I promise," I say, a cornered promise, pressured and harangued by doubt.

Manuel lets go of my hands and I slip the envelope under my shirt, snug it inside the waistband of my pants. Guillermo stashes the lock box back on the shelf.

Manuel's breathing rattles; he coughs and slumps, but when Hernan comes back with the map, he asks to be propped upright. He spreads it across his lap. It's creased and soft and he smoothes it outward from the center.

The drawing depicts a twisting route over rugged terrain, each landmark precise: an unusual curve in a river, a snow-covered peak, the lopsided crest of a butte. I catch myself stiffening, holding my breath. Manuel and this map—something déjà vu so sharply felt that I wonder if I'm losing my grip. God help me, it wouldn't be the first time.

Guillermo's watching me. "Is something wrong?"

I glance at him without answering.

"Manuel," he says, "You called Megan the mapmaker. What can she have to do with any of this?"

Manuel shrugs. "I can only tell you what happened to me."

Alma slips into the room and waits for the least intrusive moment to check on her father. Manuel asks for water; she dips some from a bucket. He's shivering; his teeth tap the metal cup. Alma climbs onto the cot to warm him. She nestles in the crook of his arm and arranges the blanket around them.

Manuel kisses the top of her head. He's weak but determined to speak.

"Two years ago, I left Alma in Cumbe with my grandmother and went to work in a silver mine south of Quito. I hated the work, but I needed money. Every day, deep in a hole, picking at rocks. Always in the dark. It was like being buried alive.

"The mine was old, from even before the Spaniards. I'd heard stories there were ghosts, but I tried not to think about it. Sometimes we'd find a bone or an odd tool, a broken piece of pottery . . .

"One day, an earthquake rattled the mine. Dust and clods of dirt shook loose from the ceiling. I put my axe down, crouched, and waited for more. But nothing happened. I listened for sounds from the other miners. I yelled, but all I heard was water dripping and my own breathing. And then, for no reason, I was afraid. and I took a step back against the wall. 'Who's there?' I said, and shined my lamp around.

"The figure of a man stood watching me from a fissure in one of the walls. His face was hidden by shadow and the hood of his cloak, but I could see the silver disk in the lobe of his ear.

"He spoke Quechua and he knew my name. 'Manuel,' he said. 'I have a task for you. What will you ask in return?'

"I pretended to be bold. I told him I wanted to be free of the mine—that I wanted to be a rich man with my own silver and gold. I waited to hear what he would say.

"'A thief took some things that belong to me,' he said. 'I want you to get them back.'

"He must have seen fear in my face because he gave a scornful grunt. 'Don't worry,' he said, 'He won't put up a fight.'

"I must have passed out. The next I knew, Hernan and another miner were lifting me out of a cart and onto a grassy slope away from the mouth of the mine. It was sundown and rain was beginning to fall. There was thunder, and a flash of blue lightning nearly struck me where I lay. The smell of something burnt filled my nose and I worried that my heart might stop. I almost wished it would. If I'd agreed to something, I didn't know what it was. I decided the thing I had seen in the mine was only some air-starved trick of my mind. What else could it have been? "But the cloaked figure entered my dreams that night, not as a man, but like wind behind weather. He swept me along old Inca highways and hidden mountain paths. 'Remember,' he would say about this stone, this view of a valley, this stump of a tree. 'Remember. Remember. Remember.' That morning I woke up outside the barracks, shivering and wet with dew. This," Manuel says, stroking the paper across his lap, "was tucked up beneath my shirt and I had the foreman's ink pen in my hand."

Manuel stops to search our faces. "You're not the first to doubt me," he says. "Hernan saw me put the pen back on the foreman's desk before I went back to my cot. He accused me of stealing and I told him everything. Without the map, he would never have believed me.

"Hernan and Jorge were in a fever to come with me. We stole a bag of cornmeal and some potatoes from the mess hall, took our miners' lamps, and left the next day. Just started walking into the countryside. We caught fish and ate bird eggs, whatever we could get.

"We walked east and south. On the eighth day, we came to the steep cliff marked with the trail of footholds we were looking for. We had to hack through dense brush to get to the rock underneath. I went up first.

"The cavern was shallow and empty. We might have given up, but a bird flew into the cave and I saw it go into a small opening high on one of the walls. Hernan lifted me on his shoulders and I looked into the hole where the bird had gone. It was too dark to see and it stunk of dung, but it didn't matter. We had already decided to tear into the wall.

"By late afternoon we'd made an opening big enough to climb through. We found ourselves in a cramped cavern that led to a chamber stacked with impossible things—gold and silver figurines, idols, death masks, arm bands, head dresses. Hernan and Jorge were in a holy frenzy. They made bundles of their jackets and started gathering relics. They kept changing their minds, leaving one thing and picking up another. They left to set camp with more treasure than they could hope to carry.

"I had found the place but I still didn't know what I was searching for, and I worried that Hernan or Jorge might have taken whatever it was already. I was tired and making myself crazy. It would be getting dark soon and the smell and closeness of the cave was making me sick. I had decided to come back in the morning. But when I turned to go, the light from my lamp swept across the painted-on face of a mummy. He was propped in a carved-out niche, a squat bundle wrapped in coarse woven fabric. I had a sense that the black circles that pretended to be his eyes were watching me and I jerked backward and was startled from behind by the cloaked spirit I'd met in the mine.

"Bring him down,' the spirit said. 'Tear away the shroud.'

"The bundle was lighter than I expected. I lifted it to the ground and split the covering with my knife. The layers of cloth came away in patches. The corpse was a man bound in a cramped position, musty and bitter smelling. His hands were fisted tight against his shoulders and he was wearing a ring on the middle finger of his right hand.

"'Take the ring,' the spirit said.

"I had to use my knife to cut away the fingers. When I finally held the ring in my hand I could feel its dark life, unpredictable and dangerous, like clutching a scorpion.

"'Keep it for me,' he said, 'until I come in the flesh.'

"How will I know you?' I asked.

"He turned so I could see him in the lamplight—not the face of a man. It was you, a gringa with strange green eyes."

Manuel offers me his hand. "Take it," he says.

His hand is swollen. The finger that wears the ring bulges, lurid purple, constricted at its base by an etched gold band.

I turn his hand palm up and see that the ring's honed edges are dug into the skin. I use the Vaseline lip gloss I carry in my pocket, grease his finger, twist, and pry. There's a smear of blood and Hernan warns me off. "It's no use," he says. "You'd have to cut the finger off."

But when I pull, the ring loosens its grip.

"Please," Manuel says. "You must put it on."

The ring slips on my finger, slightly loose at first but my finger swells or the band tightens. The design is exquisite, ancient etchings in gold—a puma and serpent fly at each other to merge in a single shared obsidian eye. I can see shadows flash and swim beneath the eye's polished surface.

Hernan thrusts an open hand at me. He tilts his head, peers into my pupils. His breath is sour and damp. "A dealer would pay through the nose for that. I didn't risk arrest, or claw through crumbling caverns to make you a gift."

I peer back, summon a focus that's clear and cold and sharp with adrenaline. When I speak, my voice feels strange in my mouth—Quechua words, unswerving and dangerously sonorous. "And I, *Hernanito*, am not here because you wished it."

Hernan brushes his palm against the leg of his pants, takes a cautious step backward.

Guillermo's lips are pale. "What just happened?"

But I'm at a loss, remembering the moment when I might have answered but not the answer. I glance around the room. Hernan is gone.

17 THE TALISMAN

Guillermo comes back through the curtain. "The bastard's locked us in. He's bolted the door from the outside."

He places a crate below the room's single window, tests for balance and steps up to peer through the narrow shuttered opening. "They're under the hood of the car," he says. Guillermo lingers where he stands, looking down on Hernan and Jorge at work. "Maybe Hernan will leave us here to rot—probably not. That business with the ring—he's not going to let that go."

I try to get Manuel to focus, cup his face in my hands, ask him what we should do. But his eyes roam without seeing. He trembles and stiffens—racked with spasms, riding waves of pain.

Alma hovers at the head of his cot. She winces every time he groans. She dips and wrings a rag in a bowl of water, blots her father's face and forehead. She begs, and I relent.

Guillermo steadies Manuel's arm while I insert the needle— administer the last of the morphine.

The muscles around Manuel's mouth relax. His agitated rasps slacken to whispers. Now we wait—and hope that the morphine manages to outlast the patient's need for it.

Outside, Hernan and Jorge are trying to start the engine. The motor cranks and sputters, a tedious repetition that finally ignites in a gunning roar that smudges the air. The vehicle lumbers, then rests. The engine idles. A car door slams. The hut's outer door rattles and scrapes. Hernan is coming.

He enters, scanning the room with his gun as if it's a flashlight. He looks past Guillermo, Manuel, Alma—I'm the one. He points the gun at my head, thumbs the hammer back.

I resist the urge to shut my eyes, but my breath catches in my throat—anticipating the bullet.

"If you come past the curtain," he says, "I'll kill you."

He motions Guillermo into the next room and follows. Alma and I hear Hernan giving orders, rustling movement, the sound of footsteps.

Alma furrows her brow. "They're moving the baskets."

I brush the tips of my fingers along the bottom of my vest, feeling for the position of my scalpel and the unsheathed syringe of tranquilizer hanging loose in my pocket. My hands are trembling.

Hernan shoves Guillermo back into the room, striking him between the shoulder blades with the heel of his hand. He orders Guillermo to step against the wall, hands away from his body. Guillermo raises his arms, but instead of stepping forward, he pivots and makes a lunge for the gun.

Hernan jerks and fires. The bullet spatters blood in an indiscriminate arc. Guillermo recoils and drops, dazed, but not unconscious. Hernan is incensed, mumbling profanities through clenched teeth. He grabs Guillermo by his shirt collar and strikes him across the cheekbone with the barrel of the gun.

Hernan yells for Jorge who comes hefting a rifle and a coil of rope. Guillermo groans and shudders as Jorge trusses him into a fetal position, wrists and ankles together. I lean forward, aching to object. The gesture incites Hernan and he kicks and pushes Guillermo with the toe of his boot, forcing him backward until he's crammed into a recess beneath some shelves.

Hernan wheels around to confront me, but he hesitates, searches my face. He's not sure. He wags his gun. "I'll take the ring."

I move to comply. The metal warms to my touch, eases off my finger, strangely supple—like a living thing. I glance and am caught—the glistening black of the stone's polished surface clouds and swirls to a radiant center, a black nucleus that looks out, alert and prescient, from a field of limpid green. For a piercing breathless instant—it's as if I'm peering into my own eye.

Hernan plucks the ring between his thumb and forefinger and deposits it in his shirt pocket. Then, with the quickness of a strike, he grabs the front of my vest and jerks me hard against him. The edges of his belt buckle press against my stomach. I cringe and arch backward, my hand frantic in my pocket, positioning the syringe. I stab him in the forearm, press the plunger—half delivered. A gunshot shakes the room. Hernan groans and swears. He bats the syringe, breaks the needle off in his arm. He grasps the side of his head, pulls his hand away to look. It's smeared with blood. The rim of his ear is hanging by a piece of skin. A second blast—Manuel, propped on an unsteady arm, still points the pistol. Hernan staggers for the door.

Outside, truck doors slam and a gearshift grinds. A streak of light travels across the wall opposite the window and Manuel's arm collapses. The gun he holds drops to the floor. I'm trembling. The backs of my eyeballs feel scorched. Alma is crouched behind Manuel's cot. She's crying.

My eyes open, blink, and search the scattering darkness. Alma sleeps heavy in the crook of my arm. She breathes in starts and soft rhythmic whistles. We've been hours in one position. My feet are cold, numb in my boots. I stretch, shift in increments, trying not to wake her. She squirms then nestles—resettles her small copper hands, one above the other on the folds of her skirt.

Last night she acted the good soldier and did everything I asked. It took both of us to drag Guillermo to the middle of the room and onto my tarp. She held the lantern while I used my tweezers and magnifying glasses to pick debris from his ravaged shoulder. We flushed the wound with the last of her father's liquor and Guillermo slipped into a stupor.

Alma left the hut and came back with potatoes, shriveled in their skins, the pulp dry from being buried too long in the ashes. We sat on the floor facing each other, coaxing our desiccated supper down our throats with unpurified water from tin cups. There was a moment before I had taken a drink, when I thought to get iodine from my pack to treat the water, but Alma had already emptied her cup with such decisive confidence—to question her gifts seemed ungracious.

We'd finished eating, and still she sat with her dark eyes trained on me, silent in the alert and abiding way cats are silent.

"What is it Alma?" I asked.

She was quick getting to her feet, stepping to the side of Manuel's cot. "Tayta." Her chin quivered.

In the aftermath of gunshots, I had gone to Manuel's side, tried to find a pulse, closed his eyes and covered him while Alma stood by, mute and fiercely aloof.

"Forgive me, Alma," I said.

We heated water and washed Manuel, lathered and rinsed and combed his hair. Alma found his wool slacks and a white shirt. We struggled with a pair of scuffed brown oxfords that even in life must have been awkward on his feet, then shrouded his body in blankets.

Alma took a rosary from a pocket in her skirt and climbed onto my lap. She began praying, Hail Mary, word on word, bead on bead, over and over. She wrapped her arms around my waist and we held each other and slept.

"I'm going for help," I tell Guillermo.

He nods, feverish and glassy-eyed, and I hesitate—second-guessing, yet again, the only decision that makes any sense.

I stuff my jacket pockets with stale tortillas and ask Alma to fill Manuel's canteen with water for me. She follows me through the adjacent room and halts at the threshold. I step outside into wan morning light.

"Keep the door bolted," I say. "And make sure the gun is where you can reach it." Strange directives to give a child, but I tell myself that I'll hurry, that, somehow, Alma and Guillermo will be all right.

I step onto the path of tire tracks that brought me here. A band of light behind crimped pink clouds is fading and the sky brightens to a fragile blue. One of the dogs comes to sniff my legs. He trots ahead of me for awhile, then veers off into the tufted expanse. Later, I catch sight of him in the distance, loping back toward the hut with something in his mouth—going home to Alma. It's still early. I check my watch, almost seven. The tire tracks have disappeared and a vast stretch of rocky terrain looms in front of me. The morning seems oddly placid.

I hike the low side of a rise, keeping to places that are broad and flat enough for a car or truck to travel. My sock is bunched in the heel of my boot and I sit on the ground to straighten, re-lace, and take a drink. A shadow passes overhead and I look up. A condor, huge and black, comes again, swoops low and exam-ines me with a predatory tilt of his head. I stand and yell, wave him off, and start walking. He extends his wingtip feathers like rows of out-stretched fingers and rides upward on a current of air. I watch him glide just beyond the hump of the hill, not far, circling, and hovering. When he makes his descent, there's a sick flutter in my stomach. I pick up the pace.

From the top of the knoll, I spot the truck, pitched and top-pled on the incline of a shallow ravine. I pull out my binoculars. The baskets and boxes Hernan forced Guillermo to load at gun-point are strewn down the hillside, their contents scattered. Several yards from the truck, I locate the condor perched on the torso of a man. The bird's head bobs and tugs, picking at the face and neck. I search, quadrant by quadrant. Hernan and Jorge left the hut together; one of them is missing. I let the bin-oculars fall on their strap around my neck and take off running down the hill, damning Hernan every step of the way. Guiller-mo's probably dying. I don't have time for this.

I step around the truck's cab, stooping to peer through the windshield. Vacant—the glove box gaping and nothing but a filthy pack of cigarette papers and the metal hull of a thermos that rolls back-and-forth across the window of the earthbound door when the wind blows.

I remove my jacket and come at the bird waving and snap-ping the fabric. He pulls his head back to strike and unfurls his wings, beats them at me and squawks. And I back off, but now I'm sure the body is Hernan's—the same regulation boots—too tall and lean to be Jorge. I consider leaving Hernan to the bird. And then I remember the gun. The gun's not in the truck. If it's not on Hernan, Jorge must have it.

I pry a broken slat from the back of the truck and take the emergency whistle out of my backpack, get mentally ready, and make a running, high-pitched charge at the bird. This time he shrieks and flutters, takes long, barely airborne hops across the ground and settles not more than twenty feet away, still watching.

The bird's picked at Hernan's mutilated ear and one of his eyes. Nothing's left but a socket. The other eye is all pupil, fixed on the sky. His shirt is ripped and the sparse hair on his chest is matted with dry blood, there's swelling. I look for an injury, maybe sustained from the steering wheel when the truck lost traction. Instead, between the breast bone and left nipple, I find two distinct puncture wounds that look like snake bite. It's a puzzle; snakes usually strike ankles or fingers, some extremity. And then I see, his right hand and arm are disfigured, horribly swollen, still clutching a piece of torn cloth.

I pull the fingers back. The fabric is adhered like a bandage, stiff with blood. I peel it away. The center of Hernan's hand has been savagely bitten. The ring falls through a frayed hole in the shirt pocket and drops to the ground between my knees. I pick it up, sticky with blood, and wipe the face of it on my pants. Hernan's blood is on my hands, staining my cuticles, under my fingernails, viscous, the smell sticky sweet.

Unobstructed sun beats down. I wobble, feel sickened, dizzy. I see the ring become limber in my hand, begin to stretch and curl, turn into a bright yellow snake the length of my forearm. I stare, stunned and perversely fascinated. The snake twines around my wrist and up my arm, then angles back. The animal lifts its head from my palm, gazes into my eyes. Images of Hernan begin to reel through my mind—I see him squirm and flinch against the movement in his pocket, the strike on his chest. He bats, yells. The truck swerves. Hernan yanks, then tears at the pocket of his shirt. He stiffens, jams his foot on the brake. Jorge is hollering. The vehicle flips. Hernan is wild, trying to catch his breath, clawing at his chest. He scrambles out the truck's open window with Jorge pushing him from behind.

"Enough!" I shout. The word is hoarse in my throat. I shut my eyes and feel the serpent shrink in my hand. It slides and nuzzles, then twines itself around my finger.

I'm crouching, trembling and weak-kneed beside Hernan, my field of vision eclipsed to a throbbing sunspot—maybe the beginning of a migraine. I press my eyes shut and wobble to a stand. I stare down at Hernan's chest, disbelieving—the puncture wounds are gone—no fang marks, only a bloody gash. I look, and look again, then stoop to check his palm. It's abraded and swollen around an intentional looking slice that cuts the lifeline—nothing else. But the ring is on my hand; its etched hollows caked with Hernan's blood—observable and solid—an implausibly perfect fit.

I want shade, to lie down and shut my eyes. Instead, I turn away and stumble off, leave Hernan's body to the bird. Jorge is out there somewhere, headed toward the highway—or back to the hut. He's got a gun. I try to anticipate what he might do, but without Hernan, Jorge's a cipher. I don't even know if he's dangerous.

I keep moving, unsure that I'm headed in any helpful direction. The caress of the snake's skin haunts my arm. I rub and rub, but the feeling persists. I try to focus on Koyam, hold on to the prospect of her help, or understanding—or I don't know what. As if just being in her presence will make sense of something.

Faint, but unmistakable—a dog barks and someone answers. I rush toward the sound, a downhill balancing act with my pack. Minutes later, I spot an Indian boy and his dog, funneling slow-moving sheep along the bottom of a narrow ravine.

Loose stones warn the boy that I'm coming and he halts to watch my descent.

I speak choppy, urgent words in Quechua, tell the boy that I'm looking for the highway, that my friend's been hurt, that he needs help.

"*La Hacienda Sangradiste*," he offers. "There's a road to the highway." He points in the direction the sheep are headed. "Not far," he tells me. "Señor Esteban will help you."

He beckons to me and rejoins the dog. He looks back to make sure I'm coming, then wields his stick and harangues the sheep, dealing sharp blows and a tirade of curses.

Soon, the gorge drops away to pasture and croplands swarming with men picking and hustling to dump their baskets into trucks that move among the rows at a snail's pace.

The boy hollers and points past a broad complex of orchards and vineyards, paddocks and stables and gardens, to a huge house, painted white with rows of carmine-colored shutters and cantilevered balconies.

"*Gracias*," I say. "Thank you." And I dodge around the rumps of his trotting sheep and pick up the pace, heading toward the house.

I mount the steps and walk the width of the columned veranda. The doorknocker is a heavy iron ring. I deliver three decisive strikes—and wait, listening for footsteps, but the wind's kicked up, sighing and clamoring through the tops of the trees that crowd the house, sweeping the porch with incessant whispers. My nerves feel like they're on the outside of my body.

I knock again, fierce pounding this time. Almost at once, a Latina woman in a stiff maroon dress and white apron pulls the door ajar.

"*Cómo*," she says—more scold than question.

"*Señor Esteban*," I barely start.

"*Señor Esteban no está aquí.*" She dips her head, as if to say our business is finished and moves to shut the door, but I push it back with the heel of my hand.

"Wait," I insist. "*¿Usted habla inglés, o Quechua? Es muy importante. Por favor.*" A quiver is building at the edge of my voice. Desperation makes me angry. My cheeks are hot.

She relents, steps backward. "Un momento," she says, and leaves me holding the door, staring into a cavernous vestibule of polished wood and antique rugs.

The hollow clanging of a brass bell comes from the back of the house. Minutes pass. I'm about to call out—to knock again, when an older man with skin that looks permanently sun-burned, pushes through the swinging doors beyond the stair-case. He's fresh from the stables, carrying a beat up cowboy hat in one hand and brushing dust from the arm of his shirt with the other. Flecks of straw and dry manure cling to his tooled boots. He smells of horse sweat.

He tells me his name is Sandoval in English so tortured by a Spanish accent that it's hard to penetrate, but it's clear, he's a person in charge. I follow him to a sun porch off the main par-lor. He points and I sit in one of the wicker chairs. He takes a seat facing me and settles his hat in his lap.

I speak slowly, enunciate, watching the flint centers of his eyes for signs of comprehension, or disbelief. Even rendered at the bone, my predicament sounds surreal—that I've been walking since sunup, looking for help, that my friend's been shot and I've left him in a remote hovel alone with a child and a dead man.

Sandoval pats the cigarettes in his shirt pocket, eases his forefinger and thumb inside, shakes the pack, and clutches a protruding cigarette at the corner of his mouth. He rises, drops his hat in the chair and moves to face one of the screened windows. I watch the back of him—striking a match, cupping the flame with his palm. He inhales and mulls the smoke, blows in a smooth stream, gazing outside—while the pendulum of the huge clock in the adjoining room makes me crazy repeating its metered arc.

Finally he turns, stubs the butt of his cigarette in the terra cotta ashtray. He picks up his hat, fingers the rim, and looks at me.

I straighten in my chair.

He suggests we retrace my route on horseback and instructs the maid to take me to the storage locker where they keep supplies and livestock medicines. "Take what you think you need," he says.

I ask if it's possible for me to use the telephone first.

He leads me into the next room and points to the end of a library table. "I'll tell the housekeeper you'll come find her when you're done," he says. He steps away, over the room's threshold, and slides the mahogany pocket doors closed behind him.

I rummage in my backpack for Guillermo's wallet, remove and sort through the small packet of papers stuffed in the front fold. Not much: his university ID, a photograph of two girls in summer dresses with the names Elena and Charisa penciled on the back, the stub of his train ticket to Cuenca. And Eduardo's business card with an extra telephone number and the letter c scrawled in the margin.

The operator listens while I manage the numbers in Spanish. When the phone begins to ring, a sudden pulse throbs in my throat. I can barely breathe.

"*Hola. Está es el Departmento de Antropólogía.*"

"*¿Habla inglés?*" I ask. "I need to speak to Dr. Sircusa."

"He's in a meeting," she says. "Would you like to leave a message?"

"It's an emergency," I say. "Please, tell him it's Megan Kimsey. He'll want to speak to me."

She hesitates but relents. "Please, hold," she says.

My palm is sweating. I pass the receiver to my other hand, wipe the dampness on my pants.

Eduardo comes on the line. "Megan? What's happened?" His words sound thick, tentative.

"Guillermo's been shot. It's bad. I left him early this morning to find help. Now I'm on my way back."

"Where are you?"

"A hacienda. It can't be far from Cuenca, called *La Sangradiste*. Do you know it?"

"I'll figure it out. Where's Guillermo?"

"About seven hours from here, on foot. Due north about two hours and then northeast. A man named Sandoval, the foreman here, is getting horses. I don't think there's a road."

"What's your plan?"

"We're headed back to the hut with medicines. If Guillermo's still alive, I'll do what I can and Sandoval will go for help. But it's not just Guillermo. I've left him there with a child. There are two bodies to bring out and a truckload of artifacts."

"Good lord, Megan. Bodies and artifacts?"

"It's complicated. I'll tell you what I know when I see you. One of the men was killed in a truck rollover several miles from the hut. There are Inca relics strewn over a hillside and down a ravine."

"I'm coming. I'll arrange a helicopter and get there as soon as I can. Whatever you do, don't get the police involved, not yet. Antiquities theft is a serious offense. I don't want you and Guillermo implicated. Keep the foreman with you. I'll take care of the rest."

In the supply room, I pack a pair of saddlebags with bandages and medicines then go to wait for Sandoval on the trellised patio that overlooks the stables.

The housemaid offers a glass of water and a plate of food. I gulp the water down, but I have no appetite. Anyway, there's no time. I see Sandoval and one of his men leading three horses through the gate. He beckons and I run to join him.

Sandoval swings astride of the saddle of a tall chestnut gelding. He secures the lead on the packhorse, and I mount the horse he's outfitted for me.

"*¿Dónde están?*" he asks.

I point and we head out at a gallop.

Sandoval draws his horse to a halt and sits high and still in his saddle. I bring my horse next to his. The shallow valley is folded in late-day angles of shadow and light, and below us, in a stark slant of burnished sun, is the wrecked truck and the tumbled debris. A lone fox streaks through the dormant chaos into the parched grasses.

Sandoval flicks the reins and clicks his tongue, coaxes his horse down the sloping hillside. I follow a beat behind. He dismounts and leads his horse around the truck, halts to look at what's left of Hernan's body, then turns away to wander among the spilled baskets. He surveys as he walks, sometimes pushing or turning a thing with the toe of his boot. Once, and again, I see him stoop, pick up something, and slip it into his jacket pocket.

"We're wasting time," I say. "We need to go."

Alma's silhouette haunts the hut's entrance. She stands, still as a mannequin, one arm poised to shut the door. I ask Sandoval to wait and I ride out ahead of him, dismount, take a few steps, and call her name. Alma comes running. She throws her arms around my waist, clinging and crying hot, moist tears that saturate the fabric of my shirt. I stoop and gather her into my arms, shush a kind of comfort close to her ear and ask, "Is he still alive?"

The room is closed, oppressively hot, and ripe with the rank-sweet odor of festering flesh. Alma has a fire blazing. I lay a hand on Guillermo's forehead. His eyelids flutter. He breathes in labored rasps through cracked lips. In spite of the heat, he's shivering. I administer a hefty dose of antibiotics and give him codeine, prop his head, grease his lips, pull the stool close and settle in. I feed him water, half a spoonful at a time. Again and again, I tell him that he must swallow, that Sircusa is coming, that soon we'll get him to a hospital.

Sandoval hovers but his interest is perfunctory and Alma makes him nervous. He can't help glancing toward the wooden shelf where she sits, cross-legged—her elbows on her knees; her head propped in her hands—eyeing Sandoval with the fierce unsettling demeanor of a gargoyle.

"It's hot as hell in here," he says and heads outside.

Faint but unmistakable, a droning distant, wop-wop-wop.

"*Está aquí,*" Sandoval shouts from outside the hut.

Alma rushes to the door ahead of me, then comes back to grasp my hand.

The helicopter is a bright speck in a darkening sky. But soon the glass and metal hulk closes in, blazing lights hovering, descending in a whirl of its own wind, churning dust and bits of dry grass into the air. Eduardo's face is refracted in the curved glass. He lifts a hand and I wave back. He leans to speak to the pilot, then pushes out the door and hurries to loosen the straps that anchor the stretcher. I let go of Alma's hand and run to help him, so glad he's here I have to swallow hard to keep from crying. We stand at either end of the litter, glancing at each other, words useless next to the idling engines.

I've prepared Guillermo and primed Sandoval and Alma in how this will go—what must be done. Alma leads the way to Guillermo's cot and he's lifted onto the stretcher. Sandoval and Eduardo take him to the helicopter and secure him for the flight. I touch Guillermo's face and begin to step away but Eduardo catches my arm. His hand is on my shoulder. He leans close. His voice strains to be heard.

"I'll hurry," he says. "Stay here. Wait for me."

Sandoval and Alma watch with me until the helicopter is nothing but a glint on the horizon.

"I've got to get going, "Sandoval says. "I could leave a horse."

"It's okay," I say. "Eduardo will be back soon, probably with his colleagues and the police—and their Jeeps, or trucks, or another helicopter. Go. You've literally saved my life. Thank you. Alma and I will be fine."

I stand outside the hut's doorway watching Sandoval leading the horses behind him, their lumbering haunches rising and falling as they plod through the long grass. The wind billows my jacket, beats it like a sail.

18 CAPAQ-ÑAN

I wander back into the hut and look over at the empty cot, the blankets thrown back beneath the fractured shaft of light that streams through the high shutters. A cloud of dust motes drift and glint, as if the air is some viscous solution. My eyes settle on Alma, sitting in a shadowed corner on the floor, her knees drawn up beneath her skirt—darning the sleeve of a sweater. I cross my arms, grip my flesh and bone shoulders, hoping for substance. Alma and I could be ghosts, how would we know?

One of the dogs prances in carrying a rabbit in his mouth. He makes a beeline for Alma, lays his quarry at her feet, and she leans forward, her mouth softening in a rare smile. She sets the sweater aside and ruffles the dog's fur, wraps her arms around his shaggy neck, then stands, regal and in charge. She lifts the limp rabbit by its back legs.

"*Mihuy?*" she asks—Am I hungry?

"*Arí,*" I say—sure. I'm not, but we should eat. It's what the living do.

The dog follows her outside and I go to rummage through the cans and boxes of supplies left from Sandoval's saddlebags—evaporated milk, rice, dried apples. A few minutes, and she comes back with the carcass, gutted and skinned, prepared for the fire.

Alma and I lift our heads, both of us silent, listening—barely breathing. Outside, the dogs are barking. In the distance, something with a motor lumbers toward the hut. It can't be Eduardo; it's too soon. I take Manuel's gun from the shelf, pull the hammer back with my thumb and go to stand in the doorway.

I watch the Land Rover manage the last quarter mile of rutted track with the dogs lunging at its windows and nipping the tires.

Close in, I recognize Corbin, big as life in khaki work clothes and a flat-brimmed leather hat. Henriette sits beside him, looking so bleak and tense that I imagine she is literally holding on to her seat.

The vehicle comes to a stop in front of the hut, and the dogs, as if they have an agreement, take up separate positions at each of the passenger doors, bristling their hackles, menacing with low snarling growls.

Corbin lowers his window a crack. "For god's sake." he says. "A little help here."

Alma looks to me for a sign. I uncock the gun, drop the arm that holds it to my side, and she calls to the dogs.

Corbin thrusts the Land Rover's door open. "Some welcome," he says. "Who are you gunning for?"

"Maybe you," I say, "What are you doing here?"

"Eduardo radioed us last night. He said you were in trouble. We've come to catalogue the artifacts." Corbin peers beyond my shoulder, then strides past me and hunkers low enough to fit through the hut's door. I follow him inside.

"The artifacts aren't here," I say.

He scans anyway, checks the walls, the corners. "What's under the tarp?"

"A man's body—on the verge of becoming unpleasant. Want to take a look?"

"Really. God. What happened?"

"I'd rather wait until Eduardo gets here. It's complicated."

"Then tell me where to find these artifacts," he says.

Corbin probes my memory for uncertain directions, but it's not that simple. He ushers me into his vehicle. Alma begs to come too, but I send her back to the hut, implore her please, to wait here for Eduardo. I perch between Corbin and Henriette straddling the Land Rover's gearshift. He cranks the engine and we lurch forward across the puna. Ahead, the terrain rises and falls over an ocean of rocky ledges and hillocks. We pitch, shoulder thumping shoulder, suffering a rough intimacy that none of us wants.

Three times now—always the knoll and then the wreck.

Corbin is out of the Land Rover and halfway down the hillside before I can scoot across the seat.

Henriette and I walk to the lip of the incline together, not a gasp from her or a word between us.

I can't help but look to the place where Hernan's body still molders in the tarp Sandoval and I trussed around him—the place where the snake climbed my arm and I saw through its eye. I push my hand deep inside my pocket.

Corbin runs halfway up the hill hollering for Henriette to bring him his ledger and journal. She goes to reach over the vehicle's tailgate and gets them, then descends the hill a few steps behind me, both of us walking toward Corbin. His face is flushed. He's intensely focused, snatching artifacts from the ground, using a magnifying glass or sometimes holding one up to the sun to assess a detail or look at a marking. He arranges small groupings on the grass. Henriette hands him his books.

"Should you be doing this?" I say. "Maybe I've seen too many American television shows, but aren't you interfering with a crime scene?"

"The crime would be to let these disappear. Besides, we aren't taking anything, just cataloging what's here so nothing disappears. Think of it as a service to the authorities," he says. "I hope I brought enough boxes. Both of you—go back and get an armload. Let's get them down here, see what we've got to work with. Henriette?"

Henriette keeps her back to him and stoops to handle a small terracotta figurine. "I'll do it," she says. "Just give me a minute."

She looks up at me. "Where did these come from?"

"Manuel said he found them in a natural cavern, somewhere south of Quito."

"A shame," she says, "so much information lost. It's best when we find these in context." She puts the little clay man back where Corbin had placed him. "I suppose we should get Jasper his boxes."

Corbin barks directions all afternoon, and the three of us work. At dusk, I threaten to start walking back by myself and he relents. We trudge up the hill and climb back into the Land Rover. Corbin shifts from first to second gear and turns on the headlights. The last distance is all incline. I sit high in my seat, straining my eyes. Eduardo must have made it to the hut by now. I should have been there, but Corbin is a jackass. Everyone's concerns sublimated to his prime directive, getting every last artifact tagged, wrapped and methodically tucked into exactly the number of boxes he brought, a feat as improbable as the loaves and fishes.

The hut's window is a slice of light. The Land Rover's head-lamps pan past an unfamiliar Jeep parked next to what's left of Hernan's scavenged car.

"That must be Eduardo's," I say. "I need to get out."

Henriette fumbles with the handle, throws the door open. Her feet barely meet the ground and I'm sliding out behind her.

Eduardo meets me at the door. He's smiling, looking more relaxed than I've ever seen him—no suit or tie or crisp white shirt. He's wearing a brown leather jacket, creased and worn soft, over a denim shirt and jeans, hiking boots instead of pol-ished oxfords.

"Well?" I say. "How is he?"

"Guillermo's going to be okay," he says. "It was touch-and-go last night, but he was stable when I left. They've scheduled him for surgery on his shoulder tomorrow morning. A few days in the hospital in Cuenca, then he'll be transferred to Guayaquil, closer to his family."

I'm so relieved I'm weak. Sudden tears flood my eyes. I throw grateful arms around his neck and he holds me. His em-brace is firm. I register the caress of his hand on the middle of my back, and I feel soothed and supported—and loved.

"Thanks for coming yesterday," I say, "for everything," There's so much I want to tell him. I wish we were alone, but we're not.

Corbin closes the Land Rover's tailgate with a slam and walks to the hut's door where we're standing. Henriette trails behind him. He clears his throat, emanating impatience.

We shift our attention; put our hands in our pockets.

"I realize this has been an awful business," he says, "but it's getting late. Eduardo, we should talk. I need to know what kind of deal were you able to make." he says.

"All good news, "Eduardo smiles and glances to include Henriette and me "We got what we asked for. I've arranged with the curator of the Native Cultures Museum in Cuenca to certify and hold any artifacts. The police have agreed, but we have to let them spot check everything and see the manifests before we take anything out of here. They'll need to be taken to the wreck site."

"But we retain control, right?" Corbin says, "This is big, Eduardo. Ruminaui big. But we'll need to do this right. Help me bring in some boxes. You won't believe this."

Eduardo glances at me.

"Go," I say. "I should find Alma. Where is she?"

"Inside with a cup of warm milk. She's had a tough day. The police took her father's body. They'll be back tomorrow to look at the wreck site. They want to talk to you."

Henriette follows me beyond the door. "Forgive me for asking. It's none of my business." She hesitates.

"It's okay," I say. "What?"

"You and Eduardo, are you—seeing each other?"

"Is there some reason why we shouldn't be?" I ask.

"Oh no, nothing like that. It's just—I've worked with him a long time."

We stand there, as if something else needs to be said, but the air's gone stale between us.

Alma and I sit together beside the fire pit gazing into the flames; both of us are tired.

Corbin's battery operated lamp makes bright edges around the curtain that separates the rooms. Voices rise and fall, most words distinct if we choose to hear them. When Alma is ready for bed she looks into my face and confesses, "I gave him Tayta's map."

"That's okay," I say. "We were done with it."

Eduardo crouches beside me, then sits on the floor, tailor-fashion, with his legs crossed. Alma is snoring in soft raspy whispers. He looks at her, and then we smile at each other— maybe because we have a pact to let her go on sleeping, or because this tenuous aloneness makes us feel awkward.

"The water is hot," I say. "There's still some evaporated milk, even sugar to put in it if you like it sweet."

"Not unless you have some," he says.

I set two cups on the flat slab of stone next to the fire pit, pour milk out of the punctured can, then use a folded towel to grasp the water pot's handle and fill each cup, almost to the top.

"Guillermo asked me to tell you that he's grateful. And that he's sorry he wasn't more help. He also told me to ask you about the map."

I add a spoonful of sugar to the milk in my cup, take one sip, and then another. "Alma confessed that she gave you the map. I'm glad. Maybe it will lead you to the cave that Manuel found."

"Alma's a smart girl. It's a miracle she's not more traumatized. She told me about her father and Hernan and Jorge. About the mine and the map, the story of the strange visitation and the bargain for the ring, about how you put it on and challenged Hernan. We had quite a time together. Did you know, she thinks you're a ghost?"

I wrap my hands around my cup and absorb the warmth. "And what do you think?"

"So much has happened. At first I felt like I should ask forgiveness from my profession for taking you seriously, but you keep surprising me."

I sit across from him. I don't speak. I'm not sure what to say. We look at each other in the firelight.

He leans forward, as if something's just occurred to him. "Megan, listen to me. We have our expedition. You practically dropped it in our laps. Join us. Let's follow this map. You come along as a resource, really more of a guide. There's money to pay you. Corbin and I are ready to put whatever it takes into an expedition to locate this cavern. We would be crazy to go public with this set of amazing pieces without trying to locate where they were taken from. Every scavenger looking for a quick buck would try to beat us to it. What do you say?"

"You have the map. I'm sure Corbin already has a journal article half written. You can send me a galley before it goes to print. I'd like that. But I'm going to Baños as soon as I can get Alma settled. I promised her father I'd take her to the nuns in Cuenca. After that, before I do anything else, I need to see Koyam."

He takes a sip from his cup and stares into the fire. "I'm not going to be able to change your mind, am I?"

"I don't think so."

"Okay," he sets his cup down, sighs, and rubs his chin. "Change of plan. Let me take you to Baños."

I hesitate, ready to decline.

"At least hear me out," he says. "Koyam may not agree to see you. She has huge demands on her time and she's a person who prefers solitude. She's been known to send pharmaceutical reps and journalists away with their tails between their legs. I've worked with her for a long time; we're friends. If she needs convincing, I can do that for you."

I'm stunned silent—remembering Koyam on the airplane. Even then, we seemed to be part of something together.

"Please," he says, "let me do this for you. Let me be there with you. I won't interfere."

Corbin pulls the curtain in the doorway back. He's been standing behind it listening. "If Eduardo's offering, you'd be a fool not to take him up on it. It's no small feat to get to her."

He ducks into the room. His eyes go straight to the ring on my finger. I feel my vertebrae stiffen, bracing for a confrontation.

Instead, he says, "I'm coming to Baños with the two of you. I wouldn't miss it. Henriette can soldier through these boxes and get the early work done. We won't be gone long and she'll have everything cleaned and organized by the time we get back."

I watch for Eduardo through the windows of the hotel lobby. It rained last night, torrential rain that spattered against the roof and coursed the gutters. There are puddles in the street and a cool sheen on the bricks beneath the lamp post. When the sun comes up, everything will look washed and new.

Eduardo pulls the car, not his little Austin Healey, but a boxy blue sedan, close to the curb. I push out the hotel door with my bags.

"Good morning," he says, leaning in with a brief kiss and a tired smile.

"Is it morning?" I say, and he deposits my suitcase and backpack in the trunk.

He steps to open the front passenger door for me. I open the back door instead.

"Corbin can have the front seat," I say. "It's okay. I prefer the back."

The scenery slips past the car's window. I try to be a good tourist but my mind is already at Koyam's door. If she doesn't know why I've come, how will I explain? I straighten in my seat, sit back against the leather upholstery and look past the back of Corbin's head to the road ahead of us. I pull the map from its zippered pocket, unfold and spread it across my lap, locate and trace the yellow line that marks the highway with my finger. Three hundred and nine kilometers; it will take us six, maybe seven hours to get from Cuenca to Baños.

We climb, dip, and climb again, creeping along hillside roads that are narrow and precipitous, navigating endless, repetitive turns with sunlight flickering through the canopy of trees. The three of us stiffen and lean in unison, as if keeping the car from sliding over the edge is a balancing act.

I doze for awhile then wake with a wave of nausea hanging in my throat. I think I might need to ask Eduardo to stop and let me out. I roll the window down a crack. The breeze rushes in and I lean back against the seat, position my face to meet the coolness, and close my eyes.

"*Allí.*" Eduardo's voice startles me. He's pointing.

I jerk forward, tremulous and still dazed with sleep. I grip the back of the front seat, rise slightly so I can see. There, in the valley below us, is Baños, small and ethereal, smudged by wisps of fog.

In town, we stop at the mayor's office and take on a thin young man named Luis who wears a blue suit and talks to us in heavily accented English. Luis explains that he is the mayor's assistant, that it will be his great honor to drive the car back from the trailhead. He assures Eduardo that the car will be parked at the mayor's house.

"Even," he says, "in the mayor's own garage."

Twenty minutes outside of town, Eduardo takes us off the road. The car lumbers and sways over shallow clefts and rocks embedded in a grassy meadow. We stop not far from a fast-moving river.

"This is it," Eduardo says.

On the river's far bank, like a necklace that hugs the base of the mountain then curves upward to ascend its shoulder, is a path bordered by a strand of white stones.

"*Capaq Ñan*," I whisper—the barest of utterances, and I wonder if I'm dreaming, how else to explain this sense of recognition, the spasm of soaring affection, the embarrassment of tears. "You're looking at a wonder," Sircusa tells me, "a well preserved Inca Road. Part of a system of roads the Inca called *Capaq Ñan*."

Eduardo opens the trunk and we take our backpacks, struggle into them, adjust the straps at the shoulder and waist.

Luis promises that, beginning in three days time, and every afternoon until we return, he will come here to wait for us.

19 THE SHAMAN'S APPRENTICE

We head upriver, stalking the bank, and make a common decision to cross at a place where the river narrows and cascades around and between pillars of igneous rock. Each of us hesitates on the brink. Eduardo goes first.

The trail ascends quickly, in the steepest places up steps hand-fitted, stone-to-stone. We travel at a fast clip until the air turns noticeably thinner and we're forced to make frequent stops, to lean or sit beside the trail and rest in the bald heat.

None of us is immune to the light-headed nausea and throbbing headache, but Corbin feels it most. He hangs back, insists that Eduardo and I go ahead. We trek on a few yards, then stop and wait while he vomits in the brush.

"*Soroche*," Eduardo calls it – another name for altitude sickness. "Not much farther," he says. Soon he stops at the top of a steep rise and motions with a wave of his arm. "That's where we're going."

Down the slope and off the trail by at least a quarter mile, I think I see what he's trying to show me. I fumble for my binoculars and adjust for distance. Muted by mist and organic as a mushroom, Koyam's house sits on a perch of craggy grassland, a thatched relic with walls built entirely of Inca stone. I stare through the lenses, my muscles iced with sudden reluctance.

The door is a rough wooden slab, painted red. Instead of a knob, there's a stout leather handle. Eduardo raps with the side of a curled fist. He shouts Koyam's name and pounds again— nothing, only the alarmed chatter of birds nesting in the thatch above the lintel. Eduardo steps away from the house and takes out the emergency whistle he wears on a chain around his neck. He blows three shrill staccato bursts. We scan the hillside, crane our necks, and listen.

"We'll wait," he says. "Maybe she heard."

"Let's hope. It's getting late," says Corbin, looking even more pinched and ill.

I offer my canteen. "Dehydration makes it worse," I say.

"Too nauseous," he says, and waves the canteen away. He goes to sit in the shadow of Koyam's house with his back against the foundation, slumped with his elbows on his knees, his head propped in his hands.

I follow him. "Deep breathing helps," I say. "We should get you to a lower altitude while you can still walk. If you're better, we could come back tomorrow."

He sighs and lowers his head a notch. "I'll be fine," he says. "Just let me rest."

I join Eduardo on a rocky promontory not far from the house where the view is better. At first we stand and gaze, and then we pace, but after awhile, Eduardo finds a flat rock shaded by a ragged clump of trees where he can sit and lean back with his hat over his eyes.

The plodding clank of tin bells is the first sign. Seconds later, Eduardo and I spot Koyam trekking toward the house through a stand of trees, the striped colors of her cloak flashing red and white. She emerges from the tree trunks and shadows into a rock-studded clearing with three goats trotting behind her. Eduardo calls her name and waves with his arms above his head. She salutes us with her walking stick and quickens her step.

I stall on the brink, not afraid exactly, but bracing myself, the way a diver prepares to enter unfamiliar water.

Eduardo starts down the incline ahead of me, taking long strides at first, and then running. He greets her with an embrace and dutiful kisses brushed across one cheek and then the other. But Koyam only has eyes for me. She pulls away from Eduardo and gives him her walking stick. She comes and takes my hands in hers. For an instant she pauses to appreciate the ring, nods, as if to say she knew I'd be wearing it, and then she gazes into my face. Her grasp is urgent, all sinew and bone and knuckle, spare and fierce as a bird's claw. The rough pads of her thumbs caress my fingers. She nods and smiles.

"I've been preparing," she says. "Tonight we will take a spirit journey. Have you eaten today?"

"Not much," I say.

"That's good," she says. She circles my waist with her arm and we begin walking toward the house.

Corbin's spotted us coming. He's on his feet, leaning beside the door. His usually ruddy skin looks moth gray in the shadowed light. He makes an effort to smile, but the lines in his face are winced and hard.

Koyam looks him up and down. "*Soroche*," she says.

He gives a wan shake of his head. "Fix me up, will you?"

The three of us hover around Koyam with the goats bleating and nosing us from behind. The door is swollen inside its frame.

She pushes. When it doesn't give, she lifts a booted leg and slams the solid center of it with a single, well-placed kick. It swings open, a little cockeyed and listing on its hinges.

"Go in," she says, "There's clean water in the jug next to the table. I'll shut the goats in their pen."

Corbin steps over the threshold ahead of me. He ducks to negotiate the doorway and mutters, "Hobbit hole."

He's right. The ground floor is a single expansive room, barely tall enough for Corbin to stand without stooping. I watch him swat his way through the bundles of drying herbs that dangle from the ceiling as he heads for a chair beside the table. He sits, bent forward with his forehead heavy on his arms.

Koyam's house smells of animal dander and camphor, an odd tinge of brittle herbs, lemongrass and fennel. Eduardo stands in the doorway behind me. I feel his eyes on the back of my neck and shoulders. I turn to meet his gaze and he looks back with unabashed interest and a doe-eyed expression that makes me blush. Then, seemingly out of nowhere, and like the wrath of god, a muscular-looking white bird with a sleek topknot shrieks and dives at us. We startle, crouch, raising our arms to protect our heads. The bird jeers and flutters, swoops, traveling back and forth from the top of a suspended cage set wagging on its rope, to the ornate lip of a heavy mirrored credenza. The bird perches and scolds us, then stops to admire its reflection. The commotion sets off a scramble of skitters accompanied by urgent-sounding wheeks and whistles that come from the far side of the room.

Eduardo and I start laughing.

"*Mira*," he says, "come see."

I keep an eye out for the bird and follow him across the room to a place where the floor drops a steep step down to an animal run. Guinea pigs, more than a dozen, converge beneath our shadows, crowding and scratching up the wall to be fed.

Eduardo stoops and grasps a caramel-colored animal with a white face by its scruff and lifts it out of the enclosure. He sets it in my hands and I hold it next to my stomach and use two fingers to stroke its back. It settles on my arm with a drunken purr.

"I wouldn't get too attached," He says with a smile. "It's never a good idea to make friends with your supper."

Koyam hustles back inside carrying a bundle of grass and leafy stalks. She makes a methodical sweep up and down the guinea pig enclosure scattering fodder as she goes. When she's finished, she gives me a few stalks to feed to the animal I'm holding and goes to slip out of her cloak and hang it on a hook that's fixed to the back of the door.

As the cloak drops away from her arms she tells me to come and help her see to Corbin. I hand the guinea pig to Eduardo and cross the room, scanning the rafters for the bird, preparing to be harassed. There are white feathers and down lodged in the slivered surface of the beams, but the bird is nowhere to be seen.

Koyam thumps Corbin's shoulder with the back of her hand. "Sit up," she tells him and he rouses, lifts his head from the table and rears upright looking stunned and pathetic. Koyam probes the flesh over his cheekbones with her fingertips then pulls a lower lid away from an eye. She moves quickly, grabs two tin cups from a shelf behind one of the credenza doors and pours water into one. She tells Corbin to take a mouthful, to swish and spit into the empty cup. Then she unhooks two of the bags from her belt and thrusts them at me. "Take what he needs from these," she says.

I'm left standing next to Corbin with the two pouches in my hands, one less than four inches long, the other half its size. Both are made of soft tooled leather cinched shut at the top with a thin fiber drawstring that's been braided and waxed. Something about the smaller one, maybe its heft and size, or the ritual fineness of its stitching, stirs up an unsettled feeling.

"Well," says Corbin. "Are you going to do something for me or not?"

I nod and focus, insert my finger to broaden the opening of the small bag, remove a lacquered box with a lid that slides with a flick of the thumb and a tiny wooden stick with a slight depression hollowed at the end. I know before I look that the other pouch will be stuffed with leaves. I extract several, layer and sprinkle them with fine ash from the wooden box and roll the leaves into a tight cylinder the size of a bullet.

"It's coca, right?"

"Coca and ash from quinoa," I say. "Chew gently and then sort of suck. Don't swallow the pulp. Use your tongue or finger to pack it between your cheek and gum, like snuff or chewing tobacco."

"I've done this before," he says.

"Good," I say. "Then you know what to expect."

The air has turned mild and still. Koyam props the door open with a rock and several heavy-bellied flies drift inside. They pass through the bright patch of late-day sunlight like winged zeppelins, but there's no breeze. She calls my name and pulls out a chair, pats the huge slab of a table in front of her with the flat of her hand.

"Come. Sit," she says.

It's been an hour, maybe more, and I've only just begun to penetrate Koyam's virtual pharmacy; the shelves lined with labeled containers—bottles and tins of sharp-smelling herbs, black seeds, wizened scarlet berries, tiny amber crystals, shreds of curled bark, corms and shriveled rhizomes, rows and rows of tinctures in their stoppered vials.

I put the bottle that's in my hand back on the shelf – tidy it into line with its neighbors and go to sit next to Koyam in the chair she's pulled out for me.

"Bring the photographs and the tape," she says to Eduardo.

He steps across the room to his backpack and takes a stack of three by five photographs and a small portable tape player out of the front-zippered pocket.

I wonder when they had a chance to talk, but I know these photographs and the tape recording of me with the hypnotist well enough. Eduardo, Corbin, and I have spent hours pondering and re-pondering their details and deciding what to bring. Four of the photographs pieced together show Manuel's map, slightly enlarged, with its strange scrawls and notations. There are photos of the artifacts Manuel took from the cave. The rest, just three, are some of the photos my father sent to Corbin, my drawings of indigenous plants with scribbles describing their magical and medicinal uses.

Eduardo slips into the seat across from Koyam and places the photos and tape player on the table in front of him. He rearranges the order, straightens the stack between the palms of his hands and settles back in his chair. There are dark circles beneath his eyes, though the eyes themselves are bright. He looks from Koyam to me then turns his head.

"Jasper," he says, "Are you coming?"

Corbin makes a ruckus hobbling to the table, wearing one boot and carrying the other with its sock stuffed inside. He's obviously feeling better, still tonguing the bulge of coca in his cheek, his skin flushed with new blood.

"Front and center," Corbin says, and plops onto the chair sideways next to Eduardo. He lifts and guides his pale foot into his sock, taking care not to displace a piece of moleskin he's applied to the side of his big toe.

"Bit of a callus," he says, feigning a wince and smiling. He thrusts his foot into the empty boot but leaves the laces loosened, the tongue hanging out. He shifts to face the table and looks at me with a wry and tolerant grin that I find supremely irritating.

I'm so on edge I can't seem to catch my breath. I fight the urge to push away from the table, to flee this place, to run far and fast. Instead, I bring my hands together and twine my fingers, as if that will help close some frayed circuit.

Koyam reaches across the table and covers my clasped hands with one of hers. She gives a firm squeeze and rises out of her chair to stand beside the table. I watch her remove three coca leaves from her small leather bag.

"*Rastreo de coca*," she says, "a form of divination."

She holds the leaves in her palm, blows across them and tosses them onto the table. They fall in an arc, none of them touching, but their leaf-tips, like arrows, all point in the same direction. She slaps the table with the palm of her hand, takes three more leaves from the pouch and tosses them. One of the leaves inexplicably crumbles as it drops from her hand. The pieces fall among and on top of the others in a dissonant-looking pattern.

"What do you see?" she asks.

I stand up beside her and lean forward to look, astonished at first by the easy way my eyes know how to make sense, and then, abruptly, I stiffen and take a step backward. "I won't read this," I say.

Koyam circles my waist with her arm and yanks me tight against the table.

She traces the trajectory of the leaves from disrupted arrow to disrupted arrow with her finger as if she's following a line of print. She speaks in a hoarse whisper. "Bound in life. Bound in death. Bound in life," a brutal-sounding prognosis that seems to carry the force of law.

"Sounds hopeless. But what does it mean?" Corbin says.

"Yes, what does it mean?" she repeats.

We settle back in our chairs and she asks me to begin at the beginning.

I don't know where the beginning is, so I start with being a child and feeling alone and misplaced in the universe. I explain about the dreams and premonitions and memories that marked me, about Dr. Vickers' attempts to reinterpret and expunge, about the way my Dad defended me, about Bella, and that night in the La Platas—how I dreamt about the cloaked specter on the bridge. I tell her about the puma and the conch, my dreams and the moment on the mountain when I knew I could speak Quechua. I tell her Manuel's story, about the map and the destruction of Ruminaui's mummy, about Hernan and the condor, the wreckage and finding Hernan's corpse with the ring in his pocket, even the disappearing fang marks, everything. She takes my hand and examines the ring with an oversized, hand-held magnifying glass. She tells Eduardo to play the tape.

We talk and puzzle and listen while the little house takes on a kind of dugout dimness, until even that sparse daylight dissolves by degrees.

Koyam stoops in front of the cast iron stove with the firebox
door open, stirring the leftover coals, adding fistfuls of dry
grass, then slender twigs. She blows, urging the kindling until it
ignites in a sudden ochre burst that sends her shadow leaping in
an arc over the opposite wall and across the ceiling. In the glow
of the flaring firelight—maybe because I'm in a strange place
feeling raw and exhausted, I see her with fresh and uneasy eyes,
bent over in her woven shawl and heavy woolen skirts, strands
of frizzled gray hair escaping from the heavy braid hanging over
her shoulder. She looks unreadable and dangerous—like a crone
or witch out of some disquieting fairytale. She lifts her head and
we peer at each other from across the room. For an instant I
stand rapt, immobilized by her gaze, feeling like something
small and exposed beneath her dark wing.

"Your cheeks are flushed," she says to me. "Come outside."
She lifts her cloak from its hook by the door and tilts her head
toward Eduardo and Corbin, standing together, practically cantilevered over the table studying a map in a shaft of lantern
light. "They won't miss us."

Koyam lights and lifts a lantern from its hook beside the
doorway, shines it out in front of us. We walk a short distance
from the house to a small outcropping. She hands me the light
and I hold the beam up high for her while she scrambles a short
ways up the rocky shelf. She reaches the top and comes to a
careful stand, then lifts her chin and cups her mouth with her
hands. Once and again, she sends out a clear and lonesome-
sounding trill that's half shriek. She waits, listening with her
head erect and her arms hanging at her sides. Then comes a
warbled whistle.

"Huari, my cousin's nephew—he will bring the ayahuasca now," she says, and she climbs off the rocks and dusts her hands against the front of her cloak.

"I prepared the vines this morning. I added bark from the shadow side of the lapuna negra tree. We must take care, or the visions in this brew will send us straight to hell. Tonight, it will be important to invite the darkness as well as the light."

I feel myself shrink back, wanting to regroup, reconsider. I've never used mind-altering drugs. Not marijuana—nothing. If my dad were here, this is the line he'd refuse to let me cross. But I'm already mired in this thing; didn't I insist? It's like one of my premonitions—whatever's coming, it might as well have already happened. I scrutinize Koyam, wondering if she senses this inevitability the way that I do.

"But how could you be so sure I would arrive today?" I say.

"Have you not felt me?" she asks, "perching at the edge of your dreams."

She doesn't wait for an answer, but lifts a hand to rub the back of her neck and gazes up at the sky. Above us, a fast moving cloud obscures, and then reveals, a bright slice of moon.

"We should go back now," she says.

Koyam props the door open with a rock, then goes from window to window throwing open the shutters. Cool night air stirs the brittle warmth, wavers the light of the candles and lanterns. Koyam reaches into a deep niche in the stone wall and brings out a rolled-up mat and a small bundle. She sets the bundle in my hands, kneels and unfurls the mat on the floor in front of her, then sits back on her heels, rests her palms on her knees, and begins to pray, a low guttural prayer that is half song.

I stand motionless, feeling like an acolyte and holding the bundle close to my stomach. I glance, barely turning my head, to locate Eduardo and Corbin. They've stationed themselves on the periphery.

Koyam's chant ends and she stares at something no one else can see.

My legs ache. I need to move and stretch. A bobbing sense of dread has my stomach on edge. I try to pray, but it's like writing a letter when all you can come up with is the salutation.

A candle smokes and sizzles, dying in its own pool of wax and Corbin's breathing makes a repetitive nasal circle. Somewhere, not far, frogs call back and forth, insistent—kvac, kvac, kvac.

And then Koyam is pushing herself off her knees, forcing her body upright with a final, stiff lurch. She takes the bundle from my arms and speaks to Corbin and Eduardo.

"Stay or leave. Decide now," she says. "No one shall sit apart. The circle must be maintained. If you choose to leave, you can make yourself a place to sleep in the attic."

"I'll stay," Eduardo says. He looks across the room to me, his expression offering comfort.

"This is the main event," Corbin says. "I have no intention of leaving."

Koyam points, tells us where to sit, Eduardo and Corbin, one on opposite sides of the mat. I sit cross-legged, facing the night through the open door with the pattern of the weaving spread out in front of me.

I touch the mat's surface, gently, with two fingers.

It depicts the hatun laika, the master shaman, his sandaled feet planted in a belligerent stance. He looks out at the world from beneath an elaborate crescent-shaped headdress with his arms thrust wide. In each hand he clutches a writhing serpent. On either side he is flanked by wide-eyed creatures. On his left, four black cats watch, each from one of four ascending trellis-like tree branches. On his right, he is faced by four tiers of human figures with the heads and wings of condors. Above him is a stepped white arch that Koyam has positioned pointing toward the open doorway like an arrow. Only tufts of what must have been a thick swag of fringe remain along the edges at the top and bottom but the colors remain rich. The piece is obviously ancient, but remarkably whole.

Eduardo leans over the pattern and murmurs some small exclamation in Spanish. His cheeks flush with recognition. He exchanges a glance with Corbin. Right now it seems they are in perfect agreement, but it doesn't take a premonition to know there will be another argument about contraband, about another stunning and singular artifact, undeclared and not apt to be surrendered—like the ring on my finger. Only this time, they will air their differences in private. It won't be here and it won't be tonight.

Koyam clears her throat, demanding attention. Her demeanor is grave. "Tonight the ayahuasca will not be enough," she tells me. "Ask your questions, but know that the answers may come in riddles. Keep your wits about you. Be fearless. Don't hesitate. Remember, fears are like attack dogs, they have sharp teeth and a desire to maim. I will do what I can to guide you and keep you from harm, employ every talisman and power at my disposal, but you must do exactly as I say. Do you understand?"

"Yes," I say.

A breeze blows through the open doorway and I turn my face to meet it. From here, backlit by lanterns and candles, the night appears impenetrable. I try to think past this moment, to tomorrow or the day after. Tonight there will be mumbled words and purging and cascades of strange visions. I think I have always known this night would come. But beyond this cycle of light and dark lurks a disconcerting void.

I shut my eyes wanting to reset my thoughts. When I open them again, I'm looking at a man standing at the threshold. I see the edges of his dark woolen poncho, the cuffs of his white shirt. His brown hands hold a pint jar more than half full of amber liquid. He wears baggy pants that end above sturdy ankles and feet in cloth sandals with rope soles. I fix on the feet, broad and dusty with short toes and a pronounced space that sets the big toe apart—Down's syndrome toes. I glance up and see a young man, barely more than a boy, in a felt hat with his hair pulled back in a single thick braid. He watches me with a hesitant demeanor and quiet slits for eyes that are startling to look at—Brushfield spots; he has a whole universe of stars in his eyes. I stare because I can't help myself and he stares back, as if he sees something just as mesmerizing in me.

Koyam claps her hands.

"Huari, pasaykamy," she says. "Hurry now."

Huari re-centers himself, makes a reverent dip of his head to honor the figure in the weaving and maneuvers behind us to take the jar of ayahuasca to Koyam. I hear her instructing him as they move around the room refreshing the lanterns and candles.

Koyam brings the bundle and kneels at the corner of the weaving between Corbin and me, unties and carefully exposes an array of rare and sacred objects. She positions them, one at a time, on the weaving in relation to the hatun laika. A globe of rose quartz the size of a baseball is assigned to the place where the Master Shaman's heart would be. A pipe made of pale wood whose carved bowl resembles the head of a bird she aligns horizontally above his headdress. She pulls open the drawstring of a tiny cloth pouch and folds it from the top until its shouldered bottom resembles a grass-lined nest that contains a clutch of small green-speckled bird eggs—this she sets at his feet.

She attends, corner to corner. On the upper right she mounds a handful of blue-gray pebbles. "Gravel," she tells us, "from the craw of a jungle hawk." An ivory-colored conch whose inner whorl is a radiant blush of oranges and pinks goes across from it. Bottom left—the brittle carcass of a wandering spider.

She reaches into her skirt-pocket and brings out the puma's foot that I carry with me as my talisman. For an instant I'm confused, not sure when or how she got it, and then she tells me to open my hand and she lays the paw across my palm. The slip of fur and bone feels warm and supple against my skin. I close my hand around it, careful not to clutch too tightly because I have an odd sense it might begin to struggle. I put the paw where I know it belongs—on the corner below the staring figures of the bird-headed men.

Koyam stands and signals for Huari to approach with the elements. She takes a cigar from the tray he brings and bites off the narrow tip, spits it over her shoulder, licks and sucks the cigar's end to make it moist, then motions for Huari to set the tray with the remaining elements in the center of the weaving. She holds the cigar out for us to see.

"*Mapacho*," she says. "Specially prepared tobacco, it will lift you up. The ayahuasca will be swift when it takes you."

She closes her mouth around it, lights it with the flame of a candle, and draws air through in small kissing puffs until the lit end looks like a coal floating in the dimness. She fills her lungs and paces behind us blowing smoke over our heads, engulfing us in an acrid haze – harsh and bitter on an empty stomach. Not one of us can keep from coughing. The inside of my nose and the back of my throat burns. Tears stream down my cheeks, but I keep my spine erect and my hands folded in my lap.

She leaves a long stub of cigar smoldering on the tray and begins to sing a high-pitched song in a melody intertwined with bird-like whistles and fervent incantations—all praise and warning and invitation to a pantheon of gods and spirits. The song ends abruptly and she sits down, settles in between Corbin and me.

She claps her hands for Huari who stoops and sets the tray on the floor beside her. I watch her pour a portion of the ayahuasca from the pint jar into a small wooden cup that she gives to Corbin. He's quick, tossing the liquid to the back of his throat with his eyes shut tight, his face in a grimace.

She refills the cup and passes it through me to Eduardo. He reaches to take it from my hand but hesitates in mid-motion, looking at me as if there's something he should say.

I smooth a loose strand of hair away from my eye, half expecting him to tell me I have a smudge on my cheek, or how pale and tired I look tonight.

"*Cuídate*," he says. "Come back safe."

"You too," I say.

He drinks and hands the cup back.

Koyam pours for me. I swallow it all in two resolute gulps, heeding Koyam's words, facing my fear. The ayahuasca is slick on my tongue, the taste slightly bitter.

Koyam upends the pint jar and drinks what's left, shakes loose the last clinging drops and licks them from the rim.

She hands the jar off to Huari then sits with her spine straight and begins to emit an odd ethereal hum.

Huari reaches around Koyam and takes a bottle of clear liquor from the tray. He hands the bottle to Corbin first.

"*Aguardiente*," Corbin explains, and demonstrates that we are to hold it beneath our noses and inhale the alcoholic vapors.

After we pass around the bottle, Huari gives each of us a towel moistened with lemon-scented water to refresh our faces and wipe our hands. And then he retires to sit on a bench apart from us in the shadows. I look to Koyam, but her eyes are glazed and staring. She's gone ahead but still, she's singing.

We are left to our own souls and demons—waiting for the drug they call "the little death," to come for us.

I'm nauseous. I feel deserted and I worry that I'm immune. Corbin sits across from me, swaying gently side-to-side, rubbing his face with his hands. And Eduardo, lost to the world, studies the globe of rose quartz, utterly transfixed by a reflected flutter of candlelight.

Sooner or later, probably sooner, I'm going to vomit. I move to get up, to go outside, but a roar like the sound of fast-moving water rushes into my head and I sit down again. My jaw begins to feel numb and the numbness spreads up my cheekbones to my temples. I'm starting to be afraid – maybe there was a mistake, an impurity in the ayahuasca. And then I hear Koyam's song threading through the noise and the pattern on the mat in front of me is bathed in colors so fresh they have no name. Luminous specks appear and glint around me. I lift my hand to touch them and they fan into brilliant streaks that hang in the air like the trails of shooting stars. I'm breathless with wonder and then distracted with a sense that there's something important I should remember. I hear my name and glance toward the sound. One of the bird men turns his head and speaks to me from the weaving. "Hurry," he says, "go now, while these strands of light can be traveled like bridges."

I open my mouth to ask the birdman what do I need to do, but I'm interrupted, jostled and rushed outside, kneeling on pine needles and damp earth, dizzy and vomiting. The roar in my ears is unrelenting. Huari stoops beside me. His hand is on my back. I retch and retch, every convulsion becomes a confession, some willful meanness or botched intention heaved up to be dissected. When I'm hollowed out and one breath follows another, Huari drapes a moist cold towel across the back of my neck and wipes my mouth with the end of it. He lifts the lantern and looks into my face to see how I'm doing. His eyes are iridescent and I feel sorry for myself.

"The bird man was telling me something important," I say. "I was about to understand."

I've never heard Huari speak. I don't know if he can. But I hear him answer in a tone so terse and final I'm sure I've broken some rule.

"Trust the ayahuasca," he tells me, but before the words have a chance to dissipate, I'm wondering if he said anything at all.

I'm shivering and he takes the towel from my neck and wraps his poncho around my shoulders. He leads me through a copse of trees to a spacious outcropping littered with tumbled slabs of Inca stone bleached white and surreal in the moonlight.

Koyam moves among the monoliths shaking a small gourd. The seeds inside the gourd make a dry, hissing rattle.

Eduardo and Corbin are here too. Eduardo lying on the ground with his arms over his face. Corbin sits several yards away, upright with the back of his head against the trunk of a snag that looks more like a jutting bone than a tree. His chin is tilted up; his eyes are open – seeing without seeing, traveling in their sockets.

Huari stays several steps behind while I shamble among the stones and choose one that's level enough to sit on. The stone's coldness penetrates the seat of my pants and I look up at the stars, stare until their edges soften and streak, trying to bring back the light bridges. Just when I think I might be able to see them, I sense something crawling on my hand. I move to shake it off, but glance down, and stop. The snake of the ring lifts its blunt head to peer at me and test the air with its pink tongue. It slips its tail free of my fingers, plumps and stretches to nearly three times its size, then twines around my palm and begins to belly forward along the tracery of veins on the inside of my arm. I watch the way a patient watches a surgeon prepare to make an incision, holding very still, barely breathing.

The snake is on my shoulder, against my neck, behind my ear. It passes through the hairs on my scalp then drops to dangle over my forehead, taut and swinging its body in a slight arc. It stops, cocked and motionless, cantilevered between my eyes.

Koyam is in front of me, gone silent, studying the snake. Corbin hovers at her shoulder, craning his neck, squinting.

I hear Corbin's voice. "Oh God."

With a single, dart-like strike, the snake plunges into the pupil of my right eye. My head recoils, reels on my neck. I see brightness, a searing explosion, then nothing but dark weightless drift.

I am a corporeal thought, a mood, a frequency, tethered to the snake by luminous blue ribbons that undulate, fluorescent in the dark like the tendrils of some deep-sea creature. The snake shimmies forward, towing me swiftly behind him.

"What is this place?" I ask.

"Oblivion," he says. "But there, ahead. Squint a little. You will see."

We are aimed toward a breach of light. We close in, going fast, then faster. A sudden draft of frigid air catches me from underneath. I'm spinning.

There is roaring and friction. A flash, and I'm shot, head first, through a translucent crust into a glinting refracted world of thin air and sky and ice—hemmed in by a forest of ice pinnacles, high altitude obelisks called penitentes. I try to move but my feet are rooted in ice. I'm shivering, wrapped in Huari's poncho—no hat, no gloves, starting to be afraid. A desolate sense of foreboding balloons in my stomach.

"Hello!" I shout. "Is anyone there?" I stand very still and listen, but there's only absence, vast and white and everywhere. Even the snake has deserted me. The ring is gone.

I twine the hem of Huari's poncho around my bare hands and strike at the top of a penitente with my forearm. It cracks. I strike again and again until the peak topples off. But it's no help. In every direction, there are more penitentes, regiments of them looking like white-hooded monks, all facing the sun.

Tiny flecks of ice begin to collect and cling to the threads of Huari's cloak. I brush at them, and notice frost spreading across the backs of my hands. The skin around my eyes and mouth feels stiff. I touch my face, probe with my fingertips, feel frost on my cheeks, in my hair. I brush and rub and scratch at it. Then I scream and twist and rant, but the effort only frustrates and fatigues me. My movements becomes slow and heavy. Soon I can't move at all. I'm fixed, a thin slip of consciousness rimed in ice, my eyes frozen open, watching. Daylight slips through pinks and mottled grays to a darkness that's soft and immense and speckled with stars. Slumbering ice fields groan and shift. The penitentes hum like the tines of a thousand tuning forks.

Time and the qualities of light and dark are my drowsy concerns. Fog drifts in with the dawn, all mist and blurred sun, radiant and inching upward through glaring whiteness. My bald eyes long to squint. I wonder if I'm dead.

Foreign sounds mar the stillness. A plodding crunch, the scrape of feet treading ice. Three cloaked figures pass among the penitentes. I hear a thin complaint.

"Unu." A child's voice asks for water.

One of the men stops in front of me, so close, if it weren't for the ice that binds me, I could reach out and touch the fabric of his woolen cloak. He grasps his mittens with his teeth, tugs one off, and then the other, drops them on the rutted ice at his feet. He undoes the strapping across his chest and hips that secures a basket he carries on his back, then eases the carrier off his arms, positions it upright on the ice. The basket is constructed with a protective awning. As he begins to tip it back, I'm overcome with a wild and inexplicable surge of anticipation.

A child with a close-fitting cap of exotic feathers above a tousle of fine shoulder-length black braids pulls himself to a stand in the basket and raises his arms to be taken out. I know this child, and as if I've been struck by a clarifying burst of light, the moment slows and unfolds in distressingly visceral detail—the strength of the man's arms lifting the child out of the basket, the tilt required to manage his slight weight—an utterance, the deep tenor of the voice that tells the child to step and turn, to urinate where the moisture won't run back onto his feet—these motions, these words, this place . . . I have lived them. I glance at the man's hand looking for the ring on the fourth finger of his right hand. I know it will be there—it is.

"Take care," the man cautions the child. "If your clothes get wet you will have to sit in ice the rest of the way."

The child is finished, his clothes readjusted. The man reaches inside his cloak for a skin of water. He holds the flask steady, dribbles water into the child's mouth, then takes a drink himself and puts the flask away. He lifts the child back into the basket and strokes his head.

The child stands upright holding a piece of jerky in his mittened hand, eyes skyward, tracking the clouds. When he lowers his chin, he catches me gazing at him through the ice.

"Pin?" he asks his father. "Who is it?"

His father is distracted. He motions for the child to turn and sit so he can lower the awning.

He glances at his companions—his mind is lurching. One of them raises an arm, a signal of impatience.

Hate and a knot looped with desperation begin to gnaw beneath my breastbone—feelings so intense and personal, I know I am this man, and that these are General Ruminaui's henchmen, ordered by Atahualpa to goad and press me from behind. They are my keepers, not my friends. In the mind's eye of my frozen lurking self, the hours inexorably reel out in sequence.

My distress at what I see and fear and cannot undo builds like a head of trapped steam against the walls of my chest and roars in my ears. Streaks of blue-white light flash across my vision. The penitentes begin to emit a high-pitched hum that grows louder and louder. Ice begins to heave and crack.

20 THE NECK OF THE MOON

I blink, and blink again. My head aches. I lie very still looking up at the steep underside of a thatched roof, not sure where I am. The room is dim and musty, full of the smells of stored grain and animal fodder. I try to think. My breath catches in my throat. The last thing I remember—Ruminaui's men, being caught from behind, a sudden painful jerk, struggling, wild with adrenaline and desperate to breathe.

I span my hand and grasp my neck. It's warm and whole. My pulse repeats, rapid but unfazed. I inhale, exhale—one lung-full of air and then another. I've been unconscious— how long? Kantu! I lie stock-still, listening. Needles of panic ice my fingers. I make a fist, look down. The knuckles are pale, the wrist slender; all wrong—hopeless. Prescient or too late—always out of sync. Tears flood my eyes. I lift my head. A flickering bar of angled sunlight makes a streak across the blanket near my feet. Eduardo is standing at the window, gazing out. I rise up on my elbows, trembling and still charged with alarm.

"Eduardo." My voice is choked.

He turns; his expression is stark and winced with concern. "Megan," he says. "Thank God." He's so glad to see me it breaks my heart, and a strangled sob erupts from deep in my chest. I cover my mouth. Hot messy tears blur my vision and stream down my cheeks. I can't stop crying. He crosses the room and sits beside me, presses his handkerchief into my hand and strokes my hair.

"I bet you feel like hell. I should get Koyam." He's up, his stride thumping the floorboards. He pulls the curtain back, leans out the window and shouts, "Koyam, *ven ahora*! *Por favor*. Megan's awake."

Sharp throbbing pain zings right to the top of my head. God it hurts. I drop onto my back and lie with my forearm over my eyes. Outside, I hear rustling and voices—and then the creak and motion of someone ascending the ladder that leads to the attic window.

Eduardo grabs Koyam's hand and she hoists herself over the window sill. Corbin comes close behind her. He hangs back next to the wall by the window, but Koyam makes a beeline straight to me. I open my mouth to speak but she shushes, puts a hand on my forehead and examines my eyes. "*Allin,*" she says, with an exhale that's all relief.

She grins up at Eduardo and Corbin, and nods, then extracts a bottle of drugstore aspirin from her pocket and demands my palm. I pull myself upright and extend my hand. She shakes out two tablets then pulls a metal cup and a flask from a bag attached to her belt, and fills the cup with liquid that's clear and green. I'm stunned and sluggish, slow to move.

"Go on," she says, "take it."

I bring the aspirins to my tongue and down them with several quick swallows. The drink tastes fresh, like celery, but slightly sweet.

"Finish it," she says. "Rest for awhile and then come down. You'll need to eat."

Corbin keeps his distance, eyeing me as if I've become something dangerous and strange. I mean to ask him what he sees, but Koyam motions, and one at a time, the three of them step out the window and disappear down the ladder.

I lie with the blankets pulled up to my chin. My mind is tumbling and raw—stuck on that instant of recognition—the child's eyes engaging mine. "*Pin?*" he asks—that thin sweet voice. And though there is ice between us, and entire lifetimes— I'm stricken with a parent's anguished craving. "Kantu," I say his name out loud. What happened to you? Was I the instrument of your death? Is that what I need to find out?

There's a dark wobble at my core, and gloom as thick as fog settling in my stomach. I keep asking myself what good can come from any of this. I press my eyelids shut and try to picture my dad. If he could be here now, I wouldn't ask much— just the touch of his hand on my shoulder. But instead, my pressured thoughts veer to Dr. Vickers. I picture him seated in the huge blue wing chair by his office window, leaning toward me over crossed legs, pursing his lips. He pegs me with an unremitting gaze and emits a weary grunt. "Ayahuasca was a reckless idea," he says. "And chasing hallucinations is always a madman's errand. Go home, Megan. Get therapy and mourn your father. Get your head on straight."

"But what about Kantu?" I pose the question.

"Nothing but a functional hallucination. You completed a rotation in psychiatry; somewhere in that brain of yours you know he's a figment. You're displacing unresolved guilt about

Bella—inventing this fevered need to find some hopelessly lost imaginary child, and hurling yourself toward some grand self-destructive act. Last time, your father kept you from pitching yourself into the river. When it happens again, who will save you from yourself?"

Everything I imagine Dr. Vickers saying about me is probably true. I should be frightened. But mostly, I'm stuck wondering if anyone can be saved from themselves. And if they are, who would they be?

I wipe my nose with Eduardo's handkerchief, sniff and sit upright. I'm restless and my head itches. I prod myself, "Buck up, Megan," a little self-talk to get me moving—not my dad's voice, but it's what he would say.

I brush my teeth with water from my canteen and smooth my hair. I'm preoccupied—probably losing my mind. I put my toothbrush away and take the pocket mirror from a zippered compartment of my backpack. Then I go and sit cross-legged on the straw mattress where I woke up this morning and examine my reflection. My face looks tired and pale, but mostly unremarkable.

"*Mihuy.* Eat,*"* Koyam says. And like compliant children, we take up our spoons.

The stew is pepper-hot and oily-tasting, cooked so long the pieces of meat and vegetables fall apart without chewing. The milk is not the sweet, cold milk I expect. It's tepid and thicker, sharp-tasting, like warm yogurt or buttermilk.

The business of eating consumes us and we don't speak. But after a while, I sense I'm being watched. When I lift my chin, I'm looking into Corbin's steady gaze.

"What?" I say. "I know. I don't look well."

He peers straight into my eyes. "Last night you were in my hallucination. I saw a snake dangling off your forehead. I swear to God, it plunged right into the center of your eye. Your head jerked, but you didn't make a sound. It seemed so real, I find myself looking for a sign, some swelling or hemorrhage. And this morning—all that time you barely had a heartbeat. Do you remember anything? Where were you?"

"You make it sound like I almost died." I look from Corbin to Koyam.

"You were unconscious," she says. "Huari found you out under the trees. We brought you in here by the stove and wrapped you in blankets. Eduardo was already out the door, going for help. A seizure brought you back."

"A seizure," I say, stuck on the thought, imagining myself writhing in tremors, frothing at the mouth.

Eduardo leans forward on his elbows. "Megan, what happened? What do you remember?"

I sit gazing at my hands—pale slender fingers and well-trimmed nails, folded together and resting on the table. I wonder how my own body can feel so much like a stranger. I touch the eye of the ring, twist its golden circle around on my finger, astonished, yet again, at the way it fits, the way it seems to desire my hand—a crazy thought, who would believe me? And then, from somewhere, and because I need him, I hear my dad's soft and steady voice, "Meggie," he says to me, "just because something's crazy doesn't mean it isn't true."

I tell them—about the snake and the forest of ice pinnacles, about standing in that high, lonely place with wind beating past my ears and frost accumulating on my skin, about seeing three men and that I knew one of them was me, that I carried my child up the mountain in a basket on my back.

"*Capa cocha*, Eduardo says. "It has to be. Why else would you be carrying a child?"

"But only three," says Corbin. "A ritual sacrifice would demand an entire entourage. It's only near the summit, when scaling the mountain becomes too dangerous, that the holiest of holy men and the living sacrifice proceed without the others."

"The important question," Koyam says to me, "is—what do you think it means?"

"It's about something I have to do," I say. "I'm going there. Do you know the mountain Cotopaxi?"

"A volcano," Corbin says. "There's a nature reserve with the same name on the outskirts of Quito. So you go there—then what?"

The images vibrate in my head, urgent and visceral and exhausting. My legs are so restless I can't sit still and I get up from the table to go look out the open doorway. It's midafternoon. Bees are cruising among the blossoming scrub just beyond Koyam's door, and on the hillside, the cobbled Inca trail is bathed in bald sunlight.

"I think I'm looking for my child," I say.

We leave Koyam's little house at sunup. The air is moist and cool, and the valley below is a caldron of fog. In places the stones are dark and slick with moss and dew. We step off, single file, Koyam leading with her walking stick.

By early afternoon the mist has lifted and the humid air shimmers with sunshine.

As promised, Luis is waiting for us in the meadow across the river exactly where we left him. He spots us coming down the hillside and gets out of the car, waving his arms above his head.

In Baños, Eduardo drops Luis and the car at the mayor's office and we lug our backpacks and bags several blocks to the *Hospedaje Soledad*. The hotel door is thick glass set in a wooden frame that opens into a lobby flooded with afternoon sun. There are no rugs; just green plants in huge ceramic pots grouped around two plump couches upholstered in faded pink damask. Our hiking boots make a hollow clomping sound on the wide planks of the wooden floor. Eduardo speaks Spanish to the attendant. One at a time, we sign our names in the register, take our keys, and climb the stairs.

My room is as spare as a monk's cell, just a narrow bed with the covers pulled into tight geometric corners, a straight-backed wooden chair next to a small writing table, a standard hotel luggage rack. But on the wall that faces the street, there's a tall window with heavy drapes and sheer gauzy curtains that puff with the breeze. And behind the adjacent door, my own bathroom with stark white tiles and twenty-four-hour hot water. I hoist my suitcase onto the luggage rack, take off my boots. I think I'll lie on the bed, just for a minute, and then I'll get up and take a bath. Instead, I sleep.

I dream of that other life—and Citllali. I see her walking through mist in the humid bowers of a jungle. I call her name. This time she hears. She stops and turns, quiet and expectant among the palms and acacias. As if all my prayers and wanting might be satisfied, we stand face-to-face. My eyes scald and blur with glad tears and I open my arms to embrace her. But she takes a step backward, glances around and behind me. "Our son?" she asks. "Where is Kantu?"

Just before seven, I meet Corbin and Eduardo in a small restaurant whose vinyl covered booths and rough-sawn wood walls remind me of diners back home. Eduardo scoots to make room, and I slide into the booth beside him. He's fresh from a shower, still smelling of hotel soap. His hair is damp, and the stubble he's been ignoring the last few days is gone, replaced by a tidy mustache."

"You shaved," I say. I run my finger above my lip. "This is new."

"Do you object?"

"It suits you," I say. My eyes are full of him and for one besotted instant, he gazes back.

Corbin clears his throat. "We've ordered beer. Do you want something to drink?"

"Bottled water," I say. "Where's Koyam?"

"Staying in tonight," Corbin says.

"Is she alright?"

"Just tired." Eduardo smiles. "She's famously uninterested in expedition details. Don't worry. She'll be at breakfast tomorrow."

"Were you able to contact the hypnotist?" I ask.

"He's coming," Eduardo says. "He'll meet us tomorrow in Quito. I offered him a stipend, but he's so intrigued by the case, he would have come anyway."

"The case," I repeat the words, everything reduced to the clinical.

Corbin leans forward on his elbows, a smirk on his face. "We need to keep a low profile. This past life regression business. Getting our leads from a reincarnated Inca with an ayahuasca hallucination seems like a stunt, more worthy of the *National Inquirer* than the *National Geographic*."

Eduardo half smiles but turns sober. "We may have a more serious problem. I called the ranger station at Cotopaxi. Another two weeks and they stop issuing permits. Right now the weather forecast looks passable but that could change. It's late in the season."

"We could rethink," Corbin says. "Of course, a child sacrifice, especially if we have some leads on who the child was, would be the more spectacular find, but the timing borders on reckless. We could plan the Cotopaxi expedition for next spring and refocus our current efforts on the map and finding the cave where those pilfered artifacts came from. That may be more urgent. We know it's been ransacked at least once."

The three of us sit upright and silent while the waitress sets frosted bottles of beer on small, square paper napkins in front of Eduardo and Corbin. She puts a basket of fried bread in the center of the table and pulls a pad and pencil from her apron pocket.

The menu is a blackboard posted above the cash register with the daily offerings scrawled in chalk. Eduardo orders and I say I'll have what he's having, chicken-something with avocados.

"*Bistec y las patatas*," Corbin announces with a halting accent. The waitress looks confused. He says to Eduardo. "Tell her I know steak and potatoes aren't on the menu, but that's what I want. Tell her I'll pay extra."

Eduardo relays the message and the waitress goes to ask the cook. She comes back smiling.

Corbin flashes her a grin, and then he's back to business. "About redirecting our energies, what do you think?"

I interrupt. "I don't want to put anyone in danger," I say. "I'll help locate Manuel's cave in any reasonable way that doesn't interfere with my own goals. But permit or no permit,

I'm climbing Cotopaxi. Don't worry; I'm perfectly capable of doing it on my own."

"Megan, slow down," Eduardo says. "I hope you know I'm invested. I spent a good part of yesterday afternoon getting my provost on board about Cotopaxi. Unless there's a blizzard or an avalanche, I'm not about to call him back and say I've changed my mind."

He turns to Corbin. "Consider dividing our efforts. You and Henriette hunt down the source of the artifacts in Cuenca and I'll go with Megan and Koyam to Cotopaxi."

"I'm not going to miss being there if you find that child." Corbin lifts his hands and emits an irritated sigh. "All right, let's throw caution to the wind. Cotopaxi it is. For the record, I think it would be better to wait. But I'm coming. I'll shut up."

Our dinners arrive. For long minutes, we eat in silence until Eduardo takes a small spiral notebook from his shirt pocket and we begin to lay out plans. Already we know we will launch the climb from a house in Quito reserved for visiting faculty on campus at the Universidad de San Francisco, and that Henriette is coming to make contacts and manage details.

Long after the substance has been settled, Eduardo and Corbin are still parsing. Will we take one donkey or two—or maybe a llama, to haul any artifacts? How many graduate students must be included to justify spending university money?

I don't care, as long as I get there.

The cashier comes out from behind the register and changes the sign in the window.

"They're closing," I say. "I'm ready to call it a night."

"It's only nine," Corbin says. "I was hoping for a drink, something stiff and alcoholic. I'm too keyed up to sleep."

"I can find my way back," I say. "I'll see you both at breakfast."

"There's a bar across the street," Eduardo tells Corbin. "Start without me. I'll walk Megan to the hotel."

The evening is warm and soft. Street lamps are blinking on.

We talk, casual conversation, then grow silent walking through the hotel lobby and up the stairs. In the hallway outside my room I fit my key into the lock, give the door a measured push, and turn to say goodnight.

Eduardo steps close. With a curled forefinger, he lifts my chin and studies my face. The pupils of his eyes are liquid and intense.

"I'm in love with you," he says.

"I know," I say. He bends slightly and kisses my mouth, a light soft brush on the lips.

"*Dime*," he says, "Tell me. Is there hope for me?"

"I want there to be," I say.

He pushes a stray hair away from my cheek. "Then I'm going to follow you wherever you'll take me and give you every reason to say yes." He kisses me again, and for an instant, we stand there, reluctant to say goodnight. "Well," he says, "Jasper's waiting. Go inside and lock the door. I'll see you in the morning."

The campus guard at the security kiosk tells Eduardo that the keys were picked up earlier.

"*¿Quién es?*" he asks.

The guard consults his clipboard. "*Se llama Professora Polmo*," he says. He takes a map from a stack at his elbow, circles the visiting faculty house in red ink. He hands the map through the car's open window.

We drive past a maze of dormitories and lecture halls to the northern edge of the campus. The house is one of three imposing Spanish-style residences on a compound behind a spiked iron gate. Ours is sand-colored stucco with the veranda and shutters painted dusky green.

Eduardo parks the car beneath the vine-covered carport and we pile out, glad to stretch our legs. Corbin, Koyam and I follow Eduardo onto the wide veranda that fronts the door. He thumps the door with the twined iron knocker. Henriette answers. For an instant, she stands stock-still, smiling, so glad to see Eduardo. I think she's going to comment on his mustache, but she notices me behind him and glances at her feet.

"Come in," she says, and she ushers us into the tiled vestibule.

Corbin wanders ahead toward the kitchen calling over his shoulder to Henriette. "Are you roasting nuts or something? It smells wonderful."

"I don't know what you think you smell," Henriette says. She looks at her watch. "Check out the house. Let's decide where everyone's sleeping and you can deposit your things. We'll need to double up, but most rooms have two beds."

"Have you heard from Felix?" Eduardo asks.

"He's here, outside in the garden. He came by cab about an hour ago. He's says he'll sleep on the couch in the study. Shall, I show you around? I brought gin and vermouth," she says. "It's late enough, I could fix martinis. The caterer will be here with dinner at 6:00."

Talk at dinner is all about hypnotism and past life regression.

I listen, enduring glances and smiles, mostly without comment.

When dinner is over, I lay my fork across my dessert plate and refuse a second cup of coffee. Henriette signals for the caterers to begin removing the china.

"Take half an hour," Eduardo says, "and then we'll meet in the study."

Everyone rises from the table. Henriette and Dr. Lester step out onto the stone terrace beyond the French doors with their cigarettes. I go upstairs to the bathroom, and then across the hall to the room I'm sharing with Koyam. The lamp is on and she's lying on the coverlet of one of the twin beds with her shoes on and her arm over her eyes.

I walk softly across the room to the window. It's dark outside. All I see is my own reflection in the glass.

She rises on her elbows watching me. "Some things require an act of faith," she says.

Dr. Lester meets me at the study door. "I understand you want to focus on specifics."

"Yes," I say. "Please, help me find the child. Somewhere on Vulcán Cotopaxi, I think that's where he is."

I take a seat in one of the high-backed Chesterfield chairs angled by the fireplace and the group converges. Koyam sits in the corner of the sofa directly across from me. She gives a reassuring nod and I try to relax, put that act of faith to the test.

Dr. Lester asks if I'm comfortable. I nod and he begins, droning in wide repetitive circles. His voice, soft and monotonous, slips like silk. He repeats and repeats—until I begin to drift, suspended and slack and nowhere.

"Tell us," he says. "About Cotopaxi. What happened? Where is Kantu?"

There's a sudden ache in the back of my throat and I shake my head. My fingers clutch the arms of the chair. *"Manan!"* No, I say. *"Allichu ama!"* Please, I can't.

He coaxes and soothes, his singsong voice patiently swinging like a metronome, until my breathing settles and coils in effortless loops. And then he asks again. "Tell us. What happened on Cotopaxi? Where is Kantu?"

I lift a hand to my chest, my fingers grasp and worry a button on my shirt. I remember sunlight on mud-brick walls. "They came for Kantu and me at the end of summer. Atahualpa sent runners and servants with provisions from his own household to escort us from Tumbes to Quito, and on to the base camp at Cotopaxi. An endless trudge whose days were filled with nothing but the road ahead and too much time to think. Mostly I watched Kantu and tried to imagine a future. I had seen the omens but I worked against them; I wanted to hope. And I kept thinking about Citllali that last day—the mute way she'd lifted Kantu and brought her nose to his. She kissed his forehead and told him to be good, then passed him into my arms. She was fighting tears, keeping a brave face for him. I put an arm around her and we stood for a moment, the three of us together, but soon she stiffened and slipped out of my embrace. She squeezed my hand and touched Kantu's cheek. 'Be kind to him,' she said to me. 'Please go now.'

"Emissaries and citizens from towns along the way greeted Kantu with armloads of flowers, and small gifts. He accepted their fawning and curiosity with shy smiles. I watched his dark eyes study their faces. I was impressed and proud—only four years old, so young, and already gifted with such presence.

"Atahualpa had a palanquin specially made for Kantu to ride in, but he refused, preferring instead, to lead one of the llamas or walk beside me. Sometimes, late in the day, he would ask me to pick him up and I would carry him with his arms clasped around my neck. But our nights were a misery. He would startle awake, breathless and sobbing, begging to go home and crying for his mother. I would bring him onto my lap and hold him, but soon he would crawl back onto his cot and cover his face with his hands.

"I moved through our days in a state of high alert, scrutinizing each detail and rehearsing a remedy for every conceivable misstep. Atahualpa's war had made me a traitor and a liar, and I was at the center of so many secrets and deceits that now traveled on the backs and instincts of others—it was as if I had released a bag of snakes and I was always waiting for one to slither back and bite my ankle.

"On the evening before the final climb up Cotopaxi, a small regiment of Ruminaui's soldiers surprised the camp at dusk. I heard the commotion of new arrivals and left my tent to see who it was. The afternoon had been dull and overcast, and now the clouds sifted down in a cold wet haze. Fires in pits around the camp struggled to burn in the moisture-laden air. A pall of smoke and the smells of damp wood and ash made the air acrid and hard to breathe. Minutes before, I'd heard scurrying and a thread of agitated chatter, now there was only mist and a blind kind of white light. A lone old man came at me through the fog and grasped my arm. 'Soldiers are here,' he said. 'Their captain—a man called Rafa, is asking about you.'

"I swallowed back a sour taste in my mouth and gave him a blank nod. I did my best to feign indifference, but my fingers had gone cold and I caught myself making fists. I knew Rafa—a hulking warmonger whose face had a devastating battle scar that puckered the skin around his left eye and cheek and gave him the appearance of a constant sneer. He was a favorite of

Atahualpa's, a notorious fighter, unhesitating and brutal—and now he was here.

"I went back to my tent, pulled my dagger from its sheath then put it back. I was feeling cornered and I wanted to fight, to tear out someone's liver, but more than that, I was tired. I felt as if I had been slogging into a gale-force wind for so long the effort was wearing me down. Earlier that same day I had been hopeful, only one more bold and final hurdle I'd thought, and I could begin to imagine that same wind at my back. I took in a ragged breath and massaged my forehead with my finger-tips. When I looked up, Kantu was watching me with a worried expression on his face.

"He was sitting on his cot playing with a guinea pig, a nervous little thing with russet-colored fur and a white face. He held it in his lap stroking it between the ears and feeding it grass and plant stems.

"'It's only the fog,' I said. 'It's giving me a headache. I'll be better in the morning.' I went and stooped beside him to run a finger along the guinea pig's back. 'Does he have a name?'

"'I call him *Phisku*,' he smiled, 'because he's so jumpy.'

"'Maybe we should find a basket with a lid where *Phisku* can sleep. We don't want him to get loose in the night.'

"Kantu hugged my neck. 'Yes, please,' he said.

"I brought him a wicker basket I used for plied thread and yarn but Kantu worried that the guinea pig would chew his way out, so we found a small wooden box instead and lined it with soft fabric and dry grass.

"'Soldiers are in the camp,' I said. 'Did you know that?'

"Kantu shook his head.

"'Their captain will come to us tonight. He has a scary face but I'm here and you don't need to be afraid. He was cut in a fight and to save him, to help him heal, the curandero had to burn the wounds.'

"As if my words had summoned him, the bright shadow of a torch passed outside the tent, and without greeting or invitation, Rafa pushed his way inside with his bedroll under his arm. I stepped to block his way and push back against the insult of his presence. For an icy instant, we were eye-to-eye. I was looking for signs that I had been betrayed. I wondered how much he knew. In this, one of us was blind, and I worried that it was me. He had been sent with a show of force for a reason. At the moment, I had no defense but bluster. Beyond that, I had no idea what I was going to do.

"'You're a long way from the war,' I said. 'Why are you here?'

"'To be Atahualpa's eyes and ears,' he said. 'You and I, we have no quarrel—as long as we want the same thing.'

"'And what same thing is that?'

"'For Atahualpa to assume his proper place as *Sapa Inca of Tahuantinsuyu* blessed with all the promises that are rightfully his.' He turned his head and assessed Kantu with a sharp and lingering stare.

"Caught in the gaze of Rafa's bulging predatory eye, Kantu flinched and stared down at his feet.

"'Kantu,' I said. 'Come here.'

"Kantu sucked in his bottom lip and gathered the guinea pig close to his chest. He skirted Rafa, came to me, and I lifted him in my arms.

"'This is Captain Rafa,' I said. I tried to appear indifferent, but underneath that calculated facade I cursed him. I wanted him distant and lifetimes away from my child, and in my thoughts I bound him to an image—Rafa at the bottom of a frozen ravine, that ugly eye of his perpetually fixed on the sky.

"Rafa spread his bedroll beside mine. All night, while he twitched and snored, I lay awake thinking about Citllali and Rhian, wondering if Tumbes had been sacked and burned, and whose head was on a spike. Tomorrow, Rafa and two of his soldiers would hound me to the summit. I would be outnumbered, but the mountain was a fickle and treacherous place. I could call down an avalanche if I had to. I looked over at Kantu, curled on his side with his face in his hands. I don't think he slept. If he had night terrors, he kept them to himself.

"The morning was brisk and unnaturally clear. A sheen of dew gave everything an oddly sharp focus. I remember being struck by the absence of clouds and feeling exposed. I wondered how such weather was possible, what it could mean.

"Kantu's attendants pushed him out of the tent wearing a red mantle of fine-spun wool marked with the black and purple insignia of Atahualpa's court. He was made to stand at the center of the camp and kneel before the crowd. He was trembling and trying not to cry. I kneeled so I could look into his face and crowned him with a jeweled and fanned headdress of brilliant yellow and orange feathers. I grasped him gently by his shoulders and kissed him on each cheek.

"'Just today, Kantu,' I whispered. 'Just today.'

"The people cheered and clamored. They reached to touch him and put their hands to their hearts or their fingers to their lips and blew kisses.

"I raised my arms and turned toward the mountain. The entire company fell in line behind me, and we began the trek to the first platform. Ruminaui's men marched among us.

"The trail traversed the low face of the mountain in a series of switchbacks that ended at a broad stone dais. Two of the attendants came forward and lifted Kantu to a high rock ledge that formed a natural altar. He stood alone, peering down at the crowd, looking like a chick lost from his nest, small and flightless and weighted down by unwieldy plumage. I climbed the rocks and knelt and took and squeezed his hands. His fingers were cold. The murmuring crowd hushed, and I rehearsed with Kantu the greetings he must speak to the gods. The gifts Atahualpa had provided to be offered with Kantu were handed up and arranged at his feet—many small fine things: gold and silver statues, twined bundles of coca leaves, vessels of quinoa, miniature ears of dried corn. At the last, the assembled company recited the solemn blessing. I knelt and tied a small leather bag to the sash of Kantu's tunic. The bag contained every hair cut from his head or collected from his pillow, clipped nails from his fingers and toes. Had he been older, there would have been baby teeth. I rose to my feet and asked the crowd, 'Do you give this child and these gifts, whole and without reservation?'

"The celebrants raised their arms above their heads and shouted, '*Ari! Ari! Ari!*'

"Kantu was brought down and the crowd formed a line. He held out his hand. Each person touched or grasped or kissed it as they passed on their way down the mountain. Only Rafa and two of his men remained to travel with Kantu and me to the summit. The wind had picked up, it beat past our ears and we had to yell at each other to be heard, but howling wind seemed a good thing to me. Cotopaxi was a dangerous place, and I had murder on my mind.

"I bundled Kantu against the cold and lifted him into the pack basket, then stooped, adjusted the straps and stood upright. I filled my cheeks with coca leaves, began to moisten and work them with the tip of my tongue and started walking into the wind. I chose a steep and difficult route and moved at a quick pace. Often, I glanced over my shoulder to see how Rafa and his men fared.

"In early-afternoon we came to the base of a jutting cliff near the top of Cotopaxi. Rafa and one of his men were tired and light-headed from the altitude. We pressed our bodies against a recess in the mountain's stone face to get out of a biting wind. The sacrificial site was above us. We could look up and see the underside of the rocky ledge. A heavy knotted rope tied with red and yellow flags dangled over the cliff's edge, tossing and whipping Atahualpa's colors in the wind.

"My eyebrows and lashes were coated with frost and my face was numb. I called to Kantu and he gave back a muffled grunt. I eased the pack off my back and pulled back the basket's awning. Kantu was slumped inside, peaked and drowsy. I pulled him upright, fed him sips from a bladder of coca tea and herbs that I carried close to my body. I pinched his cheeks and blew air warmed from my lungs into his face. I kissed his forehead.

"Children brought for sacrifice were predictably numb and lethargic. The high altitude stupor had become part of the ritual and was considered a blessing. It made them compliant—and at the end, when the offerings had been arranged and the parting blessings sung, a single well-delivered blow to the back of the head easily fixed them in place.

"Rafa and his men watched me coax the liquid into Kantu's mouth. If they wondered that I worked to revive him, they didn't say. I settled Kantu and one of them caught the rope and pushed it at me.

"'We are soldiers, not holy men,' he said. 'We'll wait for you here. We'll tie our bundles to the rope. You can pull them up.' He panted, out of breath, and pushed the rope at me again. 'Be quick. Worse weather's coming.'

"I wanted a blizzard, something to make them careless and miserable. I secured the basket, centered Kantu on my back and began to climb. My cloak billowed and flapped, and the wind made a shrill whistle through the gap at the top of the basket. The wild, thin air made it difficult to breathe. For the first time, the weight of Kantu in the basket seemed more than I could bear.

"I hoisted my body onto the rocks and hunched low to steady myself and see where I was. The place was a shallow basalt shelf that abutted a natural cave. Most high holy sites required hours of digging and preparation but here was a place right and perfect in its natural state—so perfect, that before they had been drafted as soldiers, Atahualpa's craftsmen had begun work to make this a monument.

"The wind bellowed and hissed across the mouth of the cave. I stood in the dim recess waiting for my eyes to adjust and feeling the sudden still warmth of protective walls. Provisions had been left—bundles of firewood wrapped in oiled skins, hand torches, jars of quinoa and ground corn, chunks of ice brought up to melt for water, a lidded ceramic pot for cooking, everything grouped together.

"I lowered the basket and lifted Kantu onto his feet. He was unsure and timid and he wobbled from being carried so long. I held his mittened hand and we walked back and forth. We sat on the wrapped bundles of wood in the chill vague light and I took him onto my lap and warmed him close to my body with my cloak stretched around us. I prepared coca tea and we ate some salted jerky. He was tired and homesick and he cried, begging again for his mother. 'She's in the jungle,' I said. 'Soon we will be there too.' I hoped it was true.

"Kantu watched me haul up the bundles of ceremonial offerings and carry them to the cave.

"We started a fire. I lit a torch and led Kantu by the hand. He resisted, afraid of the dark at the back of the cave. A shallow burial pit had been gouged in one corner of the floor and natural hollows in the walls of the cave had been enlarged to receive some of the offerings. 'See,' I said, holding the torch high to spread the light, 'just a secret place away from the wind.'

"I situated him near the fire and put some ice to melt in a ceramic pot.

"'Rafa and his men are waiting for me,' I said. 'Keep your fingers and toes warm and make sure the fire doesn't go out. I'll be back as soon as I can.'

"'Tayta, how long?' he asked.

"'Not long, Kantu. Stay out of the wind.' I hugged him and kissed his cheeks then touched his forehead and blessed him. I stood to leave, but he grabbed my cloak and I knelt and held him again.

"'Tayta,' he said. He pulled at his mittens, dropped them at his feet and pushed back the layers of clothing to get at his belt and the bag that contained his nail and hair clippings. He picked at the knot until it came undone and held the bag out to me. 'If you have it when *Inti* comes, he won't make me go with him.'

"I took the bag, tied it on my own belt, then stooped and straightened his cloak, pulled it snug around him and put his mittens on his hands. I had bitten my bottom lip and I licked the blood with my tongue. 'I'm coming back for you,' I said. 'Wait for me. Nothing will stop me. I promise.' And then I turned my back on him and went to join my enemies.

21 PALE FIRE

Dr. Lester's voice, vague at first. He claps his hands. I startle, pull my spine upright, and—as if forward motion has been interrupted by a sudden stop, my head slaps against the back of the chair. I open my eyes. Henriette, Eduardo, Corbin, Koyam, Dr. Ortega, all of them—watching, their gazes fixed and expectant. Perhaps I have something to declare, but I can't think what it might be. I glance down at the mahogany lap desk that rests across my thighs. My hand grips a buff-colored mechanical pencil. Apparently, I've made a sketch, a rough map.

Dr. Lester crouches in front of me peering into my face. "Megan. Is this Megan? Who are you? Talk to me."

I feel cudgeled and numb and rudely poked, yanked away from a dream of urgent business. A spike of annoyance goes straight to my gums and teeth. If I were a dog I would bite somebody. "Yes," I tell him, "I'm here."

He releases a moist exhale that fills my nostrils with the sour taint of old coffee, and the curve of his shoulders slumps. He rocks back on his heels then stands and runs his fingers through his hair. "Jesus, Mary, and Joseph," he says, with a terse snuff of a laugh that's all bitter relief.

I glance around the room and see Corbin and the others through the warp of strangeness. For an instant it seems possible that this, and not my Inca life, is the phantom world.

Eduardo calls my name from the corner of the desk. He wants to know, am I thirsty. I nod and he lifts the faceted pitcher, pours water into a glass and brings it to me.

"You seem distant, not yet among us," he says. "Please come back."

His expression is soft and admiring. He touches my arm.

I can't help but notice Henriette who sits across from me. Her attention veers from me to her lap. All evening, I've been the subject of her steady observation. Now, with Eduardo standing at the arm of my chair, she can't bear for me to see her looking. She delves into her skirt pocket and brings out her cigarette case. She lights up, inhales, and leans back into the deep cushions of the couch. She blows a leisurely stream of smoke that curls and clouds and smudges the air between us.

Henriette and I like each other well enough. It's just that, as far as she's concerned, I've done nothing to earn Eduardo's regard. If we were to discuss it, we would agree; it's not fair.

All evening, the ring on my finger has been unnaturally warm. Sometimes I think it has a heartbeat. Later tonight, when we are alone in our room, I'll talk to Koyam about it. I turn my head to reassure myself of her presence but she's vacated her chair. The door to the walled garden is open. I can see her silhouette on the patio.

Corbin clears his throat. He rises to his feet and adopts the stern posture of a professor. He calls everyone back to their seats—all for the good of the order. What must we know? That we are on the cusp of a climbing window and in several weeks the weather will change—afterward, the trek will be more dangerous; we could be denied permits. He recommends a small exploratory expedition; still, he says, getting permits will take time. If a site is located, more work can follow in the spring. I think—as long as there's an audience, he will talk all night.

I'm restless, barely skimming the surface. My thoughts haunt that shallow cave near the summit of Cotopaxi. I imagine a small thin voice piercing the icy silence—like a ringing in my ears. That voice is long since gone. I know that.

We are released and I climb the stairs, shut the door behind me, and go to sit on the window seat. I push the heavy curtains aside and open the window. The night is warm and clamorous with the seesawing chirp of insects, the repetitive shriek of a bird. Moths and huge flying beetles are drawn to the light. They batter themselves against the screen.

I talk to Koyam about the ring. She examines it and my hand, then shakes her head. Maybe what I'm sensing is important, she says, maybe it's not—only hindsight will tell. She rummages in her bag then says she's going to the kitchen. When she comes back, she brings a tray with a pot of chamomile tea. She sets the tray on the dresser by the door.

"There's news," she says. "Henriette just heard on the radio, there was an avalanche on Cotopaxi. Two German climbers, technical experts, were buried. Eduardo is on the phone verifying, but he's worried there won't be a permit. The university won't support a climb when conditions are this dangerous."

The door's ajar. Eduardo raps, then pushes it open. "I see you've heard. I've been on the phone with the university. The provost wants the expedition be rescheduled. Just two months,

Megan, December. We don't have a choice. I'm sorry." He waits for me to say something. I shrug and he steps close and wraps me in his arms. I lay my cheek against the lapel of his sport jacket.

I feel like I'm in some kind of limbo, iced-over and numb. "I'm sorry," I say. "I can't get my head around any of this right now."

"We'll talk in the morning," he says. "We're all tired. Get some rest." He kisses me on the forehead.

"Take care of her," he says to Koyam, and then he steps away and shuts the door behind him.

Koyam pours and hands me a cup of tea and some capsules of pulverized valerian root that she takes from the pocket of her skirt. I wince and she tells me to hold my nose.

"I know," she says. "Valerian smells like vomit, but swallow it. You need sleep. The university's expedition can come later, but what's happening with you won't wait. I know someone who can help. We should leave before sun-up. I'll wake you when it's time."

I get into my pajamas and under the covers, drowsy and wondering if it's disloyal not to talk to Eduardo, but I don't want to put him in danger or make him have to choose between me and the university. And I don't want to argue. I fall asleep watching Koyam pull the few things I've hung in the closet off their hangers.

I sleep and dream, not of Kantu, but of Bella—Bella on the porch, Bella heavy in my arms, Bella, her angel face inert and dusted with snow. In my dream, I'm wearing a flannel night-gown, nothing underneath but my skin and my hiking boots. I'm breathless, trudging, bearing the weight of her. The wind sears the calves of my legs and chafes the place where my boots rub my ankles—they burn and I ache. My bones feel brittle. The high altitude atmosphere is thin and blue and the terrain is a maze of never ending meringues, snow crusted with fine crystals of ice, up and up a spine of grey-black rock.

Koyam flicks on the reading lamp. A sudden arc of light fractures the darkness and I cover my face with the sheet then roll to face her. She's already dressed. I think she must have slept in her clothes and not under the covers, because, except for the imprint of her head on the spread-covered pillow, her bed is undisturbed. She's standing by the dresser in her stocking feet pouring steaming maté into the lid of a thermos. She sets the tea on my bedside table. Not a word passes between us. I get up and into my jeans and sweatshirt, find my zippered grooming kit, then slip down the hall to the bathroom. I come back and Koyam slides past me at the door with a bar of soap in her hand. I make my bed and sit on the edge drinking tea and feeling reckless and half-blind about what I suspect is ahead, but also strangely reconciled.

Before we leave the room, I write a note to Eduardo, black ink on a sheet of lined blue paper that I pilfered from the hotel Flores in Cuenca. The words:

Eduardo,
I know you are doing what you have to do, and so am I. You were right last night when you said we don't have a choice. Neither of us does.
Tell Corbin not to worry, I'll leave things the way I find them. Thank you for everything. I hope you understand; I'm not running away from you. This is not about us.
Te amo,
Megan

Koyam lights our way down the stairs with her flashlight. In the kitchen, the small fluorescent lamp above the stove casts a weak glow. Eduardo's sport coat is where he left it, draped over the back of a chair by the table. I fold the note and put it in his pocket so it sticks out at the top.

We leave by the back door, walk around the house and down the driveway to the iron gates to wait beneath a dark sky still blazing with stars. Koyam checks the time on my watch with the flashlight then she puts the flashlight in her bag. She's silent, standing like a sentinel looking up the road. In a few minutes the headlights of the taxi come around the university commons and up the hill.

Saquisili is two hours south of Quito and not even a published stop on the bus route to Ambato. I worry. What if the bus driver forgets? What if we fly past without stopping? But when it's time, Koyam gives my arm an urgent poke and I'm up, struggling into my backpack, taking a wide stance against the motion of the bus, unsteady and bumbling up the aisle with Koyam's bag nudging the seat of my jeans. The driver veers the bus to the edge of the highway and stops. The door opens with a hydraulic hiss. Koyam and I step off into glaring sunshine behind three indigenous women in their skirts and shawls and felt hats. I squint. Ahead of us is a walk into town on a narrow dirt road. Beyond, obliterating the horizon, is Cotopaxi, blanketed in snow, massive and stark against blue sky.

Thursday is market day in Saquisili, and the atmosphere is electric with commerce. The town's plazas have been over-run by native vendors who have managed to bring, whether by vehicle or pack animal, or by physically carrying on their own backs or heads or in shoulder slings, seemingly everything marketable in Ecuador. The morning is heating up and in every direction goods are being handled and buyers and sellers are coming to terms. Delicacies and handmade treasures crowd alongside everyday common things—red bananas and mandarin oranges, drifts of quinoa, rice, and corn, honeys, teas, potions and oils, jugs and dishes, stacks of straw and Panama hats, taffy and jerky hanging from lines strung between posts, the stewed heads of pigs, plucked and eviscerated poultry, sugared pastries. But my focus is on Koyam, a fast three steps ahead of me, constantly moving, like a mole along the pathways. She turns and waves for me to hurry, "*los animales,*" she insists.

The livestock market is a dusty expanse bordered by animal enclosures and pickup trucks, and shoulder high mounds of cut green hay. The odor of fresh manure is a smack in the face. I take my hat off and use the stiff brim to keep the air moving and shoo flies.

It's still early, just past 9:30, but already sellers are pulling up stakes. Pigs and cows, alpacas, llamas and sheep are being taken away, some skittish and objecting, coaxed or yanked and prodded into trucks or led down the road on their own legs, back to barns or fields or off to slaughter, somewhere out of the heat.

"We'll find him here," Koyam says. She slows her pace and begins to scan faces.

Not long, she stops and points to a short stocky man who's urging a reluctant sheep up a ramp at the back of an old farm truck. "That's him," she says.

He's about my age, wearing a hooded gray sweatshirt and a pale blue baseball cap. We watch from where we're standing while he secures the animal behind a wire enclosure banked with bags of grain and bales of hay at the back of the truck's flatbed, and then we step out to meet him.

"*Oye.* Armando," Koyam calls.

He turns, surprised. "*Madrina*," he says. He takes several quick strides and hops off the back of the truck, folds her in a dutiful hug and brushes each of her cheeks with ritual kisses. Then he pulls back and looks at her as if he's assessing for soundness.

"*¿Qué pasa?*" he asks.

She puts her hand between my shoulder blades and gives me an abrupt push toward him. "I've brought Megan. She's looking for an outfitter and a guide who knows Cotopaxi. I need you to help us. This is important to me."

He tilts his head. I can tell he's leery, but Koyam has given him just enough information to make him curious. He takes off one of his gloves and offers me his hand. His handshake is firm; the palm is moist and warm. He has the face of an Inca, an aquiline nose, bronze skin, and wide spaced teeth that seem almost too white.

I feel awkward and rude, even ridiculous, dropped on him from out of the blue—but I forge ahead.

"Will you take us?"

"That depends. When do you want to go?"

"How soon can you make it happen?"

He takes a deep breath and purses his lips. "Do you have a permit?"

"No, but I'll pay you more than you usually charge. It's more expedition than climb. I may want to stay on the mountain several days. I'm looking for something. Will you do it?"

"Are you an experienced climber?"

"Good enough. I won't be a problem."

"Don't doubt her *hijo*," Koyam says.

"Do you listen to the news? There's been an avalanche. It's not safe."

"I'll pay extra. Name your price."

Armando warns us to be careful of slivers. The flatbed of his truck is pocked with holes and rust, and he's covered the floor with a sheet of worn plywood. Koyam and I hoist ourselves in behind one of Armando's friends, a man named Florio and his nine-year-old son, Javier.

The truck is packed with sacks of grain, bales of hay, and animal crates and cages stacked like apartment houses, mostly empty except for half a dozen black-speckled white hens and a single contentious rooster, a magnificent bird with a glistening mane of orange hackle feathers and an arching black tail. The rooster screeches and flaps at us, and the boy, Javier, pulls a stick from a bundle of firewood and pokes at the bird through the pen's wire mesh.

"Put the stick back." His father speaks sharply in Quechua. He watches to see that it's done and then he tells Javier to get sacks of grain from the stacks, one for each of us.

Koyam and I arrange ours adjacent to bails of hay so we have a place to lean our backs, and then we sit and wait.

Armando's wife comes to the tailgate to urge Koyam, yet again, to come up front and ride in the cab with Armando and her mother-in-law. Koyam waves her off with a smile but her tone is unmistakably firm. "I'm happy where I am," she says. "Go back and ride with your husband."

The passenger door shuts. Armando cranks the ignition once, and then again. It chugs and sputters. There's a strong smell of gasoline. Koyam and I sit very still, listening, as if that might help, while Armando tries again. This time the engine catches and he coaxes, pressing down and easing up on the gas pedal. He lets the motor idle for a few minutes then he steers the truck in a wide arc over the pot-holed parking expanse, weaving among the market trucks and onto an unpaved road barely wide enough for two lanes of traffic. We bounce and lurch then settle into a smooth rhythm, moving along at a clip, vibrating to the hum of tires on gravel.

Other trucks and a few old cars pass us by, but mostly we have an open road through hillocks and grasslands pocked with granite stones and clumps of shrubs, a house in the midst of a field or a line of fence posts and a stand of lanky deciduous trees. The breeze smells sharp and grassy with a thin sweetness.

Koyam is upright, shielding her eyes from the sun, staring down the road.

"*Mira*," she says. "That's Jasper's Land Rover. Henriette's driving. Jasper and Eduardo are with her."

The Land Rover closes in, crowds the truck, hovers behind just long enough for them to be sure. Henriette pulls up beside Armando. She honks the horn, several shrill, staccato blasts. Florio is on his feet grabbing a rough piece of lumber to use as a bludgeon. Koyam bumps his shoulder passing, going to the cab's rear window. She pounds and yells at Armando through the glass.

"*¡Sayay! ¡Sayay!* I know them. Stop."

Armando drives the truck off the shoulder into the weeds at the side of the road and gets out. I watch at an angle through the cab's rear window, Armando and Corbin standing and talking in the shadow of the open door. Corbin gives a final nod, gets out his wallet, and gives Armando some bills. Armando climbs back into the truck and pulls the door shut.

And then Corbin and Eduardo are jumping on the rusted trailer hitch, flinging their backpacks ahead of them. Corbin's skin is so ruddy he looks like he's been running. Florio drops his makeshift weapon. He grasps Eduardo's hand and then Corbin's, and gives one and then the other a steady hoist up and over the tailgate into the back of the truck. Eduardo's eyes catch mine. He smiles, an uncertain glancing smile, and I feel a stab of remorse for leaving the way I did. He hasn't shaved and I don't think he's slept. I pat the truck bed beside me and scoot to make room for him. I know he's here against his better judgment, but he came, and I can't help being glad to see him.

Corbin feigns irritability but his expression is unmistakably smug. "So here we are again, forced to put ourselves at the mercy of whatever the hell you think you're doing."

"You're an opportunist, Jasper. Don't pretend you've come to save me."

For once he's awkward, stuck in a beat of silence, one hand gripping the open zipper of his jacket. How is it possible that I feel like I'm the one who's been rude?

"How did you find us?"

"Henriette was standing at her bedroom window when the cab picked you up. We called the cab company and then the bus station. We knew you'd be looking for a guide, that if you were getting off the bus at Saquisili, Koyam was probably taking you to Armando."

"We keep showing up like a couple of bad pennies." Eduardo's expression is earnest, apologetic. "I hope you aren't offended that we tracked you down."

"Not unless you're here expecting to change my plans."

He sighs. "We're here to come with you."

"You do know, I intend to climb Cotopaxi—in spite of a dangerous weather forecast and without a permit? Won't there be hell to pay with the university?"

"Believe me, Jasper and I have discussed all that ad nauseam. We're both officially on sabbatical and we've left liability waivers with my attorney that should, at least in theory, take the university out of it. None of that means that there won't be consequences if things go south, but—well . . . We're here, and we're coming with you."

Misery loves company, and shouldn't I be glad? Instead, I'm struck with a bright shock of realization and the flutter of panic—the onus of other people's lives harnessed to mine. An image of Mama with an eyebrow raised and a stern curl on her lips, blows through my mind. Stop being so oblivious, she'd tell me. I asked for this—and she'd be right. Now it's on me.

"I don't want to put anyone in danger," I say to Eduardo, an observation so stale and obvious and out of touch I'm embarrassed, but I say it anyway. "What if, because of me, something happens to you—or Corbin, or Koyam, or Armando? How would I live with that?"

"You can't think of it that way," he says. "We made our choices."

He takes my gloved hand in his and I'm glad of it, but I wonder—why would anyone choose this?

I look over my shoulder at Koyam, expecting something from her. But she keeps her own counsel, sitting back on her bales of hay, a benign expression on her face like some carved god.

The slam and rattle of wind buffeting the truck renders speech inaudible. Eduardo puts his arm around me but still I'm cold. I wish I'd worn warmer clothes. The barren landscape falls away behind us, vast and restless, too windswept and unforgiving for anything to grow but stunted scrub and ankle-deep tufts of grass. Low-hanging clouds in the distance cast shadows that roam like ghosts across the pumice-covered tableland.

Florio and Javier are up, gathering their packs and bags. They go to squat on their heels near the tailgate. Almost immediately, we are passing through a village of one-story dwellings constructed of high mud walls with peaked tile roofs. Scattered among them are outbuildings and animal enclosures. The road that passes for a main street is unpaved and rutted; slow-going. Bump and halt. Armando honks the horn and children rush from doorways to shoo chickens and a huge spotted pig out of the way. Florio and Javier toss their belongings over the tailgate and climb out. "*Adios,*" Florio says, and then to me, "*que Dios te acompañe.*" I wave, and the truck begins again, jog and jerk, trundling on until we stop at a house that looks like all the others.

Armando's house has only a few shuttered windows and a floor of pounded earth. He leads us through a narrow hallway to the kitchen. It's dim and chill with the earthen smell of a cavern. He strikes a match and lights an oil lamp that dangles from a slim metal hook over the wooden table, then he turns to the hearth and gathers the still-living coals into a heap. He builds a tent of kindling and dry branches then stoops and blows. The coals begin to smoke and glow, to curl and nibble the edges of the brittle grass. A draft stirs through vents in the wall. There's an audible whoosh and sudden heat. For an instant, the room is bathed in tongues of light and shadow and I feel my face flush with the warmth.

We sit on benches that border the table. Corbin hands Armando the map I made under hypnosis. He spreads it on the table then unfolds and smoothes a map of Cotopaxi beside it.

We hover and lean in, comparing the two in the lamplight. Miraculously, there appears to be congruence. I reach out and run my finger along the clefts and ridges represented on Armando's map.

"The trail was here," I say. "The outcropping, if it hasn't been sheered off by erosion or a volcanic eruption, and the cave should be in this general area," I touch the spot—so fixed and certain I get a shiver and a desperate swimming intuition that I'm stuck in a loop of grim repetitions. I can't help but think of Bella, huddled in the corner of her porch, snowflakes accumulating on the soft ledges of her eyelashes.

Armando studies the map. Without looking up he says to me. "You expect to lead. Is that what you want?"

"Yes," I say, "but I need your help, your caution and advice. I could get us into trouble."

He chews the corner of his lip and considers, long enough that I half expect him to say no. Finally he gives a subtle nod, more thought than answer, and begins a pointed and serious interrogation: how long do we plan to be on the mountain, are we experienced climbers, are we acclimated and prepared to climb in high altitude conditions. And then he scribbles quantities and adds items to the bottom of a standard list of supplies printed on a carbon copy.

"This will take money," Armando says to me, "There are provisions to buy and we'll need a pack animal and an extra hand to set up a decent base camp. I know a man named Sanchez. I've climbed with him before and he has a mule we can hire."

Eduardo is ready, like a bidder at auction. "I'll pay for everything."

"Then these are for you." Armando tosses him the keys to the truck and hands the list across the table. "You can get most of these things at the general store in Latacunga. I'll see about Sanchez."

Eduardo lifts his hand, keys clutched in the palm, "Megan, *ven conmigo*." He smiles and coaxes with a tilt of his chin.

And I'm on my feet. For once I make an effortless decision, and I feel like a schoolgirl. God, let it be that simple. I can't think of anything I'd like more than to be alone with him in the cab of a truck traveling just about anywhere away from here.

Just then, Armando's mother comes into the room and makes a beeline straight to her son.

She's swift and shy. She speaks to him in Spanish, quick low tones, so soft and quiet he has to lower his head to hear her.

The message is for Koyam. "*Madrina*," Armando says, "the people from the village know you are here. They keep coming. They won't leave."

Koyam slides out from between the bench and the table. "Megan, I could use your help."

Eduardo snaps his hand closed around the keys. "Go. It's okay," he says to me and drops his arm.

I follow Koyam.

Just outside the house, squatting close together along the foundation where the hard corner of the house deflects the wind, are more than a dozen patient souls in their woolen hats and ponchos, waiting to show Koyam their warts and wounds and sick children.

The base of Cotopaxi is a barren place, no trees, only rocks and ravines tufted with low growing brush and sparse grass. Sanchez and his mule are waiting for us near the crumbled ruins of a solitary shepherd's hut. Armando halts the truck and we toss our gear to the ground and climb out. It's a relief to stand and stretch. The early chill is evaporating and the afternoon will be clear, perfect for climbing. I squint upward. The snow-covered crown of Cotopaxi stands in relief, stark and white against an untroubled sky.

This morning, waking up in the smoky chill of Armando's living room, thinking about the day, I was overcome by an almost paralyzing reluctance that I can't seem to shake.

Armando speaks to Sanchez, and then he walks with his wife to the cab side of the truck. I watch them standing together, facing each other, saying goodbye. She scowls, but relents and gives him a kiss. Yesterday and this morning there were no sharp or sorry words between them. There were barely any words at all, just her mother-in-law muttering to her to be patient. Next week, she'd said, Armando would have more time. There would be more money. Then, he would take her to see her sister in San Lorenzo. His wife climbs back into the truck, this time behind the steering wheel, and settles into the depression between the brittle springs of the old leather seat. Armando thumps the door shut and she stretches to reach the gas pedal, starts the engine. She shifts gears. The vehicle makes a sudden lurch then begins a cumbersome lumber over the uneven scrubby terrain, heading away from us toward the road. I stand with my backpack at my feet ready to offer a wave, but she doesn't look back and the five of us set off.

I walk ahead of Armando with the others in a line behind. A quiet steady trek, nothing but the faint rustle and chirping of insects, the sounds of our boots and the plodding clomp of the mule's hooves scuffing earth and loose rock.

Even low on the mountain, the air is noticeably thin. Tomorrow we will climb in earnest, but this afternoon we move in long snaking switchbacks searching for a fragment of stone wall or a stretch of cobbled pathway, a remnant, anything that might have been part of the tampo or ceremonial platform.

Miles of relentless plodding into a raw and steady wind, and we find nothing. But there is a moment when I stop in my tracks, overcome by the view and a keen sense of recognition. For nearly an hour we scour the site, rummaging through volcanic gravel, searching the ground, but there are no stone structures or rough pavers, no matted grass, no ancient pieces of wooden post.

"We've barely scratched the surface," Eduardo tells me.

"I know," I say. Mostly he's offering comfort. I know that too and that it's time to move on.

In the last bright hour before dusk we unload our gear and pitch our tents in the hollow of a low mounded ridge that shields us from the brunt of the wind. Armando heats water on the camp stove. We help him spread an oiled tarp on the ground and set out the cold supper his wife sent for us, not the usual backpacking rehydrated something, but stacks of hand-made flour tortillas to wrap around shredded roast pork and cabbage, a soft white cheese that tastes like fresh mozzarella, and pears, bruised and sticky from hours of being jostled in the saddlebag. He fills our cups with boiling water and passes a tin filled with teabags and packets of hot chocolate. We sit on the edges of the tarp and eat, mostly in silence, dazed from the altitude and miles of walking into the wind.

Armando wipes his gloved hands against his pant legs and removes his map from a zippered pocket. He spreads it on the tarp. Daylight is turning murky and Corbin shines his flashlight. We hover, watching while Armando plots our location and the path we'll take tomorrow. We make a plan to leave in the hour after midnight, to do most of our climbing in the dark before the sun has a chance to soften the snow.

Earlier, before the tents were erected, Koyam had chosen a place for a ritual fire near the edge of camp not far from a deep and treacherous fracture in the mountain's stone face. She directed Sanchez to lay kindling and build a scaffolding of firewood above it. Now we follow her there.

"Here," she says and passes me her bundle and flashlight. She tells us to sit. We settle in a semi-circle, squatting more than sitting because the ground is so cold. She kneels and strikes a match against a rock, cups the flame with her free hand, guides it to the loose nest of splintered wood and paper, and blows. Fire begins to nibble and curl the edges of the paper. There's smoke, a sudden whoosh, and a flicker of blue-orange flames begins to lick and char the wood.

Koyam rocks back on her heels, squatting. Seeming entranced by the fire, she starts to emit a deep and guttural hum that turns to chant, and then to song. She sings in Quechua mixed with another more ancient language, praising *Apu* Cotopaxi, asking permission to climb and to search for the unclaimed child. She begs for safe passage. In exchange, she tells the *Apu*, we offer gifts.

Still singing, she opens her bundle and organizes the contents, takes a thin woven cloth and spreads it on the ground in the firelight. She arranges three perfectly formed coca leaves at the center of the cloth in a triangle and begins adding items from the bundle in a painstaking pattern—raw nuggets of silver and gold, dried maize kernels, a single starfish, an assortment of small shells and tiny sand dollars, several buttons of incense, quinoa seed, a small pottery jar filled with llama fat, and the dried fetus of a llama.

"Now," she says to me, "add something you carry with you always, something personal and painful to part with."

She hasn't prepared me for this, and for a moment, I am at a loss; I brought so little with me. But I unzip my coat and get at the flat zippered pouch that contains my passport and driver's license, a list of telephone numbers, several photographs. My fingers find my gift before I know what I'm after. I bring out a fading Polaroid of Dodie pushing Bella on one of the swings at Mason School's playground—Dodie with a broad smile, and Bella, hair in a swirl, laughing, hurtling toward me and my camera. I add the photograph to the despacho, and Koyam hands me the small brass hammer from her bundle. She doesn't need to tell me what to do. I smash the pottery jar. And the llama fat, warmed by the fire, oozes among the offerings.

"Finish it," she says. I grasp the corners of the cloth, tie them together and carry it by the knot. I hold the flashlight ahead of me to light my way and drop the despacho into the wide fissure in the rock. It descends without a sound. I watch it drop into the crevasse, casting my light, but all I see is the glossy shine of black rock.

We drift back to the camp in silence and squat around the fire, too tired to make small talk but reluctant to leave the warmth. Corbin brings out a flask of peach schnapps. It passes hand-to-hand. Everyone takes a sip except Corbin who accepts the flask's return, screws on the cap, then puts it back in his pocket.

All evening he's been under the radar, none of his harrowing stories or lectures. In the firelight, I think he looks pale.

"You're not having any?"

"Not tonight," he says.

Sanchez begins his rounds, hollering through the flaps of our tents, I'm already awake and up in an instant. I finish getting dressed, get into my coat and boots. I know the drill—strike my tent, roll up my sleeping bag, arrange and tuck until it all fits inside my backpack.

Moonlight gives everything an icy sheen. My boots are cold. Everything is cold. Even our shadows have hard edges.

Sanchez has simmered water and made coffee on the camp stove. The coffee is strong and thick with grounds. He passes a tin of condensed milk to cut the bitterness. I sip and blow. He's baking biscuits in the Dutch oven for breakfast and boiling eggs and fist-sized potatoes to keep our pockets warm and eat for lunch. We slather the biscuits with butter and honey. I eat too fast.

"*Vámonos*," Armando says, "Let's go." And the five of us come together like good soldiers. Armando ties us to his rope and we set off up the slope, our headlamps bobbing in the darkness.

We hit the snowline in just over an hour, stop to plot our position, then strap on our crampons and continue. The night is clear and cold. Moonlight reflecting on endless white, crevasse after crevasse, mounds and banks and drifts of ice and snow. There's barely a sound, no wind, just the occasional groan of ice cracking. It's as if God is holding His breath.

Higher on the mountain, scarves of mist turn to freezing fog and a bitter unobstructed wind begins to blow. Our clothes and gear are rimed in ice. I'm bone-tired but tireless—a zombie walking.

Corbin stops to vomit, not the first time. He's been sluggish, panting and pale—a drag on the climb almost from the beginning. Still he insists he's well enough.

Armando motions and we assemble to take stock and catch our breath while Corbin squats, head down. Koyam produces more coca for him to chew and a finger-full of lime to smear on the back of his molar.

Armando perches, knees bent with his back against a bank of ice. "*Mala suerte*," he says to me and glances at Corbin. He could be talking about the weather, but I know he's not. He drinks from his canteen and eats most of a chocolate bar, then pulls his compass and the map from his coat pocket. He studies the map, then looks up and out toward the west.

"What are you thinking?" I ask.

He hands me the compass and points. "When the fog lifts we should be able to see the face of your bluff."

Chance and luck, or because what I know to be true really is, the mist clears and we see where we're going.

Armando and Eduardo give Corbin an assist up the last few feet onto the rocks. Corbin squats, prostrate and rasping. Koyam helps him drop his backpack, gives him his canteen. "Drink," she says. "You're too sick to be here."

"Yes, well." He takes a gulp of water, breathes and coughs, gets to his feet. He pivots away from Koyam and comes to stand next to me at the lip of the precipice. "My god," he huffs, "These sites, always, the endless, heart-stopping outlook."

The fog has vanished entirely and Cotopaxi's brother peaks, Illiniza Sur, Illiniza Norte, and Corazon, stand like placid sentinels in the pale blue distance.

I'm lightheaded, reeling with apprehension and altitude, and the sense of stillness in this stark and eternal place.

"I'm sick and getting worse," Corbin tells me. "Somehow I'll have to get back to base camp, but first, I need to see what's in that cave. We should get on with it."

The cave's entrance is a slender cleft in the cliff's stone face, a sideways squeeze and several cautious steps down an uneven cascade of rocks to the cavern floor.

Someone's slipped foot dislodges a sudden rain of pebbles. There's an audible intake of breath, and then silence—so vast, it's like a ringing in my ears.

"*Noqa-kaypi*, Kantu," I say. "Where are you?"

"That smell," Eduardo says, "Even frozen, the dead have an unmistakable scent."

The initial chamber leads to a cramped tunnel that spills into a larger space. Our headlamps cast a murky light.

Koyam puts a centering hand against the small of my back, a message that she feels it too, the something here that's stale and sad and unspeakably lonely.

Corbin brings out his flashlight and pans the beam in a slow arc. "Unbelievable," he says. "Look at this. They meant to construct a monument."

The floor is covered with mats of ichu grass, and the far wall is pocked with the beginnings of a series of stone niches, some smoothed and sculpted, most unfinished. The center of the cavern is stacked with firewood and supplies: pottery vessels, digging implements and chisels, satchels and bundles. And in the midst, slouched upright among the bundles and sacks, and facing the weak stream of light that seeps into the cavern—is Kantu, cloaked in blankets, his head slouched to one side.

A knot swells in my chest and my boots feel like they are made of cement. I take the last numb steps and fall to my knees in front of him, remove my glove, run my fingers over the sleek tousle of his fine braids. In the museum at Cuenca, I had read that the cold dry mountain air kept the processes of decay at bay. I had seen the photographs of the child they found in Chile on the mountain El Plomo. Still, I'm unprepared. Despite a mottled discoloration of his skin and a fine grit of dust and frost on his cheek, it doesn't seem impossible that he might rouse and open his eyes. I touch his face, his lips. I utter his name, half expecting something to happen— but what would that be? I sit back on my heels, put my hands in the pockets of my coat and clutch at the misery ballooning in my stomach—and weep.

Less than half an hour in the cavern and Corbin has to be forcibly helped to the outside. He's coughing up blood, getting paranoid and barking demands, convinced our concern is a plot to exclude him from the find.

Eduardo and Koyam work to get him to stop struggling while Armando and I fit the mask and emergency oxygen tank. And then we watch and wait to see if he will improve and how many of us it will take to get him down the mountain.

Corbin gulps bottled air like a thirsty man drinks. Soon he's less agitated. His skin goes from pallid to pink.

Armando lightens Corbin's backpack, everything out but survival gear and food. "Put it on. *Vámonos*, Dr. Corbin," he says. "You and me, let's go."

"Rotten time for me to be sick," Corbin says.

For a long time, when we look down from the precipice, we can make out the blue and orange of their parkas threading down the mountain.

We watch until we can't see them anymore and then we make our way back to the cave. Corbin and Armando's departure leaves us dispirited and tired, but we go through the motions. Eduardo takes a few photographs and then he and Koyam carry some of the sacks and bundles into the daylight to begin cataloging the artifacts.

I wander the cavern like a diver grasping at the timbers of a sunken wreck, hefting a cup, tracing a finger along an unfinished pattern etched in the wall. I choose a sachet of incense from the bottom of a basket and hold it to my nose. Cold and time have dulled its smell but I understand by its wrapping, this is the one I want. I empty the three pressed buttons onto a shallow dish and light them with matches from my coat pocket. I blow and coax until they smolder and smoke. I carry the dish, set it beside me, and sit with Kantu, the way a parent sits at the bedside of a comatose child. I talk, random talk, whatever comes into my head—the story of his life and of my life, the way my life is now. I sing to him, recite rhymes and riddles until my voice is hoarse and I only have a few words left. And then I begin to recite the words he spoke to me the day that Bella died.

"Little beetle, little beetle
Back so shiny black,
Little beetle, little beetle . . ."

I don't have the heart to finish. And I turn off my headlamp and sink into a smoke-induced stupor, wanting to feel numb and distant, beginning to believe I'm a ghost here myself.

Late in the day clouds begin accumulating at the top of the mountain and strong gusts of wind force us to move our tents inside the cave. Koyam uses the camp stove to melt snow and prepare dehydrated packets of lentil soup for supper. The melted snow smells like sulfur and so does the soup, but it doesn't matter. We're too tired to eat.

I startle awake—sure someone has called my name. I lift the tent flap and shine the flashlight.

Koyam sits upright in her sleeping bag, watching me slip my stockinged feet into my boots and rifle through my backpack. I pull out the emergency blanket and stoop to leave the tent.

"Lord Illapa," she says. "Is that you?"

I pause and turn. "Arí, Koyam," I say, "I am here."

Eduardo rises on his elbows, squinting into the beam of my flashlight. "Megan? What's wrong?"

"I'm cold—mostly lonely. Would you mind? Can I get in there with you?"

Even as I'm asking, he's opening the bag's zipper. He holds the gap wide and I slip into the crook of his arm. We work the bag around us, spread the blanket over the top and tuck in the edges. I flick off the flashlight. I'm shivering. He rubs my arms and wraps himself around me, and then we lie together, warm and very still. The darkness is absolute. I lift my chin and he kisses my mouth, my neck, the curve between my neck and shoulder.

I touch his face; give him a kiss that's soft and hungry.

And his hand, warm and dry, moves to the skin beneath my undershirt.

"*Te amo*," he says. "I love you."

Before dawn, I leave Eduardo dozing in his sleeping bag and take the flashlight. I gather the emergency blanket around me, and scramble up the rocks and out of the cave.

The night is canopied in bright clouds that pulse with veins of lightning. Wind whips the edges of the blanket and the sound of thunder comes in peals. My hair is wild with static. I know the secrets of the universe the way one does in dreams. I hear the current that hums in the space between atoms. The eye of the ring has turned an opalescent milky green, emitting its own eerie light and my heart is quivering in my chest. I'm chanting, a monotone urgent hum. I command and the image of my child appears in a swirling iridescent blur. I hold up my arms and shout. "Kantu, I am come for you." And we are together, parent and child again, engulfed in blue light.

Epilogue

Megan Kimsey
c/o Koyam Sapaki-Kallpa
General Delivery
Baños, Ecuador

Charlie Kimsey
294 Lipton Way, Apt 3B
Littleton, Colorado 80111

Dear Charlie,

I know I should have called or written before now. It was unkind of me not to, but it's taken me awhile to settle in one place. Anyway, I hope everyone at home is well and that there hasn't been a lot of concern or worry about me. I'm living in the mountains above Baños, Ecuador. It's an unspeakably beautiful place, subtropical, everything wild and rugged, and so lush and green, also the most amazing wildlife (iridescent hummingbirds in such bright and unexpected colors). In many ways the country reminds me of Colorado. I can't stop thinking how much

Dad would have liked it here. (Yesterday I caught four nice-sized trout that I fried for our supper.)

I'm living with an indigenous medicine woman, but calling her a medicine woman makes her sound more voodoo-ish than she really is. Koyam is a legend in Ecuador for her knowledge of herbs and traditional healing practices, maybe even a national treasure, and I am so blessed that she's willing to teach me. She is getting older and needs my help, and I want to learn everything I can from her, so my being here is a mutual benefit.

One other thing, not a small thing, I'm pregnant, almost three months already. No, I'm not married. Tell Mama the father is anything but a deadbeat. He's an important man in archeological and political circles here and in Colombia and I know he loves me. I haven't told him about the baby yet. Frankly, I'm a little skittish about marriage. (I'm sure Mama will be scandalized.) He's coming later this month to see me and I plan to tell him then. Please write to me and give everyone my love. Try to be happy for me.

I love you,

Megan

ACKNOWLEDGEMENTS

I would like to thank my family and friends for their kindness and support through the many lurches, stalls and small triumphs it took for me to find my way to the end of this novel, to Mary Drew who helped me get the Spanish right, and to my editor, Erin Brown, whose thoughtful criticism and eagle eye made the novel so much better than it might have been.

ABOUT THE AUTHOR

Ginger Bensman is a life-long student of the human condition with a deep interest in philosophy and ecology. She holds a Ph.D. in Human Development/Child and Family Studies from the University of Maine in Orono and has spent more than 25 years working in family support and child abuse prevention programs.

She lives with her husband in Salem, Oregon. This is her first novel.